D0432316

The Mistress of
Windfell Manor

By Diane Allen

For the Sake of Her Family
For a Mother's Sins
For a Father's Pride
Like Father, Like Son
The Mistress of Windfell Manor

DIANE ALLEN

The Mistress of Windfell Manor

MACMILLAN

First published 2016 by Macmillan
an imprint of Pan Macmillan
20 New Wharf Road, London N1 9RR
Associated companies throughout the world
www.panmacmillan.com

ISBN 978-1-4472-8730-8

Copyright © Diane Allen 2016

The right of Diane Allen to be identified as the
author of this work has been asserted by her in accordance
with the Copyright, Designs and Patents Act 1988.

All rights reserved. No part of this publication may be reproduced,
stored in a retrieval system, or transmitted, in any form, or by any means
(electronic, mechanical, photocopying, recording or otherwise)
without the prior written permission of the publisher.

Pan Macmillan does not have any control over, or any responsibility for,
any author or third-party websites referred to in or on this book.

1 3 5 7 9 8 6 4 2

A CIP catalogue record for this book is available from the British Library.

Typeset by Ellipsis Digital Limited, Glasgow
Printed and bound by CPI Group (UK) Ltd, Croydon, CR0 4YY

This book is sold subject to the condition that it shall not, by way of
trade or otherwise, be lent, hired out, or otherwise circulated without
the publisher's prior consent in any form of binding or cover other than
that in which it is published and without a similar condition including
this condition being imposed on the subsequent purchaser.

Visit **www.panmacmillan.com** to read more about all our books
and to buy them. You will also find features, author interviews and
news of any author events, and you can sign up for e-newsletters
so that you're always first to hear about our new releases.

Dedicated with all my love to Ronnie.
Forty-one years married, my love,
who said it would never last?
I love you.

A Weaver's Lament

Come all you cotton-weavers, your looms you must
  pull down.
You must be employed in factories, in country or
  in town,
For our cotton-masters have found out a wonderful
  new scheme,
These calico goods now wove by hand they're going
  to weave by steam.

A VERSE FROM A NINETEENTH-CENTURY
BROADSHEET BALLAD

1

Wesley Booth stood with his hands clenched behind his back and looked out of the parlour window of Crummock Farm, admiring the early-morning view over the dew-clad dales towards the hamlet of Eldroth. There wasn't a better view in all Yorkshire, he proclaimed to himself, as he turned and glared at the young maid as she put too much coal on the newly lit fire.

'Not a finer sight tha'll find, Mary, than looking out of this window on an early spring morning. God's own county, that's what we are in, lass. Mark my words, God's own county.'

'Yes, sir.' Mary looked up at her new master for a brief second, remembering to curtsy just in time, before smoothing her apron.

'Go easy with the coal, lass; anybody would think we were made of money.' Wesley scowled at the young lass from the village of Austwick as she added another piece of coal, before brushing the hearth.

'Yes, sir; sorry, sir.' Mary blushed.

Wesley smiled to himself; it felt good finally to be in control of his family home. By God, he'd waited long enough for this day, and now it was here. He stretched and yawned; it had been a long night, and he had thought his father was never going to die. Eighty-eight was a bloody good age for the old bugger, and he'd been sickly for years, but would not give up control of the three hundred and sixty-five acres of land that belonged to Crummock Farm. The words his father said nearly every day echoed in Wesley's ears: 'Three hundred and sixty-five acres – one for every day of the year – and all containing the sweat off my back.' Sweat off his back, my arse, grinned Wesley; it had been *his* sweat, that and the sweat of the farm labourers he had employed, and his father had just stood leaning on his stick giving the orders.

Anyway, the old bugger was dead – cold as the grave, in his bed up above – and Wesley was master and owner now. He breathed in heavily and looked once more out of the window. The view was grand, the sun shone clear, and playful beams filtered through the budding branches of the sycamore tree at the end of the garden. It was going to be a good day, despite a death in the family. It had been expected, and no one should cry over someone who had reached that age. After breakfast he would ride around his inheritance; not that he didn't know every inch of it already, but now it was his, and that made all the difference. As if on cue, Mrs Cranston entered the parlour.

'Breakfast is out in the dining room, and Miss Lottie is waiting for you. She seems a bit upset, if you don't mind me saying so.' Lucy Cranston looked at her new master; she'd known him as both man and boy and realized how much he had waited for this day.

'Upset, my arse. The only thing she'll be upset about will be losing the odd guinea that the old devil used to give her. Our Lottie is as cunning as a vixen – God help the man she marries.' Wesley smiled at Lucy Cranston. He could talk plain to her, and she knew it. There were no secrets between him and the cook, who had served him and his family well.

'Well, she does look a little pale. I've told her to put some more rouge on. No doubt we will have callers all day, once word is out that Mr Booth has died. And we want her to look her best, especially if that Archie Atkinson comes calling.'

'Now, Mrs Cranston, are you matchmaking with that nephew of yours? Our Lottie will do just the opposite of what you want – you know how strong-willed she is. Besides, I doubt he'll have enough brass for my lass, for she's been used to the finer things in life.' Wesley put his hand on the old cook's shoulder. 'I know you mean well.'

'Aye, you've spoilt her good and proper. It doesn't seem five minutes since her mother died, but it must be all of twenty years. Such a pretty thing she was. Lottie is the image of her.'

'Ah! My darling Isabelle, there isn't a day goes by without me thinking of her. I thought that we would never be parted.' Wesley's voice faded, as his memory recalled the day his wife had been knocked to the ground and killed by a runaway horse and buggy, sacrificing her life for that of her baby, as she pushed Charlotte to safety.

'Life's been hard for you, but you should be proud of your Charlotte, she's not a bad girl.' Lucy touched her master's hand gently in sympathy, as she saw his usually joyful face cloud over.

'Indeed I am, Mrs Cranston, you are quite right. Count your blessings, and I'm sure the right man will come along for our Charlotte – and it won't be long, if I have my way. But when he does, I will ask him if his intentions towards my daughter are honourable, and if he can support her in the way I think appropriate, just as I was made to quiver like a simpering jelly in front of Isabelle's father. As you say, it does seem like only yesterday.' Wesley lifted his bowed head and smiled at the old cook with a heart of gold. 'Now, what have we got for breakfast? Some of your scrambled eggs, I hope, and perhaps a rasher of bacon. It's been a long night and I'm starving.'

Charlotte Booth sat at her usual place at the immaculately polished dining table. She was building herself up to her father's entrance; now that he owned the family home, it was her father that she would have to play to, in order to secure her spending money. She glanced at her reflection in the silver-covered serving bowl. If she pulled a lock out of place from her lovingly styled hair, it would give her the advantage of looking more distressed by the death of her grandpapa. She carefully teased a golden tress out and made it fall down strategically in front of her eyes, smiling at her reflection as it showed the desired effect. Then she practised the sob, the one that she had refined in her bedroom, before making her woeful descent down the twisting stairs of the old farmhouse. It had fooled Mrs Cranston, so it would fool her father, too. Lord knows how heartbroken she was over the death; it was quite obvious for the entire world to see. Hearing the sound of footsteps and her father's voice, she started her play-acting.

'So what have we here then, my lovely daughter? It's too fair a day for a young lass like you to be crying. Your grandpapa wouldn't hold with this; he was old and ready to make peace with his maker.' Wesley kissed his daughter on both cheeks, noting the lack of real tears as he bent down to comfort her.

'I'll miss him, Father. I was so close to him, you know I was.' Charlotte added an extra sniffle as her father pulled up his chair to the dining table.

'Close to his wallet perhaps. That's what you are more bothered about – never mind that the poor old bugger's not yet buried.' Wesley lifted the lid on the silver server and helped himself to the warm scrambled eggs, before reaching over for a rasher of bacon from another tray.

'Father, I'm not like that, and you know it. I loved my grandpapa, I really did.' Charlotte gave a sly glance from behind her handkerchief and knew she wasn't going to win with the fake adoration of her grand-father.

'Aye, well, he's gone, lass. There's just me and thee in this rambling old farmhouse. Thee and me and Mrs Cranston, who seems to think that she has a suitor lined up for you, in that Atkinson lad from Butterfield Gap. I've told her he's not got enough brass to keep you in shoes, never mind anything else.' Wesley ran his knife through the bacon, lifting it to his mouth while watching his daughter's face as it suddenly brightened.

'He's alright, is Archie, he keeps me amused.' Charlotte played with her napkin.

'I didn't invest my money in giving you a decent education, and introducing you to some of the leading gentry of this area, for you to be simpering over some farm lad. You'd not last a minute; as soon as your skirts got dirty, you'd be running back home. I might be a farmer myself, but set your stall for someone a bit higher up in society, our Lottie. Besides, your grandpapa has left you a small inheritance. Nothing special, just twenty guineas a year, but it's better than nowt. And I don't want to see it going to waste on keeping you out of poverty on a rough fell-land farm. I'll set up an account for you at my bank. Miserable old Brown will not be happy when I ask him for an account in your own right, but he should be grateful we are putting money into his bank. I could always bank elsewhere in Settle.'

'Good old Grandpapa, I knew he'd have thought of me. All those boring days of reading to him have paid off; the hours I was bored, and the tales I had to endure, were unbelievable. Thank you for going to see Mr Brown, Papa. I can't believe that women are looked upon as not having any sense with money. He's such a stuffy old devil.' Charlotte's mood changed instantly, as she thought of how she could spend her inheritance.

'By God, lass, you should audition for the stage in Leeds, you're such a good actress. Now listen: you make nowt of that Atkinson lad. I've got my eye on a fella for you and, believe me, you'll want for nowt.' Wesley leaned back in his chair and patted his stomach. 'As long as I've got Mrs Cranston, I'll not want for owt, either. But we've got to get you wed. You're not getting any younger, and neither am I, come to think of it.'

'I hope you're not lining me up with one of your miserable old cronies, Father? I couldn't bear being married to some dithering man of fifty. The thought of someone like old Eric Sowerby breathing over me, and dribbling at the merest suggestion, makes me feel quite sick. Filthy old man!' Charlotte sipped her tea and wrinkled her nose in disgust at the thought of one of the richest eligible landowners in Yorkshire groping her in their wedding bed.

'Give over, lass – Eric's longer in the tooth than I am. That doesn't make him any less able to take on a young filly like you. But no, behave, we need to find you a respectable man: someone younger, with fresh ideas and plenty of brass. And I met just the right man the other night, when I had my meeting with the councillors at Settle. I looked across the table at the fella and

7

I listened to him talking about his newfangled mill, and I thought: *He's the man for my lass.* He wasn't frightened of owt or anybody; he said what he wanted, said what he needed to do and left them old buggers on the council speechless. That lad will go far, mark my words. Not that he isn't already worth a bob or two, from what I understand.' Wesley chewed on his bacon and watched his daughter's face.

'A mill owner! But that means he's not from around here. And how do you know what he's like? He could have come from nothing. At least I know where Archie comes from and that he's like us: a farmer born and bred in these dales. You'd marry me off to someone we know nothing about?' Charlotte looked horrified at her father's acceptance of a complete stranger, just because he'd stood his ground with the local councillors.

'Aye, lass, you'll think different when tha sees him. He's nowt like your Archie; you'll be blown to the four winds when he walks in through yon door. On that I'll eat my hat. You are my lass, and the one thing you have inherited from me is knowing when something's worth spending time on, especially when it involves money. Anyway, you can make your own mind up, because he's coming to supper next Friday.' Wesley leaned back and belched loudly.

'Well, you'll need better manners than that when he's here, if you aim to impress,' Charlotte chastised her father.

'Nowt wrong with belching – it's the sound of appreciation of good food.' Wesley grinned at his vexed daughter. She was angry with him now, but things would change once she saw their guest. 'I'm off on a ride around my new kingdom. I'll be back for the undertaker. Don't you get under Mrs Cranston's feet, and make sure you entertain anybody who comes paying their respects before my return.'

Charlotte watched as her father stood up from the table and made for the door. 'Just one thing, Father: you've forgotten to tell me our visitor's name. And how old is he?'

'Oh, aye, I'd say he's about thirty, and his name is Joseph Dawson. And before you ask, he's from Accrington. Not a million miles away, lass, so don't you fret that pretty head of yours.'

Wesley closed the dining-room door after him, knowing full well that his daughter's head would be full of questions for his cook. Lucy Cranston knew everything about anybody; where she learned it from, God only knew, but her source of gossip was to be admired. If he wanted to know owt, he had only to ask Lucy. And what he'd heard from her regarding Joseph Dawson was all good. Aye, he was the right man for his lass. Besides, it was time she was wed and out from under his feet. He had his own life – he and Lucy. If he could, he'd wed his cook, but that wouldn't be seen to be acceptable in polite society, so he aimed to share the house with no intrusions, once Lottie was gone. There was nowt wrong with having your cake and eating it, and how true that was in Lucy's case. He smirked to himself. She was good in the kitchen and knew how to keep a bed warm on the coldest of nights, and he'd be lost without her. Her and that ample figure, in which he found comfort and pleasure.

He blushed at his own thoughts as he shouted for his dog, which had been asleep next to the hearth in the warm kitchen. With his father gone and Lottie to be married off, he could at last find solace in Lucy's arms as and when he wanted. To hell with whatever the servant lass thought; he was the owner of Crummock Farm – he could do what he liked, when he wanted to, and you could be sure that's just what he was going to do.

'Off to view my land, Lucy. I'll be back mid-morning,' Wesley shouted through the kitchen door.

'I'll make sure to keep you warm one of these scones I'm making.' Mrs Cranston wiped her hands on her apron and smiled at the love of her life as he closed the kitchen door behind him. She turned and noticed the snigger on the face of Mary, the parlour maid, as she wiped the kitchen table. 'Get a move on and clear the dining room, you. We can expect visitors this morning, and I want it all tidy and in its place.'

'Yes, ma'am.' Mary grinned. It was common gossip down in Austwick that it was more than a warm scone that old Booth got from his cook and housekeeper, since the death of his wife. But why should she worry? That left her free of any advances, unlike her friend who worked at Clapham Hall; she should be thankful that the master didn't have an eye for a young lass that he could easily take advantage of.

*

10

Charlotte lingered over her cup of tea, running her finger around the rim of the delicate gold-lustre china. Who was this Joseph Dawson that her father seemed convinced was right for her? And, even if he was, how was she going to prove it to him? After all, he might already be married; indeed, he might not even be wanting to look at marriage. And what if she absolutely hated him. Hate him! How could she hate him, if he had money? Money was everything in Charlotte's life, and she knew it.

Her thoughts returned to her dead grandfather. Good old Grandfather: twenty guineas a year was not to be sneezed at, though he could have made it a round hundred. Still, she'd buy material for a new dress next week, ready to wear once she had got out of these terrible drab mourning weeds. Then the awful thought came that she would have to be dressed in black when she met the wealthy Mr Dawson. What would he think of her? She could have worn the beautiful blue dress that showed her eyes off so well, greatly preferring to use her charms and looks than her brains. Instead, this time she'd have to find something out about him, so that she could show an interest in the same things as him and hold a decent conversation. She'd ask Mrs Cranston; she would know about Joseph Dawson – she knew everything about everybody. That's what she would do, and she would do it now.

'Aye, Miss Charlotte, will you stop quizzing me? I already told you, I don't know a lot about him. We don't exactly move in the same circles, Mr Dawson and I.' Lucy Cranston bustled around her kitchen table, emptying her newly made scones out onto a wire rack to cool. 'I know he's stopping at The Eagle in Long Preston until he finds a home for himself, and folk say he's got big plans for the cotton mill at Langcliffe, but that's all I know.'

'But you must know what he looks like, Lucy. I need to know . . .' Charlotte attempted to pick up a still-hot scone, only to swear when she nearly burned her fingers.

'Will you leave those scones alone? You're not too big to be in my bad books.' Lucy put her hands on her hips and scowled at the nuisance in her kitchen.

'I know what he looks like, Miss Charlotte. I saw Mr Dawson coming out of the bank last Tuesday in Settle.' Mary wiped the mixing bowl and looked smug, as she teased both older women with her knowledge.

'You wouldn't know him if you fell over him, Mary, and well you know it.' Lucy Cranston dismissed the young parlour maid's confession.

'But I do. The bank clerk ran after him down the steps and shouted his name as he walked across to the town hall. I think everyone in Settle stopped to look at him; he's the talk of the town, with saving the mill.' Mary smiled and placed the gleaming bowl back in the cupboard in which it lived.

'And . . .' Both Charlotte and Lucy hung on her words.

'He's alright; a toff's a toff to me. Quite tall, dark

hair, spoke different to us, a bit posher. Oh, and he wore a gold watch on a chain that hung down on his waistcoat.'

'And his face?' Charlotte asked.

'Couldn't really see; he'd a top hat on and that shaded it. I only know he had dark hair because I saw it on his shoulders as he walked away.' Mary grinned at the two women as they sighed in exasperation, sensing a story going nowhere.

'You tell us only half a tale, lass, that's no good.' Lucy walloped her maid lightly with her tea-towel and then filled the kettle and placed it on the hearth to boil, stopping for a moment as she heard the knocker on the front door. 'Go on and see who that is, Mary. It can't be the undertakers; they'd come round to the back door. Take them into the parlour, if they've come to pay their respects. Mr Booth will be back shortly, and in the meantime Miss Charlotte here will keep them company.'

'Oh! Do I have to? What if it's some of my father's cronies? I'll have nothing to say to them.' Charlotte watched as Mary ran out of the kitchen to open the front door.

'You'll act like a lady, Miss Charlotte; you know your father would want you to, no matter who's in that parlour.' Lucy shook her head. Sometimes her mistress needed a wallop too, but she didn't dare give her one. Charlotte – or Lottie, as her father called her – was the jewel of Wesley Booth's eye, and she knew better than to overstep her duties too much.

'It's only Archie Atkinson. He says he's come to give his condolences, and he's got a bunch of primroses in his hand.' Mary smirked and looked at Charlotte.

'It's "Mr Atkinson" to you, Mary.' Lucy looked at Charlotte. 'I suppose you'll be alright holding court now, in your father's absence?'

'Of course. Could you bring Mr Atkinson and me some tea in the parlour, please, Mrs Cranston.' Charlotte turned as she walked out of the kitchen. 'And two of your scones wouldn't go amiss; that is, if you aren't going to feed them all to my father.'

Mary stifled a snigger as Mrs Cranston huffed and puffed at the cheek of her mistress. 'That lass will be the death of me. And that lad needs to know his place – knocking on the front door! He's nobbut a farm lad. Next time, Mary, tell him to use the back door.'

Charlotte smiled at Archie Atkinson as he held out to her a freshly picked bunch of primroses, which he had hurriedly picked from the mossy bank leading down from the fellside of his farm.

'I didn't know what to do. I knew you'd be upset that your grandfather had died, and I thought you might like these, especially the one or two violets that are mixed in with them – they smell so sweet.' Archie blushed. He wanted to add, 'Just like you', but he didn't dare.

'Archie, they are beautiful. Primroses are quite my favourite flower.' Charlotte took them from his trembling hand and looked at his red, blushing cheeks, framed by a mop of shocking blond hair. 'Do sit down. I've ordered some tea, and I'm sure you'll not say no to one of Mrs Cranston's scones.' She sat with the small bouquet in her hand and looked at the fidgeting lad, who she knew was sweet on her. 'I tell you what: let's not bother with tea. It's lovely out there this morning, let's go for a walk up the knot behind the house.' Charlotte instantly sensed the relief coming from Archie. She knew he wasn't at ease in her decadent surroundings, and knew also that a walk up the small hillock known as 'the knot' would be more to his suiting.

'Are you sure? What about the undertakers? What about Mrs Cranston?'

'They'll be alright. Besides, I could do with a breath of fresh air. There's a feeling of death beginning to seep into the air, and I'm not going to let that spoil a beautiful spring day. My grandfather was old, he was ill, but life goes on, Archie. That's what he would have wanted.' Charlotte placed the primroses carefully down on the polished sideboard. 'I'll put them in a vase when we come back. Come on, we'll sneak quietly out of the front door.'

She reached for Archie's hand and urged him along the passage and through the front door, closing it behind them.

'There, that's better – fresh air!' She breathed in deeply, the sharp spring air biting at her lungs, as they stood on the paved path that ran around the farm's large garden.

'But you'll freeze, you've no coat,' Archie shouted as Charlotte ran to open the garden gate onto the farm-yard and duck pond.

'No, I won't. This is grand weather. It's spring, Archie, you can smell it on the air. The fell around us is waking up after its winter's sleep. I love the smell of the sphagnum moss and the primroses that you have lov-ingly picked me – it's part of me, and always will be. Come on, catch me if you can; race you to the top of the knot.' Charlotte picked up her skirts and ran over the rutted farm track and up the smooth grassy fellside, laughing at Archie as he tried to catch her. The breath from her running clouded around her in the cold air as she clambered her way to the top of the fellside hillock, only to collapse in a heap on the summit.

'Your dress, Charlotte! You'll get it filthy, sitting down like that, and the ground is still rock-hard with frost.' Archie clambered up the side of the steep hill and stood next to her, breathless.

'Stop wittering like an old woman. Just look at the day. No wonder my father decided to ride around his land this morning.' She sighed and looked around her at the outstretched dales, shining and sparkling as the frost on them began to thaw with the warmth of the sun.

'Aye, I must admit, it's on days like these I'm glad to live here in the country, not in a town with its grubby streets and mill chimneys.' Archie put his hand on Charlotte's shoulder and looked out towards his home, Eldroth, nestling amongst the sprawling fells and dales in the distance.

'You mean like Accrington? I hear that the new mill owner at Langcliffe is from there. Have you met him yet?' Charlotte pulled herself up with the help of Archie's hand and looked into his eyes.

'No. Why should someone like me have met him? But I have heard plenty about him. He sounds a bit full of himself. He's going to update the mill, renovate the mill-pond cottages for the workers, and thinks he can bully the town council. My father says he won't last long – that he's all talk.' Archie didn't like the way his Lottie was showing interest in this offcumden.

'My father's asked him to dinner next week. He seems to have taken a shine to him.' Charlotte grinned. She could see the jealousy creeping over Archie's face. 'He says we should get to know him well, because he's got power.'

'Power's not everything. Some of us are happy just being content with a roof over our heads and a full belly. But if that's what you are after, Lottie, I wish you well.' Archie watched the undertaker from Austwick coming up the rough stony track, with his team of black horses nearly at a gallop.

'Why, Archie Atkinson, is there a hint of jealousy in your voice? I haven't even met the man yet, and he's my father's friend, not mine,' Charlotte teased.

'I know you: I'll never be good enough. Sometimes I think it's only because you are bored that you bother with me at all.' He shuffled his feet and put his head down.

17

'Poor little farm boy, does nobody love you?' Charlotte shivered as a cold northern wind suddenly whipped her for her scathing torment of Archie.

'No, but I love you, and you know it.' He grabbed her hand and held it tight.

'Don't be silly – let go. The undertaker can see us. What will he think? And my father's just riding into the yard.' Charlotte started off back down the hill, stopping after a few steps. 'We are just friends, Archie. I'm very fond of you, you know I am; but to talk of love, that's not for me.'

'Well, I do love you,' Archie yelled as she strode out down the hillside, leaving him standing in the biting wind. He watched as her black chiffon mourning dress shimmered in the sun. She didn't give a damn about him, and he knew it. He was just a poor farm boy, in her eyes.

2

'Aye, stop your blubbering, our Lottie, a few tears are enough. You don't want to spoil that bonny face of yours, not when he's here.' Wesley Booth whispered fiercely into Lottie's ear as she sniffled yet again into her handkerchief while she watched her grandpa's coffin slowly being lowered into the ground. 'First impressions and all that, lass. He doesn't want to think he might be courting a blithering idiot.'

Lottie sniffed loudly and stared at her father. 'It's what you do at a funeral, Father. And who said Joseph Dawson will want to court me, if I don't show any grief for my grandpa's death?' She muttered between sobs and smiled weakly at the curate, as she picked up a handful of heavy clay soil and sprinkled it onto the dark oak coffin. Afterwards she sobbed and pretended to be feeling faint at the sight of her beloved grandpapa being covered by the dark earth.

'For lawk's sake, Lottie!' Wesley could nearly have

laughed at his daughter's acting, but a graveyard was not the place.

'Are you alright, Lottie?' Archie rushed to her side, worried that the love of his life had nearly swooned into the open grave, and that her father looked uninterested at her despair.

'I'm fine, Archie, thank you for your concern.' Lottie could have sworn; it wasn't Archie she had wanted to save her, but the tall, dark stranger she now knew to be Joseph Dawson, who stood not more than a few feet from her.

'Can I get you a drink of water? Do you want to take my arm and we'll go and sit in the church?' Archie looked alarmed and held his arm out.

'She's right, lad. Go back to your father, I'll look after our Lottie.' Wesley dismissed the young lad who was going to spoil his plans, if he had his way. He linked arms with his 'grieving' daughter and led her away from the grave's edge, giving Archie a black look as he watched him head back to his father's side. 'Bloody well behave yourself,' he told Lottie. 'He was eighty-eight. Folk expect you to die, at that age, and you are just looking foolish.'

'But, Father, I was only trying to attract—'

'My condolences, Mr Booth.' Wesley looked up at the tall figure of Joseph Dawson, who must have heard him chastising Lottie, and smiled a humble smile. Joseph bowed and held out his gloved hand for Wesley to shake. 'And you must be Charlotte? I'm sure you miss your grandfather terribly, and funerals are so upsetting, aren't they, Wesley?'

Charlotte smiled. She could feel herself blushing from her toes up.

'Aye, my lass and my father were awfully close. She thought the world of him, didn't you, Lottie?' Wesley grimaced a smile, meanwhile thinking 'close to his wallet, more like'.

'I loved my grandpapa. My father is correct: I'll miss him terribly, he was such a kind man.' Lottie dared to look up into the handsome face of Joseph, who smiled as he noticed her flutter her long blonde lashes at him.

'Still, life goes on, does it not, Miss Booth? He was a good age, I understand, and had a rich life; made all the better, I'm sure, by a doting granddaughter.' Joseph had to hide a snigger as the young woman in front of him fluttered her eyelashes at him again.

'You'll not forget supper with us on Friday night, will you, Dawson? The invitation is still standing. As you say, my father was a good age, and he wouldn't want us to mope over him.' Wesley was determined to have Joseph sit down at his table, to prove that he was worthy of his company.

'Indeed I will not. I'm looking forward to it. Will you be joining us, Miss Dawson, or will our talk of business and local gossip bore you?' Joseph flashed a smile, showing Lottie a row of perfect white teeth, made more perfect by his slightly dusky skin.

Wesley butted in quickly before his daughter showed

herself up even more. 'She will indeed. She's got a good business head on her, has my lass, and likes to know what's going on. I sent her to finishing school at Harrogate, and what she didn't learn there, I taught her. There's not many lasses as clever as our Charlotte.' Wesley sighed and looked at the pride of his life. At that moment Lottie looked as daft as a milksop.

'Well, I look forward to seeing you both. Did we say around seven?' Joseph smiled at them both, as he caught Wesley scowling at his dumbstruck daughter.

'Aye, that will be grand. Mrs Cranston, my cook, will not see you go hungry.' Wesley shook Joseph's hand warmly.

Joseph smiled and bowed politely to the smitten Charlotte. He might have been new to the area, but people gossiped. He was in no doubt whatsoever that Mrs Cranston would give them a good supper – and more besides, to her master. He was also sure there was more to the little actress Charlotte; he had heard that she was as sharp as a needle, and not at all the dim-witted farm girl she was portraying.

'Now think on, Lottie. You act normal tonight. I want none of your daftness. We've to impress Joseph. I need him, because I bet he's got contacts in Bradford and Accrington for my wool. And you, missus, could do with him for his money and lifestyle; you'd want for nowt, with that 'un on your arm.'

Wesley looked around the large dining room. The parquetry floor had been polished to within an inch of its life and a good blaze roared in the fireplace, reflecting in the shining silver and crystal that adorned the heavily dressed dining table.

'If he's not impressed with this spread, then I'll eat my hat.'

'I've heard nothing but panic in the kitchen all day. You'd think the Queen was coming, never mind a mill owner, if you'd heard Mrs Cranston flapping. He's only a fella – nowt special.' Lottie pinched a grape from the fruit dish that was piled high on the sideboard, and played with it in her fingers before placing it in her mouth.

'He took your eye, so don't give me that. Anyway quiet now, lass. I can hear Mary talking to someone in the hallway. I should bloody well have hired a butler for the night. What will he think of, being served by a common village lass?' Wesley sighed and then painted a smile on his face, before giving Lottie a warning glance to behave herself.

Joseph smiled at the blushing maid who took his top hat, gloves and cane. She was a sweet-looking thing, he couldn't help but think, as she curtsied and placed his belongings on the hall-stand.

'Ah! Joseph, welcome to my home. I trust you found us easily enough and that my stable lad is looking after your horse?' Wesley patted Joseph on his back and held out his hand to be shaken.

'Indeed I did. I hadn't realized you were so far out of Austwick – you are quite remote out here.' Joseph shook the hand of the robust, red-faced man strongly and looked past his shoulder, to see Charlotte standing behind him. 'Miss Booth! Are you recovered from your grandfather's funeral? I was quite concerned for your well-being.' He smiled.

'Quite recovered, thank you, Mr Dawson. I'm afraid I made a fool of myself, with the grief overcoming me. I hope you'll forgive me for being so empty-headed.' Lottie quietly felt her heart jump as Joseph took her hand and kissed it lightly.

'Now then, you two, let's go into the dining room and I'll shout to Mary to tell Cook that we are ready for some supper.' No sooner had Wesley spoken than he bellowed out his instructions from the hallway to poor Mary, banishing any thoughts of refinement in the Booth household. Seeing the look on Joseph's face, and one of horror on Charlotte's, Wesley quickly made an excuse to his guest. 'We are a little short-staffed tonight, as the butler's off sick.'

'Good staff are so hard to find nowadays. I completely understand.' Joseph followed Charlotte into the dining room, admiring how small her waist looked in her mourning dress and how the black complemented her long blonde hair. 'Well, this is a grand room and, even though it's a spring evening, that blaze is welcome.'

'Aye, Lucy – I mean, my cook – has done us proud. She knows how to lay a table. Wine, Joseph? I bought a bottle or two when I was last in Settle. I can't stand the stuff myself, I'd rather have a gill of ale, but our Lottie tells me I should be more refined.' Wesley pulled a face at the bottle of claret he had been bullied into buying by Lottie.

'Ale will do fine. Perhaps Charlotte would like a glass of the wine, seeing as she has recommended it?' Joseph sat down in the chair at the head of the table that he had been ushered into, as Wesley placed a tankard of ale next to him. He watched Lottie's face as her father completely left her out of the offer of drinks.

'I would indeed, Father. I do like a drink of claret.' Lottie took advantage of Joseph's hint and held her wine glass up to be filled, as she made herself comfortable in her seat between the two men.

'Aye, well, watch it doesn't go to your head. There's nowt worse than a giggling, drunk woman.' Wesley poured a half-measure into Lottie's wine glass and then firmly placed the bottle on the sideboard.

Joseph caught Lottie's eye and winked, as her father sat down in his chair at the other end of the table.

Mary came in, all flustered, carrying a tray laden with three bowls of steaming soup, and served Wesley first, completely forgetting the order Mrs Cranston had told her earlier in the day, and the protocol required for the evening.

'So, lad, tha's got big plans for that mill of yours, have you? I can't say I've ever been near it. Not got much use for cotton mills up here. Now, if it had been wool, that'd be a different matter – I'd be selling you mine every autumn.' Wesley looked up, after slurping a mouthful of soup and dipping his bread in it, and looked at Joseph for an answer.

'I have indeed, Mr Booth.' Joseph put down his spoon and leaned on the table, clenching his hands and leaning on them as he spoke. 'Ferndale Mill at Langcliffe is empty at the moment. I aim to take out the old weaving looms and replace them with spinning and perhaps even doubling machinery. I'm looking at fourteen thousand spindles, if I've done my homework right. That'll bring employment back into the area and fill them cottages up that are standing empty in Langcliffe, and the original rows of cottages at the end of the mill-pond. It's just what this area needs. The slump in cotton that hit everybody bad, back in 1849, is hopefully over, and it's time to look to the future.' Joseph's eyes glazed over, thinking of his ambition, before coming back to reality and reaching for his spoon to continue with his soup. 'Then I hope to upgrade the derelict mill lower down the river; upgrade it to a top-class weaving mill. That'll give the other mill owners something to think about.'

'These are grand ideas, lad. I hope tha's got enough brass, it'll cost a bob or two.' Wesley made light of his answer, but really he was wondering how much money his guest had.

'I've no worries about finance; my wife made sure of that.' Joseph sipped his soup and patted his lips with his napkin, before looking at Lottie.

'Your wife! I didn't know you were married.' Charlotte heard herself gasp, as all her dreams of becoming Joseph's wife, and living a life of style, drifted away.

26

'I was. We were happily married for a whole year, and then unfortunately May caught consumption. I watched her go from a healthy, pink-cheeked young thing to an old woman within a few months. It broke my heart. That is why I decided to make a new life for myself in the country, instead of among the mill chimneys of Accrington. Fortunately, May bequeathed me all of her parents' small fortune, which she herself had been left. So there's no problem, Mr Booth. I do have "a bob or two", as you say.' Joseph watched the obvious relief on Charlotte's face, giving her game-plan away.

'Aye, I'm sorry to hear tha came into money through bereavement. I know what it's like to lose the woman you love, at such a young age. I lost Lottie's mother when she was but a baby – broke my heart, it did. Perhaps you'll find solace in this new project. I take it you weren't lucky enough to have any family?' Wesley sat back and watched as Mary quickly cleared the empty soup dishes, nearly dropping the spoons as she did so.

'No – no family. I am on my own, to do with my life as I will.' Joseph smiled at Charlotte and leaned back comfortably in his chair.

'It's a bad do that you are all alone, Mr Dawson. Life must be hard sometimes.' Lottie watched Joseph stretch his long legs under the table and gaze at his hosts. He was indeed worth money, and he was very handsome, but there was an undercurrent of arrogance about him. Lottie felt as if he knew what she was thinking when she smiled across at him, while making pleasant conversation.

'Life's what you make it, Miss Booth. I've no time for folk who feel sorry for themselves. I hadn't a penny to my name a few years ago. Now I'm comfortable and, when it comes to friends and relations, they come and go. I've learned to be independent. Folk need me more than I need them.'

'Well, lad, my lass Lottie means the world to me, and I don't know what I'd do without friends. Happen us farmers depend on one another when times are hard. Your life sounds different to ours, lad, but as long as you're happy.' Wesley rubbed his hands and looked at the roast blade of beef that Mary had just placed on a plate in front of him. He remembered butchering the bullock that the beef had come from. A finer beast he'd never owned, and he knew that the beef in front of him would be succulent. 'Give me a full belly and a happy daughter, and I ask for no more. Now, let's get stuck into this beef, it's a shame for it to go cold. Mary, fill mine and Mr Dawson's tankards, and pass the tatties, lass. I've been looking forward to this all day.'

Joseph smirked at his host. The man had no social graces or skills.

'My father appreciates good food. After all, it's like you producing good cotton: that's what our trade is about.' Lottie had caught the look on Joseph's face and decided to squash his disgust.

'And you, Miss Booth, what do you do with your life, up here on this remote farm? Do you not get bored?' Joseph tilted his head while chewing a mouthful of beef.

'She's like a mountain hare, that's what she is. She wanders the fells, knows every one of my sheep, and keeps up-to-date with all the gossip that's talked in the kitchen. But when it comes to doing my accounts and watching where I spend my brass, I can't fault her. Better eyes than old Brown in the bank at Settle, that 'un has.' Wesley Booth butted in and summoned Mary, who was standing in the corner, to clear some of the empty plates.

'So you are good with figures, Miss Booth. That's unusual in a woman. You will be an asset to any forward-thinking husband you might take in the future.' Joseph lowered his eyes and took the last mouthful of his dinner.

'Aye, but she can spend it and all – she likes the finer things, does our Lottie.' Wesley laughed as he watched Joseph finding out about his daughter. 'Got a good eye, though; doesn't spend money daft. She gets that from her mother.'

'Father, will you be quiet. I am here, you know!' Charlotte was mortified by her father's outburst, likening her to a mountain hare. 'I do seem to be good at bookkeeping. I learned it at Harrogate. It wasn't my first choice of subject, but I found I had a head for figures. But, like my father says, I also like to wander the fells. I love my home.' She felt her cheeks flush as she took a delicate sip of her wine for comfort.

'Mmm. A woman of good taste. You must come and look around Windfell before I start to furnish it. I would like to have some advice from a female perspective. Us old males could do with some help on curtains and the like.' Joseph grinned at Charlotte and her blushing cheeks.

'Windfell!' Wesley and Charlotte echoed together.

'Yes, didn't I mention that I'd bought Windfell, in between Stainforth and Langcliffe? I signed the deeds for it just this morning. I thought it was time I got myself a home, and Windfell Manor should do the job. It needs some money spending on it, but it is a good house for someone in my position and will make a fitting home if I ever decide to take myself a wife and family.' Joseph sat back and watched both the Booths mentally trying to calculate exactly how much money he was worth.

'Aye, it'll be a grand house that. It's set in some good grounds and has a grand view down to the River Ribble. I remember when Tom Redmayne built it. Shame he only got thirty years living in it, before he died. His wife got even less – I don't think she saw it completed. Could happen to be buying a bit of bad luck there, lad.' Wesley pictured the large, pillared hall set in its own grounds, surrounded by beautiful copper beeches.

'I'd love . . . I'd love to come and look around Windfell.' Charlotte stuttered over her words, eager to accept Joseph's offer to give him some advice, and to be given the chance to get to know a little better the man sitting across from her – and without her father's interference.

'Well, that's a deal then, Miss Booth. We will make an afternoon of it, and I will arrange some tea.' Joseph leaned over to slice a piece of cheese from the selection that Mary had placed in the middle of the dining table. She left the room, stifling a giggle, after eavesdropping on the ongoing conversation at her master's table.

'Please, Mr Dawson, call me Charlotte. I'm sure my father won't mind.' Charlotte glanced at her father.

'I'm not bothered. Can't be doing with standing on ceremony. Call her what you want, lad, as long as you are civil.' Wesley Booth rose from his chair and charged Joseph's tankard. 'Tha's a slow drinker – are you sure you like ale? I've some port on the sideboard. Do you fancy a glass of that?'

'"Charlotte" it is, then. And yes, a glass of port would be most welcome. I look forward to showing you around. Would Monday next week fit in with your plans?' Joseph raised his glass of port without thanking Wesley for it, and waited for a reply from the bewitched young woman.

'That would be perfect. I'll look forward to it very much. But now I'll leave you to talk with Father. I know your business matters will be far over my head.' Charlotte rose from her chair. She would have liked to have stayed longer, but it would not be deemed polite. She'd got what she had wanted: an invitation into the world of Joseph Dawson, with a visit to Windfell Manor as an added bonus.

'I look forward to that indeed, Charlotte. And I'm sure that anything your father and I discuss tonight will not be too intellectual for your pretty head.' Joseph stood up from his chair and watched the perfect figure of Charlotte saying her farewells.

'Goodnight, Father. Goodnight, Mr Dawson.' The rustle of black taffeta followed her out of the room. She stopped just outside the door, not quite closing it behind her, and listened to both men for a few brief seconds.

'She's a bit of a one, is our Lottie. Got her own mind, and as sharp as a vixen,' she could hear her father saying.

'I'm sure she is, Mr Booth – and beautiful with it, may I add, if I'm not being too presumptuous.'

'Aye, I know I've got a winner there, lad. That's why I've got to get the right bull in the pasture. No good her going with a fella with no breeding,' Wesley muttered quietly.

Charlotte could have died. Would her father never learn any manners!

3

'You look lovely, Miss Charlotte. Not to worry that you are in mourning – black quite suits you.' Mrs Cranston stood back on the pegged rug in the kitchen and admired the daughter she had never had.

Charlotte reeled around and grinned like the cat that got the cream, as she adjusted a small silver hair-slide. 'How many bedrooms do you think Windfell has? And how many servants will he be taking on? What did you think of him, Mary? Is he not truly handsome? I think I'm going to be lost for words when I speak to him.' For once Charlotte was acting her age, and already she had plans in her head to be lady of the manor.

'He was indeed handsome, Miss Charlotte. I'm quite envious. You will have to tell us everything when you come back home.' Mary giggled at her mistress and clapped her hands as Charlotte pulled on her long velvet gloves, adding the final piece to her apparel.

'Aye, well, you'd better get a move on, as his carriage is here. And it'll not wait.' Wesley Booth entered the kitchen and looked at his only child, noting the flutter she was in. 'Anybody would think you were wedding him, not just having tea.' He pulled his hanky out of his pocket and blew his nose, his eyes on the brink of tears at the beauty of his beloved daughter. 'Now behave yourself, don't act like an idiot and try to impress him, our Lottie.'

Charlotte kissed her father on the cheek and secured the small lace-frilled bag on her arm. 'I'll not let you down, Father.' She gave a parting grin to the two servants as she picked up her skirts and left the three of them watching her. All of them thought this was the day she had upped her game, for the man of her dreams.

'I have a funny feeling about this, Lucy. I think I might just have opened a can of worms, introducing Joseph Dawson to my lass. His brass would keep her in a good lifestyle, but as I talked to him the other evening, I don't know if I liked what I heard. I think he could perhaps be a hard man.' Wesley looked out of the kitchen window, watching the carriage that was carrying his daughter down the rough farm track.

Lucy caught his arm gently. 'She's only going for tea. She's not eloping with him, and Lottie has a mind of her own. She'll soon find out if he's not what he seems.'

'Aye, you're right, but that lass is all I've got, and I'd rather she stopped at home all her life than be unhappy. She means everything to me.' Wesley sighed.

'Come here, sit next to the fire. Mary, put that kettle

34

on and make your master a cup of tea. I don't know, Miss Charlotte goes for her first proper invite out and the house falls apart. It's going to be a long year, if she does take his eye, God help us all!' Lucy puffed. 'I've never known such a precious lass.'

Joseph Dawson stood outside the front doors of Windfell Manor. He gazed up at the fluted columns and cast-iron balcony above the entrance to his latest purchase. He silently admitted to himself that he had come a long way, since being a snotty, ragged kid in the back streets of Accrington, begging for a crust from passers-by just to fill his belly. He'd vowed, on the day that a rich merchant had hit him with the back of his hand, after Joseph put his filthy hands on his plush jacket, that he would not remain poor, and that he would play the rich at their own game.

By luck, cunning and good looks, he had managed it. And now he was starting a new life, comfortable in a wealthy lifestyle in the quiet Yorkshire Dales, where nobody knew of his past and where money talked louder than actions. Windfell was part of his dream, a mansion house built by the brother of a silk merchant. What a house that man had built, and now Joseph owned it, along with Ferndale Mill – thanks to his docile, trusting, dear wife. It had been a good day when he had met May, when she had opened her heart to him on the death of her parents, as he had sipped his coffee in the coffee house on Wellington Street. Fate had smiled at him, as May borrowed his handkerchief to wipe away her tears and then looked into his eyes. He could still see those almond-coloured puppy-dog eyes, the ones that – even now – bore into his soul and would make him wake at night, screaming.

He breathed in deeply. There, that was all in the past. It was time to move on. He had a guest coming, and he must not be seen wallowing in things that were now buried and gone. No sooner had he gathered his thoughts than he heard the sound of his coach approaching, turning its way into the gateway of Windfell to come to a standstill a yard away from him. The horses pounded and snorted as their driver dismounted and opened the carriage door to reveal Charlotte. Her head of blonde hair shone, as she politely thanked the driver for the help of his hand in assisting her.

'Charlotte, so good to see you. I trust the ride was not too uncomfortable?' Joseph held out his hand and smiled at his guest as she stood on the pebbled driveway and admired his home.

'It's beautiful, Joseph. I've always looked at this house from the road, but hadn't realized it was so large! It must be three times the size of my home, and I thought our farmhouse was large. I'm sorry – I'm forgetting my manners. I didn't even answer your question and say good afternoon, but I truly am in awe of the grandness of your home. The ride was comfortable; it made a pleasant change from my father's plodding pair of nags. I must tell him to put his hand in his pocket and get a team of horses with some style, instead of practicality.' Charlotte turned and looked at Joseph, who appeared even more handsome in the cold light of day and blended in with his surroundings perfectly.

'Yes, the Redmaynes knew how to build a house alright. But let's not stand here. Come, let me show you the rest of the building. I'm afraid only one of the rooms is furnished as of yet, but my housekeeper has lit the fire in the parlour and has prepared some tea for us, once you've looked around my new home.'

Charlotte walked up the entrance steps into the large hall and gasped as she surveyed the huge, sweeping staircase before her. Her eyes surveyed the grandness of the hallway, the beautiful glittering chandelier that was the centrepiece of the ceiling, and the rich tapestries that hung at the windows. Never had she seen such luxury.

Joseph breathed in deeply. The smell of perfume surrounded him as Charlotte brushed past and stood in the centre of his hall. She looked the perfect picture. Even in her mourning dress, she seemed as if she was in her natural setting.

'It is marvellous, Joseph. Look at the staircase and this hallway. How many rooms do you actually have?' Charlotte twirled around, filling the room with the smell of violets, and Joseph smiled as he read on her face her impatience to be shown around.

'Take my arm and I'll show you round. I can't quite believe it myself that this is to be my home. Mrs Dodgson, my housekeeper, is grumbling already, thinking how many servants I'm going to need to keep on top of it, once I've got all the rooms prepared. Now tell me, I thought this would make a perfect morning room, where I could write all my correspondence. And perhaps, if I take a wife, she could sit and sew in here. The room catches all the light in the morning.'

Joseph opened one of the doors leading out of the hall and revealed a large, spacious room, with windows overlooking the driveway and an Adams fireplace taking pride of place on the centre wall. Elegant cornicing ran all round the ceiling, surrounding yet another chandelier hanging in the centre.

'This is one of the smaller rooms, but every one of them has these beautiful decorated ceilings. And you get a good view from every room in the house, apart from the kitchen, but even that isn't bad. The Redmaynes made sure their kitchen was up-to-date in its fixtures. I thought perhaps a warm flock wallpaper in here? What do you think?' Joseph stood next to a bedazzled Charlotte.

'Flock – what's flock?' Charlotte turned and looked at her host, waiting for an answer.

'It's wallpaper with a velvety pattern on it, rather like your gloves, Charlotte.' Joseph reached out and touched the softness of one of her gloved arms. His hand lingered on her arm as they looked into one another's eyes.

'That would be different. I've never seen that before.' Charlotte looked into Joseph's eyes and found herself lost for words.

He smiled and placed his hand back down by his side. 'It's in all the best homes; it seems to be the latest trend. I've also asked Gillow's of Lancaster to show me their latest catalogue of furniture. They are a good company, and local.'

Charlotte gathered her thoughts; her heart had missed a beat when Joseph placed his hand on her arm. 'Have you some furniture from your old home, over in Accrington? Would it not fit in anywhere?'

'I've left the past behind, Charlotte. It would only remind me of life back there, if I brought it with me.' Joseph's face clouded over.

'I'm sorry I've reminded you of bad times, with the death of your wife. I do apologize.' She bowed her head; Joseph was obviously still in love with his wife.

'The only thing coming from Accrington is my housekeeper, Mrs Dodgson. She has known me all my life, and looks after me like my own mother. I couldn't have done any of this without her. My wife's gone, and I never discuss her death if I can help it.' He walked over to the window and leaned against the sill, looking down the drive. 'Sorry, Charlotte.' He turned and put a smile back on his face. 'They were trying times – I hope you understand.'

'Of course I do. I apologize if I upset you.' She was more upset at thinking she had blotted her copybook when it came to Joseph.

'No, forgive me, I'm too sensitive. Come, take my arm and view the rest of the house and then we will have some tea. You can meet Mrs Dodgson. She's an old dragon really, but her bark is worse than her bite and I'd be lost without her. She's just who I need to run a house like this, when I'm busy at both mills, and I can trust her.'

'I'm sure she's delightful. We'd be lost without Mrs Cranston; she knows our needs and runs the house like clockwork. Father would be heartbroken if anything happened to her.' Charlotte patted Joseph's hand gently.

'Servants, aye, more like family – it just shouldn't happen. They should know their place and we should remember to keep them in it.' Joseph squeezed Charlotte's gloved hand and raised it to kiss it.

Charlotte blushed and let her hand linger in his for a brief second. 'Now, let us look at the rest of the house. I'm getting ready for that tea, and meeting your Mrs Dodgson. She must be quite a character, if she earns your respect.' Joseph was not letting the grass grow under his feet. Had she read the signs incorrectly or was he totally smitten with her?

'So, Miss Booth, your father owns Crummock, at Austwick. Is it a large farm?' Mrs Dodgson poured out the tea in the grand parlour. The room was sparsely furnished, but had a fire blazing in the hearth.

Charlotte looked at the prying housekeeper. She was surprised that Mrs Dodgson didn't know her place and was so presumptuous, with someone who was obviously above her station. 'Yes, it is quite large, one of the biggest in the district.'

'Is it sheep or dairy?'

'It's sheep; my father breeds sheep. That's why he was hoping that Joseph – I mean, Mr Dawson – was

40

going to open a woollen mill, not a cotton mill. As it stands, we will still have to supply the Jacksons at Long Preston with our wool.' Charlotte felt as if she was being interrogated by the scrawny, tall, dark-haired woman, who had a menacing air about her.

'That will be all, Mrs Dodgson, thank you.' Joseph scowled at his servant and shooed her away with his hand.

Mrs Dodgson curtsied sharply, keeping her face plain and without expression. Her chatelaine belt rattled as she walked away, and she stopped briefly at the doorway, before making her way across the hallway.

Joseph leaned over and offered Charlotte a selection of tempting confectionery, which Charlotte found hard to choose from. 'I do apologize. She can be nosy when she wants to be.'

'It's alright; she didn't ask anything that local folk don't know. I was just a bit surprised.' Charlotte bit into a slice of sponge cake, taking care to use the delicate bone-china plate that had also been handed to her.

'As I say, she is nearly family. Talking about family, have you recovered from losing your grandfather? I did feel for your loss at his funeral. Your father will have inherited Crummock, I presume, along with other assets?'

'Yes, my father owns Crummock now and has been left quite comfortable. Perhaps not as wealthy as yourself, but he has enough to be happy with. And of course my grandpapa left me a small allowance. I always did love Grandpapa.' Charlotte bowed her head and stirred her tea, wondering what this actually had to do with Joseph, but she supposed he had to know that her family were not penniless.

'And who was the young man who rushed to your aid at the funeral?' Joseph smiled and bit into his slice of sponge while waiting for Charlotte's reply.

'Oh! That was Archie – Archie Atkinson. He farms over at Eldroth, at Butterfield Gap. We pretend to wave to each other first thing in the morning, because I can just see his bedroom window across the dale from high out of my window.' Charlotte laughed.

'Do you love him? He seemed concerned for your well-being,' said Joseph.

'Oh God, no – not in that sense. I've just grown up with Archie, and he's Mrs Cranston's nephew. My father says Archie couldn't keep me in shoes. So no, he's only a friend, and always will be, I hope.' Charlotte was ashamed to admit that she would have made the Devil her bedfellow, if it led to being asked back to Windfell and the company of Joseph Dawson.

'Ah, I see. I thought perhaps he was your beau. I didn't want to come between star-crossed lovers.' Joseph smiled at the blushing girl. He'd dug deep into her personal life, but he had to be sure of her commitments.

'Come between us – why would you be doing that, Mr Dawson?' Charlotte looked teasingly at Joseph. She knew why he'd asked, and she knew where it was leading.

'Well, I thought afternoon tea together could be a regular thing, Charlotte, if you are in agreement. I think we keep quite good company together.' He looked across at the blonde beauty and thought that he had chosen well, especially as she had an allowance.

'That would be more than agreeable, Joseph. I'd look forward to our teas together.' She could have run around the great parlour, letting out hoots of delight, but instead she remained calm and genteel.

'Would Friday afternoon suit you? Perhaps we should meet at Mrs Armistead's on Duke Street in Settle? I'm given to believe she runs a good tea room. Besides, it saves you being cross-examined by Mrs Dodgson, who gets a bit protective of me.'

'That would be delightful. I'll look forward to that very much.' Charlotte couldn't wait for Friday to come, and going to Mrs Armistead's was an added bonus. High-tea was such a treat, and Mrs Armistead had the most beautiful fancies; she'd seen them in the window as she walked by.

'Right, Friday it is. And now, if you'll excuse me, I'll get Mrs Dodgson to tell my man that you are nearly ready to return home.' Joseph smiled at his excited guest and walked out of the room.

Charlotte sat back in her chair and looked around the huge parlour. One day this might belong to her; she might be the lady of the manor. Damn it, there was no *might* about it – she *would* be the lady of the manor.

4

Joseph Dawson sat back in his chair in his newly refurbished office at Ferndale Mill. He'd not wasted money on making his office plush and comfortable; that was to spend on his home and not his place of work. He looked out at the newly reinstalled Arkwright water frames and muttered a silent prayer. They'd cost him a small fortune, along with the now-working water wheel that was going to power the water frames that spun the cotton. The raw cotton was waiting for collection by carters on the docks at Liverpool, and should be stacked up in the warehouse by the end of the week.

Thank God he'd kept his connections in New Orleans. His suppliers there had been only too happy to sell to him, no questions asked, as long as his money was good. He'd have to try and get out there again, spend a few weeks on the Natchez plantation; watch the black slaves working in the fields, while he sat sipping port on the porch with the hard-talking Richard

Todd, who would boast of how good his working 'Negroes' were, compared to those on other plantations. He'd enjoy that. Folk respected you out there, if you were white and had brass. It was a pity he couldn't treat the folk in his mill like Negroes. But his overseers would see there were no shirkers, that he knew; he hadn't chosen the men who were going to be his 'eyes' for their kindness. Another week and he'd not be able to hear himself think, as the mill filled up with workers, old and young; as long as they could work, he wasn't bothered.

He listened to the conversation in the next room, where the local doctor was examining a batch of eleven-year-olds for employment in the mill.

'Name!' The doctor bellowed out.

'William Walton,' a voice replied.

'I said "your name", boy,' the doctor bellowed again.

'William Walton.'

'Get out of my sight, boy, you've failed. Next!'

Joseph breathed in deeply as he heard the next interviewee.

'Name, boy?'

'James Mitchell, sir.'

'Put out your tongue. Age?'

'Eleven years and two months, sir.'

'Can you write your name, lad?'

'I can, sir.'

'Report for work at five-thirty on Monday morning at the main gate. Don't be late.'

Joseph smirked, appreciating that for the lad to

45

know his place in society was more important than whether he could write; as long as he knew when to show respect to his elders and betters, he might just survive in his mill. If he had his way, he'd have had children younger than nine working for him. At least they could work next to their parents while they were at the looms and shuttles, instead of the parents wondering what their offspring were up to at home. The Factory Act of 1833 had a lot to answer for, in his view; at least the younger children had been making a bit of money for their parents, or helped out the parish if they came from the workhouse, before the Act was brought in, no matter how meagre their pay.

Joseph stood up from his desk and looked out of his office window across the yard at the millpond. A few hundred yards further along he had families moving into the empty mill cottages that would house his workers. Families from Lancashire, Skipton and an occasional Dales family, fed up of eking out a living on a small piece of land that had probably been in their family for centuries. Now they were going to be slaves to the mill bell – fed by him, housed by him and even told by him how long to pray. The fools! Their lives were his to do with as he pleased, and no one was going to stop him. On their backs he hoped to have a lifestyle beyond belief and, if his plans were to succeed with the smitten Miss Booth as his soon-to-be wife, he would also be a landowner in a while. Life couldn't be much better.

He turned sharply as he heard a timid knock on his office door.

'Yes, who is it?'

The door opened slowly. Before him stood a slim-figured, dark-haired young woman with cheeks as bright as her cherry-red lips. She stood there hesitantly, realizing that she was in the wrong room.

'Sorry, sir. I think I've got the wrong office.' She turned and started to close the door.

'Are you after employment here?' Joseph took in the dark good looks of a local beauty.

'I am, sir. I was told to go upstairs to the offices, but I think I'm in the wrong one.'

'What's your name, girl?' Joseph watched as she wrapped her shawl around herself tightly, showing her figure off to its full extent.

'Betsy Foster, sir.'

'Have you worked in a cotton mill before, Miss Foster?'

'Yes, sir. I work at Belmont Mill in Skipton, on the carding machine, aligning the cotton fibres.'

'And what brings you here, Miss Foster?'

'I've seen that there are cottages available to rent, and I have a younger dependent brother. We lost our parents to the cholera two years ago, and I've vowed ever since to move out further into the countryside. I don't like our Johnny running wild on the streets.'

Joseph walked to his desk and scribbled a hasty note. 'Give this to the man in the next office. It informs him to give you the last empty cottage on the row of mill cottages, and to put you on the carding machine, come Monday morning.' He passed it to her and noticed her hand tremble as she accepted.

'Thank you, sir. Thank you, sir, I won't let you down. God bless you for your kindness.' Betsy could not believe her luck as she closed the door behind her. Everything she had ever wanted since her parents' death had suddenly become hers.

Joseph smiled; he couldn't believe he had a true beauty at his beck and call, and one who now owed everything to her employer. He had thought life couldn't get any better. Well, now it was definitely complete!

Charlotte sat on the rugged limestone outcrop of rock that covered Moughton Scars, a high fellside that rose out of Crummockdale. It was her favourite place on the entire farm. She could gaze for miles in all directions, and sit and listen to the skylarks that sang their familiar song above her head.

Life had been a whirlwind lately. She'd had two months of flowers, fine dining and being treated like a lady by Joseph Dawson. She sighed deeply and breathed in, smelling the late spring air and feeling the warm sunshine on her face. She did love him, truly she did, but things were moving so fast – too fast for her. She did want to be mistress of Windfell, to be married to Joseph, to have his children and be a woman of substance, but how she would miss days like today. A day when she had wandered out of the farmhouse in her ordinary everyday clothes, not bothered about how her hair looked or whether she had rouge on her cheeks. If she was to marry Joseph, everything would change. On the other hand, look at what she was gaining. Any other farm lass would not be able to believe her luck. So why was she losing her fascination with all aspects of Windfell and its occupants?

She stood up on the edge of the scar and shouted to the world, 'What do I do: do I say "yes"?' An echo bounced around the scar, almost mocking the desperation in her situation, as it answered the last word repeatedly. 'Hmm, so that's your reply,' she muttered to herself and continued with her thoughts: I know I'm being daft; I'll give Joseph permission to speak to my father and set a date, if he's happy to give us his blessing. Dear Father, I will miss him so much, but it's not like he's a million miles away – just over the next dale. Besides, he can make his house his real home, once I'm out of the way. I believe he and Mrs Cranston think I was born yesterday! Charlotte grinned, thinking about the love between her father and Lucy, the cook. They must think she was deaf of a night. Someone should tell them that the slightest sound carried around the old farmhouse.

Slowly now she clambered along the limestone clints and grikes, making her way back to the green-grassed pathway that had been used for centuries by travellers between Crummockdale and Horton-in-Ribblesdale. The newly sprung bracken edged the path back down into the valley, and the small stream that evolved out of the limestone bedrock sparkled and meandered in front of her. Despite never knowing her mother, she had been privileged enough to have a perfect childhood, growing up in such a glorious place. It was this that she was going to miss, along with not having any responsibilities, except occasionally chastising her father over his bookkeeping, which she knew he hated.

Her walk hadn't helped her decide at all. In fact, if anything it had confused her even more; she didn't want to turn her back on her beloved home, no matter how big and grand Windfell was. She made her way along the fellside, following the limestone wall, and eventually came to the gate that led into the farmyard. She was just in the process of tying the rope that secured it when she heard the voice of Lucy Cranston, who was laughing and talking on the steps of the farmhouse kitchen to someone just inside the doorway. Charlotte made her way across the yard and to the kitchen.

'Miss Charlotte, I'm so glad you are back from your walk. Look who we have visiting – it's our Archie, and this is his fiancée, Rosie. They've walked up from Austwick to tell me their news. They've just been arranging for their banns to be read by the vicar. It's such a surprise, I didn't even know he was courting.' Lucy Cranston gave the pretty brunette girl by Archie's side a huge hug and then wiped a tear away from her full cheeks.

'Fiancée! Archie, that was quick work. I didn't realize, and now you are getting married? You've kept that quiet!' Charlotte looked at the lad she had once had feelings for, and at his bride-to-be. She couldn't help but feel a pang of jealousy, but at the same time an air of superiority washed over her as she looked at the young, quivering farm lass who stood by his side. Who was she, to stand arm-in-arm with a lad she hardly knew?

Archie blushed. 'Aye, well, it's a bit quick, I know – but we have to, you know?' Archie tilted his head towards Rosie and looked down at his feet, embarrassed. His girlfriend jabbed him in the ribs with her elbow while smiling at Charlotte.

'Well, I wish you all the best, and congratulations. Have you found somewhere to live?' Charlotte smiled. So that's how it was; he'd got the lass pregnant. Poor bugger, he'd all on to look after himself, let alone a baby.

'Aye, Rosie's father says we can live with them, just until the baby comes and we get set up on our own feet. It's going to be hard, making a living for us all, but I'll try and get somewhere of my own to rent as soon as I can. My father and mother say they'll help out, too. Rosie's family have a farm over near Bentham, so my family know what I'm marrying into.'

'They've got twenty acres on the edge of Mewith Moor,' chirped Rosie, before going quiet again.

'It will be nice living there.' Charlotte thought about the edge of Mewith Moor and how wild it was; there wouldn't be much of a living to be made there. Archie could have done so much better for himself.

'Aye, well, as long as you love one another; and a

baby always brings its own love into the world.' Lucy Cranston smiled at her nephew. She knew he had once had feelings for Charlotte, but had also known that nothing would ever come of it. She could read the disappointment and hurt on her nephew's face. The silly lad should have kept it in his pocket and tried harder for Lottie's hand, proving that he could have farmed Crummock well and made Wesley proud of him. But no, precious Lottie had to marry into society, which had been her destiny as soon as her father realized how clever his daughter was. At the end of the day, he'd lost sight as to who would look after the family farm.

'I'm sure you will be very happy. Don't forget to give me an invite.' Charlotte brushed past the threesome and was relieved to reach the sanctuary of the kitchen. She could feel tears welling up in her throat. She hadn't realized how much Archie had meant to her, and now it was too late. So much for his announcement of endearing love on the morning of her grandpapa's death. He must have jumped into bed with that dimwit of a farm girl nearly straight away. Still, the news had made up her mind about what to do with her life. She wasn't going to be left struggling to make a living on a godforsaken farm. She was going to live the life of a lady, accept the hand of Joseph Dawson and make her home at Windfell Manor. She was going to be a woman of substance, someone to look up to and recognize in high society.

5

'Don't you think you're moving a bit too quick, lad? You've not known our Lottie six months yet!' Wesley Booth looked across at the swanky, headstrong mill owner. 'Your wife's not been dead that long, either. Are you sure you are ready to take on my lass?' At his first meetings with the forward-thinking young man, Wesley had thought Joseph would be ideal for his daughter, but recent conversations with the locals had raised doubts.

'I've never come across a lovelier creature. She suits me well, and it is as if I have known her all my life, Mr Booth. I can give her the lifestyle and position that any other woman would be envious of. I can assure you that Charlotte will want for nothing.' Joseph looked at the old man who was going to be his father-in-law. He was an unhealthy specimen of a farmer, too fond of his food and drink, and his lips and cheeks were coloured purple, a sure sign that his heart was not that strong.

He wouldn't have to wait too long for the farm to fall into Charlotte's hands.

'But do you love her, lad? You can buy owt with money – anything, that is, but love, and that's the most precious thing in a marriage.' Wesley held onto the back of his favourite chair and looked squarely at the man who was going to take his daughter away from him.

'I do indeed, sir. And of course she would be free to visit you any time she wishes.' Joseph patted Wesley on his shoulder, assuring him that his intentions towards his daughter were honourable.

'Well, you have my blessing, lad – or should I say "son". By God, that sounds strange; I never thought I'd have a son. What's mine is yours, lad, as long as you do right by my lass.'

Wesley wiped his nose and looked at the dark-haired man in the high collar with a diamond stud in it. Well, he'd got what he'd always wished for: a man with brass for his Lottie; but was Joseph a good man? Only time would tell him that.

'You can come in now; I know you are hiding behind that door.' Wesley knew Charlotte had been trying to listen to every word, through the thick oak door that separated the parlour from the passageway. 'Aye, he's all yours. I've given you my blessing, and now we've to talk about a dowry and set a date. You'll both have to go and see the vicar, get a date set, and we'll take it from there.' Wesley's breath was nearly knocked out of him as Lottie hugged him tightly and kissed him all over his cheeks.

'I love you so much, Father. Thank you for giving us your blessing. I love Joseph, really I do, and we will be happy until the day we die.' Charlotte reached for Joseph's hand and hugged both her men.

'Yes, thank you, Mr Booth. And please, I don't expect a dowry; your daughter's hand is enough for me. And when it comes to the wedding, I prefer to keep it quiet. I've not much family, and what I have are all down in Lancashire. Do you agree, Charlotte: just a quiet marriage?' Joseph squeezed her hand and looked at his new fiancée.

'I don't mind if it's just us three there, as long as I've got you. But I must have a dress; all covered with Nottingham lace, with gloves and veil to match. 'Oh, and a cake. Mrs Cranston will have to make a cake.' Charlotte was excited about her wedding day and her mind was racing.

'Perhaps you should leave the cake in my hands, my dear. My new cook comes highly recommended from her last employment with the Sidgwicks at Skipton. And, as you know, I now have several members of house-staff who can easily manage to host a wedding breakfast at Windfell.' Joseph was determined that the wedding would be planned by him, not by the cook and Lottie's parlour maid at Crummock. 'Would you like Mrs Dodgson to accompany you to choose your wedding dress? I'm sure she would enjoy every minute.' Even though the offer of his housekeeper's help with the dress choice must have sounded ridiculous, he wanted to make sure he was marrying his bride in something respectable.

'Oh, Joseph, Mrs Cranston will be so disappointed if she can't make the cake. She's a superb cook and, to be honest, I think I might like her to come with me to choose the material for a dress. She's the nearest thing to a mother I've got.' Charlotte was shocked that control of her wedding was slipping out of her hands already.

'Charlotte, you are going to have to realize that marriage to me will come with expectations – and saying that the family cook is a substitute mother to you is not recommended.' Joseph showed his disgust at the lack of distance between the classes.

'Now then, lad. Lucy Cranston means everything to my lass and me. She's been there through rough and smooth and, like Lottie says, she has been good to her. Now, let your fancy cook make the cake; but if the lass wants Lucy with her when she looks for a dress, you let her – and let that be an end to it. Else you can think again about marrying my lass.' Wesley looked at his future son-in-law. Life was not going to be a bed of roses for his lass from now on. She might have standing in the community, but that would be about it, if Joseph Dawson had his way.

'I'm sorry. I just wanted it to be right and, to my eyes, a cook helping choose my bride's wedding dress doesn't sit well in polite society.' Joseph knew he'd gone too far.

'No, and neither does a housekeeper's help. Your

Mrs Dodgson doesn't know the first thing about my lass! Don't you fret, Lottie's got a good eye, and I'll take her over to Harrogate and get her fitted out properly, with Mrs Cranston's help.' Wesley stood his ground. 'Aye, and I've a few friends and relations that I might like to invite. Never mind a small wedding; this is my only daughter's wedding and it's a thing to celebrate, I hope! If brass is an issue, which I'm sure it isn't, you've just to say. I'll pay for the do – after all, it's a father's privilege.' Wesley didn't like being dictated to.

'Excuse me, it is *my* wedding.' Charlotte stood with her hands on her hips and glared at the men in her life. 'My wedding breakfast will be at Windfell, and Mrs Cranston will come with me to Harrogate to choose my wedding attire. Both of us will put a list of guests together and see how many we come up with. And then, dear Father and Joseph, you can come to an arrangement about payment. However, before all that, we had better see Reverend Richardson to find out if he is willing to marry us at Austwick church, and check which dates are available.' Charlotte nearly stamped her foot in temper. This should have been one of the most enjoyable days of her life, and instead she was being torn apart.

'Aye, lass, that's alright by me.' Wesley turned and looked out of his parlour window, hiding from his daughter his growing doubts about Joseph.

'If that's what you wish, Charlotte, then we will go and see the vicar. And if you want to put a guest list together, I will be happy to accommodate it. Paying for it is not a problem. I just hoped for a quiet affair.' Joseph put his arm around Charlotte's waist and then released her, as she pulled away and stood between him and her father.

'How about an October wedding? The twenty-seventh: it would have been my late mother's birthday? If the vicar can undertake it then.' Charlotte looked at her sulking men. 'We will have known each other exactly six months then, Joseph.' She reached for his hand and squeezed it.

'Your mother would have liked that. The twenty-seventh is grand with me.' Wesley smiled at his daughter. If Joseph thought he was going to bully his daughter, he'd soon learn different.

'That's fine, my dear: the twenty-seventh of October it is, if the vicar can comply.' Joseph smiled. The sooner he could get her away and under his roof, the better. She'd soon realize that his way was all or nothing.

'Breathe in.' Lucy Cranston yanked hard on the cream laces that bound Charlotte's bodice.

'I can't breathe – how much tighter are you going to pull? I feel like a trussed chicken ready for the pot.' Charlotte could feel the heat rising in her cheeks, as the old cook pulled and tugged her waist even tighter.

'Sorry, Miss Charlotte, but we've got to tame that waist and bosom of yours, so that man can't take his eyes off you as you walk down the aisle.' She finally finished and tied the laces in a delicate bow, before standing back and admiring her mistress in her bloomers and bodice. Charlotte's waist was about the size of one of her thighs, thought Lucy, as she caught her breath before adding the next layer of clothing.

'Phew, I don't know if I can stand all day in this. I can hardly breathe.' Charlotte bent over and tried to get her breath as she looked at herself in the mirror.

'It'll get slacker, the longer you wear it. Besides, you'll forget all about it being on, once you are walking down that aisle and you see dashing Mr Dawson waiting for you. Come on, arms up: underskirts next, and then your dress.'

Lucy slipped the full cotton underskirt over Charlotte's head and then reached for the cream Nottingham-lace dress that had been hanging up behind her bedroom door. They had seen a copy of it in one of the flash dress-shop windows in Harrogate and had known straight away that it was the dress for Charlotte, who had stood patiently while the dressmaker painstakingly measured and pinned her, before hand-making the perfect wedding dress for her big day. The lace was so delicate, embroidered slightly with rosebuds and falling leaves, with a high enough neckline to be a little revealing, but not too brash. Lucy buttoned up the back while looking over Charlotte's shoulder, as she looked at herself in the long mirror in her bedroom.

'You look beautiful, Miss Charlotte – or you will, when we get that hair out of those rags. I'll give Mary a yell; she's better at doing your hair than I am. Besides, I want to make sure your father is dressed and isn't letting the side down, before I put on my hat and your veil. Mary!' Lucy stood at the bedroom door and looked round at Charlotte. 'Your mother would be proud of you. You are so bonny and are doing so well for yourself. If you always act like a lady and treat folk right, you'll not go far wrong, Miss Charlotte.' Lucy could feel her eyes filling up with tears, for she loved the lass. 'Mary . . . where are you?'

'I'm coming, I'm coming. I've just been putting some flowers in the horse's mane, while talking to the lad from the smithy. He says there's crowds of locals already waiting for you, Miss Charlotte, and the local children are to tie the church gates to get your guests to throw their coppers, so that they'll untie the gates and let you get out. I might join in with them. There should be some brass thrown, if your fella's got as much as he says.'

'You'll do no such thing, Mary. You'll stand with me at the back of the church and be a lady. You are no longer a child, and you are part of this household and, as such, should be respectable. Now get on and take Miss Charlotte's rags out of her hair. We'll then leave, before her and her father go down to the church with Sam in his buggy.' Lucy was feeling the pressure of the day; she might not have been Wesley's wife or Charlotte's mother, but she had been expected to fulfil both roles on Charlotte's special day.

Mary sighed, lifted the hair brush up from Charlotte's dressing table and watched as her mistress sat in front of her in her beautiful dress. 'You do look pretty, Miss. I wish I could have a dress like that when

60

I get married.' She carefully untied the first knot that held the long strip of cotton rag with Charlotte's blonde hair twisted around it. They had washed and then parted and twisted her hair around a number of rags the previous evening, in order to make it fall into ringlets for her big day. Mary pulled gently and the thick hair fell perfectly down into a tight curl. 'Well, that one looks alright, Miss. I'll take them all out and then just tease them out with the brush, to make them look thicker. I bet you'll be glad to get them all out – I know they aren't that comfortable.' She continued to pull the next ringlet out.

'It's this one here; it's driven me mad all night. It must have some hair more tightly bound than all the rest, because it's pulled on my head all night.' Charlotte put her hand on her head and tugged on the cloth-bound tress.

'I'll take it out now. You are looking lovely already, Miss Charlotte. Mr Dawson doesn't know how lucky he is.'

Charlotte patted Mary's hand. 'What am I going to do, without you and Mrs Cranston? You are both like family to me.' She looked in the mirror at the reflection of herself and the young parlour maid. How she was going to miss home!

'You'll be fine, Miss. You'll have more servants and be more pampered than you'll know what to do with; and me and Mrs Cranston will look after your father, so you don't have to worry about him.' Mary teased out each ringlet and then stood back and admired her handiwork. 'You look perfect, Miss, and your veil will sit splendidly on your long locks. What do you think?'

Charlotte looked at herself in the mirror. It didn't seem to be her reflection looking back at her. She saw a nervous bride-to-be, filled with doubt and concern. She could have cried; she didn't want to leave her home, and her life was going to change beyond belief. For the better, she hoped, but could she be sure – and would she be happy? She didn't need a lady's maid and a housekeeper, along with numerous other servants at her beck and call. She just needed Joseph, and a friend in her new home. And she couldn't see Mrs Dodgson, his housekeeper, ever becoming as close to her as Lucy, or even as Mary.

'There, your father's looking like a real dandy. I'm all ready, and Mary looks like she's worked her magic on you. Now let's put this veil on, and then that's mine and Mary's job done and we'll be off.' Lucy Cranston shuffled back into the room, the feather in her hat announcing her arrival before her. 'There, you are complete.' She pinned the small pearled comb with the delicate veil into Charlotte's hair and stood back. 'A bonnier bride I've never seen. What your father will say, I don't know.'

Lucy sniffled a sob, while Mary gasped as Charlotte stood up.

'I think it should be "Lady Charlotte" from now on, you look so bonny. Come on, Mary, let's us away. Mr Booth is waiting at the bottom of the stairs. We need to get our seat at the church before they arrive.' Lucy stopped in her tracks as she left her mistress. 'Good luck, Miss Charlotte, may God bless you. I'm always here for you.'

'Thank you, Mrs Cranston. That means a lot to me, and I'm not that far away, so you must come and have tea with me.' Charlotte walked over and gave her faithful cook a kiss on the cheek.

'I don't think Mr Dawson will be happy with that. A cook having tea with the lady of the manor. Nay, lass, you'll have to learn your position in life from now on.' Lucy's hand lingered on the door knob. 'Charlotte, you do love Joseph Dawson, don't you? You're not just marrying him because of his position and his money? It isn't those aspects that are ruling your head?' She knew she was talking out of place, but she was concerned for the girl's happiness, and that of her father.

'Oh, Mrs Cranston, bless you. I love Joseph with every inch of my heart. I love his dark hair, his blue eyes, the way he dresses – the very smell of him. He cares for me, and loves me as I love him. How can you ever question our love for one another?' Charlotte was shocked. Joseph was the perfect gentleman, who loved her and had promised her the earth. They would live happily until the end of time, as far as she was concerned.

'Aye, lass, I just thought happen he'd turned your head, and I hoped you'd not live to regret this day. Marry in haste and repent in leisure, as the saying goes. Your father would be broken-hearted if Joseph wasn't the right man for you.' Lucy looked at the blushing bride and watched a shadow cross her brow.

'I love him, Mrs Cranston. He is a man of honour, who will love and cherish me. My father would not have brought him to the house if it had been any other way. Besides, over the last six months we have grown stronger in our love every day. Please be happy for us – it is our special day.' Charlotte squeezed Lucy's hand tightly. 'I love him, truly I do, and he's a good man.'

Lucy smiled and squeezed Charlotte's hand back, trying to fight back the tears that were welling up in her eyes. 'Take care, lass. I've loved you like my own. I wish for you all the happiness in the world.'

'Thank you, Mrs Cranston, your wishes mean a great deal to me. And don't worry, we are in love, and this day is to be celebrated.' Charlotte kissed the old cook on her cheek again. How could she ever doubt the love that she and Joseph had between them?

Lucy made her way down the stairs, shaking her head. She was going to watch a marriage that she knew was not going to be a happy one. The lass should have married her nephew – that would have been a better match. Joseph Dawson was a nowter, a man who got what he wanted by fair means or foul, and Charlotte was going to have to find that out the hard way.

Wesley's eyes filled with tears as he watched his only daughter glide down the stairs; she was the image of her mother when he had married her. If only she'd lived to see this day, she would have been so proud. 'Now then, lass, take my arm and make an old man feel like a millionaire.'

Charlotte smiled. Her father had scrubbed up well, and for once looked like the wealthy farmer he was. 'You don't look too bad yourself.' She linked her arm into his and they walked down the passageway arm-in-arm, picking up her bouquet of lilies from the hallway table before walking out into the hazy autumn sunshine.

'I love you, my lass, I hope you know that. But today you start a new life with that man of yours and, like your wedding vows tell you, you've got to love, honour and obey; and what's yours is his now. That doesn't mean to say that if he treats you badly I'd turn my back on you, and you know where home is, if you want me.' Wesley helped his beloved daughter up into the flower-adorned gig and watched as she brushed a tear away from her cheek.

'I love you too, Father. I'll miss you so much. Crummock will always be my home, but, as you say, a new life with Joseph awaits and I love him so much that it hurts.' She looked at her father and then at her family home. Far away in the distance she could hear the church bells ringing, her wedding bells beckoning her to the church. 'Oh, Father, am I doing the right thing? I do love Joseph, but I don't want to leave home and you.'

'It'll be right, lass, you've a grand home and a good man. We've all to grow up sometime, and just be glad you're not farming on some godforsaken strip of land, like you would have been if you had married that Archie. And you love the man, else you wouldn't be marrying him.' Wesley patted her knee.

Charlotte smiled and kissed him on the cheek.

'Right, come on: we've a wedding to go to and it can't begin without us. Those poor buggers that are ringing those bells will be cursing us. Their arms are going to be dropping off, if we don't get a move on. Not to say that that man of yours will be wondering where we are.'

If Wesley could have said 'Stay', he would have done, but he'd played a part in this matchmaking and now it had come to fruition. He had to make the most of it, for Charlotte's sake, regardless of being heartbroken at losing his daughter to Joseph Dawson and his brass.

6

Charlotte smiled at her new husband, who sat by her side. It had been a wonderful wedding in the village church at Austwick. Her heart had nearly leapt out of her chest as she'd walked down the aisle to stand by his side. He truly was the most handsome man she had ever set eyes on. And when he placed the wedding ring on her finger, she had to fight back the tears of happiness as he gently kissed her on the cheek and whispered how much he loved her, whilst the vicar looked on.

This was the happiest day of her life, with the man she loved. Although there had not been many guests on either side, the villagers had made up for the lack of them and had cheered the young couple as they left the church. They cheered even more as Wesley, Joseph and best man Bert Bannister, the mill overseer, threw handfuls of coins for the children of the village. Charlotte loved seeing the children running and scrabbling for every farthing and ha'penny they could find amongst the cobbles, before untying the churchyard gates to let the newly married couple escape. When she and Joseph had finally been able to get to the safety of his coach and horses, he had lent gently over and kissed her with passion, telling her how much he loved her. All her doubts about doing the wrong thing in marrying him disappeared in that second. Of course he loved her, and she him; and life was going to be marvellous from now on.

The coach and horses turned into the driveway of Windfell Manor and the coachman quickly pulled the team up just outside the steps, as he had done on previous occasions.

'We are here, my darling, at your new home.' Joseph leapt down and reached for Charlotte as she climbed out of the coach.

On either side of the grand steps the new staff of Windfell stood, welcoming their master and new mistress on their wedding day. Parlour maids, butler, gardeners and footmen all bowed and wished the newly-weds con-gratulations, while the housekeeper, Mrs Dodgson, stood at the head of them all, looking sombre and unsmiling.

'Make way, make way.' Joseph lifted Charlotte off her feet and carried her, laughing and screaming, over the threshold with all the staff cheering.

'You'll hurt your back doing that. Where's all the rest of them?' Mrs Dodgson growled as she followed the newly-weds inside, directing serving girls, butlers and the cook back to work.

'They are on their way.' Joseph laughed as he placed

Charlotte down on her feet in the middle of the grand hall. 'Is all in hand, Mrs D.? Have you done us proud on our wonderful day?'

'We've done as much as we can, and I hope it meets with your satisfaction. Go in and see for yourself.' Her face never changed expression as she looked Charlotte up and down.

'Doesn't Charlotte look beautiful? Every bit the lady of the manor.' Joseph summoned the underbutler to open the doors to the guests, whose carriages he could hear approaching, while he talked to his housekeeper.

'She'll do. Now, if you'll excuse me, I've a wedding breakfast to organize.' Dora Dodgson glared at Charlotte, without wishing her any congratulations or making her welcome.

'I don't think your Mrs Dodgson likes me – she never has a kind word for me,' Charlotte said to Joseph.

'Nonsense, that's just her way. And she was close to May; she hasn't got over her death yet. She probably thinks I'm marrying too quickly. I'll have a word with her later. Now come, let's take our places in the dining room, my darling. I think you will be impressed with your wedding breakfast.'

Charlotte's face filled with awe as Joseph opened the heavy walnut doors into the dining room. Two long tables were covered with cream tablecloths decorated with swags and roses, and both were laid with the finest of silver and crystal. The tables were fit for a king to dine at. The sideboards were laden with dishes of fruit, delicate desserts and a selection of drinks, so that the serving staff could quickly fill any empty glass that needed replenishing. Three timid maids curtsied to Charlotte and Joseph as they entered the room, and the butler bowed and smiled to them both, then pointed to their places in the centre of the largest table.

'We will greet our guests at the doorway, thank you, Yates, and then if you can show them to their seats.' Joseph linked his arm through Charlotte's and stood proudly next to her, eager to greet their guests to the marital home.

'It is beautiful, Joseph. I'm so happy, and I'm glad that we kept it quite small. I thought at one time my father was going to invite everyone in the district. However, sense prevailed, thank goodness.'

'Yes, I know. We have thirty guests, but it is quite intimate. Thank heavens he saw my reasoning for not asking Mrs Cranston. It would have been embarrassing for him. The poor woman would have been most uncomfortable; she would have been out of her depth.' Joseph shook the hand of the Mayor of Settle as he walked in with his wife on his arm. She curtsied to Charlotte and looked her up and down, before they were ushered to their seats.

'You are right, my dear, but she is more like family. She has more right to be here than the Mayor of Settle and his wife.' Charlotte smiled and shook the hand of another dignitary who wished them both well.

'Charlotte, we have to impress by having the right connections. Being best friends with a cook on an outlying farm is not going to impress anyone. Besides, I don't want to be seen condoning your father's affections for his servant – it is not done in polite society.' Joseph shook another councillor's hand and turned to look at Charlotte.

'You mean, you know that my father loves Mrs Cranston? Does everybody know about their "understanding"?' Charlotte looked horrified.

'I'm afraid so, my dear. Let me say that it does not bother me in the least, as long as he doesn't flaunt his infatuation. And inviting her here today would have done just that.' He patted Charlotte's hand for comfort, sensing the horror on her face, which betrayed the fact that she thought the skeleton in the family cupboard was not public knowledge.

Charlotte smiled at the arriving guests, but behind her smile lay worry. Her father was obviously the talk of the district, with his love for the family cook. How could she hold her head up and act like a lady? It would perhaps be better if her father was to marry Lucy Cranston. Either that or sack her. Either way, it was the cause of talk and gossip among the local gentry.

'By heck, tha's put on a good spread here, lad. Tha's right, we couldn't have put this on up at our place, could we, our lass?' Wesley Booth looked down at the line of cutlery and wondered where to begin, as the footman placed a steaming bowl of soup before him.

Charlotte leaned over and whispered in his ear, 'Start at the outside of your cutlery and work in with

71

each course,' as her father looked puzzled as to which spoon he should use first. 'And that is your side plate.' She felt embarrassed by her father. How could he show her up on her wedding day?

'This must have cost a fair bob or two, Joseph. I bet tha's glad tha doesn't do this every day.' Wesley watched everyone eating their soup and tried to copy their manners. He could sense that Lottie was watching his every move and he didn't want to let her down.

'I don't ever aim to do this again, Wesley. Your beautiful daughter is the only wife for me.' Joseph sipped his soup and smiled.

'Here, here, Joseph, and a beautiful wife she is,' the Mayor of Settle cheered. His wife gave him a warning glance as she delicately wiped her lips with her napkin.

'Glad to hear it, lad. You've got a grand home here, just needs filling with a few bairns running around the place, livening the spot up a bit. But I'm sure you'll not need my advice on how to remedy that. Eh, lad?' Wesley grinned and sat back in his chair.

'Father!' Charlotte was horrified. He wasn't talking about his sheep, now that he was at her wedding breakfast. And it was she who would be producing the grandchildren he was hinting heavily about.

'I don't know if I want children. I need to focus on my business, and children would only get in the way. However, it is for Charlotte and me to discuss, and not dining-table conversation.' Joseph sat back and looked at his father-in-law. He really was a crude, rough, uneducated man. Thank heavens Charlotte had manners.

72

She was not out of place in any society, but at the same time he was sure she would do as he bade, if only to keep her in the lifestyle that she craved. As for children, he wasn't fussed; they would only hinder him and be a drain on his finances, and he didn't really want any. He was not the sort of man to sit, of an evening, bouncing demanding children on his knee.

Charlotte looked at the two men in her life. They never would agree; they were two different breeds, and neither of them was thinking of her. She would like a family, some children to love and nurture; but children – or the lack of them – had never been discussed before the wedding. She was now the wife of Joseph, whom she loved dearly and had just promised to obey. If he didn't want children, then she would have to obey his wishes, for that was her lot in life now. It would be a pity if she was never going to be a mother. However, Mother Nature would probably play her hand and children would come along in the end, of that she was sure. She had expected that, once married to Joseph, parenthood would surely follow. A pang of disappointment came over her. She would love to have at least two children to call their own.

The last guest had gone, and Joseph and Charlotte were finally on their own as they sat in the parlour.

'Well, Mrs Dawson, we have had quite a day. I think we impressed everyone with our home and the wedding breakfast.' Joseph sat in his high-backed chair next to the fire and looked across at his beautiful new wife.

'Yes, my love, we did indeed. How can I ever thank you? I'm sorry my father sometimes overstepped the mark. He's used to talking to his farming friends, and they always say it as it is.' Charlotte sensed that Joseph was not happy with her father and felt she had to apologize on his behalf.

'It makes no difference to me, but if he wants to go up in society, he's going to have to change his ways, and I won't have my private life discussed. I suggest, my dear, that what goes on within these four walls stays within these four walls.' He stood up and placed his hand on the large Adams fireplace.

'Of course, I understand.' Charlotte bowed her head. Gone were the days when she could be open with her father, for her first loyalties belonged to Joseph now. She looked up as the parlour door opened.

'Ah, Mrs Dodgson, thank you for joining us.' Joseph cupped his hands behind his back. 'I just needed to have a word with you. Charlotte is now my wife, and I wish you to respect her as much as you did the late Mrs Dawson. She is your new mistress and, as such, you will do as she wishes.' He turned before the house-keeper could answer, and gazed at the oil painting above the fireplace.

'I will do as you wish, sir. I know I'm only here to serve you, and now the new mistress. Lily, the lady's maid, is waiting for Mrs Dawson. She needs to discuss her needs and see what else is expected of her.'

Charlotte could have sworn she read hatred in Mrs Dodgson's eyes as she glared at her. 'Thank you, Mrs

Dodgson, I'm sure we will become used to one another in time. I'll go and join Lily and let her know my daily routine. Do we have anything planned for tomorrow, Joseph?' She rose and stood by the side of her husband.

'No. I'll have to go and make sure there are no problems at the mill, and I thought you might like to acquaint yourself with the staff and the house. Mrs Dodgson, would you mind staying with me for a while, once Charlotte has gone. I need to discuss a small problem that we have.' Joseph held Charlotte's hand and kissed her lightly on her cheek. 'I'll be with you shortly, my dear.'

'I'll leave you two to discuss things. Good evening, Mrs Dodgson. Don't be too late, my dear.' Charlotte squeezed Joseph's hand and then walked quickly out of the parlour, past the dismissive housekeeper. She lingered next to the closed parlour doors, in the hope of hearing the conversation between master and servant, but the door was too thick. So she quickly made her way up the grand stairs to the master bedroom, where her lady's maid was waiting for her.

'Good evening, ma'am.' The young, pretty, blonde-haired woman curtsied and smiled.

'Good evening, Lily, you must be my lady's maid, I take it?' Charlotte looked at the young lass standing before her, not quite knowing who was the more nervous between them.

'I am, ma'am. I've laid out your nightwear and have pulled the sheets down. I'm here to help you undress and make you ready for bed.' Lily blushed, knowing that it was Charlotte's wedding night.

'Thank you, Lily. I'll let you into a secret: I've never had a lady's maid before. So this is all new to me.' She smiled.

'It's new to me as well, ma'am. There isn't much call for ladies' maids in Settle, but my mother says I'll be good at it, and Mr Dawson seemed to think that I'd suit you.' Lily blushed again and stoked the coal fire, so that the fire was nice for her new mistress to undress in front of. 'Your dress is beautiful, ma'am. I'd love to get married in something like that. All the staff were speechless when you stepped out of the carriage with Mr Dawson.'

'Thank you, Lily, it has been a perfect day. Now, would you like to unbutton and unlace my dress. I've felt like I'm going to faint all day. Mrs Cranston laced me up so tight this morning.' Charlotte stood in front of the mirror and looked at herself and the young maid. The reflection showed two young women in grand surroundings, both of whom were going to have to get used to their new roles in life. 'That's better, Lily, at long last I can breathe.' She smiled at her young helper as the maid carefully laid out the wedding dress and underskirts, then gently slipped a nightdress over her head.

'The downstairs maid has filled the wash jug up with warm water, ma'am, if you need a wash in private.' Lily pointed to the marble-topped washstand, with a jug and bowl waiting for her to use. 'I'll take your shoes down to the footman to polish, while you are making yourself comfortable, and then I'll come back and brush your hair before you get into bed.' She had the sense to know that her mistress needed time to herself and smiled, thinking of her mistress's wedding-night antics, before disappearing with the shoes down to the servants' quarters.

Charlotte quickly took the opportunity to wash herself while alone. At least her lady's maid respected her privacy, she thought, as she washed herself with the warm water, feeling it refreshing her. She then sat on the edge of the bed and gazed around her. The bedroom was beautiful. She'd helped Joseph choose the heavy curtains at the windows, and the Gillow's furniture complemented the warm decor of the bedroom, just as they had imagined. It was a long way away from her whitewashed bedroom at Crummock. Her mind flitted back there for a short while. Her father had gone home more than a little merry. She didn't blame him, for it was after all her wedding day, but she wished he had been more careful with what he said. She could see that was going to be a sore point between her and Joseph. Oh, Joseph! Tonight was their wedding night. What was she to expect? The most she had ever done was kiss him. And for him to say he didn't want children! If they were to be intimate, then children would definitely follow; and of course they had to be, for that's what marriage was all about. Besides, her father was right: she'd like some children, especially a daughter to spoil and pamper in this beautiful home, otherwise what was the point of their marriage?

'Have you finished, ma'am? Mr Yates is just undressing Mr Dawson in his bedroom.' Lily smiled as she watched the expression on Charlotte's face.

'Mr Dawson's bedroom? I thought this bedroom was for us both.' Charlotte's face must have told the maid everything.

'Don't worry, ma'am, I'm sure he will come to you. Mr Yates told me that Mr Dawson doesn't sleep well of a night and is concerned that his restlessness might keep you awake.' Lily brushed Charlotte's long hair and watched her new mistress panic as she sat in front of her dressing-table mirror. 'Just because you have separate bedrooms doesn't mean you can't . . . you know – you know what . . . Sorry, ma'am, if I'm talking out of turn here, but you look so worried.'

'I'm just concerned that we won't be together tonight. After all, it is our wedding night and it is expected.' Charlotte felt as embarrassed as the maid.

'I'm sure he will be counting the minutes, and will be in your room as soon as he knows I've left you.' Lily placed the silver-plated hairbrush back down on the dressing table. 'Would you like me to help you into bed?'

'No, I'm fine, thank you, Lily. I'll no doubt see you in the morning?'

'Yes, ma'am. Would you like breakfast in bed or down in the dining room?' The maid waited at the bedroom door.

'I'll have breakfast with Mr Dawson in the dining room, thank you, Lily.' Charlotte walked across to her bed.

'That will be at six then, ma'am. He always eats early and then he goes down to the mill.' Lily waited and watched as her mistress debated the early time. 'Perhaps if you have breakfast in bed tomorrow, ma'am, and then I'll come and dress you?'

'Yes, perhaps that would be better. Thank you, Lily.' Charlotte sighed.

'Anything you want, ma'am, just pull on the bell-pull, and either me or Mazy, the scullery maid, will come. And don't worry, ma'am. Mr Dawson will be with you shortly. Goodnight.'

'Goodnight, Lily, and thank you.' Charlotte could have cried as her maid closed the door behind her. She was alone, awaiting her lover, but would he come? She climbed in between the cool cotton sheets – sheets that had been woven at Ferndale Mill, along with the towel that she had dried herself with. This was now her way of life: servants and cotton goods. What a change from the warm, friendly home she was used to. She pulled the sheets up to her chin and gazed at the ceiling, turning her head as she heard the bedroom door open.

'Charlotte, my Charlotte, are you waiting for me?' Joseph closed the door quietly behind him and walked stealthily across the carpeted floor to her bedside. He sat on the bed's edge and took her hand, before kissing her passionately on the lips and running his hands under her nightdress, feeling the firmness of her pert nipples.

Charlotte had never let anyone touch her there, and her body rippled with pleasure while her mind raced, wondering what pleasures were to follow and hoping that Joseph would be a gentle lover. Mrs Cranston had touched on what to do on your wedding night, as she had laid out Charlotte's nightdress, ready for her first night as a married woman. She knew that she should pleasure her man, but was frightened at the thought of what to do.

Joseph slid into bed beside her, taking his time to pleasure her, his hand moving down between her legs, playing with her most sensitive areas, where no man had been before. He gently guided Charlotte's hand to his private parts and urged her hands to pleasure him in the same way he was pleasuring her.

Charlotte felt herself quiver with delight, and wanted to shout and scream as she dug her nails into the broad back of her lover as he brought her to a climax. She knew he would expect the same, and opened her legs wide so that he could enter her without resistance. But he declined the invitation, lay back and placed her hand once again on his throbbing penis. Charlotte kissed him delicately on his lips and chest. She wanted him to enter her, she needed it so badly; but still he insisted on her satisfying him, without giving herself totally to him. She lay by his side, doing as he bade, until with a loud groan his last thrust was spent. The pair of them lay on the bedcovers side-by-side, not saying anything for a brief second that felt like hours to Charlotte.

'Thank you, my dear, you did not disappoint.' Joseph reached over to Charlotte and kissed her gently on the lips. 'I'll go back to my room now and let you have a good night's sleep.'

She pulled on his arm gently as he tugged his night-shirt down and sat on the edge of the bed. 'Stay with me, Joseph, it is our wedding night.' Her eyes pleaded with him. She needed to feel him by her side, and perhaps perform the same act of love again in the morning.

'I must go. It will soon be morning, and the mill and my employees will not wait. We have all our lives, Charlotte, to lie in one another's arms.' He stood up and looked down at his bride. She was beautiful, but he had no intention of sleeping with her through the night. He wouldn't have been able to control his urges for that long.

'I understand.' Charlotte turned her head, her eyes brimming with tears as he walked across the bedroom floor, quietly closing the door behind him. The mill and his business were his first love, and she must learn her position in the life of her new husband.

Mazy, the scullery maid, bobbed and curtsied before leaving the room as the newly lit fire sparked into life. Charlotte watched her from the comfort of her bed as she waited for Lily to bring her breakfast. The skies outside looked heavy and grey with threatening rain, and Charlotte couldn't help but think that her heart felt the same. Did Joseph expect them to live in separate beds while married?

She recoiled from her thoughts, as a further knock on the door told her that Lily had arrived with the breakfast.

'Come in.' Charlotte puffed up her pillows and made herself sit upright in her bed. She might as well enjoy the privilege of breakfast in bed, a luxury that had never been heard of, back home at Crummock. She could just imagine Lucy Cranston giving her a good tongue-lashing if she had suggested such an extravagance.

'Morning, ma'am. Did you sleep well?' Lily smiled as she placed the walnut bed-tray over Charlotte's covered legs. 'Cook didn't know what you liked for breakfast, so she's sent you toast, porridge, veal cake and some Finnan haddock. She says anything you don't like, you've just got to let her know.' Lily smiled as she watched Charlotte lift up each serving platter lid and examine the contents.

'I don't like veal, Lily, if you can let Cook know, please. It reminds me of the poor little calves I used to hand-feed if they had lost their mothers. How anyone can eat them, I don't know!' She looked at the slice of veal terrine, delicately layered with sliced egg and bacon, and thought of the doe-like eyes of the orphaned calves that she had fed with warm milk, remembering how they sucked on her hand as she coaxed their mouths into taking their first drink from a bucket. 'Everything else is fine.'

'I'll tell Cook. She'll make a note. She wondered why you left your calves' sweetbreads yesterday at your wedding breakfast. She was quite upset, but she will understand now, I'm sure. There's always veal on the menu – it's Mr Dawson's favourite.' Lily walked over to the wardrobe in the corner of the room and flung the doors open. 'Now, ma'am, what are you doing today, and what would you like to wear?'

To Charlotte's amazement, the wardrobe was filled with fine clothes, which were obviously to be worn by her.

Realizing that her mistress knew nothing about her new outfits, Lily smiled. 'Mr Dawson had them all specially made for you. Mrs Dodgson helped him with your sizing, and he had them brought here from Accrington the other day. He thought it would be an extra surprise for you. I think this blue day-dress would be perfect. If you are to stay home today, it will complement your eyes beautifully.' Lily ran her hand over the dress and held it up for Charlotte to inspect as she ate her toast.

Charlotte pushed her breakfast tray away. 'Where are all my clothes from home?' She rushed to the wardrobe and pulled back the hangers of quality outfits, looking for her familiar daily apparel.

Lily hung her head. 'I think Mrs Dodgson gave them away. She said that you would not be needing them, now you are living at Windfell.'

'She what? Without even asking me?' Charlotte turned and glared at the fretting lady's maid, who looked

83

as if she knew Mrs Dodgson had overstepped the mark.

'Mr Dawson told her to, I think, ma'am. There are some beautiful garments here, ma'am, just look at them.' Lily tried to defuse the situation; she didn't like Mrs Dodgson, either. The housekeeper had an air about her, one of lording it over the rest of the staff. Plus, she was always favoured by Joseph Dawson, far too much.

'Give me that dress there. I suppose I'll have to wear the damned thing. I've not a lot, other than what that stupid woman has left me with.' Charlotte snatched the dress that Lily was nearly crying into, and held it up against her. 'At least they've got good taste, but that's not the point. The dresses were mine from home, and I loved them.' Charlotte could have cried.

'Ma'am, I shouldn't say this, but everyone has to do as they are told at Windfell. Mr Dawson likes everything to be just so, and it is the worse for everyone if he doesn't get his own way.'

'Well, give me time, Lily, and that may change. It is I that he married, not Mrs Dodgson, and perhaps the two of them get their way too often.' Charlotte stepped into her bloomers and threw her nightdress onto the unmade bed. 'Now, today I'll meet all the staff and get to know them one by one. I'll inform Mrs Dodgson that I will speak to everybody individually in the morning room after ten this morning, starting with the cook.' She looked at herself as Lily buttoned up her new blue dress. It did fit and suited her perfectly, but it was the principle of the matter; she should have been asked, before her clothes were disposed of.

'Yes, ma'am. The staff would appreciate that, I'm sure.' Lily sighed. These were going to be volatile times. If Joseph Dawson thought he'd married someone who would do his bidding, she could sense that this time he had got it wrong.

7

'Get that bloody lad out from under that machine,'
Joseph yelled at the two workers who were stricken
with panic as a young lad, with four of his fingers lost
in the carding machinery, screamed and writhed on the
floor. 'What the bloody hell was he doing? Look at the
blood on that length of cotton. What a bloody waste!'

Joseph hadn't any time for the eleven-year-old boy
who was slowly bleeding to death, for the sake of
doing his job of cleaning the fluff and dust from under
the carding machines. Instead he was more concerned
about the loss of cotton, and time, while the machinery
was stopped, in order to haul the crippled lad out from
under the fast-working machine. Time was money, and
he hadn't enough of either at the moment.

'I kept telling him he's too bloody slow. I gave him
a whack with the strap yesterday morning because he
was nearly asleep on the job.' Bert Bannister stood next

to his boss, shouting above the constant rattle and noise of the machines racing back and forth.

'Hah! It was better when you could employ the young 'uns. They were more nippy, especially for cleaning the fluff and debris from under the carding machines. Bloody government and well-doers. An eleven-year-old is too big, especially these farm lads who come just to make more income at home.' Joseph swore under his breath. He watched as the lad was carried out, slumped between two workers, drips of blood staining the dark wooden flooring of the mill floor. 'I'm up in the office if you want me, Bert; we'll have to find a new lad to take this one's place. I'll put an advert together and get it posted down in Settle. It'll not take long to find a replacement.' He looked around the busy mill floor. None of the workers had stopped for the accident; they were too scared to lose payment because of a second of sympathy, especially with the owner there.

There were five floors to Ferndale Mill and all were working full out, carding, spinning and weaving the raw cotton from America into cotton sheeting, to be supplied to businesses all over the country. In the six months since Joseph had taken on the derelict mill he had employed more than two hundred people from all walks of life. The folk who worked there had a lot to be thankful for: they had money in their pockets, a roof over their head and worthwhile employment. The least they could do was work hard and show him respect.

He walked out of the carding room past his workers.

None of them dared raise their heads to look at him, for he was the boss. You didn't catch the eye of the owner, in case he took a dislike to you or singled you out for extra work. Joseph himself knew that and took full advantage of his privileged position, putting the fear of God into his staff as he walked by. He stopped at the bottom of the stairs leading to his office as a young girl came running up the lower flight of stairs.

'Where have you been, girl?' Joseph stood sternly and awaited her answer.

'Sir, I've been down to the warehouse, Mr Bannister sent me with a message, and he said it was urgent and that my legs were faster than his up and down these stairs.' Betsy Foster stood afeared of her employer, even though she had been doing no wrong.

'I see. As long as you've not dallied. The Devil makes work for idle hands, we all know that.' Joseph looked at the lass, whom he now recognized as the one he had taken on from Belmont Mill and made a tenant in one of his cottages. 'Are you and your brother comfortable in your new home?'

'Yes, sir; very much, sir. We are very much obliged for your kindness.' Betsy avoided eye contact with Joseph. She didn't want him to see how much she despised him being in control of every aspect of her daily life.

'Is your brother of working age, girl?' Joseph stared at the pretty, dark-haired woman in front of him. She really was a beauty.

'No, sir. He's going to school at Langcliffe until

summer, and then I hope for him to get a job as a joiner's apprentice. I've already spoken to Colin Ward, the joiner at Long Preston, and Johnny's been promised a position with him after his next birthday. He's good with his hands, like our father was.' Betsy was determined not to have her young brother working in a mill, doing the hours she worked, only to be treated like the young lad she had just seen being carried out onto a donkey cart with missing fingers.

'Good with his hands – that's just what I need. Perhaps you should rethink your brother's position in life.' Joseph stood close to Betsy and looked at her face, slowly running a finger through a lock of her dark hair, making it fall out of the tight bun it was held in. 'After all, if it wasn't for me, you wouldn't have a roof over your heads or food on the table. Perhaps we could come to some other arrangement!' He sniggered. 'After all, you are my employee, to do with as I see fit.' He ran his finger down the side of her face, lingering for a while at her lips.

'Betsy, get back at your machine. Stop dallying on the stairs. Get out of Mr Dawson's way, girl.' Bannister bellowed at his messenger, who had been missing for all of five minutes. 'I beg your pardon, sir; I need her back at her machine.' Joseph watched as Betsy nearly ran back to her carding machine, her cheeks flushed and her eyes brimming with tears.

'I'd watch that one, if I were you, Bannister. She's got spirit and lacks respect.' Joseph watched Betsy as she put her head down and got on with her work. If he couldn't have the brother, he would have her – and in more ways than one. She was his to do with as he liked, and she knew it.

Bert looked at Betsy. He'd seen Joseph Dawson talking to the girl and knew what it was about. The lass was vulnerable, and Joseph was a bastard with no heart. He might have brass and respect, but he was certainly no gentleman. He'd watched his master eyeing the young lasses as they went about their work. And him with a new bonny wife – you'd think he'd be satisfied at home. Bert spat out a mouth of chewed tobacco and walked down the length of the carding room. All bosses were bastards – the world was full of them and there was nowt he could do about it; he was just a boss's monkey, doing as he was bidden.

Charlotte sat in the morning room. Yates placed the made tea upon a silver tray and positioned it on the highly polished walnut table next to the long window, which looked out onto the drive and the graceful grey-barked beech trees that bordered it. She watched as the copper leaves twirled and raced in the breeze before falling to the ground. Autumn was passing quickly and winter would soon be here.

'Should I pour, ma'am?' Yates stood over her and awaited her instructions.

'Please do, and then take a seat, Yates. I'd like to take the time to know everyone this morning, and I may as well start with you.' Charlotte looked at the stuffy butler. His face never changed expression, but his voice was soft and kind for the size of the man.

Yates poured Charlotte her tea and then dutifully sat where she suggested.

'Tell me a little about yourself, Yates. Are you married, have you any children?' Charlotte sipped a mouthful of tea and watched the surprise on the butler's face.

'Me, ma'am, married? God forbid, I like to be my own man.'

'And do you live with us, here in the servants' quarters? I'm sorry this seems an obvious question, but Mr Dawson hasn't informed me as of yet who lives in with us and who doesn't.' Charlotte felt embarrassed that she had no knowledge about who was housed under the roof of Windfell, and she hadn't seen the servants' quarters.

'I do, ma'am. The rooms up near the attic are quite roomy and comfortable and I have my own fire, so I can make myself a drink of tea in my own privacy. I'm thankful for the employment because, as you can see, I'm not getting any younger.' Yates smiled. His new mistress at least cared. In some of the houses he had worked in, they hadn't given a damn.

'I see, and you are happy here, Yates?'

'Indeed, ma'am. I'm used to a larger household, but this suits me fine at this age in life.'

'Good. Well, I hope to be a good mistress. You'll find me fair, as long as you are right with me.' Charlotte had rehearsed her closing lines in her mind over and over again. She was going to be shown to be caring but firm, and that was what she hoped to be.

'Yes, ma'am. Can I say, ma'am, how refreshing it is for someone to show an interest in their servants.' Yates looked at the young woman who sat across from him; she was the opposite of her husband, who expected everything without a care. 'Although none of us have been serving Mr Dawson long, we are a good team and we aim to please.'

'Thank you, Yates, I'm sure we will all rub along happily. Could you send Mrs Batty, the cook, up to see me next, if it is convenient for her?' Charlotte rose from the table and walked to the door to open it for Yates.

'Of course, ma'am, but you sit down. I don't expect doors to be opened for me – that's my job.' Yates smiled as his new mistress blushed slightly.

'Of course, Yates, thank you.' Charlotte felt stupid. She was the mistress now and she had to remember that. She sat back in her chair and sighed. She felt out of her depth. Dora Dodgson had looked at her like a schoolchild earlier in the morning, as Charlotte had tackled her about her dresses from home being given away. When she had informed Dora that she wished to speak to all the servants individually, the housekeeper had sneered and virtually told her that it was not her concern how the servants lived, or whether they were happy in their positions. But in Charlotte's eyes, it was her concern, for a place could not run smoothly if people weren't looked after.

She could understand that she and Dora Dodgson were never going to see eye-to-eye. How she wished for the jovial laughter of Lucy Cranston and Mary, the parlour maid at Crummock. However, as her father would have said, 'She'd made her bed and now she must lie in it.' Even though that bed was perhaps not as full of love as she had first thought. She could feel a hatred for Dora Dodgson growing, but she knew that Joseph would hear no ill of her, so she would just have to bite her tongue and grow in strength, to outplay Dora at her own game.

The kitchen was abuzz with gossip about the new mistress. She'd spoken to all the staff personally that morning, and now they were making their minds up on how they felt about the new lady of the manor. Mrs Batty had listened to all the comments and decided to share her views.

'Well, I think she's a right grand lass – she's not much different from any of us. After all, she's only a farmer's daughter!' Mrs Batty stopped stirring the lunchtime vegetable soup for a second and added her fourpenn'th about Charlotte.

'She hasn't had the breeding, I think you mean. She actually opened the door for me. Now that's a first!' Yates scoffed as he waited for the soup to be placed in the silver serving tureen that he was about to present in the dining room.

'That's called manners, Mr Yates, and don't you knock it. You wouldn't get him opening the door for anyone!' Mrs Batty poured the soup into the tureen, splashing herself as she did so. She muttered under her breath as she reached for the bicarbonate-of-soda, to put on the burn to cool it.

'Him as got a name, and don't you forget he keeps us housed and fed.' Yates looked down his nose at the straight-talking cook, whose face was as red as the pickled beetroot that was to accompany the next course.

'Aye, and he likes to keep us all in our places. Which I don't mind – I know my place in life. I'll never be lady of the manor, but I'll not be treated like a dog.' Mrs Batty stood with her hands on her hips and watched as Yates carried the lunch towards the stairs leading up to the dining room.

'Just watch what you are saying. Mrs Dodgson could be listening and she tells him everything – the woman's got bat ears, I'm sure.' Yates looked at the blustering cook. He admired her strengths, and the woman could certainly cook, but she was in the same situation as him and needed her job.

'I think she's alright, Mrs Batty, she was really kind to me. She asked me about my brothers and sisters, and where in Settle I live. I think she'll be good for the house.' Mazy gave the candelabra that she was polishing an extra-vigorous rub and reached for the next item to be cleaned.

'Aye, well, we will take her as we find, that's the best way. If she's right with us, it'll be grand, and we'll look after her when it comes to him. God knows, she'll need it.' Mrs Batty plated up the sliced baked ham for the next course and stood back and admired her handiwork.

'Who'll need God's help? Who are you gossiping about now?' Mrs Dodgson entered the room and quickly gazed around the room, sensing that she was not going to be included in the conversation that was taking place.

'Oh! Mrs Dodgson, we were just commenting about Mazy's youngest sister – she's got influenza. Hasn't she, Mazy? She's right poorly; she's in bed with a temperature.' Mrs Batty passed Yates the platter of carved ham as he came back into the kitchen and noted his disapproving stare.

'That's right, Mrs Dodgson. My mother just hopes that we are not all going to go down with it.' Mazy coughed slightly, to add substance to the lie.

'Well, you can keep it to yourself. Get a move on and clean the dining-room silver after you've done that.' She sneered at young Mazy. Typical that her family had influenza. They probably lived like rats in the gutter. 'Mrs Dawson will be eating alone this evening. Mr Dawson is going to a meeting and will dine out. He's just informed me.'

'Would she like a light meal, Mrs Dodgson, or should I make her the full three courses that I had planned?' enquired Mrs Batty, as the hoity housekeeper started to leave the room.

'I'll ask her. Not that she's used to answering such questions; I think the cook just did what she liked at

95

her old home. Next week, when we are in a routine, she will have to start to look at the menus and see if they are to her liking. When you have the time, put your suggestions for next week's meals together, please, Mrs Batty, and give them to me.' Dora was still fuming that Charlotte had given up her morning to talk to the staff and get to know them. She'd even been to the stables to talk to old Bob, the groom, and the stable lad, whose name Dora could never remember. Why would she? He was not part of Charlotte's world. She knew as soon as she entered the kitchen that they were all talking about the insipid milksop who was now more important than her, in their eyes. 'And make sure you price everything up. We run to a budget, and it's best she knows that; and that it is us servants who have to be responsible for the money.' Dora lifted her skirts and climbed the few steps that led into the hallway. She stood by the doorway listening to any backchat from the servants, which she had no time for. But it was silent as she listened – too silent for her liking; they must have known she was eavesdropping. She crossed the hallway and entered the dining room.

'Cook would like to know: would you like a full dinner tonight or something lighter, as Mr Dawson is dining out this evening?' Dora waited for a reply, noticing that Charlotte looked upset as she finished sipping her soup.

'I'll have something lighter – a sandwich or some more of this soup, if there is any left. I didn't realize I was going to be on my own.' Charlotte flashed a querying look at Joseph, who sat across from her. Why did the housekeeper know before her where her husband was going to be? Nobody had told her that life with Joseph Dawson was going to be so lonely. There had been no offer of a honeymoon or of time together, alone. Instead, so far, all Joseph's time had been spent with his work, or telling his housekeeper his daily plans, instead of her.

'Very well, ma'am, I'll tell Mrs Batty. I presume you would like afternoon tea in the drawing room? The late Mrs Dawson always enjoyed her afternoon tea in the drawing room, when we lived at Accrington.' Dora smiled, remembering her previous mistress.

'I prefer the morning room, please, Mrs Dodgson.' Charlotte glared at the housekeeper, who was still living in the past.

'Do as Charlotte requests, Mrs Dodgson. She enjoys the view in the morning room.' Joseph pushed his soup bowl away and waited until Yates, who had been standing next to the sideboard, quickly cleared it away. He turned and smiled at Charlotte. 'I'm sorry, my dear, I should have told you first that I am dining out tonight. I do apologize. The first Monday of the month I usually meet with my fellow businessmen and we have dinner in the Talbot Arms in Settle.' Joseph patted his lips with his serviette and looked at his wife, who seemed displeased at his confession.

'I forgive you for not telling me, but can I not come with you? I'd like to learn about local business.' Charlotte held back her disappointment and hoped

97

that Joseph would invite her along with him. She could have sworn she heard Mrs Dodgson mutter something under her breath as she turned to leave the room.

'My dear, the Talbot Arms is no place for a lady, when we men get together. I'm afraid we would bore you to death with talk of business. Plus, some of my so-called business colleagues get a little leery after a gill or two of the Talbot's excellent beers.' Joseph threw his napkin down on the table and waited until Yates served the roast ham, boiled potatoes and beetroot, then ordered him to leave them both.

'But, Joseph, I want to help with the mill and learn more about it. If it is to keep us in this style, then surely I should contribute to its running.' Charlotte was used to helping on the farm and knowing the everyday running of it.

'The mill is my business; it is not for a woman to know how it runs. Yours is the house to run, along with Mrs Dodgson. You should not worry your head about things you don't understand. Be glad for what you've got, and stop interfering in things you do not know about.' Joseph sliced into his cold ham with his knife and stared at his new wife.

Charlotte looked across at her husband. The house would take no running – not with all the staff and Dora Dodgson, who ran things so strictly no one dared breathe. She would learn about the mill, and he wasn't going to stop her. After all, it was part of her new life and she had every right to know how their income was earned. If Joseph didn't want children in his life, then he should look at her as a partner in his work, to stop her from losing her sanity from boredom, if for no other reason.

'But, Joseph, I need my life fulfilling, either with children or with you at your side at the mill. I realize I don't know anything about cotton, but I could learn . . .'

'You know nothing. I don't want you anywhere near that mill, do you hear? You keep away and leave it to me.' Joseph raised his voice loudly and his eyes flashed as he banged his knife down in his fist upon the table. 'As for children, I don't like them. However, if it would keep you content, we should perhaps try for a child. A male heir would perhaps be an asset. It would at least give you some purpose in life, else I can see that you are going to be forever whining around my feet. It is our first day of marriage and already you are dis-contented with your lot.' He glared across at Charlotte, noticing that she was on the brink of tears.

'I'm not ungrateful, Joseph. I'm just used to having something to do, and I would love a child to call our own – isn't that what any couple want?' Charlotte wiped away a tear that had escaped from the corner of her eye. Was she being unreasonable? After all, this was only her first day of being married, and Joseph had to carry on with business commitments, regardless of his personal life. But if he'd agree to try for a baby, then she would be content. It was a security that she longed for and had not yet been given, with the marriage not being consummated.

'For heaven's sake, Charlotte, do you not know how

much I love you? I'm just a selfish man and wanted some time alone with you, without the burden of children around our feet. You need time to enjoy the house and the gardens, when spring comes – that's all, my dear. Forgive me for raising my voice, I didn't mean to upset you.' His temper subsided and was replaced by a sympathetic purring. 'Come here, my dear. Let me kiss you.' Joseph held out his hand for Charlotte to embrace. She rushed to his side and knelt down on the floor, putting her head on his lap as he stroked her blonde hair. 'I'm just a grumpy old man, forgive me.' He tilted her chin upwards and kissed her passionately on the lips. 'You know I'll do anything you want – just look at this fine house, and the servants at your beck and call. Just let me be selfish a little bit longer.' He smiled and looked into Charlotte's tear-filled eyes.

'No, it's me who's selfish, pushing you to do things you don't want to. I'm trying to run in my new life before I can walk. Wanting it all before I know anything about everything.' Charlotte wiped a tear away and smiled at her husband. 'I do love you.'

'And I you, my dear. One day we will look back at this, our first tiff, and laugh.' Joseph kissed her on her brow. 'Now, my dear, I've some business to do. I will see you tomorrow, but please do not wait up for me. It's usually after midnight before I return from my tedious meeting, and I'm generally the worse for drink, like the rest of them.' Joseph kissed her again and noticed the look of disappointment clouding his wife's face again.

'Take care, my love.' Charlotte's hand lingered in his as he walked away from her through the dining-room doors. She was alone again; she was going to have to make the best of her life, if this was how it was going to be. Tomorrow she would take a ride into Settle and would treat herself to a new hat; and the day after that she might even go back home and visit her father. Home! This was her home now, so she had better make the best of it.

Joseph looked at the squat little man who sat across from him in the dim candlelight of the Talbot Arms.

The room was filled with heavy tobacco smoke, and next to the open fireplace a young servant boy turned the handle of the spit that held a side of pork, which was gently cooking over the open fire. The boy's gaze took in all the drinkers and gamblers who frequently spent their lives in the Talbot Arms. He saw all, but said nothing; it was his job in life to turn the spit and do nothing more, unless it was worth his while.

'What the hell do you want with me, Simmons? I thought I'd left you back in Accrington.' Joseph sipped from his tankard and waited for an answer from his late wife's solicitor.

'It's funny you ask me that, Dawson. News travels fast, you know. When I heard from one of my clients that you'd started a new life up here in the Dales, and saw the announcement of your marriage to the lovely Charlotte Booth, I thought I'd better remind you of your past. I owe it to your new wife, if nothing else. We

can't have another mishap – or should I say disappearance – now can we?' Simmons took a long drink from
his tankard and watched him over the brim, as Joseph
Dawson studied the face of the man who had suppos-
edly found out his secret. 'I should add that, if you are
thinking of doing the same to me, there is a letter in the
hands of my partner telling him of my suspicions, if I
do not return from visiting my old friend in Yorkshire.'

Simmons sat back and waited for a reply. He hadn't
liked the man May Pilling had married, so when he'd
tracked down the loyal kitchen maid of the Pilling
family who had owned the Helene Mill on Grange Lane,
and heard her side of the story, he knew his suspicions
had been well founded and that Joseph Dawson was a
no-good imposter and rogue.

'You know nothing – you are bluffing. And keep
your bloody voice down. This isn't Accrington; everyone's local and they all know me.' Joseph bent over the
table and breathed heavily into Simmons's face. 'What
do you want from me, you bloody snake?'

'I want that pretty new wife of yours to be kept safe.
But most of all, I want my bank balance to look a little
healthier – say, around thirty guineas healthier – just to
help me in my old age!' Simmons waited, watching the
handsome face of Joseph cloud over with suppressed
anger. 'After all, you wouldn't want the information I
hold to get into the wrong hands. The cells at Preston
are waiting, if I were to open my mouth, and what a
shame for a man of such high status in the community.'

He leered, and liked the look of panic on that bastard Dawson's face. He knew he'd got what he came for.

'You bastard! Breathe a word and I'll break your bloody neck.' Joseph lent back in his chair. 'Twenty guineas. I'll give you not a penny more. My stable lad will bring it to you in the morning.' He wasn't prepared to lose his lifestyle for the sake of this worm from his past. 'You then get out, and stay out, of my life. Do you understand?' Joseph rose from his chair and swigged his gill back.

'I understand perfectly. It's a pleasure doing business with you, Mr Dawson.' Simmons held out his hand to be shaken, but was ignored by Joseph, who put his hat on and pushed his chair back. 'By the way, how is that sister of yours? I presume she's here with you; after all, you couldn't leave her back in Accrington.' Simmons knew he had Joseph Dawson by the balls. The man should think himself lucky that he wasn't asking for more, considering the information he had on the loathsome guttersnipe.

'Shut your mouth and piss off, back to the hole you've come from,' whispered Joseph, while holding the back of his chair as his knuckles turned white with rage.

'Good evening, Mr Dawson. As I say, the pleasure has been all mine.' Simmons sniggered. It was good to see Joseph Dawson worried. He and his sister had crawled their way out of the gutter at the expense of poor May. He only hoped that Dawson's new wife had a bit more sense about her. He'd heard that her father was wealthy – that was obviously what had attracted that rat Dawson. He watched as Joseph made his way to the door, giving him a backward glance with his hand on the latch. 'Regards to your beautiful new wife.' Simmons laughed as Joseph slammed the door behind him, stopping the drinkers' banter instantly. He raised his tankard to the other drinkers and laughed. 'Must have been something I said.'

8

Costly thy habit as thy purse can buy,
But not express'd in fancy: rich, not gaudy;
For the apparel oft proclaims the man.

FROM HAMLET BY WILLIAM SHAKESPEARE

Charlotte walked across the market place of Settle, stopping to talk and say hello to the various people who knew her as she made her way to the bank. The town was thronged with shoppers, Settle being the market town for northern Craven and the outlying Dales.

'Good morning, Mrs Dawson, how may we help you today?' The bank clerk smiled as Charlotte fumbled with her bag. 'Both you and Mr Dawson look to be suited to married life. I told him so myself this morning when I served him.'

'Joseph was here this morning? I thought he was at the mill all day today.'

The little man smiled at her. 'Yes, he was here first thing. He caused a bit of a stir by withdrawing twenty guineas from your account. I had to get the manager's permission before I could serve him. I'm not authorized to handle that amount, you see, but my manager assured me that if it was for Mr Dawson, it would be acceptable.'

'Oh! It must have been for a delivery of cotton from Liverpool, which I know he has been expecting. But that does seem strange for him to pay in cash, and out of my account.' Charlotte took her gloves off in order to count the money she was about to withdraw from her account. How Joseph ran his business was his affair – he had made that perfectly clear yesterday. 'May I make a withdrawal, Mr Wells?' She watched as the clerk gave her a look of disbelief.

'I'm afraid he also transferred your remaining funds out of your account into his.' He watched as Charlotte's face clouded over. 'I presumed he had discussed it with you and that, now you were married, your husband was handling all your affairs. After all, now that you are a married woman, it goes without saying that all your assets and money are his.'

'My account is my affair. Now kindly transfer my money back to me and reopen my account.' Charlotte was fuming, and embarrassed. How dare Joseph help himself to her money, without even asking her?

'I'll get the manager, Mrs Dawson, but I think you will find that I'm correct in saying you can no longer be in charge of an account with us.' The clerk quickly left his post and Charlotte could see him talking to the manager through the glass window of his door.

She watched as the clerk explained the position that she was in. Her frustration brought colour to her cheeks, both in annoyance with Joseph and at knowing there was a queue forming behind her, who were taking an interest in every word being exchanged.

'I'm sorry, Mrs Dawson, but it is as I feared. Mr Dawson was quite within his rights to transfer your account to his, and to withdraw any money he wishes. It is the law, Mrs Dawson, I'm sorry.' The clerk looked embarrassed.

'Very well. I'll talk to Mr Dawson tonight and ask him to set me up an allowance. I can see I'm not going to get any more help from you, and the manager hasn't even bothered to come out to talk to me. You can tell your manager that I'm still the Charlotte Booth that was; just because I am now married doesn't mean I have gone dim-witted and can't handle my finances. The manager smiled plenty and was eager to talk to me, when my father and I deposited my grandpapa's legacy.'

Charlotte pulled on her gloves and tugged at the strings on her draw-bag, glaring at the timid clerk, who was only doing his job. She pushed out her chin, stood tall and stamped out of the bank, past the earwigging crowd. When she reached the frosty air of the market place she sighed deeply. Her life was going from bad to worse; now she didn't even have any money to call her own. She hadn't realized that, once she married, all she owned belonged to Joseph. It was something she had not accounted for, and it wasn't a position she was going to be comfortable with. She would speak to him about an allowance at least. Surely he'd agree to that; he must see that she would need to have a little spending money?

Feeling slightly embarrassed by her ignorance, Charlotte looked around the busy market square and noticed some familiar figures wandering aimlessly amongst the crowd. It was Archie and his wife Rosie, and in her arms she could see a bundle that she presumed was their baby. She was nearly on the brink of tears as a beaming Archie spotted her, waving to her, and then turned to Rosie, before the couple pushed their way through the busy crowd towards her.

'Lottie, it's good to see you. Just look at you, a true lady now.' Archie grinned and looked Charlotte up and down.

She smiled at them both, before laying eyes on the small baby, which was wrapped up tightly and securely in a hand-woven shawl in Rosie's arms. 'Never mind about me, look at you two – both parents. Are you going to introduce me to him or her?' Charlotte swallowed hard, fighting back the emotions she felt for her old friend, and the pang of jealousy she had for Rosie and her baby.

'This is Daniel, our little boy. He takes after his father and is always hungry.' Rosie smiled and pulled back the shawl from around her baby's face, to reveal a small but perfect face, with the brightest pair of blue eyes that Charlotte had ever seen.

'He's beautiful, you must be so proud.' She sniffed back an escaping tear and smiled at the devoted parents.

'Would you like to hold him?' Rosie offered the squirming bundle over to Charlotte, who eagerly accepted.

'He's gorgeous. Look at these little fingers and the milk-spots upon his nose.' A tear escaped from her eye and blessed baby Daniel's head, as she watched him looking at her.

'Aye, Charlotte, don't cry. We are just glad he's alright. Rosie struggled having him and, as it is, he's only a lil'un because he came early. My father says he's a right runt, but he's a survivor because, like Rosie says, he's a good eater.'

'He's perfect, and you are both so lucky.' Charlotte handed the baby back to Rosie and wiped the tears away with the back of her hand.

'"Lucky," says the woman who's married the most eligible man in Craven and who lives in one of the biggest houses in the district.' Archie grinned.

Charlotte smiled, but she could feel herself welling up again inside and decided to change the subject. 'Anyway, Mr Atkinson, you never sent me a wedding invite – what happened to that?'

'Oh, Lottie, you know why – we only had our parents there.' Archie blushed. 'It was a quiet do. Wasn't it, Rosie? I think Rosie's father nearly thought of bringing a shotgun – he was that concerned I wasn't going to go through with it. But he should know now that I'm a man of my word; and besides, I love my Rosie and this lil'un.' Archie squeezed Rosie's waist tightly and bent down and kissed baby Daniel's head.

Charlotte recalled that early spring morning when he'd shouted his undying love for her as she ran down the fellside. He'd obviously been having his way with Rosie even then, else the child wasn't his. 'I know, and don't worry, I understand. Between Father and Joseph, I didn't have much say in who came to my wedding, either. Your aunty probably told you. Bless her, I miss Mrs Cranston; she's a lot plainer cook than the one at Windfell, where everything is in sauces and garlic. Mrs C. hates garlic.'

'Aye, she said it was a fair wedding, but that she hadn't been invited to the reception. Don't worry – I think she was thankful she wasn't asked. She said you only had the great and the good there, and that she'd have been out of her place.' Archie grinned again. 'You look a little down, Lottie – what's up? It's not like you to look down-in-the-mouth.'

'Oh, I've been an idiot and left my money at home, and I'd set my heart on a new hat. I'm going to have to go home without anything, or go and get my money from home, and I don't have the time.' Charlotte felt guilty, but she smiled at Rosie as she tickled baby Daniel's chin.

'Surely you could go into any shop in Settle and put it on an account. If you can't, whilst married to one of the wealthiest men in the district, then God help anybody else,' said Archie.

'My father would never do that. "Neither a lender nor a borrower be," he would say. And putting things on an account never entered my head.' Her mood quickly lifted. Why hadn't she thought of that? Archie was right: every shop in Settle would be glad of an account with Joseph Dawson; and after all, he'd left her with no other option than to buy things that way.

'Go and get yourself a hat. He won't even miss the price of it, from his huge bank account,' Archie teased.

'Yes, go and treat yourself. Archie, we will have to be going now, I'm beginning to feel a little tired.' Rosie's colour had faded from her cheeks and she looked pale and wan.

'Sorry, Rosie, I wasn't thinking. I got carried away with talking to Lottie. Here, give me the baby.' Archie took Daniel from her arms and cradled him lovingly, while smiling reassuringly at Rosie. 'Rosie is still weak. As I said, she had a bad time having this bundle of rubbish.'

'I understand. Rosie, I hope you are soon feeling better.' Charlotte took a final look at the baby nestling in Archie's arms. 'Here, wait a minute.' She rummaged in her drawstring bag. 'I thought I had one: here, a silver florin for luck, as the gypsies say.' She thrust the silver coin into the tiny baby's clenched fist and he held onto it eagerly. 'Here's hoping for good luck for both of us, baby Daniel.' She kissed him gently on the head.

'Lottie, you shouldn't.' Archie looked at the woman he still loved.

'No, you shouldn't, but thank you.' Rosie held onto Archie's arm.

'Yes, I should. Put it in his savings, from his Aunty Charlotte.' She smiled and watched as the couple walked arm-in-arm through the crowds, Archie glancing back at her for a brief moment.

The silver florin was the least she could do for that baby; he was going to need every penny, to get him through life on a bleak hillside. It had been the last of her money, but Daniel needed it more than her. After all, in Archie's words, she was married to 'one of the wealthiest men in the district'.

'Afternoon, Mrs Dawson.' The owner of the butcher's shop on the Shambles brought her back to her thoughts and reminded her of the purpose of her visit. A hat: she came for a hat, and she would go back with one – especially as Archie had said Joseph would never miss from his bank account the pittance it would cost. After all, some of that money was hers now. She made her way past the market stalls and hawkers, heading straight for the haberdasher's and hatter's. There, in the window, she spotted the loveliest creation she had ever seen. A red velvet hat, with fake winter berries adorning it and a red ribbon to secure it around her chin. She had to have it; it was the perfect hat for winter, and Joseph wanted her to look the perfect lady. The shop bell tinkled loudly, like her heartbeat, as the prim shop

112

assistant handed her the hat to try on, announcing that it 'must have been made for her'.

Charlotte preened herself and cocked her head to one side, taking in the back view, the side view and admiring how the huge red bow showed off the colour of her cheeks to perfection. She looked at the price tag. It was the most expensive thing she had ever placed on her head. Should she? Dare she? Of course she should; she was the wife of prestigious mill owner Joseph Dawson, and there had to be some benefits to being a mill owner's wife.

'Does madam like it?' asked the shop assistant.

'Yes, very much, it's such a lovely colour.' Charlotte admired herself again.

'Has madam noticed the fur muff and red kidskin gloves to match? They would be the perfect accompaniment.' The shop assistant handed them over to Charlotte, from the bottom of the shop window, and smiled at her, knowing that she had caught her customer hook, line and sinker.

'Oh! They are beautiful.' Charlotte held the red sheepskin muff next to her cheek, feeling the softness of the fine wool. 'I really shouldn't – what would my husband say?'

'I'm sure he would say they were made for you, and that you look beautiful in them.' The shop assistant smiled. 'They are all the rage in Paris.'

Charlotte looked at herself again in the mirror. She had to have them. 'Can I put them on account, please? My husband, Joseph Dawson, owns the mill at

Langcliffe, so there will be no problem with payment.'
She felt herself blushing. She had never asked for credit
before.

'Of course, madam, we know Mr Dawson. He
bought nearly the same gloves for his sister the other
month, when it was her birthday, but they were in
brown.' The assistant took the hat from Charlotte and
placed it in a striking hat box full of tissue paper.

'I don't think they will have been for his sister – he
doesn't have one.' Charlotte handed her the gloves and
muff to wrap, and thought nothing more of the shop
assistant's comment.

'I must have misheard, madam. I'm sorry. We'll send
the bill for Mr Dawson's attention, shall we?'

'Yes, please.' Charlotte smiled as she was handed
her treasured new possessions. She hadn't meant to
spend that amount of money; she wouldn't have done,
if it had been her own money. But seeing as Joseph had
helped himself to her money, it was his debt now.

'Thank you for your custom, Mrs Dawson, please
call again.' The shop assistant opened the door for her,
jingling the merry bell again.

'Oh, I will, thank you.' Charlotte had never enjoyed
shopping so much. She might have no money of her
own, but she had Joseph's good name to get credit on.
Only if she must, of course!

'So what have you done today, my love?' Joseph lifted
his head up from his bowl of soup and looked down
the table at his wife. Her cheeks looked flushed in the

milky candlelight and he couldn't help but admire her beauty as she politely sipped her soup, patting her lips with her napkin as she left the right amount for a lady to leave in her bowl, for the servants to clear away.

'I went to Settle, Joseph. I need to talk to you quite urgently regarding my bank account.' Charlotte hesitated. 'Or should I say "lack of one"!' She could feel her heart fluttering with a slight fear as she broached the subject that had annoyed her all day.

'If you mean to ask me why I transferred your account into mine, I'd have thought that is patently obvious to you.' Joseph stared at his wife and knew then why there was so much colour in her cheeks. 'You are under my roof, I feed and clothe you, you want for nothing. You are my wife – what's yours is now mine.' He laid his napkin down and ordered the soup bowls to be cleared and for Yates to leave the room.

'But you could have told, or asked, me first. I went to withdraw some money this morning and I wasn't allowed. The clerk looked at me as if I was simple!' Charlotte decided to speak her mind. 'Besides, that money gave me a little independence, some spending money of my own.' No sooner had she spoken the words than she regretted them.

'Independence, Charlotte! You are my wife; you don't need independence, just as you don't need to be part of the running of the mill or to know my accounts. Yes, Mrs Dodgson told me that you asked for the key to my desk, after your jaunt to Settle. The desk and its contents in the study are private; they are nothing to do with you.' Joseph took a drink of wine from his crystal glass and watched Charlotte try to explain her request.

'I merely wanted to see if I could understand your accounts. The clerk said you had withdrawn a significant amount of money this morning, and I was curious about why you needed it. After all, as you say, I'm completely dependent on you, and if I can help in any way with my good head for figures, surely you would let me do so.' She could see that a storm was brewing and sighed. Why couldn't she just have sat and sewn or read, like any ordinary fine lady would have done, on her return from Settle? But curiosity over Joseph's need of her money and the large withdrawal had got the better of her. So much so that she had plucked up the courage to ask for the key to his desk, to the shock and horror of a disdainful Dora Dodgson.

'Damn it, woman, how many times have I to tell you to keep out of my affairs. There's nothing in that desk anyway; the accounts are all held down at the mill. Why do you think we have offices there? What I do with my money is my business, do you hear? And yes, my dear, your money is now mine – not yours – because you are now my wife and my property.' Joseph's voice lowered as Yates entered with the next course, a shoulder of mutton with boiled potatoes.

Charlotte dared to look across at the husband she was beginning to wish she had never married, as he spooned out his portion of potatoes from the silver tray Yates was holding. She dared not mention the hat

116

and accompanying apparel that she had charged to him. With a bit of luck, the bill would not come until the end of the month and he would have calmed down by then. 'I'm sorry. You must remember it's a new life for me.' She smiled across at her glowering husband as she too helped herself to potatoes.

'I've had a hard day, Charlotte. I don't want to come home to be quizzed about my every move. Now, let's just eat our dinner and then I'll be away to my bed.' Joseph put his head down and stabbed at a potato as if he meant to kill it.

'I do love you, Joseph,' Charlotte whispered quietly over the table, out of earshot of Yates, who was standing waiting next to the doorway.

'I know. I'm tired and grumpy. The mill takes it out of me. Forgive me; I'm used to doing things my way.' He sighed, sat back in his chair and looked across at his days-old bride. He'd done nothing but argue with her since the wedding. Perhaps he should not have been so rash as to marry her, especially as it turned out she didn't have as much in her bank account as he had anticipated. He watched as a tear slowly dropped down the blushing cheeks he'd just admired. 'Stop crying, Charlotte. I apologize, I'm not the easiest man to live with. I love you too, my dear. Now excuse me. I can't keep my eyes open any longer.' He rose from his chair and kissed her on the nape of her delicate neck before leaving the room.

Charlotte sat at the dining table and looked at her plate of untouched dinner. She hadn't expected married life to be like this. She cast her mind back to earlier in the day, when she had met Archie and Rosie and seen the love and concern they had shown one another. That was what a married couple should act like; not like this sham marriage that she was now in. The big question was: what to do next? 'To love, honour and obey' – the words of her wedding vows ran through her head. Obey; did she really have to obey? That was the vow that she had most difficulty with.

'Lottie, how grand it is to see you, but shouldn't you be in the arms of your love, not trailing back home to see your old father?' Wesley Booth hugged his only daughter and then stepped back to admire her in her fancy finery. Noting that her face looked pale and drawn from lack of sleep, he wondered if perhaps there had been too much in the way of lustful nights, but her eyes told him otherwise. 'Tha's missing Crummock's clear air, by looks of them cheeks. What's up with you, lass?' Wesley wasn't going to beat around the bush. He'd always been there for his Lottie and he knew when something was wrong.

'Oh, Father, I've made a terrible mistake. I should never have married Joseph. We aren't right for one another. He's not the man I thought him to be.' Charlotte fell into the chair next to the kitchen hearth and broke down in sobs.

'He's not hitting you, is he, or demanding too much . . . you know – you-know-what? 'Cause you are still my lass, and I'll come and sort him out.' Wesley clasped his hands behind his back and waited for an answer while he summoned Lucy Cranston to go out of the kitchen and leave them in peace, as she tutted and made herself busy eavesdropping on the news of Charlotte's unhappiness.

'No, Father, he's never laid a hand on me. And as for the other, he's hardly touched me.' Charlotte blushed; sex was not something that was discussed.

'Well, what's up with that, lass? Tha's dolled up like a dog's dinner, got your own coach and driver outside. And I don't think you'll be going hungry, not like the poor buggers that work for your fella.' Wesley scowled, wondering just what was amiss with his precious daughter.

'He's taken over my bank account, Father. I've no money, and he expects me to sit at home and just be a lady all day. He shouts at me if I ask him about his business, and he says it is to be expected that he runs my affairs as well as his own.' Charlotte sobbed into her handkerchief and began to realize how petty her problems probably sounded to her father's ears.

'Is that what tha's bloody sobbing like a baby for? What did you think would happen when tha married him? Many a woman would envy your position. You don't have any worries about putting bread on the table, don't have to scrub floors for a living, and are married to the wealthiest man there is around here. You've got to grow up, Charlotte, you are a married woman now. You don't need your own money, and a man's business is his own.'

119

Wesley looked at his daughter, who stared back at him with hurt in her eyes as she sobbed.

'I taught you too much about my business. A woman shouldn't bother her head about such things. I should never have sent you to Harrogate; you came back far too independent, for a farmer's daughter. Your job is now to look after your husband and make sure he's satisfied. Surely you can do that?' He paced back and forth and watched as his daughter's eyes filled up with tears again. 'Tha's not my lil' lass any more – tha's Joseph's wife. I'll always be here for you but, like I told you, you've made your bed; now you must lie in it.'

'That's just it, Father. My bed isn't made, because he won't lie in it, and I don't know what to do!' Charlotte blurted out between sobs and hid her head in her hands.

'You mean he's not . . .' Wesley stood still and gazed at his beautiful daughter, not quite knowing what to say.

Charlotte shook her head and looked up at her father.

'By hell, I wish your mother was alive, she'd know how to tell you what to do. I can't understand the man – that is, if he is a man? He looks the part, but you never know. Lucy! Get yourself in here and stop hiding behind the door. I know you've heard every word said, so come and give my lass some advice.'

Mrs Cranston shuffled back into the kitchen, making no apologies for eavesdropping, and sat down next to

Charlotte, placing her ample arm around the sobbing young lass.

'This is women's talk, and you've used your charms plenty enough on me in the past. Give the lass some guidance, when it comes to men. That is one thing they mustn't have taught her at Harrogate. I'll make myself scarce.' Wesley felt even more embarrassed than his daughter. He'd never previously admitted to bedding Lucy, but his temper had got the better of him today. He looked round at the pair of them. If Lucy's advice didn't get Joseph into bed and make him perform, then there must be something wrong with him. When they had married, his main worry was thinking of his only daughter in bed with the man. Now he found himself insulted that the same man had not even touched her. Joseph must be blind, or something was very wrong in his life.

9

'The Angel in the House'

Man must be pleased; but him to please
Is woman's pleasure; down the gulf
Of his condoled necessities
She casts her best, she flings herself . . .

She loves with love that cannot tire,
And when, ah woe, she loves alone,
Through passionate duty love springs higher,
As grass grows taller round a stone.

COVENTRY PATMORE, 1854

'You alright?' Sally Oversby glanced across at her new friend Betsy, who looked to be struggling with her work-load, and hoped that she could either hear her or read her lips over the noise of the frames going backwards and forwards.

Betsy nodded and wiped her running nose on her

sleeve. She looked anything but alright, as she concentrated on the job in hand and at the same time kept an eye on the all-seeing overseer Bert Bannister.

'See you outside when we have our bait,' Sally mouthed, as Bert walked between the carding machines and scowled at the talking women.

'Get on with your bloody work; you've no time to gossip,' he growled.

'Kiss my arse!' Sally mouthed behind his back, making Betsy smile for the first time that morning. He'd no need to complain, and he knew it.

'Well, are you going to tell me what's up, or have I to drag it out of you?' Sally leaned over the small metal bridge spanning the mill race that fed the huge water wheel powering the machines inside Ferndale Mill. She bit into her bread and dripping and waited for her new-found friend to tell her the woes that were obviously weighing heavily on her shoulders.

Betsy sniffed hard. 'It's our Johnny.' She stopped for a second, wondering if she should tell Sally Oversby her worry. Since she'd moved to Langcliffe she'd realized that everybody was related to everybody else, and she was careful about saying anything about other families in case she offended anyone.

'Well?' Sally threw her dried crusts to the ducks that were circling in the muddy waters, in anticipation of dinner, and watched as they squabbled over the meagre offering.

'I don't know if I should say – you might be related

to those that have got him into bother.' Betsy caught her breath and looked hard at Sally.

'Bother? I thought your Johnny was an angel, a right good scholar, with his head screwed on.' Sally waited to hear the news that had obviously shattered Betsy's world.

'Aye, well, he's got in with those Wainwright lads. I told him they'd get him into trouble, but he didn't listen. Or should I say: he listened to his hungry belly, and them egging him on. I could bloody kill him.' Betsy blew her nose hard and looked at Sally. 'He got caught poaching over at Knight Stainforth, on the manor's land, by Thomas Maudsley himself. Needless to say, the Wainwright lads made themselves scarce, leaving my Johnny holding the rabbit they'd snared, making him look like an idiot. Maudsley is demanding payment of five shillings, in compensation for the rabbits he says Johnny's poached over the last few months, or he will put our Johnny up in front of the magistrates in Skipton. Oh, Sally, how am I going to pay him five shillings? Weavers only make two shillings and sixpence a week, and us carders make even less. I can hardly put bread on the table, without paying any fines.' She leaned over the bridge and waited for her friend's response.

'Those bloody Wainwright lads are a bad lot, but you can't blame 'em – they've had a hard life themselves, with their mother walking out on them when they were babies. As for Thomas Maudsley, I'm surprised he'd be that hard on your Johnny. He lost twins a few years back, when they were just babies; and his daughter Jennet with a fever, when she was in her early teens. Then as if that wasn't a big enough blow, his wife died. He's just got the one lad called Henry, who's the apple of his father's eye. Perhaps if you go and see him, and explain your Johnny means the same to you, I'm sure he'd understand. A few rabbits mean nowt to him – he's got enough brass.'

'I don't know. He lives in Knight Stainforth Manor and I daren't go there. He's gentry; he'll not listen to me. I'll just have to find the money from somewhere. I've a bit of savings put away for Johnny's tools that he'll need when he leaves school next summer, and perhaps I could ask Mr Dawson for a loan, or extra hours? I know one thing: my Johnny is not going to court. I will find the money somehow.' Betsy sighed.

'Well, I wish you luck, lass. I'd help, but you know what it's like at our house. Five mouths to feed, and rent to pay. There's never a penny left by the end of the week. But I will say something: you mind yourself with Joseph Dawson; don't play into his hands. He plays a hard game, does that one, and it's always to his advantage.' Sally hugged Betsy quickly, feeling her thin body under her rough woollen shawl. 'Bugger me, dinner hour goes faster every day, I swear it.' She swore as the mill bell summoned the workers back to their posts.

'Aye, time waits for no man or woman, now we have a mill clock, and Bert Bannister watching us.' Betsy pulled her shawl around her shoulders. 'I just don't know what I'm going to do. I brought Johnny out of

Skipton so that he'd keep out of bother, and now look what he's done.'

'Chin up, lass, at least we don't look as miserable as her.' Sally nudged Betsy and grinned, as they both watched Charlotte walk across the mill yard and enter the heavy oak doors that led into the heart of the mill. 'All that money, posh clothes and no worries, yet look at that miserable face. But then again, I'd be miserable if I were married to Joseph bloody Dawson.'

'She's beautiful.' Betsy watched as Charlotte disappeared gracefully from view.

'Beautiful but miserable – that's what money does for you, girl.' Sally put her arm through Betsy's. 'Come on, else we'll be docked wages. Race you back!' They both lifted their skirts and ran across the yard, their clogs sparking as the metal on them contacted with the cobbles.

'Charlotte, what on earth do you think you're doing here?' Joseph looked up from his desk, surrounded by paperwork and unpaid bills.

'I've just come back from visiting my father, and he has made me realize what a child I have been. I couldn't bear to wait until you came home tonight. I needed to talk to you straight away and ask for your forgiveness. I've been so stupid.' Charlotte lowered her eyes and hoped that she looked demure enough to win the affections of her husband.

'My dear, you still shouldn't have come here – it's no place for a lady. And forgiveness for what? We've

126

both perhaps been over-hasty, and we are new to one another's ways. I'm to be blamed as much as you. I work too much, and the mill demands so much of my time.' Joseph looked at his wife, who was close to tears, and regretted being so hard on her since their wedding.

'No, my love, the blame is all mine. Here I stand, dressed in the finest clothes, with nothing to worry about, and a handsome husband working hard to keep me in a lifestyle beyond my wildest dreams, and all I do is nag and make you angry.' She walked towards him, then ran her hand over his hand and looked into his blue eyes. 'I do love you, Joseph, and you were quite right to take control of my bank account. I am, after all, your wife; and business is a man's world, and I shouldn't bother my head about such things. Just look at all the responsibility you have in your work. It's far too much for an empty-headed woman like me.' Charlotte remembered all Lucy's advice and laid on the stupid-woman act that she had been told to try on her hot-headed husband.

'I'm glad you've realized that I am only trying to protect you, Charlotte. I too love you – you must know that?'

She gently ran her hand around the back of his neck, and Joseph smiled as he sat in his chair, catching her hand when it reached his shoulder and kissing it gently.

'I know, my love. Just looking around your office, I don't quite know what I was thinking of, when I wanted to get involved with the running of the mill. The noise and the dust are horrendous; no wonder you come home and just want to go to bed, you must be exhausted. Come home to me tonight, my love, and I'll show you how much I love you. I swear I know my place now and will not pester you for your attention.' She stood by his side and watched the relief flood over her husband's face.

'I'll look forward to coming home this evening, Charlotte. I must learn to spend more time at home. In another month or two the mill will not need as much attention. You must realize that the business is relatively young and demands my time.' Joseph held onto her hand and looked into the eyes that he was starting to love, despite every fibre of his body telling him just to use her for his own ends. After all, wasn't that what she was doing to him: using him for her position in so-called society?

'I know. Until tonight.' Charlotte smiled and looked up quickly as Bert Bannister knocked sharply on the office door. 'I'll go, you are busy. I'll be waiting.' She smiled and gathered her skirts as she quickly brushed her way past the burly overseer and a pretty-faced mill girl who stood next to him.

'Afternoon, ma'am, nice to see you here at the mill.' Bert tugged on his cap.

'Good to see you, Bert. I hope all is well with you?' Charlotte smiled as the girl next to him didn't dare look up at her. Her father had been right: she didn't know how lucky she was and, if she played Joseph at his own game, then the world was her oyster.

Betsy stood in front of Joseph Dawson. Her legs felt like jelly and her stomach churned with apprehension at the possibility of her request being declined or, even worse, being told that her brother deserved all that he got.

'Well, what's all this about then? Why do you want to see me?' Joseph had dismissed Bert quickly from his office, once he realized that it was the attractive Betsy he had standing quivering behind him.

'I . . . I need your help. You are the only one I can think of that can help me and Johnny.' Betsy played with her handkerchief and lowered her eyes, not wanting to look at the man who held the power over their life or death.

'Oh? And how's that then? Why should I help you and your brother, who the other week was too grand to come and work for me?' Joseph looked at the young woman. She was a beauty – a beauty that he could exploit. She was his for the taking, and she knew it. He rose from his desk and stood next to her, running his fingers through her long, dark hair, and breathed heavily on her neck. 'Well? I'm waiting.'

'Johnny's in a bit of bother. Thomas Maudsley from Knight Stainforth caught him poaching on his land, and now he's demanding payment for the rabbits he says he's been missing from his land, or he'll take Johnny in front of the magistrate at Skipton.' Betsy trembled as

Joseph licked her neck and ran his finger around the top of her laced-up dress. She hated being used and touched by him, but daren't complain and risk being homeless and jobless.

'Why do you think I should care about that? You've a thief under your roof. I'm just glad that he doesn't work for me,' whispered Joseph in her ear. 'Of course, we could come to an understanding. How much is Maudsley wanting for his flea-ridden rabbits?' He kissed the nape of Betsy's neck and slipped his hands inside her bodice, feeling her pert breasts.

Betsy froze; she couldn't scream for help. Nobody would believe her word against the mighty Joseph Dawson. His hands squeezed each breast tighter than a vice. She caught her breath and managed to whisper, 'Five shillings.'

'That's a lot of money, Miss Foster, for a mill lass to pay. How about I lend you it, and we can come to an arrangement. I'll even go and have a word with Thomas Maudsley, to explain the situation.' Joseph pushed himself hard against Betsy's skirts and felt her tremble, as she expected him to force himself on her.

'Would you, sir? I would do anything.' Betsy could have cried. God forgive her for her sins, but she could see no other way out of the situation.

Joseph kissed her neck again and then released his hold, turning her round to face him. 'I'll see Maudsley for your precious Johnny, but you are now mine. I'll visit you later this evening, for you to make the first payment that you owe me.' He looked at the relief on

130

Betsy's face. 'What, you thought I'd take you in my office! A quick five-minute fumble is not long enough for me, Betsy Foster; you'll earn your five shillings.' He smirked.

'Thank you, sir.' A tear ran down Betsy's face and she quickly wiped it away. Her legs trembled as Joseph walked away from her and opened the office door for her to leave.

'And, Betsy, don't think of doing a moonlight flit, else it will be the worse for you. I always get what I want, and I'd hunt you both down. The trouble you are in now is nothing compared to what I could make for you.' He stared at her. 'Keep your mouth shut, and make sure you close the door on your way out.'

'Yes, sir.' Betsy wiped her nose on her sleeve and tried to control her shaking. Things had just got so much worse for her. No self-respecting girl should be submitted to this.

Joseph sat in the parlour of Knight Stainforth Manor, a modest dwelling that had been built with the hard Yorkshire winters and warm summers in mind. The walls were nearly three feet thick and the windows small and narrow, to keep the cold out.

'Now, Dawson, what did you say you've come about?' Thomas Maudsley poured an ample glassful of port, then passed it over to Joseph, before sitting across from the man he knew as a neighbour and nearby mill owner.

'Young Johnny Foster. You caught him poaching rabbits on your land. His sister is concerned that you are about to carry him off to the magistrate's and has asked me to come and settle his debt. She felt awkward coming to the hall herself.' Joseph took a sip of the port and admired the full-bodied quality of the fortified wine.

'You mean the lad I clipped around the ear and threatened with God knows what? If I'd have caught them Wainwright lads from Settle, they'd have had their backsides tanned, but they left the poor little bugger on his own. So I just made idle threats; didn't think for a minute he'd take me seriously.'

'You mean he doesn't owe you anything?' Joseph smiled.

'Nay, if I'd been fined for every rabbit I caught when I was a lad, I wouldn't have a bloody penny. Besides, he did no harm. But those Wainwrights catching my pheasants, that's a different thing – they cost me.' Thomas swigged his port back and looked at Joseph. 'You are to be commended for your concern for your staff, Dawson. Not many bosses would know when their workers have a worry, let alone speak up on their behalf.'

'I try my best to look after them all. Happy staff are more productive.' Joseph swigged his port back and looked around him at the warm but sparse parlour. 'Now, if you'll excuse me, I've a pressing engagement. The Devil makes work for idle hands.'

'He does indeed, Dawson. Tell that young mill lass of yours not to worry. I know who the real culprits were, and anyway I'd rather the lad had a full belly. Better that than dead in the churchyard, like my sons and daughter.' He slapped Joseph on the back and showed him out into the dark November night. The man was a good fella. Not at all like the things he'd heard about him. It just showed that you should never listen to gossip.

Charlotte lay naked in Joseph's bed and waited. Even the all-knowing Mrs Dodgson had been surprised when he'd not been present for dinner, but Charlotte had taken it in her stride. The mill must have been more important, but it had been then that she decided to put her plan into action. If he would not come to her, then she would go to him. And when Lily had seen her settled in her nightclothes and the servants had gone to their quarters, she had tiptoed across the landing to Joseph's room. She had thrown back the curtains, slipped out of her nightgown and into the fresh snug sheets and blankets of Joseph's bed. There she lay, listening to every sound the night made, and watched the clouds scuttle across the face of the full moon, whose light filled the room with a milk-coloured glow.

Joseph had to come home sometime and, when he did, she would be there. Tonight was the night, and she would not say no to whatever he demanded. After all, she had waited long enough. The night wore on and the moon rose higher, leaving only clouds and the odd twinkling star looking down on a drowsy Charlotte in

133

the bed. But as she fought to stay awake for her missing husband, sleep won the fight.

'What the hell!' Joseph pulled back the covers of his bed and looked at his naked, half-asleep wife. It was still dark, but the morning was not far away. Charlotte squinted her eyes in the candlelight and looked up at a surprised and tired Joseph.

'What's the meaning of this? Why aren't you in your own bed?' He sat on the bed edge and pulled his boots off unsteadily, then unbuttoned his trousers, before turning round to look at a shivering Charlotte. 'Pull the bloody covers over you, else you'll freeze.'

She said nothing. She could smell drink on his breath – and quite a bit of drink, by the way he was swaying as he pulled his nightshirt on.

'Well, I might as well have a bit of fun, if you are here waiting of me.' Joseph slid into bed beside Charlotte and ran his hands down her body, while kissing her neck and forcing himself on top of her. 'Is this what you've been wanting, Charlotte?' He held both her hands down tightly and entered her hard, without any enticement other than her lying there. His kisses covered her body, as he thrust deeply and skilfully within her.

Charlotte winced as his thrusts became harder and faster and his kisses more passionate. With her hands released from his grip she ran her fingers down his back, feeling his muscles and nearly crying with pleasure and pain. He was hers – she was in his bed and they were together. A tear ran down from her eye as he climaxed and rolled, exhausted, down by her side.

'Well, you've had me now. You might as well stay here, but for God's sake get some clothes on, else what will Yates or the maid think, when you are naked in my bed?' Joseph slapped her backside as she stepped out of the bed and pulled on her nightdress.

'I don't care. We are married, it's what happens.' She pulled her nightdress over her, climbed back into bed and ran a finger down her husband's chest.

'Aye, we are, my blonde beauty, but you've got to learn your place in my world or else we'll always be fighting with one another.' Joseph pulled her close and kissed her on the lips. 'I'll regret this night's work in the morning, but right now I've got to sleep,' he mumbled, closing his eyes and holding Charlotte tight to him.

She snuggled up next to him, caressing his back. Feeling content with her small victory, she traced the scratch marks that she could feel raised on his skin. Had she really dug her fingers in that deep? She must have, in the excitement, without realizing it. She sighed and closed her eyes. At last she could say she felt content at being married to the man of her dreams, and they were in bed together.

10

Dora Dodgson scowled at Joseph as she poured his tea out for him at the breakfast table. She'd dismissed Yates from his usual duties in order to find out why Joseph had broken from his usual routine, and why she hadn't been the first to know of the previous evening's events. It was not like him not to tell her everything, and she was now fretting for her hot-headed brother.

'Will sir be going to the mill today?' Dora nearly spat out the words and glared at the rosy-cheeked and blissfully happy Charlotte at the other end of the table from Joseph.

'Sir definitely will, but not until he has finished his breakfast and retired to the morning room to do a little business in there.' Joseph smiled down the table at Charlotte.

'And will sir be home for dinner this evening or will we not be honoured with his presence, yet again?' Dora enquired, with all the tact of a sledgehammer.

'Mrs Dodgson, it is not for you to query my presence. If I am here this evening, all well and good, but I don't have to be answerable to you for my every move.' He didn't want to explain his previous evening's absence, and sometimes his sister was a little too dictatorial in her position as housekeeper.

Charlotte smirked and quickly had a sip of her tea, in an attempt to hide the wide smile as Mrs Dodgson was put in her place.

'I only enquired, sir, so that Mrs Batty knows. She gets in a right way if she doesn't know who she's cooking for.' Dora passed the blame on to the mild-mannered cook and stood back. She knew her brother well enough not to push him into a corner.

'In that case, I will be home for dinner. Also, Mrs Dodgson, can you tell Yates to move my things into the main bedroom, along with Charlotte's. I don't aim to continue with my long hours at the mill, now that I'm married and it is starting to run more smoothly.'

Joseph watched the face of his sister as it clouded over. He knew he'd promised her not to get too involved with anyone. They were going to make their money, sell up and move on to another new life. But a night with Charlotte lying next to him, and the added attraction of Betsy Foster, had turned his head. Why should he move on from such a good lifestyle? Money was a little tight at the moment, but profit would soon come, now that Ferndale Mill was operating well. Also, now that he had paid Simmons the solicitor to keep his mouth shut, there was no need to be thinking of moving on. He couldn't see Simmons returning in a hurry; twenty guineas was a small fortune to a man like him.

'Very well, sir, if you think it's wise.' Dora served the kippers to her brother and scowled at him as he completely ignored her.

'I'd like some too, Mrs Dodgson.' Charlotte spoke up to the housekeeper, before she placed the dish of kippers back over the warming pan.

'In future, Mrs Dodgson, please serve my wife first. It is the polite thing to do when we are on our own.' Joseph looked at his sulking sister; she would have to learn her place in his household, if she was to stay. He had to appear to everyone to be the perfect gentleman, and his sister had to live up to her position within his household.

'Very well, sir.' Dora went and served Charlotte, without saying a word or giving her a second glance.

'Oh, and Mrs Dodgson, I'm thinking of holding a Christmas Ball at Windfell. Perhaps Cook, Charlotte and you could sit down and put a menu together. We had a relatively quiet wedding, so it would be nice to open the doors this Christmas to our neighbours.'

'Joseph, that would be so lovely. My father could come, and Mrs Cranston, and Archie and his wife Rosie.' Charlotte's mind raced with the names of guests that she would like to see there.

'We'll see, Charlotte; we'll go through our guest list together.' Joseph cut into his kippers and watched the happiness on his wife's face, and the darkness covering his sister's. He'd have to make his peace with her later.

'You'd a letter come for you late last evening. Yates put it in the study, when you weren't here. Looks important, sir, it being from America.' Dora stared at her love-struck brother. She'd bring him down to earth if it's the last thing she did – the fool. 'Will that be all, sir?' she asked her brother, who nodded at her while wondering what the letter from America that now lay in his hand contained. Dora turned and closed the dining-room door behind her. Joseph had better not cross her, or he'd be the worse for it. She'd stuck by him through thick and thin, and now his head was being turned by a giggling farm girl.

Charlotte sat at her desk in the morning room, writing to her father of the news of the Christmas Ball, and watched as Joseph read the letter that had come thousands of miles from Richard Todd, the plantation owner in New Orleans.

'I hope I'm not being too inquisitive, but you look worried, my dear. What's wrong?' She stopped writing and watched as Joseph stood looking out of the window and sighing.

'You shouldn't concern yourself with this. How many times have I told you not to bother about business.' He looked at the letter again and tried to hide his worry. 'Have you told your father of our Christmas Ball? I suppose Mrs Cranston really should be asked this time. I'm sure he will be diplomatic enough to instruct her to keep a low profile.' He sighed. Mrs Cranston was the least of his worries, if the letter's contents were to be believed.

Charlotte ran and hugged his neck and kissed him on the cheek. 'That would be wonderful. And Archie and his wife Rosie?'

'Oh, I suppose so, Charlotte. Now if you'll excuse me, I've got to go to the mill. I'm late as it is.' Joseph's mind was racing. He had to check the number of cotton bales he had in the warehouse and see if he could afford another delivery from Todd. Cotton was plentiful at the moment, and reasonable in price at ten cents a pound. But Richard had warned him that trouble was brewing across the Atlantic, and he had to buy now if he was to survive the coming problems. 'I'll see you at dinner.'

Joseph slammed the morning-room door and Charlotte watched him as he walked out to the stables, yelling at the stable lad to saddle his horse. There must have been bad news in the letter; his mood had changed in the blink of an eye. Why was she married to such a moody beast? She smiled as she remembered the previous night's antics, and the fact that he'd put the probing Mrs Dodgson in her place. Lucy Cranston had been right: act like a little lost soul and the world was yours. She couldn't help but wonder: was that how Lucy had got her father into bed? No, it would be her cooking, for her father loved having a full belly more than anything.

'Oh, Betsy, what have you done! How the hell have you got a shiner like that?' Sally Oversby yelled over to

140

Betsy, who had kept her head down and seemed to have ignored her all morning. Now she could see why.

'It's nothing. I hit my head against the bed end by accident, bending down to empty the chamber pot this morning.' Betsy gave a wan smile and wished Sally would mind her own business.

'I hope you rubbed it with a knob of butter. My mother always recommends that for a bruise.' Sally grinned.

Betsy nodded. She didn't want to talk to anybody today. She felt dirty and used, her body ached and her mind did too, with the guilt and pain of having had sex with Joseph Dawson. To add to the worry, she knew it wasn't over – he'd be back. He'd said as much when he'd left her curled up in a ball in the early hours of the morning. He hadn't been a kind lover; he'd been brutal, taking out his frustrations on Betsy, his hatred and lack of respect for women made obvious as he thrust and slapped her. She'd wanted to cry out, but she knew Johnny was in the next room and she didn't want him waking to find his sister acting like a whore.

'Catch up at bait time?' Sally shouted above the noise.

'No, I'm just going to run home. Thought I'd put a tattie-hash in the fireside oven for tonight's supper.' Betsy put her back into her work, as she saw Bert Bannister walking up and down the rows of carding machines, watching for anyone slacking.

'Alright.' Sally shrugged her shoulders and smiled at Bert as he passed by. You never let that bastard know what you were thinking or doing. He was the boss's monkey and everyone knew it.

Betsy wrapped her shawl around her head and ran along the side of the millpond towards the double row of cottages, one of which was home to her and Johnny. The path was white with frost and treacherous, as she slipped dangerously on the large piece of slate that acted as a bridge by the side of the sluice gate that released excess water into the fast-flowing River Ribble. She caught her breath as she gained her footing and pressed on through the snicket gate at the side of the row of cottages.

Reaching her front door, she felt relief as she passed over her doorstep into the safety of her home. She bent over the glazed earthenware sink in the kitchen and retched while her body shook, thanking God that Johnny was at school and unable to see her in such a state. Wiping her mouth with her back of her hand, she looked at herself in the mirror hanging next to the kitchen door. An egg-like lump hung over her eye, a hue of blues and purples where Joseph had hit her, when she'd scratched him for being over-zealous with his advances.

'Are you alright, Betsy?' There was a sharp knock on her door and the enquiring voice of Gertie Potts, her next-door neighbour, shouted through the letter box.

Betsy couldn't escape; Gertie had obviously seen her come home. She swept back a loose lank of her hair and checked herself in the mirror, before opening the door.

'I saw you running in home. I thought there must be something wrong at the mill. Oh my Lord, look at you!' gasped Gertie.

'Oh, I hit my head on the brass bedstead this morning. It looks worse than it is. I've just come back to put something in the side-oven for supper. Thought that now the frosty weather's come, Johnny would like a warm supper to come home to.' She smiled at Gertie.

'Well, mind what you are doing, lass. That brother of yours doesn't realize what a good sister he has. You take care of him too much.' Gertie pulled her shawl around her and turned to go back home. 'You'd better get your skates on: that's the dinner-hour whistle going, and you don't want your pay docking. That Bert Bannister won't think twice about doing that, the miserable bugger.'

Betsy pulled her door to, picked her skirts up and ran back to the mill. She'd had no dinner, and cooking tattie-hash for supper was just a dream. It would be bread and cheese for supper, and they would have to be thankful for that.

'I'm just glad that he has moved in with her – that was no way for a young married couple to act. If my old man had stopped in his bedroom when we were first married, I'd have been thinking things weren't quite right.' Mrs Batty stood with her hands on her hips and wiped away an escaping tear as she finished chopping the onions for the evening meal.

'You mean you wanted a bit of nightly entertainment?' Lily joked as she sat next to the fire, mending a shirt of Joseph's that had lost some of its buttons, which she'd previously picked up from the bedroom floor in the morning.

'Close your ears, young Mazy; and Lily, you stop your mucky talk. You know what I meant. It just wasn't right!' Mrs Batty put her chopped onions into a large dish, adding the diced lamb and carrots before placing it in the oven to cook.

'Well, they made up for lost time last night, by the looks of this shirt. That's three buttons I've had to sew on, from his shirt being ripped off.' Lily bit off the end of her thread and then admired her handiwork.

'I'd watch what you are saying. What goes on in that bedroom is none of our business.' Yates decided to break up the women of the kitchen from their gossiping session. 'Besides, walls have ears, and you know who I'm on about.'

'If you mean Dodgy Dodgson, she's gone out. Said she had a bad head and needed some air,' Mazy added quickly.

'She's "Mrs Dodgson" to you, young Mazy. Show some respect for your elders.' Yates stifled a smirk.

'I'm only calling her what you all call her. She looked as black as thunder when I saw her go out of the back door.' Mazy carried on cleaning the silver and waited

144

for the hated housekeeper to be torn apart by everyone, now that they knew she wasn't in the building.

'She'll be sulking over Mr Dawson throwing a Christmas Ball; she isn't exactly the partying kind.' Mrs Batty sat down and reached for her almost cold cup of tea from the kitchen table. 'I'm right looking forward to us holding a do here. The manor will look so bonny, with a bit of Christmas cheer. It will be something for the mistress to look forward to.'

'Aye, she looked so happy this morning, she must have had a good night, too.' Lily grinned.

'Ladies, please! Spare me my blushes and change the subject.' Yates rose from his chair. 'If you'll excuse me, I'll make sure that all is in its place in their bedroom, in readiness for Mr Dawson's return.'

'Aye, you do that, and then we can carry on with our gossip. It's very rare we have time without that eavesdropping Dodgy Dodgson listening in, and all's in hand down here.' Mrs Batty put her feet up on the small stool and looked into the fire. 'I might even have five minutes' nap while the old bat is out. I'm jiggered.'

'Mrs Batty!' Yates exclaimed.

'Well, that one deserves all she gets, and you know it.' The cook closed her eyes and listened to Mazy and Lily giggling at her comments, and thought how good life would be without Dora Dodgson.

11

'That looks wonderful, Mrs Batty.' Charlotte stood back and admired the dining-room table adorned with sparkling crystal, silver platters and enough food to feed an army. Steaming hot bowls of vegetable and beef broth were to be served fresh from the kitchen to start the meal, and then there would be carving joints along the table, with pickles and cheeses and breads in equal quantities. 'The puddings look fantastic.' She looked across at the long dresser adorned with blancmanges, jellies, pies and flans.

'Aye, well, we thought we might as well impress. Yates, Jethro the footman and the stable lad, and even Mazy can manage to serve something as simple as this quickly and easily, seeing as Mrs Dodgson doesn't seem to want to employ any outside staff.'

'I'm sorry, Mrs Batty, she's quite adamant that you will all manage, and I'm sure you will. I'd help if I could.' Charlotte looked at the fretful cook. 'I'm afraid

Mrs Dodgson is a force to be reckoned with, and sometimes influences my husband too much. But you didn't hear that from me.'

'I'm sure it will be to Mr Dawson's satisfaction.' Mrs Batty coughed loudly, attracting Charlotte to Dora's presence as she entered the room, and hoping that her mistress's last comment had not been heard over the sound of the band in the main hall striking up.

'Waste of time and money. And if he thinks I'm going to watch half the county eating at his expense and making fools of themselves trying to dance, then he can think again.' Charlotte looked shocked that Dora was talking about her employer in that way.

'I don't think Joseph will take kindly to the way you are talking about the Christmas Ball. I feel I should convey your thoughts to him, Mrs Dodgson.' Charlotte stood her ground with the grumpy housekeeper, who was most definitely overstepping her position in the household.

'Suit yourself. He already knows what I think. Besides, look at the weather: that sky is threatening snow, you mark my words.' Dora looked out of the dining-room window and bit her tongue from saying worse to the woman who was growing stronger by the day, as Joseph became more infatuated with her.

'Well, if it does snow, we've plenty of spare rooms, and most will only have come from nearby Settle. It's just a short walk, even if they don't come by carriage. I'm sure it will be a splendid night.' Charlotte smiled.

'Aye, well, we'll do our best; it'll not be for the want

of trying. I suppose you'll want me to feed the band as well? Are they to eat with us downstairs, after the ball? Because I'll be ready for my bed after all this.' Mrs Batty sighed; she'd been run off her feet all day and she knew that she'd not see her bed before 2 a.m. the next morning.

'If you could, Mrs Batty. Don't they look splendid? And listen to that divine music – my feet won't be able to keep still.' Charlotte smiled at the cook, who had gone all out to make sure the evening was a success, and she appreciated it. The music was floating in from the main hall and her feet just wouldn't stay still. 'Do you dance, Mrs Dodgson? Once dinner is served, I'm sure Joseph wouldn't mind the staff watching, or perhaps even dancing on the outskirts of the room.

'I most certainly do not. I will go to my room, once I know everyone's been fed. I've no time for flippancy. This wouldn't have happened if we'd still been living in Accrington.' Dora picked up her skirts and left the dining room. Why hadn't Joseph listened to her and kept a low profile? The stupid man. Half the district was to be at Windfell Manor tonight, and she wanted none of it.

'Sorry, Mistress, but she's just a misery. I know I shouldn't say that.' Mrs Batty waddled towards the doorway of the dining room.

'I agree, Mrs Batty. But now excuse me, I have to change. Could you ask Lily to come up to my room, please? Joseph is just coming down the stairs, so he is free to greet any early guests while I change.'

'Of course I will, ma'am, and I bet you will look the belle of the ball.' Mrs Batty smiled; she had grown fond of the lass who had first been so unsure of her role in the big house. Now she was turning into a real lady, to the dismay of Mrs Dodgson.

Charlotte walked across the hallway and smiled at the four-piece band who were gleefully playing a merry jig to an empty hallway. She met Joseph at the bottom of the wrought-iron staircase, gently placing her hand on the sleeve of his dashing red velvet jacket. 'You're looking handsome, my dear.' She smiled at her dark-haired husband as she stood at the bottom of the stairs, and waited for his reply.

'I'm sure you will look equally beautiful, if you get a move on. Our guests will be with us any minute, and you are talking to the cook. Where's Mrs Dodgson? Talking to the cook is *her* job.' Joseph watched as his wife listened to the band.

'She's gone down to the kitchen. I don't think to-night's event is to her taste. And besides, I just wanted to check with Mrs Batty that everything was in hand, and I knew Yates was with you.' Charlotte lifted her skirts and started to climb the stairs.

'Charlotte, I need to talk to you later. I've received a bill from the milliner's in Settle that I didn't authorize. They say it was your doing.' Joseph looked stern as she stopped in her tracks.

'It was only for a few things, Joseph. I've no say over my money any more; I didn't think you would mind.'

'We'll talk later. The stairs are no place to discuss money matters, but needless to say, I'm not happy, Charlotte. I will buy what you need, do you understand?' He lingered by the black-painted wrought-iron lion's head that adorned the stair end and looked up at his wife.

'I understand, Joseph. Now if you'll excuse me, I do need to change.' Charlotte knew the look that he gave her would mean a lecture later, and she could feel herself getting upset at the thought of being put in her place yet again. Especially on a night when she had been feeling happy at last with her life at Windfell Manor. She ran up the stairs and into their marital bedroom and waited for Lily, the butterflies mounting in her stomach at the thought of Joseph's black look and the way he could make her feel, over spending a few pounds on herself. Damn it, she'd never be what he wanted her to be, and she was becoming tired of acting like a brainless doll. Surely no other husband in his position would quibble over a few pounds spent on a hat and gloves, for someone they loved?

Charlotte ran her hand over the beautiful blue silk ballgown that had arrived that morning for her to wear tonight. Joseph had gone to the bother of spending all that money without her knowledge, but when it came to buying something of her own choice, it was a different matter. He just liked to be in control of everything. It would seem that he and Mrs Dodgson were birds of a feather – both out to spoil anyone's enjoyment. Her

150

thoughts were interrupted by Lily's timid knock on her bedroom door.

'Come in, Lily.' She left her bedside and sat on the stool at her dressing table, looking at herself. She'd changed this last month or two. The bloom in her cheeks had left her and now she was replacing it with rouge, to camouflage the drawn look of her face.

'Oh, Mistress, people are starting to arrive. Your father's here with his guest. And doesn't Mr Dawson look handsome? The band is playing, and everyone is smiling.' Lily could hardly draw breath between sentences.

'My father's here, and Mrs Cranston? Hurry, Lily, get me out of this and into my dress – I can't wait to see them.' Charlotte quickly finished applying the rouge and stood up, for Lily to undo the laces on the back of her bodice.

'This dress is beautiful – it is the same colour as your eyes. Mr Dawson does have good taste.' She slipped the silk dress over Charlotte's head and then asked her to hold onto the bedpost, as she pulled on the laces to tie the back of the bodice up tightly.

'Don't lace it too tight, Lily, I can hardly breathe. He should have let me go to the dressmaker's to be measured – this one's a little tight.' Charlotte breathed in and looked at herself in the mirror, before sitting down again for Lily to put her hair in place. 'I can't possibly have anything to eat if I'm to dance tonight, this dress is so tight.'

'You look beautiful, ma'am.' Lily brushed and

curled Charlotte's hair, pinning each curl into place and watching as her mistress looked at herself in the mirror. 'Mr Dawson is a lucky man, to have one so beautiful on his arm.'

'Do you think so, Lily? I think I'm the lucky one. As you say, he is a handsome man – a handsome man with very good prospects. That's what my father told me when he first met him.' Charlotte smiled at the young lady's maid as she stood back and admired her handiwork.

'Quite rightly so, ma'am.' Lily looked at her mistress's reflection and smiled.

'Time to face the music, Lily, in more ways than one.' Charlotte stood up and reached for her fan on the dressing table. 'Thank you, Lily. What would I do without you?'

'You'd manage, ma'am, I'm sure.'

'Some days I wonder, Lily, I really wonder.' Charlotte made for the bedroom door, leaving the maid to tidy her room.

'Father, I'm so glad you and Mrs Cranston have made it.' Charlotte opened her arms to hug her father and then to hug Lucy Cranston.

Lucy blushed. 'Do you think you should be doing that, Lottie? I'm only a cook.'

'Nonsense. You were like a mother to me, and I'm not too proud to admit it.' Charlotte noted Joseph's disapproving stare and covered her face with her fan as she watched him meeting and greeting their guests.

'So, what do you think? Poor Yates and Jethro took all day putting up those ivy-and-holly bowers and swags. If I heard one swear word, I heard twenty, when the holly pricked their arms and fingers. Don't you think the red ribbons just add to the effect?' Charlotte gazed around the hall and smiled as people nodded their heads in respect at her presence.

'Aye, it's grand, lass, and that fiddle player can fair play. We'll have to have a dance, won't we, Lucy, after we've had something to eat? We'll not be stopping long, though. It's threatening snow out there, and you know what a bugger it is to get back up to Crummock with snow on the ground.'

'You could always stay the night – we've plenty of rooms. I'm sure Joseph wouldn't mind. Let me ask him.' Charlotte started to walk away.

'Nay, don't bother, lass; don't go asking Joseph. We'll keep an eye on the weather. I'd rather sleep in my own bed and be back at home in the morning. Besides, there's Lucy here. He wouldn't know where to put her, because he's made it quite clear what he thinks about our . . . er . . . arrangement.' Wesley put his arm round Lucy's waist. 'Where I go, she goes now. I might even get around to wedding her yet.'

'Give over, and be careful what you say, Wesley. We are with gentry.' Lucy blushed.

'Gentry, my arse; they are all hypocrites! There's old Cartwright over there, who runs the snuff mill at Settle – everyone knows he's got a floozy at Giggleswick. And then there's Bernard Baxter right there, talking to his wife – it'll be the first time he's had her on his arm for months; he's usually occupied with the chambermaid at The Lion.'

'Father, please, these are all Joseph's friends.' Charlotte fluttered her fan, aware that her husband was making his way over to them.

'I was nobbut saying.'

'Well, don't,' said Charlotte, before reaching her hand out for Joseph.

'Are you enjoying your visit to us, Mrs Cranston?' he enquired, to the blushing, flustered woman who stood next to his protective wife.

'I am, thank you, sir,' answered Mrs Cranston quickly, while thinking of the advice she had given her young ward about how to woo her handsome partner.

'My cook has done wonders tonight; you must help yourselves at our table and enjoy the music. Charlotte has been busy all day organizing everyone – I'm surprised she isn't quite worn out.' Joseph raised his glass of wine to his lips and watched his wife as she averted her gaze.

'I'm quite fine, thank you, my dear. I'm more concerned about the weather not being kind to our guests. My father says it looks like snow.' Charlotte was trying to draw out an invitation for her father to stay the night, but it was not forthcoming.

'We will have to be vigilant to nature's wishes. I'll ask Jethro to alert me, should we indeed get snow. I'm sure you would need to get home at the first snowflake. Crummock is such a remote farmstead.' Joseph took another sip from his glass and looked at Mrs Cranston as she lowered her eyes. She knew all too well why they were not allowed to stay. 'But now, let's eat. I'll go and ask Yates to announce dinner being served. It's no good having a dog and then barking yourself.'

Charlotte felt embarrassed by her husband's arrogance. How dare he make Mrs Cranston feel unwanted, and liken his butler to a dog.

'Come, Father, you must try Mrs Batty's cooked ham, it melts in the mouth; and the plum chutney she made from the fruit in the orchard just gives it that added tang. Sit next to me, Mrs Cranston, so you don't have to make conversation with anyone you don't know. I know how uncomfortable that can feel.' Charlotte linked her arm through Lucy's and led them to their seats at the table.

'By, it's a grand spread, Lottie. I expect my eyes are going to be bigger than my belly, there's so much to eat.' Wesley watched as Yates served him a steaming bowl of chicken broth. 'Just what you need on a cold winter's night. And then I will try a bit of that ham, our Lottie. It looks bloody good.'

Charlotte smiled. Her father loved his food, perhaps a little too much.

'I shouldn't have eaten all that ham, Lucy. By, have I got a pain right between my shoulder blades. It must be wind. And it hurts right into my chest.' Wesley stopped mid-dance, bending double to catch his breath after doing an extra-fast jig.

'You're just a silly old bugger – you're not sixteen any more.' Lucy stood over him.

His red face looked up at his love and he grinned. 'Aye, but we showed these young pups how it's done, and I'll do it again just once more, before I go and get the horse and trap. Just let me get my breath,' puffed Wesley.

'You silly old fool, you will not. Everybody has seen us cavorting around the floor. Even Lottie was embarrassed by us, and I saw Joseph mutter something under his breath.'

'Aye, perhaps you are right – maybe we should call it a day. We could do with getting home. Let's just sneak out. Our Lottie won't miss us. Look, she's talking to that po-faced, unhappy-looking housekeeper. By gum, this pain is bad. I hope that stable lad has harnessed my horse. I told him to about half an hour ago, when I went outside to see what the weather was doing.' Wesley tried to straighten himself and winced as a pain as sharp as a needle went down his arm.

'Let me help you. We are going home. We'll sneak out the back door, then we won't spoil Lottie's night by making her aware that you aren't well.' Lucy grabbed his arm and walked with Wesley steadily through the long corridor to the back door of Windfell Manor.

'Bugger, it's starting to snow. But at least my horse and trap are ready.' Wesley felt the cold air restrict his chest from breathing, and gasped as the snow-filled air bit into his lungs. 'Bloody hell, lass, I'm done for. I can't breathe.'

'Wesley, Wesley!' Lucy shouted as he fell to the floor. 'Wesley, what's wrong?' She bent down beside him as he fought for breath.

'I'll go and get Dr Burrows – he's in the manor,' said the stable boy as he stood over the elderly couple and realized that there was something wrong. He ran for help.

'Wesley, can you hear me? There's help coming, the lad's gone for Dr Burrows.' Lucy held her beloved's hand; she could feel his pulse getting weaker by the minute as he struggled for breath. His breathing laboured, and then weakened to almost nothing.

'I'm sorry, lass. I love you, you know that, don't you? Take care of my Lottie, 'cause I know that I'm knackered,' Wesley whispered with his dying breath, which was hardly audible to the sobbing Lucy.

'Oh, Wesley, no. No, you silly old fool, you shouldn't have danced like that.' Mrs Cranston knelt on the granite chippings of the great driveway of Windfell Manor and cradled the true love of her life as tears fell down, mixing with the falling snowflakes onto the body of Wesley. 'I loved you, you old fool, and we were going to be married. Why, why, why?' She sobbed and cradled the dying man as Dr Burrows rushed out of the manor with a crowd of merrymakers behind him, all wondering what the fuss was about.

Dr Burrows bent down beside Lucy and felt for Wesley's pulse on his neck. Realizing that he had arrived too late, he gently closed the man's staring eyes. 'I'm afraid he's dead. A heart attack, by the look of those lips. I'm so sorry; he wasn't a fit man.'

'Father, Father, when are you going to learn to take it steady?' Charlotte pushed her way through the crowd, believing that her father had simply over-exerted himself, as the stable boy had been overheard saying.

Dr Burrows stood up from the side of the grieving Lucy and put his arm around Charlotte. 'I'm sorry, my dear, but your father's dead. There's nothing we can do.'

'No, he can't be – he was only dancing a minute or two ago. You're wrong.' Charlotte pushed past the doctor and knelt down next to Lucy. She brushed her father's grey hair with loving care, looking into Lucy's eyes for reassurance that her father was only sleeping and that nothing was wrong.

'He's gone, Miss Charlotte, we've lost him,' sobbed Lucy, holding both Charlotte and Wesley tight.

'What am I going to do? I loved him. Where can I call home now, with my father dead? He was always there for me.'

'I know, Miss Lottie. I loved him too, the silly old bugger. Why has he left us?'

At the back of the crowd Joseph Dawson watched his wife grieving over her dead father. Dora stood at his shoulder and quietly whispered into his ear, 'Have faith in the Lord, for he will provide.' She looked hard at her brother, who was now married to a rich farm owner. His money worries had, hopefully, just been answered. 'Charlotte looks fine in that old dress of May's. It was always your favourite on her, when she was on your arm,' Dora smirked.

'Shut your mouth, woman. People can hear.' Joseph scowled at his sister. She always took delight in other people's misfortunes and never knew when to keep her mouth closed. She wasn't as refined in her actions as he was, and the coldness of her heart frightened even him on occasion.

The gaiety of the Christmas season was lost at Windfell Manor, as the dark mists of a death in the family hung around all the rooms like a sneaking spectre. The day after New Year's Day had been set by the Reverend Richardson for Wesley's funeral at the little village church of Austwick. He would be buried next to his wife Isabelle, in the small churchyard surrounding the ancient church, which was the last resting place for generations of the Booth family and their descendants.

'Are you alright, my dear?' Joseph offered Charlotte his hand to help her climb into the coach and horses, which waited patiently outside the entrance to the manor.

Charlotte nodded and stifled her tears underneath the black veil shrouding her eyes from her husband's gaze.

'Be strong, my dear. It will soon be over. The grave-side's the worst, as you know, and I'm here for you.' Joseph sat next to his sobbing wife and then instructed the coach driver to whip the team of black funeral horses, which he had hired from the livery stable to match the plumed team that carried Wesley's body from Crummock Farm to the church. The show of the funeral had cost him a pretty penny, but that mattered little, with the farm soon to be his.

As arranged, the cortège met at the bottom of the lane leading up to Crummock Farm. The black horses, with their heads of feathery plumes, chomped on their bits and jangled their harness as Charlotte and Joseph's coach lined up behind the hearse carrying Wesley. Mrs Cranston and Mary, the parlour maid, stood behind it. Mary had her arm around Mrs Cranston's waist, while she sobbed beneath the black shawl that covered her head.

'Lucy, come and join us in the carriage. You too, Mary – we have room.' Charlotte could hardly say the words as she leaned out of the carriage window and looked down at the crumpled, heartbroken face of Lucy Cranston.

'Nay, I'll not bother, Miss. I'd rather walk behind him – it's our way. He was nobbut a farm lad really; he'd not think owt of a grand funeral like this. Not that he wouldn't be grateful for it, of course. I don't mean to offend, sir.' Lucy looked up into the sober face of Joseph.

'Then I'll come down to you, and we'll walk together.' Charlotte leaned over to undo the catch on the coach door.

Joseph put his hand on hers, stopping her from turning the catch. He looked angrily at her as she resisted his force.

'I have to, Joseph. It's tradition to walk behind the one we have lost. Look at all the people waiting with bowed heads for us to pass by their houses. They are paying their respects and will probably walk with us to the church.' Charlotte turned the catch and climbed out of the carriage, battling with her long black skirts as she joined Lucy and Mary.

'Damn it, woman, why do you always defy me?' whispered Joseph as he climbed out of the carriage to join his defiant wife. 'Take the team to the water trough next to Austwick Hall; it seems I'm walking to the church with my wife,' he instructed the groom and coachman, before joining the gathering throng behind the hearse.

'Thank you.' Charlotte sobbed as she stepped out meekly, walking slowly past the shuttered windows and bowed heads of the respectful people of the small village.

The innkeeper of The Gamecock, Richard Goodwin, joined the gathering as the mourners made their way down the street to the crossroads where the village church stood. 'I've put on a spread, like you requested, Lottie. I've done him proud. He was always a good customer, was your father.'

Charlotte nodded and fought back more tears as she thought of her father's favourite corner in The Game-cock, where he'd often been found sharing the gossip or playing dominoes.

'I've made sure the back parlour is empty and all and is private, away from prying eyes, like you said.

You've just to say if you want owt else, lass.' Richard caught Joseph's black look and decided he had said enough, and to walk a little slower as they neared the church gates.

A funeral tea at The Gamecock had not been to Joseph's liking. It was not grand enough, in his eyes. But when Wesley's grovelling solicitor had suggested that the man's last will and testament be read there, directly after his interment, Joseph's mind had soon changed.

The carriage came to a standstill and the pall-bearers slowly lifted Wesley's coffin onto their shoulders. The shocking blond mop of Archie Atkinson shone like a halo, as he bore some of the weight of Wesley's body. He caught Charlotte's eye as she bowed her head and slipped her arm through Joseph's. This was the worst day of her life; she was burying her father – the only man she had truly loved.

12

'My condolences, Charlotte, your father was a good man – he'll be missed, here in Austwick.' Charles Walker was a solicitor from Walker & Preston, the local solicitors. He shook her hand and then offered his hand to Joseph, who shook it before pulling a chair out for a sobbing Charlotte to sit on.

'Could we not do this business elsewhere and on another day? I think Charlotte has been through enough.' Joseph patted her hand gently, while keeping his secret thoughts to himself. Just how much had Wesley Booth been worth?

'Wesley requested that his will be delivered here and now, and it is my duty to do so.' Charles Walker pulled his chair out and sat down promptly, across from the man he had heard so much about, but had never had the pleasure or misfortune (whichever was to prove the case) to meet.

'I'm quite fine, please continue. Joseph, don't worry:

I'd rather know where I stand with my father's estate. I'm more upset at seeing so many friends and family gathered to show their respects. He was, as you say, well respected in the community. However, no amount of crying and sobbing is going to bring him back, and I've to face the future without him.' Charlotte's hands shook as she blew her nose and then composed herself. She smiled wanly at both men as they looked at her, surprised by her strength of character on such an occasion.

'Very well, then I will read the will. It is short and to the point, with only two beneficiaries.' Walker opened the parchment and looked at the couple before him: a farmer's daughter, and the mill owner whom her father had grown to dislike over the few months that he had witnessed the marriage.

'So, Charlotte, Crummock Farm is now yours. However, with your recent marriage to Mr Dawson, I am afraid it is by law your husband's. I'm sorry, Charlotte, this may come as a blow to you, as I know you love Crummock, but I'm sure Joseph here will look after your family home.' Walker watched as Charlotte's eyes filled with tears and Joseph breathed in deeply.

'You say that there are two beneficiaries. Who is the other?' Joseph leaned on the makeshift desk and stared at the solicitor.

'It is Mrs Lucy Cranston. She is to inherit all of Wesley's wealth, on his bequest. Quite a considerable amount, if I may say so. I'm afraid I've not been able to notify her as of yet, so it will come as a surprise to the poor woman.' Walker smiled. 'On the proviso that she pays any of his outstanding debts. But your father was a careful man, so I'm not expecting any. If he couldn't pay for it, he didn't buy it – as is taught to all us Dales folk, as we sit on our mother's knees.' Walker sat back and looked at Charlotte, whose tears ran freely down her cheeks.

Joseph swore under his breath and clenched his knuckles until they were white with rage.

'He loved Lucy; he should have married her, the silly old fool, and he shouldn't have listened to local gossip.' Charlotte sobbed. 'I'm glad that he's been right with her.'

'This way he's looked after both the women that he loved. And you, Mr Dawson, have a wealthy land-owner as a wife – a most attractive asset, if you don't mind me saying.' Charles leaned back in his chair and looked at the dark-haired, high-cheekboned man, who didn't look at all pleased with his lot.

'Do we have to honour Wesley's wishes? And have you included the stock in his assets?' Joseph had no way to hide his feelings. That bloody common cook had come between him and a small fortune.

'The stock is included in his assets, and so belongs to you and Charlotte. When it comes to Mrs Cranston, surely you would not want to go against Wesley's last wishes?'

'A bloody cook with all that money, it's not right!' Joseph pushed his chair back and paced around the parlour.

'Joseph, I'm just happy that we have Crummock –

be content with that. Lucy's been like a mother to me, and I'm happy that father has made her last few years bearable. You saw how heartbroken she was.' Charlotte sobbed, not daring to look at her ungrateful husband.

'Aye, well, I'm not! What am I going to do with a bloody farm? I'd rather have had his brass than some acres of land that are not worth a lot,' Joseph snarled.

'Sir, I'd hold your tongue and remember that we have just buried your wife's father. You'd be surprised at how much the price of land is. However, I would advise that you sell in the autumn, if that is your plan.' Walker looked at the disrespectful man and bit his tongue from saying exactly what he thought of the blaggard that stood before him. 'I've already spoken to your father's farm lad, and he's willing to stay on at Crummock until he's told otherwise. Providing you are willing to pay him, that is? However, lambing time will soon be upon you and you need someone else in place by then – he won't manage on his own.' Walker looked at the young woman. He knew she had a good business head and was proud of her roots.

'That will be Arthur, Joseph. I don't want you to sell Crummock; the farm lad must stay – that will give you time to grow to love Crummock as I do. Perhaps you could rent it and then you will have some extra income?' Charlotte turned around and looked pleadingly at Joseph.

'Damn you, have you no sense?' Joseph walked over to the small window, leaning on his arm, blocking the light in the room as he swore under his breath at not getting his way.

'Sir, be careful, I will not abide language of that sort within a lady's presence.' Walker's hearing was as sharp as a bat's and he was not impressed with Charlotte Booth's choice of husband; he was definitely no gent.

'My husband is not a farmer, Mr Walker; he doesn't have a love of the land, like I do.' Charlotte tried to smile and rose from her chair.

'You don't have to make excuses for me. I just can't understand why a useless cook has ended up with a small fortune and I've drawn the short straw, with worthless moorland and a rambling farmhouse.' Joseph stood next to Charlotte.

'Wesley knew that Crummock would make Charlotte happy, Mr Dawson. Money is sometimes not everything. I've seen the poorest people be the happiest, and the wealthiest be the saddest, most wretched individuals you have ever seen. Your heart and your head should always be your guide, and I'm sure Charlotte is more than happy that you now own Crummock.'

'I am, Mr Walker. It's the place I love, and I'm grateful to my father for leaving it to me.' Charlotte rose from her chair and lightly touched the arm of the concerned solicitor.

'He was a good man, your father; we will miss him.' Walker smiled and squeezed her hand.

'If your business is done, let's away. I've some business of my own that awaits my attention.' Joseph picked

167

up his hat and opened the door into the inn's main room.

'How is business, Mr Dawson? I hear there is unrest in America, that the Southern Confederate States have been using their cotton revenue to buy arms and economic power, to build a Confederate nation away from the north. Is it true their strategy is to coerce us in Great Britain to be in alliance with them, by starving us of cotton? That will surely hit your business, will it not?' Walker looked at the angry face of Joseph and knew he had touched a weak spot. Trouble was brewing across the Atlantic – he'd heard it on all the mill owners' lips and read it in *Frank Leslie's Illustrated Newspaper*, which was printed in Mississippi and had been full of the news. Lorenzo Christie, the new owner of High Mill at Langcliffe and of Shed Mill, had thrust a copy of the paper in his hand when they had dinner together, and had warned Walker and his accountant that bad times for mill owners were coming, and they would either sink or swim.

'Is this true, Joseph? Is there to be trouble?' Charlotte stopped in her tracks and looked at her husband.

'Not for us. Richard Todd at the Natchez Plantation warned me in his letter last week and I have secured a full ship's hold of cotton, just for Ferndale. It should be halfway across the Atlantic as we speak. There is ample stock of cotton on the docks at Liverpool anyway, so don't worry; these last years the South has oversupplied Britain with cotton. I suggest Mr Christie gets his facts right. Now, if you don't mind, sir, I'd like you to keep your nose out of my business and not unduly give my wife other worries on her father's funeral day. Come, Charlotte, I can no longer dally and listen to idle gossip. Lorenzo Christie is just a troublemaker and likes to have a monopoly on all the mills.' Joseph stood in the doorway and took Charlotte's hand without even wishing Walker good day.

Once away from The Gamecock and on their way back in the coach, Charlotte sat quietly, knowing that Joseph was in no mood to be approached.

'Coachman, pull up here. I'll be away to my mill.' Joseph banged on the outside of the coach with his silver-mounted walking stick as they passed the lane that led down to Ferndale Mill.

'Will you be home later for dinner?' asked Charlotte, as Joseph alighted from the coach without making his farewells.

'You'll be a lucky woman if I come home at all, after today.' Joseph slammed the coach door and strode off down the lane, without giving a backward glance at his distraught wife as she sobbed in the corner of the coach.

The coachman flicked the reins and the team trotted on. Charlotte watched Joseph striding out until he disappeared around the bend of the lane. Now that Crummock Farm was in his hands, she had to convince him not to sell it. She might be sobbing with grief and fearful of his temper, but it was her birthright and there was no way that Joseph Dawson was going to sell it – not while she had breath in her body.

*

'What the bloody hell's the problem now? You're always up in that office with that bastard. He's picking on you, girl.' Sally Oversby leaned over the railings of the mill race and looked at Betsy's worried face.

'Oh, Sally, I don't know what to do, I'm in such a mess.' Betsy Foster held her head in her hands and wiped the snot from her nose with the back of her hand. She'd wanted to tell her friend for weeks about the hold that Joseph Dawson had over her. But she could keep it back no longer.

'You mean you've been giving him it two nights a week for the last two months, for nowt! Bloody hell, lass, he's seen you coming. If he wants a bit of rough, you should make him pay for it! The bugger's made of money: charge him sixpence a time, or even more if he demands things . . . you know what I mean.' Sally looked at Betsy and couldn't quite believe her ears.

'But it was to settle a debt for payments of the rabbits that our Johnny snared.' Betsy sobbed and wiped her eyes.

'How many bloody rabbits did he snare? All of Craven's? For lawk's sake, girl, the parlour maid at Windfell was telling my sister his sleeping arrangements, but I didn't think that he was with you when his bed was empty.' Sally looked at the innocence in her friend's eyes and wanted to educate Betsy on how not to be used by the gentry. 'Gentry' – now that was a word to be laughed at. She'd never known any gentlemen, only users; and Joseph Dawson was definitely a user.

'I couldn't do that, I'd be nothing more than a

pros—' Betsy stopped, not even wanting to say the word.

'A prostitute, a prick-pincher – whatever you want to call it, it makes no odds, but you are one already in his eyes. So you might as well get money for it.'

'No, I couldn't; he wouldn't pay.' Betsy sniffed and looked at her friend, who was more worldly-wise than her. In fact Sally had been with most of the men in the mill and she never went without anything, now Betsy thought about it.

'Yes, he would. You've got him by the short and curlies, and he wouldn't want his precious reputation to be tarnished. Go on, try it! It would keep Johnny fed and shod. Better than a poke in the eye with a shitty stick!' Sally spat out a mouthful of chewing tobacco and watched the face of her friend lighten as if she had just seen the light.

'I couldn't – I'm not that sort.' Betsy shook her head.

'Well, what are you now, then? St Joan? Because believe me, girl, if he can get it for nothing he will. And bugger the job – there's plenty more. Christie would soon take you on; you're good at your job, and he's got cottages at Langcliffe. Bugger, that was a short dinner hour.' The warning bell sounded out across the yard. 'You listen to me. Play the bastard at his own game; he'll soon cough up. He's had his pleasure, now it's time to pay.' Sally picked her skirts up and made her way through the puddles of the cobbled yard. 'Come on, you, time you enjoyed the finer pleasures of life, for

171

lying on your back.' She chuckled and put her arm around Betsy. When it came to men, Betsy knew nothing; but now Sally would make sure she'd teach her the subtle arts of seduction.

Betsy quietly crept out of the side of the bed and looked at Joseph Dawson, snoring under her hand-made patchwork quilt. She could hear her mother's scolding voice in her ears, preaching at her for having sex with her master. A few weeks ago she would have agreed and thought herself dirty and worthless; but after this night, things had changed. She looked at the silver threepenny piece in her hand. It was only half of what Sally had said to charge, but it was thruppence more than she thought she would get. It was worth the slap that Joseph had given her, when she had threatened to tell his wife. His displeasure at her threat had told her everything: he might be in control at the mill, but he had a weak spot when it came to his precious wife hearing about his lifestyle.

She silently opened the secret door in her dressing table and placed the coin in a small trinket box, safe within it. Once he had gone, she would write in a journal the date and payment: *2nd January 1861. Services rendered to Joseph Dawson: 3d*. She was going to treat this like a business, with her ill-gotten gains making sure that Johnny wanted for nothing.

She walked across the pegged rug on the floor and climbed softly back into bed beside the warm, sleeping body of Joseph. She listened to him breathing and watched him as his eyes twitched in his dreams. He was such a bastard, but his looks belied his nature. He was one of the most handsome men she had ever seen. The trouble was that he wasn't *her* man. He came for pleasure that he couldn't get elsewhere, often in a temper or in lust, and that was how it would always be, for a mill girl who had nowt. Betsy sighed and looked at the frosty fern patterns on her bedroom window. She watched her warm breath evaporate in the moonlight that shone through her curtainless windows. Why was he in bed with her, when he had a beautiful young wife waiting for him, a warm grand house, and servants at his beck and call? It must be the demons that raged in him, when he lashed out in anger, that kept him unhappy. Perhaps as a result of some deep pain from his past? Whatever it was, she'd never know, and for the time being threepence for services rendered would be most welcomed.

Betsy closed her eyes and prayed that Joseph would be gone before light of day and before the neighbours caught sight of him. She couldn't abide the scandal that his presence would cause. She whispered under her breath, *Please, God, look after me and Johnny and let him be gone by the time I awake*, and then pulled the sparse cover over her to sleep.

Charlotte lay in the bed she usually shared with Joseph. There had been no sign of him all evening, and even Dora Dodgson had been perplexed by his notable absence at the dinner table. Charlotte's mind was racing

173

with the day's events. What was going to happen to Crummock? It was obvious that Joseph wanted her to sell it, but she couldn't even think about that. The best option was to rent it out, and then both she and Joseph would benefit from the extra income. What had Charles Walker said about trouble in America? Was it really that bad over there, and why hadn't Joseph told her? Why had he been so angry when Lucy had inherited her father's money? After all, that was only right. Lucy had loved him.

She tossed and turned and plumped up her pillows in an attempt to get comfortable and finally fall sleep. The few embers in the bedroom fire grate still glowed, giving an orange hue to part of the bedroom as she wrestled with the pillows and blankets. The grandfather clock in the hallway struck five o'clock. As if on cue, she heard the front door of the manor being opened by Yates, his voice noticeably sleepy as he answered his master's request for his boots to be removed, before climbing the stairs. She hardly dared breathe as she waited for the bedroom door to be opened, and pulled the covers up to her chin, closing her eyes as she waited for Joseph to enter the room and get into bed with her. Instead his footsteps went past her door, and his own bedroom door, which he had abandoned several months ago, slammed shut. So that was the way he was going to play it tonight. At least he was home and, quite frankly, she was past caring if he slept with her or not, at this time of night. He'd probably been drinking and was in a foul mood anyway.

174

Charlotte hugged her pillow and closed her eyes. What had she done to deserve a man like Joseph, and why on earth had she ever been attracted to him?

13

The ride in the trap up to Crummock was stifling. The silence was unbearable and Charlotte kept her eyes focused on the back of Jethro, as Joseph kept his thoughts to himself on the viewing of his new property. His horse trotted happily behind the trap, the stirrups jangling down by its side, glad that it was riderless. Never had the trip up to her beloved home been so agonizing as Charlotte debated how the cook she loved would have reacted to the news that she had to leave Crummock. She was hating having to enter Crummock without her father there and her stomach churned as the trap finally turned into the farmyard.

'I'll leave you to deal with your father's shame. I'm going to look at the stock with Jethro and this so-called farm man. Just make sure Mrs Cranston goes, and quickly. I don't want to have to come and throw her out myself. She's had plenty of time to pack her bags and leave.'

Charlotte looked at Joseph and decided silence was her best option as she walked away and made her way to the back door of her old home. Lucy greeted her with tears in her eyes and an outpouring of her feelings.

'Aye, Miss Charlotte, it's been the longest month I've ever known, without your father here to cheer me along. I can't say I'll be sad to see the back of the place, now I've rented myself a cottage down in Austwick, but it won't be the same as here. What's to become of the place – who's going to live here? Young Arthur can't look after all them sheep on his own.'

'I don't know, Lucy. Joseph doesn't know himself, and I have no say in it. Crummock's mine, but not mine to do with as I wish, and I miss my father so much.' Charlotte sniffed and fought back the tears.

'I'm sorry, Miss Charlotte, you must be broken-hearted too. It's just that the place is not the same without your father. I miss him sitting next to the fire with his darned socks on his feet, and I miss seeing the hay seeds scattered around, which had fallen out of his breeches after he'd fed the cattle. I miss the moaning when his bacon was a bit too crisp, and all the daft things he used to say. There will never be another Wesley Booth. The world's a sadder place without your father.' Lucy sat at the pine kitchen table and sobbed into her handkerchief. 'I know he's left me all his money, but that doesn't mean a thing without him. I got that solicitor to draw all the money out of the bank and I've kept it under my mattress. I don't trust banks – never needed them, don't need them now. But I keep looking at all this money and thinking it can't be mine. He should have left it to you, the silly old fool. There's thousands – I'll never spend it. I think that solicitor thought me daft.'

'Hush now, Lucy. Joseph will be in at any minute. Has Arthur loaded the cart with all your possessions? Because once Joseph sees you out of the door, he will not let you in again.' Charlotte didn't want faithful Lucy to know how angry her husband had been to hear that he would not benefit from Wesley's bank account. So far she had sheltered the cook from his anger, but it was plain for all to see that he was not a happy man. The last thing she wanted was for Lucy to tell him where she had hidden her money, and that she wasn't appreciative of it.

'Aye, I've packed everything I have on the cart. Arthur took most of the things yesterday, so that was a good help. And the cottage I'm moving in to is clean and tidy, and Archie said he'd pop in to see me every now and then. I might write to my sister over at More-cambe. She runs a boarding house for sailors; she could probably do with another pair of hands – it would make me feel wanted.' Lucy sighed and looked at Charlotte, remembering all the love that her father had put into her upbringing.

Charlotte put her arm around the shaking cook and kissed her gently on the quivering mob cap that sat askew on her mop of thin, grey hair. 'I'm sorry you are losing your home. It must be a big shock for you, and

I'm not helping because I truly don't know what Joseph's plans are for this place.'

'At least Mary's found herself work at Austwick Hall, and I'm glad that you are keeping Arthur on. I know he's single, but he still needs the wage and he's a good hand with the stock.' Lucy pulled her shawl around her and looked out of the kitchen window for one last time. 'I'll miss this place, but you've got to move on. Just look at you: you've turned out to be the lady your father always wanted, in your finery. You're a good 'un, Miss Charlotte. Your father brought you up correctly, and he'd be right proud of you. That husband of yours must be counting himself lucky: a bonny slip of a wife, a farm and his mill – you should want for nowt.' Lucy had shared confidences with Wesley that she also thought Joseph was not all that he seemed.

'I'm coping with my new status in life. Like you, I miss my father, and I'm not quite used to doing all the things that ladies do. I'm not into tapestry and reading. You know me, I'd rather be doing something more productive with my time.' Charlotte smiled. She wasn't going to say, *Well, actually I'm regretting the day I set eyes on Joseph Dawson*, which was just what she felt at that moment in time.

'No signs of family yet? Your father was really looking forward to being a grandfather.' Lucy squeezed Charlotte's arm as she brushed past her.

'No, not yet.' Charlotte averted the cook's attentions by picking up her full basket and walking towards the back door.

'Did you get a chance to talk to Archie at the funeral? Did he tell you they are expecting another? Baby Daniel's not even crawling yet and she's in the family way again. And she's ill with it; he nearly lost her last time, and it's dangerous having another straight away.' Lucy shook her head in disbelief at the situation her nephew was in.

'No, I didn't talk to him. Poor Rosie. She looked worn out when I saw her in Settle before Christmas and unfortunately they didn't accept my invite to join us at Windfell at Christmas. They'll be struggling up on Mewith Moor. There won't be enough living up there for one family, let alone two. There's us with everything, and there's poor Archie with nothing and soon another mouth to feed.' Charlotte dropped her head onto her breast. It hurt when she thought about the feelings she still had for the boy from across the dale. She even felt a pang of jealousy when it came to his wife, Rosie. They might not have any money, but they were happy, which was more than she was.

'Aye, if he'd have played his cards right, he could have been sitting here with us as the new owner of Crummock. If only he'd been good enough for you. Your father wouldn't have had it. In his eyes, you'd to marry somebody with status – he made that clear from the day you were born.' Lucy Cranston gave a loving look around her beloved kitchen and wiped a tear as it escaped from her eye. 'It's a shame he hasn't got a better start in life. He's not a bad lad. You and him always seemed happy together. I might be able to help him out a bit, with this brass of your father's, but he's a proud one, is Archie. I doubt he'd take it.'

'I'm sure he'd perhaps appreciate a bit of help. He's with Rosie now, and I'm with Joseph, so it was not to be.' Charlotte could feel tears welling up in her eyes as she thought of the time when Archie had shouted out that he loved her, from the knot behind Crummock. Had he meant it? And did he still love her?

'Aye, life moves on. It's a good job we don't know what life's going to throw at us, else sometimes I think we'd give in. Well, come on, let's get me on that cart. I've said my goodbyes to the old place. I'll leave it and let the ghosts that rattle around it take care of it for now.' Lucy breathed in deeply and followed Charlotte out of the back door.

Charlotte lifted Lucy's basket up to Arthur, who was waiting patiently on the cart. 'Where's Mr Dawson, Arthur?' Charlotte looked around her, as Lucy hitched her long skirts up to sit next to the farm lad.

'He's in the barn, Miss. I think he's looking at the stock.' Arthur smirked; the townie knew nowt about owt. Didn't know a gimmer from a tup.

'Alright, thank you. Take care of Mrs Cranston. Make sure she's settled when you leave her, and then come back and get your orders from Mr Dawson.' Charlotte patted Lucy's hand and climbed up on the buck-board to give her a peck on the cheek. 'Take care, I'll always love you, and I'll call in when I can.'

'Aye, take care, lass, and I'll always be there for you. If you need anything, you know where I am.' Lucy pulled her apron to her eyes and sobbed openly as the cart drew away from the place she had called home.

Charlotte stood back and watched as the cart with Lucy and all her belongings made its way past the duck pond and the wood that sheltered the ancient farm-house, then round the corner out of sight. Her breath caught in her throat and a wave of sorrow flooded over her. There was nobody left at her beloved Crummock. It was empty and unloved, apart from the ghosts that Lucy had always insisted inhabited it.

'Well, has the old bag gone?' Joseph walked up quietly behind her. 'I couldn't stand to look at her. She had your father wrapped around her finger.'

'She loved him, and he her. She's heartbroken that she's been thrown out of her home of forty years.' Charlotte turned with anger in her eyes and glared at her uncaring husband.

'As I am, that we haven't got your father's bank account. You'd better get yourself home. Jethro will take you; he's just wasting time grooming your father's old knackered nags. I'll come back in my own time. I need to look around to see exactly what I own and what it's worth.'

'It's just another possession to you, like I am. I'm beginning to think you don't care about anything and anybody,' Charlotte spat at him. She loved every inch of her previous home but was powerless to do anything with it.

'I beg to differ, my dear. I care deeply about things. It's just that, unlike you, my heart does not rule my head.' Joseph stepped away from her and shouted at Jethro to bring the trap to take Charlotte home.

Charlotte stood helplessly in the farmyard that she had played in for many a happy hour and heard herself echoing the same question as Lucy. What was going to happen to her beloved Crummock?

'You ready, ma'am?' Jethro brought the horse and trap next to her.

'Yes, let's get back to Windfell before the sun drops too much.'

Jethro tapped his cap in recognition and helped Charlotte into the trap, then set off back through the farmyard, following the road down between tall limestone escarpments that ran down to the dale bottom.

'Can we stop here for five minutes, Jethro? I want to go down this path on my own for a few minutes.' Charlotte asked Jethro to stop as they reached the last fields of Crummock land. They pulled up at a small lane that led to the hamlet of Wharfe, and to Charlotte's favourite place, called Wash Dubbs, where in summer the sheep were washed and where she had played in the warmth of the sun.

Jethro sighed. He was chilled to the bone, even more so than the horses.

'I'll only be a minute, I promise.' She climbed down from the trap. 'I'll really not be long.' She picked her skirts up and ran along the rough stone pathway. The grass hedges sparkled with frost and the hillsides shone crystal-white in the late afternoon sunshine. She took care walking over the huge embedded boulder that made up part of the pathway, which had been there since the glacier from the Ice Age had carved out its path down the valley. She finally turned the corner to her most-loved place. The ancient bridge was just as she remembered it: large slate slabs held up by pillars of concealed stones, passing over the bubbling beck that ran from a small spring high above the fells. In summer the banks were adorned with foxgloves, mountain avens and the bright blues of scabious, but today the mossy banks were littered with glistening white icicles hanging over the icy river, their shapes like fairy palaces twinkling and shining in the reflections of the water. Charlotte stood and looked for a minute, remembering happier times when she and Archie had played together in the river and she had thought those days would never end. Times when the sun shone every day, and the swallows and swifts darted high above their heads screeching their songs, and the two of them caught bullheads in the beck. Afterwards she would be told off by Lucy Cranston for being a tomboy and not acting like a young lady should. How she wished she was that young again and that she could stop there, safe and secure, without a worry in the world.

'Don't be so bloody ridiculous. I've never heard anything so stupid in all my life!' Joseph took a long, slow drink of his claret and stared at his wife, who had obviously lost leave of her senses, to suggest such a thing.

'But it makes sense. Crummock will be looked after

and we still get rent – only a little later in the year than we expected.' Charlotte laid down her knife and fork and watched her husband struggle with the suggestion she had made.

'I will not have that farm lad live rent-free, at our expense! We need the money, Charlotte. Besides, you always have been sweet on him; perhaps you should have married him instead of me. I suppose it is that witch Lucy Cranston who's convinced you of such a hare-brained scheme. I should have known, and I should have thrown her out of the house myself. If it was up to you, you would see us penniless. Did you not hear Charles Walker say that dark days were coming?' Joseph threw his napkin down onto the table and ushered Yates out of the room.

'Yes, and you assured me there was nothing to worry about. We have plenty of money, Joseph. We could help somebody less fortunate than ourselves, and Archie's been a good friend to me over the years.' Charlotte picked at her supper plate. She had no appetite, and nerves had been building up inside her, since her decision earlier in the day to suggest to Joseph that Archie lived in Crummock rent-free. That was until the back-end sales of the sheep and lambs, when he'd be in a better position to pay the rent; or, if Joseph wished, he could sell the farm.

'I'll not hear of it. He's an idiot of a lad, with no control over his ardour. He shouldn't have the habits of a rabbit, then he wouldn't be in such a situation. He's only got himself to blame. What if I need some money – have you thought of my needs?' Joseph rose from the table, overturning his chair in his anger.

'Darling, it is us I am thinking of. In the long term Crummock will be safe in his hands, and he will be able to pay us rent, once he's settled in.' Charlotte shook at the sight of her husband in such a mood and quivered as he walked towards her, his face red with rage.

Joseph raised his hand and slapped her around her face, bringing tears to her eyes and leaving traces of his fingers on her delicate skin. 'You mean *you*'ll be safe in his hands. I've seen the way you look at him. Do you think I was born yesterday? Get him and his milk-sop wife ensconced in your love-nest, and he's yours for the taking. You are just like your father: the lower the class, the more smitten you are. Yet you bleed me dry, with your fancy hats and the rubbish you adorn your-self with.' Joseph stood towering over her and watched as she trembled, then stood up next to him.

'You are wrong, Joseph, I never ask anything of you. There is nothing between me and Archie, and never has been. As for bleeding you dry, I was under the impression you had more money than you knew what to do with. If you are in financial difficulties, why don't you confide in me?' Charlotte's legs shook like jelly and she felt physically sick.

'That would suit you down to the ground, wouldn't it? Make you feel superior. After all, I'll never match your father, in your eyes. Look around you: I own this mansion we live in, woman; I own the mill, and the lives that make a living there. Even if you had inherited your father's money, it wouldn't even pay for the cotton that's waiting in the docks at Liverpool. His piddling money means nothing to me. I play with higher stakes than your father ever did.' Joseph pulled Charlotte's hand off his jacket sleeve and opened the dining-room door, before making his way across the hallway and starting to climb the stairs.

'Joseph, wait – I love you. I'm fed up of this continuous arguing. I'll do as you say. Forget I even suggested it.' Charlotte ran across the hallway and up nearly to the top of the sweeping stairs, pulling on Joseph's sleeve to stop him climbing the last two steps.

'Damn you, woman, let me be. I'm fed up of your bleating!' He turned round sharply, throwing Charlotte off-balance. To his dismay, he watched as if by slow motion she fell, tossing and tumbling the full length of the stairs. Every bounce echoed around the hallway until Charlotte lay like a crumpled ragdoll on the polished parquet floor.

'Oh, my Lord, what have you done? You've killed her!' Yates ran out from the kitchen, followed by Dora Dodgson. Both ran to where her body lay.

Joseph ran quickly down the stairs and bent over his wife. 'It was an accident. I didn't mean for her to fall. She would argue with me – she always has to have her way.'

Dora felt for a pulse on Charlotte's neck. 'She's alive and there's no blood, which is a good sign. Yates, go and get Jethro to ride for the doctor. And, Yates, don't tell a soul what you saw tonight. It was an accident, and the mistress tripped down the stairs. You understand?' She stared at the befuddled butler, her light-blue eyes belying her cold soul.

Yates shook his head and quickly disappeared out to the stables. He didn't want to lose his position in the household, for he was too old to look for service elsewhere. Besides, what went on between man and wife was none of his business, but he did pity Charlotte Booth. If she didn't say what Joseph wanted to hear, it was the worse for her; and invariably it was so, seeing as she was so headstrong.

'Don't just stand there: look as if you care. Pick her up and put her in your bed.' Dora hit Joseph's shoulder and brought him to his senses, as he stroked Charlotte's hair and watched for signs of her breathing.

'I didn't mean to – it was an accident. She wouldn't shut up!' Joseph knelt and put his arms under her small frame and looked down at the woman he had grown to love, in his own strange way.

'Shut up and get her upstairs, and just pray she doesn't die on you. We don't want to cause a scandal here, else questions will be asked about Accrington.' Dora scowled.

Charlotte moaned as Joseph picked her up gently, his arms supporting her whole body as he walked steadily up the stairs.

'I didn't mean to make you fall. I love you, Charlotte. Why do you persist in arguing with me? It just gets me angry.' Joseph struggled for breath as he carried her limp body across the bedroom and placed her in their bed, as Dora pulled back the sheets.

'I'll undo her laces and make her comfortable. You just get your story straight, because the doctor will want to know what happened tonight.' Dora's mind was racing. There had to be no sense of scandal in this new life they had made for themselves. She had to save her skin, as well as her brother's.

'But it *was* an accident.' Joseph paced the room, while Dora pulled at the dress of his moaning wife and tried to make her look as comfortable as possible.

'And the finger marks, where you've slapped her across her face? How do you think the doctor's going to view those?' Dora sighed and pulled the sheets up to Charlotte's chin.

'I tried to revive her!' Joseph looked down at his pale wife, who was breathing softly with no colour in her usually rosy cheeks and lips.

'Hah! I suppose it will do. I'll think of something to help you out – leave it with me.' Dora closed the door behind her and went to wait for the doctor's arrival. Her mind was working fast. How stupid her brother was, nearly killing his wife. His temper was always going to be their downfall; he should learn to control it, and the sooner the better.

'I came as fast as I could.' Dr Burrows handed Yates his hat and cloak and followed Dora up the stairs.

'This is the step she fell from, Doctor. I've been telling Yates to fix that stair rod for a day or two now. I just knew it was an accident waiting to happen.' The housekeeper made a point of showing him the rod, which she had dislodged just before the doctor had arrived, and the thick ruffled carpet that it had secured.

'Most unsatisfactory, Mrs Dodgson. I hope Mr Dawson shows the idle fella the door.' The doctor tutted as he stood on the stairs and looked at how far his patient had fallen.

'I should think so, but knowing Mr Dawson, he will be too lenient. He treats us servants like family.' Dora showed the doctor to Charlotte's bedroom and opened the door for him to go in.

'Ah! Dawson, a most unfortunate fall. I'd give Yates his marching orders for not securing that carpet rod securely. Now, give me some room, man, and let me have a look at the patient. That's a good sign – she's breathing evenly.' Dr Burrows strode over to the bedside and opened his leather bag, reaching in for his stethoscope.

Joseph looked up from her side as he held his wife's hand tenderly and gave his sister a questioning glance. 'Thank you for coming, Doctor. It's been a terrible accident. I love her – please tell me that she will live.' He lingered for a second, before relinquishing his grip on Charlotte's hand.

'Perhaps if you leave me to my business.' Dr Burrows looked at the ashen-faced Joseph and reached for Charlotte's pulse. 'Wait outside the door, and I'll shout if I need anything.' He breathed on his stethoscope, warming it up, before placing it to his ears to listen to Charlotte's breathing. 'Go on, she's safe with me.'

Dora and Joseph stood outside the door and waited for what seemed an age, before the doctor opened the door and bade them enter.

'You are a lucky man, Mr Dawson. As far as I can see, Charlotte is just suffering from deep concussion. She could easily have broken her neck, with a fall like that. Let her sleep the night round, and let me know if she does not wake in the morning or has any memory loss, and I'll come back to see her. When it comes to the baby, it seems to have survived the fall, you'll be glad to know. We couldn't let Charlotte lose her first baby now, could we? You must be proud to be becoming a father. You'll need an heir to that mill of yours.'

The doctor picked up his bag and looked at the amazement on Joseph's face.

'I gather by that look on your face she had not got around to telling you?' I gave her the good news last week, when she visited me at my practice in Settle. Just watch she doesn't start bleeding, Mrs Dodgson, else you will need me back again.' Dr Burrows patted Joseph on the back. 'Congratulations, old chap – let it be the first of many. I'm only sorry it was me who broke the news to you, and not your good lady, but I'm sure she will forgive me, in the circumstances.'

'I didn't know – she never said.' Joseph stood staring at Charlotte, whose eyes started to flicker.

'Ah! My patient awakes – concussion, as I suspected. Did you get carried away with trying to waken her,

191

Dawson? I couldn't help but notice the finger-marks on her cheek. I suppose you were frantic with worry.' Dr Burrows looked at Joseph Dawson, who was perhaps not quite acting in the way he had expected him to.

'Yes, yes, I got carried away.' Joseph grabbed for Charlotte's outstretched hand as she moaned.

Dr Burrows reached inside his bag for smelling salts and watched Charlotte's colour return as she slowly gained consciousness.

'Joseph, I'm sorry. I'm sorry, my love.' The faint whisper made everyone breathe a sigh of relief as Charlotte grasped his hand.

'He doesn't know his own strength, Doctor – do you, sir?' Dora butted in, before opening the door to hint that it was time for the good doctor to leave.

'Never mind, I understand. Keep her in bed for the next day or two. And, Mrs Dodgson, keep an eye on her, but I'm sure she will be fine. I wouldn't recommend she tried it again, though; it's a miracle that she didn't break anything, or lose the baby.' He patted Joseph on the back again and watched as the man bent down to kiss Charlotte on the cheek, as she shed tears on his shoulder. 'Lovely to see such a happy couple – they will make wonderful parents.'

'Yes, thank you, Doctor. Let me see you out.' Dora led the old man quickly out of the bedroom and down the stairs, where Yates waited with his cape and hat next to the doorway.

'And you: I hope you get dismissed, you lazy man. You could have had your mistress's death on your head.'

Dr Burrows gave Yates a mouthful and stepped out into the night. 'Goodnight, Mrs Dodgson, and do let me know if Charlotte doesn't improve. And remember what to look out for.'

'I will, Doctor, and thank you for coming so quickly. The mistress will be so grateful for your attentions.' Dora closed the door on the night and turned to look at Yates. 'One wrong word, Yates, and you will be out – or worse. Remember: you saw nothing!'

14

Charlotte sat in the morning room, taking in the weak late-January sunshine and watching the snowdrops' delicate heads shake in the bitter north wind that was blowing down the dale. It had been a week since her fall. Her body felt battered and bruised and her mind was confused about the evening's happenings. She knew it had been an accident. Joseph hadn't meant to push her down the full length of the stairs, but she could never forget the anger she had witnessed in his eyes, or the slap around her face when he had tried to make her bend to his will. Those eyes came back to haunt her in the night's darkest hours as she lay in her bed, thinking of the man she had married, and how she would have to protect her unborn child from his rages.

Joseph had taken the news of her pregnancy remarkably well, considering that he had made it abundantly clear in the first weeks of marriage that he neither wanted nor cared for children in his life. Charlotte could not help but wonder: would he have reacted in the same way if the fall had never happened? Perhaps it was guilt that he was feeling, as she could well have broken her neck when he accidentally pushed her down the stairs. Whatever it was, his anger had subsided, but she couldn't help but notice the worried look that clouded his face when business at the mill was mentioned. Things were not right, and she knew it.

Since her fall he'd gone back to his old ways of sleeping on his own, making the excuse that Charlotte needed her sleep and that he would only disturb her. She could hear him entering the manor at unearthly times of the night – only to be told, when she questioned him, that he had been working on new ideas for the mill and hadn't realized the hour. The shipment of raw cotton had been delivered, as per Richard Todd's promise, and Joseph had assured her that Ferndale Mill could face any upset that was to come from across the Atlantic.

Charlotte's thoughts wandered back to her father's death. She missed him so much. And now, with a baby growing inside her, she couldn't help but think how much Wesley would have loved to have been a grandfather. Things would have been so different. If only he were alive, at least she would have had a second home to run to, if things deteriorated between her and Joseph. However, her father's words – 'You've made your bed; now you must lie in it' – came back to haunt her. He'd probably have told her to go back and be the wife she should be; and then he would have worried to death, once her back had been turned, concerned that she wasn't happy. Then he would probably have discussed it with Lucy Cranston, the second love of his life.

Her mind wandered back to Crummock, the place she loved. Joseph had taken his time telling her the deed he had done, while she was too ill to complain: placing an associate from Accrington in the farmhouse. She could only wonder what a friend from his town days could have to do with farming. He might know about weaving wool, if he had to do with textiles, but breeding sheep was a different matter. She sighed; probably her profitable home was going to rack and ruin. She only hoped that Arthur would keep his eye on everything.

'Are you alright, ma'am?' Lily walked across the room and tucked in the rug, whilst fussing around Charlotte. 'Are you warm enough? That wind is vicious – it's blowing right out of the north. I'll get Jethro to bring in some more coal for the fire.' Lily looked at her mistress. Every servant was sympathetic to her plight, knowing that both she and the baby she was now carrying could have died, if the fates had decreed it.

'I'm fine, Lily, stop fussing. It's those poor snowdrops I feel sorry for – look at them shivering in the cold. A messenger of brighter spring days to come, I hope.' Charlotte placed the letter that she had been putting off replying to down on the table next to her.

'I'm sure they are, ma'am. Spring is only around the corner. It's not long now until Valentine's Day, when the birds find their mates and we are winning. That's what my old ma always says.'

'I could do with some of your mother's sense, Lily, and some hope, for things look dark at the moment.' Charlotte could feel tears welling up inside her as she thought of the previous year and the changes it had brought.

'Now, ma'am, you've so much to look forward to. You've the baby on the way, and you've the love of Mr Dawson, and a wonderful home. You are just a little upset with the fall and with losing your father. Things will get better, don't you worry.' Lily felt for her mistress. The kitchen had been awash with gossip over Charlotte's fall. Had Joseph Dawson pushed her, or hadn't he? Yates swore he had, but made everyone promise not to breathe a word of it, especially around Dora Dodgson.

'Oh, I know, Lily. I'm just feeling sorry for myself. There are people dying from hunger in the streets of Manchester and there's me, drowning in self-pity.' Charlotte patted the hand of the maid she had grown close to and smiled. 'Could you pass me my writing desk? I think I will write to a dear friend. Would you post it for me, before Mr Dawson returns from the mill?'

'Of course I will, ma'am. Jethro can take it into Settle, if you want; he's not doing a lot, except annoying Yates with his cheek.' Lily laughed and passed Charlotte her small writing desk, placing it on the table

197

in front of her and making sure she had enough ink and paper to compose her letter.

Charlotte sighed. How did you begin a letter to the man you truly loved? A man who was happily married with one child, and another on the way.

Windfell Manor
Stainforth
Settle

Dear Archie,

I'm sorry for my late reply, but I have been unwell of late. I rather foolishly fell down the stairs a week ago and have been trying to gain my strength ever since. My main concern was: what if I had lost the baby that Joseph and I are eagerly awaiting? We are delighted that we are both to become parents.

You ask if Crummock is available to rent, as your Aunt Lucy would be willing to fund you. Unfortunately my husband has already put a tenant in place. I don't know much about the man, but Joseph must have faith in him.

I do hope that Rosie is keeping well. I was surprised to hear that she was with child again. You must take care of her. Give all my love to Daniel; he will soon have a sister or brother to love.

You are always in my thoughts. I often recall our moments together.
Your dearest friend,
Lottie

Charlotte looked at the letter she had written, and wondered if she had put too much of her true feelings into it. Archie was always in her thoughts; she wasn't lying. But perhaps a little too often, since she was respectably married. She only wished that she could have let him live at Crummock. He would have been ideal, and it would make a good home for his family. Lucy must love her nephew dearly to offer him some of her inheritance, but that just showed what a good woman she actually was.

She folded the letter and sealed it into its envelope, holding it for a second in her hand, hoping that it would purvey her love silently to Archie. Her thoughts were interrupted when Lily came back into the room.

'Have you finished writing, ma'am?' She smiled.

Charlotte winced as she sat upright and pushed her writing desk out of the way. 'Yes, I have, Lily. Is Jethro available?'

'He is indeed, ma'am; he's already saddled one of the horses in readiness for his ride into Settle. In fact he said if it's a fairly local letter, he can deliver it personally, as Mr Dawson's horse could do with a good workout.' Lily held out her hand for the letter, knowing who it was for. She'd taken delivery of the letter that Archie had sent her mistress, when she had been so ill after her fall. Joseph Dawson would have thrown it onto the fire once he'd read it, so Lily had kept it safe for her mistress, knowing that Charlotte needed her friendship with him kept a secret.

'I'd be grateful if he could. And, Lily, can we keep

this to ourselves, please?' Charlotte looked at the maid, whom she knew she could trust, and smiled.

'Of course, ma'am. Neither Jethro nor myself know nothing about it.'

'Thank you, Lily, that means a lot to me.' Charlotte smiled and lay back in her chair. At least the servants were on her side.

There was a hammering at the door. Rosie Atkinson rose from the small peat fire burning in the hearth to open it. She was cold and hungry, and the baby within her was sapping all the nourishment she had in her body, making her feel weak and feeble.

'Go on, Rosie, see who it is. It must be somebody wanting summat, in weather like this.' Archie sat next to the fire and waited for his wife to open the door to their earnest guest.

'I'll give him summat, if he wakens our Daniel up,' mumbled Rosie. She was tired and needed her bed. She opened the door slightly, the wind battering her as she looked at the young lad in front of her.

'Mrs Atkinson, is your husband in?'

Jethro held onto his horse's reins and waited for Archie to come to the door, not wanting to pass the letter that his mistress had written to Archie's wife. The horse reared its head as Archie came to the door, wanting to be out of the cold wind. 'My mistress, Mrs Charlotte Dawson, asked me to deliver this to you. If you read it, I can take a reply, if you wish.' Jethro stood and watched as Archie opened the letter and read it quickly, the wind and rain blowing Archie's hair and the letter getting spotted with raindrops.

'For God's sake, close the door, lad – you're letting all the heat out,' Rosie's father yelled.

'Well?' Jethro waited.

'No, lad, I've no reply; just give her my best wishes.' Archie looked at the young groom and then screwed up the letter to him, written with love, and watched as Jethro mounted his steed and turned tail down the fellside.

'What did he want, then?' Rosie looked at the screwed-up letter in her husband's hand.

'He's Joseph Dawson's groom. He came to tell me that Crummock's already let, so I needn't bother wasting Aunt Lucy's money on it.' Archie looked at the letter in his hand and threw it quickly onto the peat fire, before anyone else asked to read it.

'Aye, well, he wouldn't rent it to you anyway – you're not in his circle of friends.' Rosie's father shuffled on his seat next to the fire. 'God knows why that Booth lass married him. She was worth more than that 'un.'

'God knows indeed. It must have been the money that turned her head.' Archie smiled at his weary wife.

'She'll never have what we have, Archie, no matter how much money he has.' Rosie pecked her husband on the cheek, knowing that he was thinking of times past. 'We will always love one another, no matter what.'

'We will, my love.' Archie returned her kiss and closed his eyes, remembering Charlotte's kisses, before looking around the hovel that he was now living in and realizing he could have done so much better.

Roger Wilson looked out of the window of Crummock and took another gulp of the port that he'd found in the pantry of the rambling farmhouse. Bloody frozen place, but still it was better than being in a police cell at Accrington. He watched as the sleet-filled rain came down in sheets across the valley, and laughed as Arthur, the farm lad, coaxed the milk cow across the farmyard into its stall to be milked. Silly bugger, he was sodden and shit-up. He'd work his fingers to the bone to keep those simple beasts fed and watered.

You wouldn't find him doing anything like that. Roger grinned, went back near the fire to put his feet up on the hearth, and sat back to finish the rest of his bottle. He toasted Joseph by swigging the port directly out of the bottle. 'Cheers, Joseph, my old mucker,' smiling to himself as he remembered the journey out of Accrington under the nose of the Peelers. They'd never find him here, in this godforsaken hole. Not that he wanted them to, not after half of Accrington was baying for his blood over unpaid bills and the theft of just a few casks of the best Fighting Cocks whisky. He'd done worse in the past, even if they did not know it; that's why he was best out of it, keeping his head down here in his old mate's new gaff. Lucky bastard, Joseph always had landed on his feet.

'What do you want?' Roger sat up in his seat, noticing Arthur entering through the kitchen door.

'I've just brought you the milk for the house.' Arthur looked at the middle-aged, rough-looking inebriated man, whom he'd been instructed was his new master.

'Milk – what the hell do I want with milk? Here, go to wherever you country bumpkins go to and get me a barrel of beer and a bottle or two of their best whisky. I'll need that to keep the bloody damp out of my bones in this godforsaken place.' Roger threw a selection of coins onto the table for Arthur to do as he bade.

Arthur looked at him and said nothing.

'Go on then – bugger off! I could do with it before nightfall; it'll help pass the hours, because there's bugger-all to do here.' Roger watched as the lad picked up the coins, hesitating before going back through the door.

'Do you want me to bring the lambing sheep down into the low pasture tomorrow?' Arthur had to ask, because it was his duty.

'You can do what the bloody hell you like, lad. Just bugger off and get me my drink.' Roger took another swig and gazed into the fire.

'Right, I'll do that then, and I'll take the horse and cart into Austwick for your barrel.'

Arthur waited for a reply, but got none. He shook his head as he walked out of the once-welcoming farm-house. His new master was an old soak, not worth a penny to the running of the farm. He might as well be on his own.

15

Spring came slowly and truly, just as Lily had said it would. The snowdrops in the driveway gave way to delicately coloured yellow daffodils, with primroses flowering in abundance on the rocky crags above Windfell Manor. Dotted between them were perfumed dog violets, which reminded Charlotte of the posy that Archie had given her the previous spring. That seemed like a lifetime ago now. So much had happened in a year.

She leaned against the window and looked out across the dale. The sun glinted on the River Ribble as it wandered down to the sea and she could just make out the red-brick chimney of Ferndale Mill, nestled down by the riverside, through the budding sycamore trees. She was bored; spring always made her restless, and not being able to ride a horse or have the freedom to wander the fells and fields around her family home made her even more so. Her hand wandered down to her stomach and she lovingly rubbed her extending abdomen. Another five months and she wouldn't be bored, she'd have a child to call her own. A little new soul to love and nurture, and to learn the rights and wrongs of the world that he or she was to grow up in.

'Can you get me my cloak, Lily, I'm going to go for a stroll.' Charlotte caught the arm of her maid as she took the morning tea tray away.

'Do you think that's wise, ma'am? It looks warm out there, but there's a real sneaky wind. Besides, what will Mr Dawson say? Will he be happy if you go for a walk alone? Perhaps I should go with you. You are still weak after your fall.' Lily hesitated with the tray and watched her mistress pacing like a caged lion.

'I am perfectly well. I wish everyone would stop fussing. This isn't the first baby to be born, and it won't be the last. Besides, Mr Dawson is at Long Preston today, visiting the Jackson family and looking at their new warehouse on the village green. So he won't know what I'm up to, unless someone tells him.' Charlotte knew that Joseph was watching her every move. Together with his spy, Mrs Dodgson, who had gone into Settle on her half-day off, so there was nobody to log Charlotte's movements.

'If you are sure, ma'am. I don't mind accompanying you. Yates is having forty winks after Mr Dawson disturbed him in the early hours this morning, and Mazy and Mrs Batty are looking at a new cookbook by Mrs Beeton. It's as big as a doorstop and tells you all the proper ways of service, and is full of fancy dishes that no doubt she'll be trying on you.' Lily waited in the doorway with her hands full with the morning tea tray.

'No, Lily, I need some time to myself. But thank you for your offer.' Charlotte followed her maid out into the hallway and awaited her return from the kitchen, smiling as Lily made sure that her mistress was warm within her cloak and gloves, before her walk. She would be lost without her sweet maid; they had both learned the ways of Windfell Manor together, and Charlotte trusted her completely.

'Take care, ma'am.' Lily opened the door and let a shaft of bright spring sunshine into the hallway of Windfell.

'I will, Lily. I just need a breath of fresh air and some time to think.' Charlotte smiled and ran her gloved hand around Lily's worried face. 'I promise I won't be long.'

'You'll turn back if you start feeling ill.' Lily lingered at the door.

'Yes, I promise. Now go and look at that new book, else Mazy will be getting ideas above her station and will start trying for your position.'

'She'd better not – her place is in the kitchen.' Lily watched Charlotte step out along the gravel driveway until she got to the gateway, then closed the door behind her. She prayed that neither Joseph Dawson nor Dora Dodgson would not return before her mistress.

Charlotte stepped out down the road that led to Settle, breathing in the sharp air and feeling all the better for it. Windfell had become claustrophobic of late. Joseph hadn't lost his temper with her since her fall down the stairs, but the deathly silence they now lived surrounded by was worse. The marriage was a sham and everyone in Windfell, including the servants, knew it.

She pulled her cloak around her. Lily had been right; the day was beautiful but very deceptive, with a cold bite in the air, once you were out of the sunshine. She stopped at the rough track leading down to Ferndale Mill and hesitated for a while. With Joseph at Long Preston, it would be interesting to take a look around the mill, without him keeping her in his office. Hopefully nobody would dare tell Joseph of her visit. After all, she was his wife and had every right to be there. Even with her worry about Joseph's rage if he did find out, her curiosity got the better of her. She had always been interested in seeing how the mill worked, and she could also see if the warehouse was indeed full of raw cotton, like her husband had said.

Charlotte dallied for a second and then set off down the track to the mill. She thought of all the mill workers making their way to work with heavy hearts every day, just to keep bread on the table. She passed the mill cottages, with their tidily kept vegetable patches, and crossed over the sluice gate that monitored the flow of water to the water wheel that powered the steam engine, which in turn powered the carding and spinning machines. The noise of the machines and shuttles within them assaulted her ears as she walked across the cobbled yard between the four-storey mill buildings. The carters tugged on their caps, realizing it was Joseph

Dawson's wife paying them a visit, as they moved bales of raw cotton up into the top of the mill by rope and pulley, through the large open doors at the very summit of the mill.

'Can I help you, Mrs Dawson?' Bert Bannister came over, after shouting at a man who was balancing on a horse and cart, trying to hook the bale bound for the top.

'Ah, Mr Bannister, I just thought I'd visit my husband. Is he here?' Charlotte was lying through her teeth, but she didn't know if she trusted Bert Bannister or not.

'I'm sorry, ma'am, he's not here. I thought that you'd know he's at Long Preston today.' Bert looked at the lass. She appeared pale and tired, and he couldn't help but think that Joseph Dawson had done to his wife what he'd done to his workers: taken the bloom out of her cheeks.

'Of course, I'd forgotten. He did tell me this morning – how stupid of me to forget.' Charlotte smiled. 'I see we are busy, Mr Bannister. Have we plenty of cotton in at the moment, to keep our machines working, and people in work?'

'Oh, aye, Mrs Dawson, the warehouse is full to the rafters. I've never seen so much cotton. I think Mr Dawson must have over-ordered. Either that or he thinks we are going to have a lot of extra orders.' Bert had wanted to say something to his master about the over-stocking of cotton, but hadn't dared to.

'I'm sure he's got his reasons. Mr Dawson doesn't spend money if he doesn't have to.' Charlotte was relieved to hear that at least he hadn't been lying about the shipment.

'Aye, you can say that again. He doesn't believe in chucking his money about, I can vouch for that.' Bert regretted what he said straight away, but his overseer's wage was paying for less and less, and his wife had been giving him earache all week.

'Mr Bannister, would you mind giving me a guided tour of the mill? I'd like to see how it all works, and I have some time on my hands.' Charlotte could see that she had Bannister in a quandary. He couldn't say no, but at the same time he was wondering if Joseph would be happy if he showed his wife his empire. 'I'll not tell my husband, I promise.' Charlotte fluttered her eyes at the burly man.

'Oh, aye, go on then. I'll not take you to where the beam engines are – the men in there will not want a woman in their way, and they only generate the power for the mill. No disrespect, Mrs Dawson. I'll show you the carding and weaving rooms, but I'll warn you, it's noisy in there!' He smiled at the young woman. She had more charm than her husband, and he respected her. Local folk talked highly of her family.

'I know it's noisy, Mr Bannister. I can hear it standing here. I don't know how the women work, or talk to one another.' Charlotte followed him up through the mill's steep stairs to the carding room.

Bert opened the heavy oak doors into the carding room. 'They learn to lipread, ma'am; you can't talk above this. This, ma'am, is where the cotton is cleaned and placed into the carding machine. When we first receive the cotton, it's stiff and contains seeds, soil and leaves and has to be cleaned. This is called "scrutching". It's placed on a wire frame in that machine over there, and is beaten so that all the waste falls out of it. It's then ready for the carding machine, which gets rid of all the impurities left in it. In the carding drum a small roller, called the "stripper", takes the cotton from the worker and, as you can see, it goes over rollers studded with wires to comb through the cotton. This aligns the cotton, making it into what we call a "rope of tow", but it still needs to be stretched and thinned, using a process of drawing and roving. If you look at the rollers, ma'am, that is what they are doing; they are making the tow thinner and thinner so that it can be wound onto a bobbin. I remember when my mother did carding by hand, by brushing the cotton over wired combs, but the process is a lot faster since this machine came along.'

The air was thick with dust and Charlotte sneezed as she watched women and children running back and forth, obeying the machine's every demand. She couldn't help but feel how selfish she had been over the last few months. She had been sitting in her elegant surroundings, feeling sorry for herself, when these women and children were labouring so hard to keep her in the manner to which she had become accustomed. She beckoned Bert to leave the giant room full of dust and noise, and caught his arm as they started moving down to the next level.

'How many children work in the mill, Mr Bannister?' she enquired, trying not to show her belief that there should be none at all – or at least not at the ages she had seen.

'I'd say we have about fifty, ma'am. They are all over the age of eleven and are mostly the mill workers' children. Although some, like Betsy Foster in the carding room, think it isn't a good enough place for their kin to work.' Bert sniggered.

'I can't say I blame her. Is Betsy at work here today? I'd like to talk to her, if I could.' Charlotte thought Betsy sounded like a proud, sensible woman, and her view of the mill would be of great value to her.

'No, her mate Sally Oversby says she's ill today. I had to dock her pay with the wages clerk this morning.' Bert knew that Charlotte should hate Betsy. It was starting to become common knowledge that Joseph Dawson was not being faithful to his wife, and that Betsy had caught his eye. And now this woman was asking to talk to Betsy. Did she perhaps know what was going on under her nose?

'The poor woman doesn't get paid, if she's ill? Surely it isn't her fault that she can't work?'

'Aye, and it isn't our fault, either. I wouldn't bother your head about Betsy, she's a survivor, ma'am.' Bert thanked the Lord that Charlotte wasn't running the mill; there'd be no children employed, and everyone would be ill every day, if they were paid to be sick. 'Here you go, ma'am: the spinning room.'

Charlotte watched as the overhead spinning wheels

drove the spinning mules back and forth, spinning the fine cleaned and carded cotton onto bobbins. Once full, they were placed into baskets, to be woven into cloth by the doffer that collected the cotton spools. She observed as the mule-minders watched their machines and the busy spindles for any broken threads, pausing the machines for a few seconds to allow the piecers to tie them together. The nimble fingers of the younger children tied them together quickly, before the carriage of the machine started moving again. The dust from the cotton filled the air and Charlotte watched in disbelief at the danger of the situation, as one of the mules briefly stopped while one of the youngest employees was sent rushing down the length of the mule under the thread, to clear the fluff that had been created beneath the carriage. His legs were barely clear before the huge machine restarted.

Bert Bannister watched Charlotte's face as she gasped at the young boy, who sat down for a second, thankful that he'd managed to escape being crushed. She cared more than her husband. You only had to look at her face to know that. But care did not make profit and keep folk fed. It was the way of the world, and she'd have to accept it. He gestured, suggesting that perhaps she would like to walk out of the huge, noisy room and make her way out to the weavers. His voice wasn't audible over the noise of the spinning machines.

'I don't think I'll see the weavers today, Mr Bannister. I've seen enough and I'll have to get back to my household. My maid will be wondering where I am.' Charlotte felt faint as she gave her apologies to Bert.

'You don't look too well, Mrs Dawson, if you don't mind me saying. I'll get one of the carters to take you back home. Better we get you back safely.' Bert held out his arm for Charlotte to take as they walked steadily down the mill stairs.

'Thank you, Mr Bannister; and thank you for your guidance. May I ask for this visit to be kept between ourselves? My husband doesn't agree with me poking my nose into his business.' Charlotte continued to feel faint and was thankful when Bert gave her a hand up next to the carter whom he'd beckoned to come to her aid.

'It's been my pleasure, ma'am. And if you need to know anything about the mill, let me know. But for now, you take care of yourself and that baby. That's the main thing.' Bert summoned the driver to walk on, and watched as the cart carrying Charlotte left the cobbled yard. Poor cow; she hadn't any idea how ruthless and uncaring her husband was to all his workers. God help them if his heir was to be anything like him; and God let the baby she was carrying be a girl, for another copy of Joseph Dawson would be hell!

Betsy lay next to Joseph and ran her hand through the dark hair on his bare chest. She leaned over and kissed him on his cheek, then laid her head back down next to his.

'So, she thinks you are at Long Preston today?' she asked as she ran her finger through his dark hair again.

'She does. Not that it's any of your business.' Joseph gazed up at the cracks running along the ceiling of the two-bedroom cottage of Betsy and her younger brother. He'd lain there a lot lately, finding love and solace in the arms of his obedient mill lass. A lass who didn't ask questions and who did what he wanted, provided he paid for it.

'Does she love you, like I do?' Betsy purred into Joseph's ear and kissed it gently.

'Again it's nowt to do with you, woman. What I do at home, and what my wife says to me, is none of your business. Be content with your lot and I'll not do wrong by you.' Joseph reached for his pocket watch, from the waistcoat strewn on the floor, and looked at the time. 'Besides, your brat of a brother will be making his way home. I'll make myself scarce.' He sat up on the edge of the bed and pulled on his trousers, buttoning his waistcoat up before fastening his pocket watch back in place.

'You could stay a little longer. Johnny always dawdles on fine days like these, and it wouldn't cost you much more.' She ran her hand up her bare leg and smiled at him. Joseph was just about a daily visitor nowadays, and she was making more money lying on her back of an evening than labouring at his mill, where she worked her fingers to the bone through the daytime.

'Get up, you whore, I'm paying you. If my bloody wife wasn't so fat and full of child, I wouldn't be coming, so don't you forget that.' Joseph buttoned his jacket up and threw a florin on the bed. 'That's more than you'd make in a fortnight, so keep your mouth shut.' He checked himself in the foxed full-length mirror attached to the wall in the badly lit bedroom and tapped his hat on his head. 'Tomorrow night I'll come, same time as usual. And change those bloody sheets – they stink. If you're going to run a brothel, run a clean one.' He looked at Betsy languishing on her brass bed and shrugged his shoulders. She'd turned into a common whore, just wanting his money and telling him what she thought he wanted to hear. All women were the same: just after his money, not really loving him at all. He'd learned that at his mother's knee, as she said the same thing to her clients in the dirty back streets of Accrington: '*Tell the punters what they want to hear, my love; take their money and then move on to the next.*' Both he and his elder sister had had to survive as best they could whilst their mother went about her trade, with men coming and going at all times of the day and night. It was then that he vowed he would never have children, and would never love a woman. They were all liars, including his sister.

'Looking forward to it, my darling.' Betsy leaned back in her bed and watched Joseph leave her for the day. Tomorrow morning he would be her boss and master, as she made a living at the mill; but come tomorrow night, he'd be her lover. Maybe one day he might even be her husband. His wife was weak, and everyone had it in mind that she'd nearly died after her accident. Whatever the outcome, Joseph no longer hit Betsy, and his passion for her was deepening while his wife's grip on him was weakening – else why would he spend a full day with her alone? A day away from the mill was a welcome break, when she was lying in her lover's arms. So what if she was going to tell tales to one and all at the mill, on her return to work tomorrow? She'd tell them how ill she had felt, and they'd fall for her lies. After all, the great and mighty Joseph Dawson would not say any different, so who were they to question it?

'Aye, that Betsy next door is riding for a fall, the stupid lass.' Gertie Potts lifted her teacup to her lips and beckoned her friend from across the way to come and witness through her lace curtains Joseph Dawson leaving her next-door neighbour's house. 'She's the talk of the mill, my Harold says. And she was such a nice lass when she first came – she and her brother Johnny. It's the lil' lad I feel sorry for. It's bad enough that he's lost his parents, without his sister being the talk of the mill. Still, you can't tell her, otherwise it will all end in tears.'

Gertie and her friend watched as Joseph closed the gate and walked down the path that skirted the mill-pond. They shook their heads at the latest scandal to beset the little row of mill cottages.

'Aye, it will all end in tears, mark my words.' Gertie sat down again, to carry on with other gossip that was demanding their attention.

16

Joseph placed the newspaper down and cursed.

'Is there any need for that on a Sunday?' Charlotte asked quietly, watching as her husband lifted his paper to read more of the news that was obviously irritating him.

'There's every bloody need, with the Americas being in turmoil. The North is now officially at war with the South, and that's bad news for us. Richard Todd did warn me. I shouldn't be surprised. I'm just glad that we managed to secure a shipment before these so-called blockades start.'

'Why would they want to blockade the sale of cotton to England? That doesn't make sense.' Charlotte looked across at Joseph and waited for his answer. She watched as he dropped the newspaper onto his knee.

'The South – or the Confederates, as they are now known – is dependent on cotton sales to finance its army, and the North is trying to stop the export of cotton. All the seaports along the southern Atlantic coast below Washington are blockaded. Cotton generates huge sums of money for the southern states and helps provide revenue for their government, arms and military. The Confederates are also fighting to keep slavery. Without the slaves, the cotton would never be picked. Damn that Abraham Lincoln and his Yankees! I hope he rots in hell – he and his high-class morals. Negroes don't know any different; they need masters.' Joseph hit his newspaper and swore again.

'Joseph! They are human beings like us, they shouldn't be treated like animals. Thank heavens we abolished slavery – it isn't right that one man owns another.'

'What do you know; you're only a woman. You won't be saying that when we are bankrupt and on the streets, and have no money to pay the wages at the mill, let alone feed ourselves. Besides, don't you realize that I own those who work at the mill: they rely on me for their pay, their houses and even how they meet their maker. Without the pay they receive they would be begging in the streets. Don't be too anti-slavery, my dear. By the time this war is over, people will be wishing they were slaves. At least they would have been fed, instead of starving.' Joseph could see nothing but gloom for the future; these were going to be worrying times at Ferndale. Things were tight as it was, without raw cotton supplies being hard to come by.

'We will agree to differ over slaves. But surely some cotton will be able to reach our shores? And, as you say, Ferndale has an ample supply at the moment.'

Charlotte stopped knitting her baby shawl and looked at the worry on her husband's face.

'It depends. I think I will cut the hours and pay at the mill. At least that will help costs, in the short term.' For once Joseph was glad he had a wife to talk to. Since his sister Dora had found a man for herself in Settle, she was no longer his confidante. Whoever the man was, he was stupid. She'd bleed him dry and leave him broken-hearted, for Dora was even harder-hearted than he was.

'But the war is not your workers' doing, yet it is they who are going to suffer the most. Do you really have to cut their hours and pay?' Charlotte remembered the workers she had seen in the mill. None of them looked healthy and well fed. In fact, some of them had looked like paupers, they were so thin.

'It will be them or us, Charlotte. We will have to make some sacrifices as well. Now is not the best time to start a family. Plus, can you understand now why giving the tenancy of Crummock to Atkinson was so foolhardy. We will need every penny, before this conflict in America ends.' Joseph sighed.

'Crummock can supply us with much of the food that we need. We were nearly self-sufficient when I lived there. Surely that man – this Mr Wilson – could supply butter, milk and mutton to us, and I'm sure he should already be raising a pig for bacon, to get them through the winter months.' Charlotte cast her mind back to a kitchen that was full of plenty and where nobody went hungry.

'I don't know if Roger Wilson is that concerned about looking after our needs at this moment in time. I think he will be getting to grips with the running of Crummock, and keeping that Arthur in check.' Joseph quickly quelled any thought of Roger Wilson keeping them in farm produce, knowing all too well that the tenant at Crummock was no farmer.

'Well, he should be – he's beholden to us. And as for keeping Arthur in check, he'll be no problem, for he knows his duties well.' Charlotte was indignant at Joseph's reply to her suggestion. 'All the more reason to have had Archie as tenant, because he'd have made sure we were supplied with what we needed.' Charlotte bit her lip, hoping that she hadn't said too much.

'It would never have worked with your precious Archie at Crummock. Besides, I cannot stand the way he looks at you,' growled Joseph.

'Don't be stupid, Joseph. He's happily married, with another baby on the way.' Charlotte blushed.

'Aye, but that was a mistake – probably a bigger one than the baby that's growing in your belly.'

'I think, on that note, I'm going to retire to my bedroom for a lie-down. I thought for once, Joseph, we were having a reasonable conversation between husband and wife. But then once again you have to spoil it.' Charlotte stood up and placed her knitting in the sewing box next to her chair. She wasn't going to let Joseph win by seeing the tears that were brimming in her eyes. This baby was everything to her and it would never go hungry, regardless of whether or not Joseph's cotton mill survived. She would make sure of that come hell or high water.

It was 6 a.m. on a cool, late spring morning as Joseph looked at the workers gathering at the mill gates and braced himself. Fewer hours worked meant less profit. However, it also meant more security for those who did work, rather than the mill running out of cotton during the first few months of the civil war. A war that could last for years. It would take ages for the cotton plantations to get back to normal.

'Right, Bert, I'm ready. They are not going to like what I'm going to say.' Joseph looked at his watch. From now on the mill gates would open at eight. Two hours less work a day might just save them all round. They could either like it or lump it. They all knew where the door was, although Joseph was sure nobody would walk. There was nowhere else to go, in this backwater of the Dales.

'As you like, Mr Dawson, but don't expect any thanks this morning.' Bert stood, opening the office door for his worried boss, and spat out a mouthful of chewing tobacco. Bad times had come to the mill and it was worrying for every last one of them, including the mighty Joseph Dawson.

'So the rat is leaving the sinking ship?' Joseph stood in the doorway of his sister's room and watched her pack her carpet bag full of belongings.

'I've had an offer of marriage from Ezera, if that's

what you mean.' Dora didn't even turn round to confront her brother. 'You didn't think I'd stay here – being sneered at and whispered about, by that wife of yours and your snivelling servants – forever? I've got a life as well. Besides, there will soon be a brat to look after, and I can't abide babies.' She stopped throwing her clothes into her bag and finally turned to face her brother.

'Tell the truth, Dora. You are going because you are frightened the money is going to run out soon, and you always have looked after number one,' Joseph snarled.

'Well, don't you look out for number one, too? And yes, I am going because the money's running out, and Ezera can offer me the lifestyle I deserve. I'll be the wife of a rich jeweller. I'll even have my own maid. What more could I ask for?'

'You could ask for your brother's blessing, as I won't be attending the wedding.' Joseph grabbed his sister's arm and squeezed it tight.

'And would I get it? Perhaps for all your scheming, thieving ways, I'm going to come off the better. That must stick in your throat.' Dora stared into her brother's dark eyes and just hoped she hadn't pushed him too far.

He shoved his sister back against the wall, pinning her to it, breathing heavily in her face. 'With a comment like that, you mention once to anybody that you are my sister and they'll find you dead in one of the back alleyways of Settle. You and I are finished. This is the parting of the ways, dear sister, and God help Ezera Bloomenber, because he's going to need His help.'

'Not half as much as you are, Joseph – you are a lost soul. Nobody loves you, nobody wants you, they just want your money. And what's funny: there isn't any. You've nearly spent it all. What then, my precious brother? Because the blonde, empty-headed thing you thought you married is not that daft.' Dora squeezed out of her brother's grip and picked up her carpet bag.

'Out, get out! I never want to see you again. Get out of my house!' Joseph yelled at his sister as she picked up her skirts and ran along the landing of the servants' quarters. 'Don't you ever show your face at Windfell again – your services are no longer required.' He sighed as Dora made her way down the back stairs. He walked across to her bedroom window and watched as she walked quickly past the stables, without giving a second glance back at the place they had planned to make their fortunes with. She was the one person who knew who he was and where he had come from. She had better keep that mouth of hers closed, or else it would be the worse for her.

'Well, I've never heard such a racket. Fancy shouting at a member of the staff to leave, in such a manner. But I'd be lying if I said I wasn't glad she's gone.' Mrs Batty rose from putting her latest concoction into the oven and looked at the seated staff around the kitchen table. 'She didn't even get a letter of reference. She'll not get into service without one of them.'

'I don't think she'll need one, Mrs Batty. From what I can gather, she's to marry the jeweller in Settle. His shop girl told me that, when I called in for a new hat-pin for Mrs Dawson this morning,' said Lily. 'She's only known him two months and he's smitten with her – he thinks she's an angel, according to Dolly.'

'I hope you put her right: that she's a vicious old dragon, with a foul mouth. As you say, we are better off without her.' Yates stood up and smiled. 'I think this may deserve a drop of sherry, to celebrate her departure tonight after supper.'

'Aye, that would be good.' Mazy grinned.

'I don't think your mother would approve, Mazy, you are a bit too young.' Yates looked disapprovingly at the grinning scullery maid.

'Go on, Edward, let the lass have a drink with us. She's fourteen now. Besides, it might be the first and last time she gets to taste sherry, if the rumours are right. We might all be gone from Windfell. How can you run a cotton mill without cotton? I know Bert Bannister says the warehouse down at Ferndale is full, but it'll not last forever. Why these Americans have to fight amongst themselves, I don't know.' Mrs Batty put her hands in her apron and slumped in her usual chair next to the fire. 'I thought I'd found the place to see my days out. And then there's Mrs Dawson carrying a baby. She must have the worries of the world on her shoulders, what with him carrying on the way he does, and her father dying. You'd think she'd get sad with it all, but she's always the same when you talk to her.'

225

'I don't think she knows about the hussy at Lang-cliffe Locks, so I'd be careful what you say. It might not be right anyway – you know how gossip spreads. Tell folk half a tale and they add the rest,' said Lily.

'Oh, believe me, I'm right. You haven't seen him come home in the early hours of the morning, like I have. "Doing his business books", my arse – apologies, ladies. It's funny business he's up to. He's a disgrace, he's no gentleman. I knew that when I saw him hit Mrs Dawson in the dining room, the night she fell down the stairs.' Yates couldn't hold his tongue.

'He did what?' All three servants gasped at Yates's confession.

'He hit her and then they squabbled, and I'm sure he pushed her down the stairs. Dora Dodgson told me to hold my tongue, else something horrible would befall me; that's why I've never said anything until today.' Yates sat back down and looked around at the aston-ished faces.

'He's nothing but a cad. He doesn't deserve the mistress, and she's such a lady.' Lily sighed.

'I've a stronger word than that for him. I've a good mind to spit in his soup tonight – that is if he's here,' said Mrs Batty.

'He'll be here tonight, Mrs Batty. He won't dare to show his face in daylight alone down at Langcliffe Lock cottages. Mrs Potts says he isn't that well liked down there at the moment, with cutting the hours at the mill. I bet they are taking it out on his bit of fun as well. She's getting paid double for her nightly exploits, while everyone else is struggling,' Mazy chipped in.

'You are too young, Mazy, to know such things. I'm surprised at Gertie Potts telling you suchlike,' said Mrs Batty.

'She didn't tell me directly. I earwigged her as she was telling the butcher's boy, when he delivered yesterday to my nana's house.' Mazy folded her arms tightly.

'He's even younger than you – that's worse than ever,' exclaimed Mrs Batty.

'Aye, but he knows everybody from Horton to Long Preston, and you know how gossip spreads.' Mazy smiled.

'Well, all I know is that that lass upstairs needs our support. I've never known such a to-do. Now come on, you lot, there's plenty to do – housekeeper or not, we've got to keep this house going, for the sake of Mrs Dawson.'

'Joseph, I'm sorry Mrs Dodgson's left us. I know you two were quite close, like family. I think you likened her to that, when we first met?' Charlotte smiled slightly. The whole house had heard Joseph shouting at his favoured member of staff as she ran down the servants' back stairs. And she was sure that the entire household, except Joseph, had breathed a sigh of relief that she had gone.

'I expected better of her: stealing my best gold cufflinks. How could I let her stay? I presume she was going to have her Ezera sell them in his jeweller's shop.

I was so disappointed in her behaviour – how could I overlook that?'

'Indeed, my dear. She's lucky you didn't call the police. That would have put paid to her wedding plans. We will not shop at Ezera Bloomenber's in the future – we can't trust where his jewellery comes from.'

'I think jewellery-buying is a thing of the past for the moment,' grunted Joseph.

'I know, I'm sorry. It was a stupid thing for me to say, when your employees can barely pay for a loaf of bread. I've been thinking, Joseph: we don't need to re-place Mrs Dodgson; between Mrs Batty and me, we can run the house. It would give me a purpose in life, instead of sitting around wasting time embroidering or reading. I'd enjoy it.' Charlotte looked across the dinner table at an unusually subdued Joseph and expected to have her head bitten off, for daring even to suggest such a thing.

'And when the baby comes, what then?' He looked up.

'Well, we will play it by ear. I'm sure we could manage. Lily won't mind doubling up as a nanny, I'm certain.'

'Whatever! The affairs of the house are not at the forefront of my mind. Do as you wish.' Joseph took a mouthful of something from his dinner plate. 'What is this stuff that's on my plate? It tastes dreadful.' He spluttered and turned to Yates, who stood behind him waiting to clear the plates.

'I believe it is called "curry of mutton". Mrs Batty

has been experimenting with what she has in the larder and what Mrs Beeton recommends in her cookbook, sir. It's from India, I believe.' Yates stepped forward.

'Well, it wants to bugger back off to India. I've never eaten anything so revolting in all my life. It's a waste of good mutton. Tell her to throw that bloody cookbook out, if that's the best she can do with it.' Joseph dismissed his plate and Yates obligingly removed the uneaten dinner.

'If you could tell Mrs Batty that this dish is usually served with boiled rice, not boiled potatoes.' Charlotte passed her plate to a subservient Yates. 'And, Yates, can you tell her that we will go through the menus for the week in the morning. Now that Mrs Dodgson has left us, Mrs Batty will be dealing only with me.' She looked across at her husband, who was quenching the taste of spices with a good swig of claret.

'I take it you don't like spices?' She nearly laughed.

'I hate anything highly flavoured. Besides, that just looked like a plate of slop – or even worse.' Joseph took another long sup and looked across at his wife.

'I'll ask Mrs Batty to look in the English section, not the Indian, if she is determined to try recipes from out of this all-singing cookbook. You were going to tell me about your day, before you decided to dislike your dinner so much. It must be hard for you at the moment, because ordinary people do not understand commerce.'

'They don't understand commerce, or war in another land, but they understand that their bellies are rumbling, bairns crying and wives complaining. Even

Bert Bannister is not happy with his lot at the moment. I'm a hard man, but even I realize we will either sink or swim with this, and that lives may be lost if it carries on for any length of time.'

'Well, I looked in our storeroom this morning. We seem to have a surplus of flour, which will only end up weevil-infested if we don't use it quickly. How about Mrs Batty and I make a few batches of bread and distribute it at the mill gates in the morning, while we survive this bad patch? It will win you some sympathy, if they feel you care.' Charlotte looked at her husband, who hated giving anything for nothing.

'I suppose that's one up on Christie: he's not cut his hours, but it'll be at his own cost. His warehouse is not as full as ours.' Joseph thought for a moment. 'Aye, go on, it might keep quiet the ones that say I don't care. But don't forget: folk have their pride, they don't like charity.'

'I know, but they'd rather have a loaf of bread than cheap words, I can assure you.' Charlotte smiled.

'Thank you, my dear, for trying to help. It means a lot to me.' Joseph patted her hand and looked more relaxed, thankful that he had someone to share his worries.

Charlotte decided that the time was right to ask a long-standing question, to which she knew Joseph might react badly. 'I thought I might visit Archie and Rosie tomorrow. Would that cause you concern, my love? It would be so nice to see baby Daniel. I bet he's grown.' She sat back and waited for his response.

'That bloody man – I hate him, you know. I can't understand your attraction to him. You can go, but take Lily with you. I don't trust him.' Joseph scowled.

'Don't trust him or don't trust me? Really, Joseph, I'm six months pregnant and I look terrible, and my husband owns a failing cotton mill. What is possibly attractive about me? He's a friend – and a friend only.'

'No, it's deeper than that with you two. Knowing you, you'll be whingeing to him about your beloved Crummock and saying that you wished he was in it,' Joseph snarled.

'Well, I wish he was. We wouldn't go hungry if he was there. But that isn't what I'm going for. Rosie is not carrying this baby very well – she's ill, and I just want to see if there's anything I can do for her before the new baby is born.' Charlotte lowered her head.

'Just go. You'd probably go, with or without my permission. After all, as you say, who's going to look at you, in your condition?' Joseph said coldly.

'Thank you, Joseph. You do know I love you more than anything else in the world.' Charlotte looked over at her husband.

'Well, you've a strange way of showing it, visiting an old lover.' Joseph sat back and stared at the woman he had married, but could never completely own.

17

Rosie's father and mother sat in the small room they lived in and listened to the screams of their daughter, as Lucy Cranston tried to help her with the birth of their next grandchild. They had faith in Lucy, for she'd brought many a child into the world, but this one seemed to be struggling to make its entrance. Rosie's mother sobbed and held Daniel close to her body, rocking him with every scream, knowing the pain of childbirth that her daughter was going through.

'Go get the doctor, Archie, something's wrong.' Lucy Cranston wiped the sweat from her brow. 'The baby's early anyway, but Rosie shouldn't be screaming like this.'

Rosie screamed again, the noise echoing around the small farmhouse like a wild banshee's wail.

'For God's sake, go, lad – else we are going to lose them both.' Lucy turned and went back into the bedroom, stopping for a second to reassure her white-faced nephew with a quick hug. She knew damn well what was wrong – the baby was early and was a breach birth – but without the aid of the doctor she couldn't turn it. Rosie was getting weaker with each push, and the bed that she lay on was wet with sweat and blood. Lucy prayed silently to herself: *God let Archie find the doctor in time.* There wasn't a second to waste.

'Lily, I know that Mr Dawson said you had to accompany me to see the Atkinsons, but there really is no need to. I would prefer to go there by myself. Besides, Jethro is taking me in the trap. I'll ask him to come into the house with me, while I talk business with Mr Atkinson. And just look at the day: it is wet and miserable. The fog will be down around Mewith, and it can be a dark, foreboding place on a day like this.' Charlotte stood in the doorway of Windfell.

'If you are sure, ma'am.'

'I'm sure, Lily. Jethro will look after me, and we'll be back before dinner.' Charlotte sighed as she stepped out towards the waiting trap and looked skywards at the grey clouds dispersing a fine mizzle of rain, while the surrounding fells were covered with low clouds, making the day dank and downcast.

'Are you sure you want to go in the trap, ma'am? It isn't any problem to get the team ready, for you to go in the carriage.' Jethro gave Charlotte a hand up into the back of the trap and covered her with an oilskin from the stable.

'I'm fine, Jethro. I prefer the trap, and I can take in the scenery better. I just love the views on the road past Clapham. The ride is so beautiful; all the fellsides are lovely at this time of the year, with the blue hues of bluebells.' Charlotte missed wandering along the fells and byways around Austwick. The trap was an excuse to be as near her beloved surroundings as a lady of her stature could be. She made herself comfortable and smiled as the trap took the turn up the road, passing the hamlet of Stainforth, and then the bay horse struggled a little as it trotted up the steep hill known as Sherrard Brow, to drop down to the turning to Helwith Bridge and then on through Austwick and Clapham. 'See, Jethro, I'd have missed all these hedgerows. Just look at them. And the hillside above Ribble is blue with bluebells, just like I said.'

'Yes, ma'am, but it's wet and miserable. Just look at Pen-y-ghent – it's shrouded by cloud.'

'Proper Dales weather, I think you call it, Jethro. I love it. Just smell the air, clear and fresh.' Charlotte smiled.

Jethro couldn't understand his mistress. She wouldn't love the weather if she had to work out in it as much as he did.

'Cheer up, Jethro, there's a bit of blue sky there. The day is improving slightly.'

Charlotte sat back and enjoyed the ride, taking in every turn and twist on the way across the wild moorland on the way up to Mewith. She'd soon be seeing

Archie. Lately she'd realized just how much she had missed him.

'For God's sake, woman, where's the doctor? I need him. My wife's in childbirth and in difficulty.' Archie's face was red with frustration as the doctor's house-keeper kept him on the step of the grand home.

'He's not in, he's visiting friends up Eldroth. He won't be back until later in the day.' The housekeeper looked at the young man on her doorstep and saw that he was in distress.

'Where – where up Eldroth? Give me the house name?' Archie was desperate. Eldroth was a good hour's ride, depending on which house the doctor was at.

'Blackbank; he's at Blackbank. I don't think he'll want to be disturbed,' the housekeeper yelled at the flee-ing lad, who jumped on his horse like the Devil himself and galloped through the streets of Austwick, without giving any thanks for her information.

Blackbank was nearly in the centre of Eldroth. Archie prayed that he would get the doctor and be back in time to save Rosie and the baby.

'Oh, Miss Charlotte, I heard the horses and thought it was the doctor.' Lucy Cranston flung the door of the small farmhouse open to her visitor.

'Doctor! Why, who's ill? Not Archie? I hope he's alright?' Charlotte flounced into the gloom of the farmhouse and cast aside her cloak.

235

'It's our lass – she's in a bad way, with this one,' Rosie's mother cried, while her father went and stood in the doorway, feeling awkward with all this women's business being spoken of around him. He loved his lass and couldn't help but think badly of the lad who had got her in this state; she was only a baby herself, without having two children – if God was willing – at her young age.

'Sorry, Charlotte, I can't stand and talk. I've got to get back upstairs to Rosie. She's in childbirth, but the baby won't come. Archie's gone for the doctor, but he's taking his time. I think he's going to be too late. I've done all I can – I can't do no more. Miss Charlotte, I don't know what to do.'

Charlotte grabbed Lucy's arm, stopping her in her tracks at the bottom of the stairs. 'What do you mean too late, she isn't . . . dying, surely?'

'She's weak, Miss Charlotte; she's been in labour for over three days now. I've seen this before. I think the baby's the wrong way around, but I can't turn it. God knows, I've tried, but I can't hurt her any more.' Lucy sobbed into her blood-covered apron and rushed up the stairs. 'She's even stopped screaming now. I think the baby must be dead.' She paused on the landing and looked at Charlotte, knowing that she was with child herself and that the sight behind the bedroom door would give her cause to worry. 'Best you stay here, Miss Charlotte, it isn't something you'd want to see.'

'Open the door, Lucy. I can't do anything, but I can be there for her.' Charlotte walked past the sobbing cook and went to the side of the pale, dying Rosie. She looked at the blood-covered bedclothes, at the wash-bowl filled with wet cloths and at the moaning body on the bed. 'Rosie, it's me, Charlotte. Archie will soon be here, he's gone for the doctor.' She wrung out a cloth and placed it on Rosie's forehead and then grasped her whiter-than-white hand.

'Charlotte,' Rosie whispered faintly. 'Charlotte, I'm dying. This baby won't come. Archie's too late.' She sighed and caught her breath. 'Promise me – please promise me – that you will look after my Archie and our baby Daniel,' she whispered, clasping Charlotte's hand tightly.

'I promise, Rosie, I promise.' Charlotte fought back her tears.

'He was always yours anyway. Archie has always loved you. I pinched him from you.'

'Don't be silly. He loves you and baby Daniel. Now no more of this silly talk. You and the baby are going to be fine.' Charlotte ran her fingers through Rosie's soaked hair.

Rosie smiled. 'Tell him I loved him.' Her voice was getting weaker and faltered. 'Remember, tell Archie that I . . .' Then the silence was heartbreaking. At peace in the knowledge that her wishes would be fulfilled, she gave up the fight to live and slipped away. She lay white and lifeless in Charlotte's arms, her struggle for breath ceased and her eyes gazed heavenwards.

'Rosie, no. Rosie, please, just wait until Archie returns.' Charlotte patted her hand and sobbed, then cried as she realized that the girl had taken her last breath on earth. 'No, Rosie, no – don't leave. What will become of baby Daniel? He needs his mother. Archie needs his wife.'

'Come away, Miss Charlotte, there's nothing more you can do now. Time for the good Lord to look after her now, and a gentler soul he'll not have in that heaven of his. She was a good lass, was Rosie; she didn't deserve this. It'll break Archie's heart, no matter what she whispered to you.' Lucy leaned over Rosie and closed her eyelids gently, while whispering, 'God bless,' before pulling the sheets over her head. She put her arm around Charlotte as she sobbed. 'It's alright, Miss Charlotte. Now, you pull yourself together, because that lad will need a friend when he comes home. He'll carry all his life the guilt of not getting the doctor in time. Just like your father did, with your mother.'

'You can't put the blame on him – his heart will be broken anyway,' sobbed Charlotte.

'No one's blaming the lad, but I know how he thinks, and he'll blame himself. The doctor must have been out on his rounds, else he'd have been here by now. Now come on, Miss Charlotte, let's wash them hands of yours, and come and sit next to the fire. I'll put the kettle on and wait for Archie to return.'

Charlotte looked down at her blood-covered hands. 'I'm frightened, Mrs Cranston. What if I die in childbirth, along with my child? Or, worse still, what if I die and my baby lives? Joseph would abandon it, I'm sure,' she sobbed.

238

'Now, don't talk daft. You are a strong lass, you've nowt to bother about. Poor Rosie there was a feeble bit of a thing; she'd nowt on her to fight with. Besides, the doctor will be with you by your side, and I'm sure Mr Dawson would do no such thing, with his own flesh and blood. It'll be his heir – all men want an heir, especially one in his position.' Lucy put her arm around Charlotte and guided her out of the room. They both looked back for a second at the body of Rosie lying at peace under the sheets. As they did so, a ray of sunshine shone through the west-facing window and lit up the room with a strange aurora. 'There, you see, Miss Charlotte. Rosie and her baby are being welcomed into heaven already. They'll not be on their own for long.'

Archie flew into the kitchen of his home and looked at the sombre group sitting around the coal fire drinking tea. He said nothing, but ran through the room with the doctor close behind him and pounded up the stairs to the bedroom, where his dead wife and baby lay.

The group sobbed when a terrible wail was heard throughout the house. Archie's world was broken, along with his heart. Lucy rocked the baby boy Daniel, who knew something was wrong and started to bawl his heart out, along with the adults. Little did he know that his mother's love and hugs had gone forever.

'Jethro, can you go home and tell Mr Dawson what has happened here today? I'll stay the night. Mr Atkinson will need a friend. Return for me in the morning.' Charlotte sobbed and looked across at the stable lad, whose cheeks were running with tears. 'I can at least help look after baby Daniel, and help Rosie's parents with their grief, if nothing else.' She stifled her tears and opened the door for Jethro to leave.

'Yes, ma'am, I'll tell him. But do you think you should stay?' Jethro questioned her judgement, for he knew it would not suit his master.

'Mr Atkinson is my oldest friend. If Mr Dawson doesn't understand why I'm staying, then he's not worthy of being called my husband,' snapped Charlotte.

'Yes, ma'am, I was only thinking . . .' Jethro stopped.

'You were only thinking it wasn't proper for me to stay, with a friend who has just lost his wife? Don't worry, I've plenty of chaperones. Not that I will need one, under the circumstances. Now go, and return in the morning.' Charlotte knew what Jethro was think-ing: that Joseph would not take the news kindly. But surely even he wouldn't deny Archie a friend in the circumstances?

'I'll be back first thing, ma'am.' Jethro doffed his cap and wiped the tear stains from his grubby face. He was thankful to leave the grieving house, but dreaded telling Joseph Dawson that he had left his wife with the man everyone knew to be his rival. He was going to get a hiding, if nothing else, for leaving her there.

'I loved her, Lottie. I know folk thought Rosie wasn't right for me, but I loved her. What am I going to do? I'm left now with the baby. How's he going to be brought up, with no mother?' Archie sat with his head in his hands, his body shaking with grief.

'She loved you too, she told me so with her dying breath. She wanted you to be happy and to take care of baby Daniel. Mrs Cranston and Rosie's parents will help you, and then, when someone else comes along to take Rosie's place, these dark days will soon disappear.' Charlotte placed her arm round Archie and looked at the pain in his eyes.

'I will never, ever forget my Rosie, and no one will ever replace her. Don't you dare say that again.' Archie trembled.

'I didn't mean any harm by my words. It might seem as if life has come to an end for you, with the death of Rosie and the baby, but it will go on. Baby Daniel will grow up, and he too will find someone to love. Life is a circle – one is never alone.' Charlotte looked around them and listened as, above them, Rosie's parents said their goodbyes to their daughter. Her thoughts flitted to memories of her father, and how she missed him. But she was right: once you loved someone, they were never forgotten; their memory lingered on and you were never alone. She wiped a tear away from her eyes. Her dear father: no one would ever replace him.

'Oh, Lottie, what am I going to do?' He broke down and sobbed.

'I don't know, Archie. I don't know what either of us is going to do. Life's not good to either of us at the moment, but we've not to lose hope. Things will change, of that I'm sure.'

It was a sorrowful sight as Rosie's family clung together on the wild skyline of the chapel's burial ground at Keasden. The late-spring wind blew through the new growth of the rushes, making them rattle together, and the lapwings and curlews echoed their cry out over the dale and over the body of Rosie and her child, as they were lowered in the coffin into the ground. Archie looked out over the grave that held his wife and bairn, and around him to the distant hills and dales. The wind whipped his blond hair against his cheeks as if chastising him for his slowness in getting aid for his wife. He was lost. A wave of sorrow washed over him and he fought it back, as the parson tried to console him.

He looked over to Charlotte and Joseph Dawson as they placed a handful of earth on the coffin. Had Joseph felt this way when he'd lost his first wife? He doubted it. That bastard felt nothing for nobody. How Charlotte lived with him, Archie didn't know. The next day after losing Rosie, Joseph had been on the steps of the house as soon as the sun had risen, to claim his wife back. A wife everyone knew he didn't love. Poor Charlotte, she was as lost as he was, stuck in a worthless marriage with a bairn on the way. What was life about?

Archie looked across to the dark shape of distant Ingleborough and watched a shower of rain as it skirted around the hill's dark flanks. 'Aye, go on, ya bugger rain, you might as well do,' he whispered to himself.

'Bless my lass, before she's covered in the ground.' It was the least God could do, seeing as he'd taken her away from him.

18

Is thy cruse of comfort wasting?
Rise and share it with another,
And through all the years of famine
It shall serve thee and thy brother . . .
Scanty food for one will often
Make a royal feed for two.

For the heart grows rich by giving;
All its wealth is living grain;
Seeds that moulder in the garner,
Scattered, fill with gold the plain.

ELIZABETH RUNDLE CHARLES

A week had passed since Rosie's funeral and Charlotte had no other choice than to throw herself wholeheartedly into helping the situation that was evolving at the mill.

'Are we right, Lily?' Charlotte looked around the kitchen of Windfell and waited for her maid.

'Aye, I'm coming, ma'am. There's another lot of dough rising in the dough trough, and Mrs Batty's going to bake it for when we return.' She hurried to her mistress's side with her basket full of warm, crusty bread. The smell of the baking dough had filled the kitchen of Windfell all morning and made everyone feel hungry.

'Jethro's ready with his horse and cart. We'll go to the mill gates and then walk on to the mill cottages at Langcliffe Locks.' Charlotte lifted her basket and waited for her maid.

'You will take care, won't you, ma'am? Some of those workers can be loutish,' Yates worried, as he held the door open for the pair, with their good intentions.

'You worry too much, Yates. How can they be loutish if we are filling their bellies?' Charlotte smiled.

'They are proud Dales folk, ma'am, and don't believe in charity. And, ma'am, should you be sitting up there? It doesn't look that comfortable for you.' Yates watched as Lily and her maid climbed up next to Jethro.

'It isn't charity; it's part payment for their hard work,' Charlotte shouted as Jethro flicked the reins and set the horse into motion.

'Yates is right, ma'am, you shouldn't be sitting up here on the cart, not in your condition.' Lily looked at her mistress.

'And if I went in the carriage, what would they

think of me then? Better the cart – more down-to-earth. Besides, these are my own people. I'm no better and no worse.' Charlotte smiled at the concern on her maid's face. 'Don't worry, Lily, I can handle a bit of bad feeling, and I'm sure there will be some. After all, their wages are down and, with the uncertainty of future work, they probably think it's all Joseph's fault. They little thought that politics in America would enter into their lives and cause such upset.' She patted Lily's hand. 'As for baby here, he's quite content. The morning sickness that I had for a few mornings early on in my pregnancy has thankfully passed and I feel well.' Times were hard, but Charlotte was determined to do her bit for the people employed at the mill.

She gripped Lily's hand as they reached the cobbled path that led down to the high locked gates of the mill yard. Workers were gathered there: the men with their flat caps and worn jackets, and the women with their shawls and long skirts, all waiting in anticipation of the large gates opening to summon them for another's day work, with the assurance of pay.

'It'll be alright, Lily. They'll know we mean well. Jethro, try and get as near as you can, and then we'll get down and walk with our baskets.' Charlotte smiled at the two people by her side as they looked worried. Truth be told, she didn't know how the offer of a meagre loaf of bread would go down, but she had to do something to help the workers of her husband's mill.

'Good morning, how are you? Would you like some bread? It was baked fresh this morning. It's free!' She smiled at the astonished faces of the mill workers, as she and Lily mixed in with the waiting workers.

The first few workers looked at her as if they didn't believe what she was saying. Then Sally Oversby spouted up, 'Don't mind if I do. After all, it's your husband that's taking it out of my baby's mouth – it's the least you can do. Come on, you lot; it's for nowt and it's from the big house.' Sally took a loaf out of Charlotte's basket and passed it back through the crowd, and then passed more to the bustling onlookers, so that soon both Charlotte's and Lily's baskets were empty.

'We've more, in the back of the cart,' Charlotte shouted, watching as the workers clambered around the cart, where Jethro stood passing out a loaf to each allotted employee.

'So, you are feeling sorry for your working classes. Give them bread and it'll keep them quiet. It takes more than that, missus. We have a right to work, and to have pride in our work, and we don't expect hand-outs from the big house.' Sally put her hands on her hips and looked at Charlotte square-on.

'I don't mean to insult anyone. I just thought a loaf of bread might help – it's the only way I could think of helping. Times are hard for everyone and it is nobody's fault. It's just that there is not enough cotton for you all to work the hours you used to.' Charlotte looked at the straight-talking woman and admired her bravery in saying her bit.

'Christie down at Bridge End at Settle is still work-ing twelve-hour days. He doesn't seem to have the same problems, and he hasn't cut his mill workers' hours.' Sally stood her ground.

'It's early days yet. Sorry, I don't know your name?'

'Sally, if you must know.'

'Yes, Sally, its early days, and the war in America could go on for years. Our cotton in America is being blocked from getting to us by the Yankees in the north, because they don't want the southern states to keep slaves, to pick the cotton. They believe all men to be free. Now isn't that a good thing? But it could go on for years, so Christie may be in trouble, if he can't get his hands on new supplies,' Charlotte explained and watched as Sally took in the information.

'So it's all about folk who don't get paid and don't have a say in their lives? And folk are trying to stop it, just like they did with the slaves over here,' said Sally.

'Partly, Sally. There's other factors as well, but that's the main one. I know I shouldn't say so, but I hope the Yankees win.' She smiled at Sally.

'So do I, ma'am. And thank you for your bread. God bless you, ma'am, 'cause no man should be a slave. Although I'm a slave to that bloody mill bell!' Sally picked up her skirts and strode off as the mill bell sounded out around the yard and the huge gates opened. She stopped and looked back, then shouted at Charlotte, 'But I hope that bell keeps ringing.'

Charlotte smiled. At least she had won over one worker. She watched as everyone raced into the mill to get into work on time, most of them with a loaf of bread under their arm.

'Well, ma'am, I think that went down well, or a lot better than I thought.' Lily stood next to Charlotte and watched the workers filing into the mill.

'Yes, I think it did. At least I got the chance to explain why this is happening. The woman I talked to will let everyone know why there's a problem with the cotton supply, and hopefully they won't look at Joseph in such a bad light from now on.' Charlotte patted Lily on the back. 'Thank you, Lily, for your help. I know it was above and beyond your duties as a lady's maid, but I have to help my husband keep his mill and his staff. After all, we all depend on him.'

'It's Mrs Batty you need to sweet-talk. Did you see her face? I thought she was going to burst, with the heat from the kitchen.' Lily smiled.

'Yes, perhaps baking that much bread once a day is a bit too much to ask. We'll make it once a week, I think. We just need to show we care, which we do. Those poor people. Their lives are in the lap of the gods – as well as ours – if the mill doesn't keep working.'

'It'll not come to that, ma'am, I'm sure,' said Lily.

'I don't know, Lily. Things are bad, and the trouble is there's nothing anyone can do about it.'

Charlotte knocked on the door of the last cottage in the row of Langcliffe Lock cottages and waited for a reply.

'I wouldn't go there, ma'am, she'll not be in.' Gertie Potts, who was on her dinner break, waited and watched on the doorstep, clutching the loaf of bread for which she was more than thankful. She knew damn well that Betsy was otherwise employed in her lunch hour, with Charlotte's husband. 'She doesn't deserve one anyway.'

'What do you mean? She works at the mill, doesn't she?' said Charlotte.

'Aye, when she can be bothered to.' Gertie instantly regretted interfering with the charity work of the big house, and decided to listen and watch from the safety of her lace curtains, as she heard the bolt on Betsy Foster's door being pulled.

'Yes. What can I do for you?' Betsy came to the door and looked at the woman she knew was her lover's wife.

'Are you too ill to work today?' Charlotte asked, looking at the state of the woman's undress as she propped herself up against the doorway.

'Aye, you could say that. Going to that mill often makes me feel worse for wear nowadays.' Betsy looked Charlotte up and down. The poor bitch hadn't got a clue.

'I'm sorry to hear that. You must really be feeling the pinch, with illness and a shortage of hours. I'm just delivering my husband's workers a loaf of bread each. It's our way of helping in these hard times. Would you like one?' Charlotte offered Betsy one of the newly baked loaves and waited for a reply.

'That would be grand, thank you very much.' Betsy took the loaf quickly and started to close the door.

'I hope you feel better shortly,' Charlotte shouted after the door closed in her face. Closing the garden gate, she saw the next-door neighbour's curtains twitch. Nothing would escape that one's eyes, but she couldn't be that good a neighbour if she was so callous about her ill friend. She shook her head. It took all sorts to make a world. She walked towards Jethro, who was standing patiently next to the horse and cart at the bottom of the lane leading to the locks.

Betsy placed the loaf of bread on her kitchen table and then climbed the stairs to her bedroom.

'Now, where were we, before your wife so rudely interrupted us?' She giggled. 'Poor cow, she thought I was ill.' Betsy leaned over Joseph, her breasts enticing him to play.

Joseph caught her by her hair and twisted it. 'You don't call my wife a cow, and you show her some respect. She's ten times the lady you will ever be.' He had been thinking for some time that the moment to stop visiting Betsy for his pleasures was upon him. She was beginning to think she could do what she wanted, and was starting to take advantage of being his whore. 'Get bloody well dressed. Your brother will be back for dinner, and I've squandered too much time lying in this filthy bed.' He pulled on his clothes and looked out from the low-set cottage window. 'This will be the last time I'll be coming for a while, as the mill needs my attention.'

'Ah, don't take on so. I was only jesting about your wife.' Betsy lay on her bed and watched as Joseph

251

smoothed back his long dark hair. 'You know you'll miss me.'

'I'll not miss you, Betsy, because you'll be in work, like every other one of my employees – unless you want to starve, like half this dale will, before this cotton famine is over.' He looked at his watch: twelve-thirty, dinner time at the mill. He had to make his escape now, before the other mill workers came back for their dinners. 'See you tomorrow, Betsy, eight o'clock, and don't forget that pay is only three-quarters at the moment.' He ran down the stairs and out of the door, slamming the garden gate behind him.

'The bloody cheek of the man. Him in her bed, and his wife on the doorstep handing out bread.' Gertie Potts shook her head and pulled back her net curtains. Just wait until her Stan came back for his dinner; he wouldn't believe his ears.

'I think our offering of bread went down well, Joseph. Did anyone say anything at the mill today?' Charlotte sat in the parlour across from her husband, watching him close his eyes in the flickering candlelight.

'Sorry, what did you say? I'm sorry, I'm so tired this evening. The worry and pressure of having so many to provide for are taking their toll on me, I'm afraid.' Joseph tried to look interested in the conversation his wife was attempting to make.

'Did the bread go down well?' asked Charlotte.

'Yes, indeed it did. Bert Bannister said I must congratulate you on such a splendid idea. He'd heard a girl called Sally, in carding, singing our praises, so it's definitely done us some good. What else have you done with your day?' He yawned.

'Go to bed, if you are tired. It makes a change for you to be at home. Are there no meetings, or friends to drink with, tonight?' From the small table at her side, Charlotte reached for the letter she had received earlier in the day.

'No, I'll be at home a lot more now, I fear. Everyone is safeguarding what money they have in their meagre purses. I heard the bank is wanting to foreclose on the cotton mill at Bell Busk. The Garforths, poor buggers, must be mortgaged to the hilt. The mere hint of trouble, and the bank soon withdraws any help.' Joseph gazed into the fire and watched the glowing embers, wishing for better days.

'I had a letter from Archie today. He sounds a bit brighter, but I don't think he will ever get over the death of Rosie. He sounds so broken-hearted. He's also offered to rear us a pig, to see us through the winter months, if you are interested. He'll need paying, of course. He says he's started lambing time, and that there are plenty of twins, so he's busy.' She passed Joseph the handwritten letter to read.

'Farming talk – do you think I'm interested in farming talk? No wonder I spend so much time in other company, until the early hours of the morning.' Joseph yawned. 'It's boring, talking of pigs and sheep. You really know how to keep a man enthralled. You and that darling Archie.' Joseph dismissed the letter and looked at his wife, who appeared blooming in the glowing firelight. Pregnancy suited her – apart from her stomach, which was growing larger by the day. 'Come to bed with me, come and make love to your husband,' he whispered into Charlotte's ear.

'Joseph, the baby!' she whispered back.

'I'll be careful. Come.' Joseph pulled on her out-stretched hand and urged her to join him. 'Just lie by my side, like we should. After all, we are man and wife.'

Charlotte smiled and followed her husband up the stairs. She was glad he was back in her arms. Perhaps the lack of money had made him realize what was precious to him. You could never buy love. Perhaps he knew that now.

19

By May and June the realization about just how bad things were going to be had finally sunk into the business people of Settle and all the districts involved in cotton in Yorkshire and Lancashire. The price of cotton, if it was accessible, trebled and the Union Yankee soldiers burned bales of it along the docksides of New Orleans.

'Damn those Union Yankees!' Joseph swore as he read the paper, before pacing back and forth in front of the bay window of Windfell. 'Damn the weather as well. Look at it: it's flaming June, and the weather is wretched. It poured down last night, the river is in full spate and I even had to get a man to open the lock gates this morning because the millpond was so high.'

'Joseph, please – the maid will hear you.' Charlotte leaned and pulled herself up by the fireplace.

'Aye, well, damn her as well, if she doesn't get here quickly with my drink.' He had no patience with anything. His life was not going as he had planned it and he was angry with the world.

'She's here.' Charlotte sighed. 'Thank you, Mazy. Is Yates feeling any better now?' she asked, as Mazy bobbed in recognition of her master's temper after placing his glass of port in front of him.

'Yes, ma'am, his fever is subsiding. Mrs Batty gave him a mustard plaster for his chest and he seems to be recovering.' Mazy shot a quick glance at Joseph as he took a long swig of his port, and then made good her retreat.

'There's bugger-all wrong with him. He's a soft lump, he wouldn't last a day at the mill. You pamper him too much, Charlotte, just like you pamper every-one too much. Folk only take advantage of you, if they think you are weak.'

'The poor man caught a chill, delivering the bread the other morning. He was only doing me a favour because he knew my back hurt, with carrying this one.' Charlotte rubbed her hand over her stomach and stood next to her husband. 'It won't be long now, Joseph. Dr Burrows says all looks well. I can't help but think of poor Rosie and her baby, and I pray that this one will be no problem when it comes into the world.'

Joseph looked Charlotte up and down. She was seven months pregnant and he was struggling to keep everything together at the mill. He'd never felt more trapped. To make matters worse, he'd heard that his sister had married her rich jeweller and was now quite well-to-do, living at Ingfield House on the outskirts of

Settle. The bitch! She'd always looked after herself before anyone else. 'Did I tell you there's a town-council meeting in Settle tonight? The Reverend Tiplady is going to be telling the great and the good, plus us mill owners, that we should all do more for the poor, especially the poor struggling mill workers.' Joseph tipped back the last mouthful of port and rang the side-bell for his glass to be refilled. 'The bloody hypocrite. He doesn't go hungry, he's often eating in the Talbot Arms.'

'Joseph, what is wrong with you tonight?' Charlotte walked steadily to her chair and watched as he summoned Mazy to refill his empty glass. 'Should you not attend such a meeting, just to portray our side of things?'

'What's wrong with me? Where do I start? How about our stock of cotton is going down quicker than I thought. I can only thank God that we weave as well. At least I can deploy some of the workforce there, and try and drag out what stock we have. Do you know raw cotton has gone up from ten cents a pound to one dollar eighty-nine? It's that scarce. But what fool is going to pay those prices? That is if it gets through the blockades.' He drank deeply again and looked out at the dark limestone outcrop known as Langcliffe Scar across the valley from Windfell Manor. Rain lashed against it. No matter what anyone said, he was in no mood to be amicable.

'But we are still here, Joseph, and there is always Crummock to fall back on. Surely the man you put in there is making money; he should be knee-deep in newborn lambs by now.' She looked at the positives, as her dark, negative husband leaned against the frame of the bay window.

'Crummock – don't make me laugh; you won't be able to see the bloody place for this low cloud. Wilson hasn't been in touch with me for days, and I haven't time to go up there and check things out. As for living there, the answer is: over my dead body. Now, if your father had left us his money, we would have been sitting pretty with nothing to worry about. I feel like closing the mill down and calling it a day.'

'Oh, Joseph, things will get better. We've the baby to look forward to, and your mood is only dark like the day. Things are worse down in Lancashire; the cotton mills in Manchester have been hit hard. At least Mr Todd had the decency to foretell you of the coming problems.'

Joseph sighed. 'You are right. Bugger it, I'll join old Tiplady and catch him filling his belly while I have a gill in the Talbot Arms. You don't mind, do you, my dear?' He turned and looked at Charlotte, who was yawning and looking tired as she sat listening to him complain. 'Don't wait up. I'll sleep in the spare bedroom – you look tired, my dear.'

'No, that's fine, you go and fight our corner. I must admit, my feet hurt and I'm tired this evening. You know if I can help, my dear, in any way, you've just to ask. Now go and enjoy your evening.' Charlotte smiled at her husband. This was the first night he had not slept with her for a month or two now, and she would welcome having the bed to herself.

'I'll see you in the morning, my dear. Although I might go to the mill early. I need to look at the accounts and see if I can scrape together enough funds for this white gold called cotton, which keeps everyone fed and housed.' Joseph yelled for Mazy to give him his cape and top hat.

'Do you need Jethro and the cab?' Mazy enquired.

'No, damn it, Mazy, I'll walk. A bit of rain never hurt anyone.' He patted his hat and stepped out with his silver-headed walking stick in his hand, kissing Charlotte on her cheek before leaving the house.

She watched out of the window as he strode out down the pebbled drive. His hand steadied his hat against the wind and rain, and his cape flapped in the gusts of strong wind. At least the prowling, growling man had left the house. Whatever state he came back in, the house was at peace for a short while. She yawned and stretched. Even though it would still be light for a while, she was going to have an early night, as she felt drained. Besides, if Joseph was going to have a night with the town council, it could be in the early hours when he returned, depending on the company he kept and the amount of drink he had. Without Yates, he'd have to get himself to bed and that would not be without noise.

'Mazy, can you tell Lily, please, that I'm going to bed.'

'Yes, ma'am, I'll go and get the bedpan to warm your bed.'

Charlotte looked out of the window once more. Her husband must be slightly mad, walking down to Settle in the wild weather battering the beech trees that lined the drive. If it blew out the demons that were blighting him, perhaps the walk would be a blessing. Anything was better than the dark mood that had possessed him all day, she thought, as she mounted the stairs up to bed.

Betsy Foster looked down into the swirling waters of the mill race and pulled her shawl over her head. Her stomach churned with the anticipation of Joseph arriving at any moment, as arranged earlier in the day. He'd promised to lie to his wife about his whereabouts and meet her as the mill clock struck eight, when she had pleaded with him to meet her out of sight of the prying eyes of her neighbours, with her important news. She looked across the yard and spied him striding out across the cobbles, head down and cape wrapped tightly around him for protection from the relentless rain. The phrase and speech she had rehearsed a hundred times flitted around her brain, making her tongue-tied as he stood in front of her, standing a matter of inches in front of her face.

'Well, what's so important that you have me coming down here on a godforsaken night like this? Don't tell me you want some money, because you'll be out of luck on that one.' Joseph tapped the silver-mounted cane next to his leg and waited for the pale-faced Betsy to reply.

'I don't want your money, not yet anyway.' Betsy swallowed hard.

'What do you mean "not yet"?' Joseph leaned near her, watching as her lips quivered with anticipation.

'I'm pregnant. I'm having your baby,' she spouted, as if it was a relief to expel the words that she had mouthed all day.

'My baby – I don't think so! It could belong to half the district, from what I hear. You are nothing but a slut who sleeps with anyone for money, so don't blame me for your misfortune.' Joseph walked along the edge of the millpond and turned just before reaching the sluice gate, as Betsy pulled on the edge of his cape.

'You know that's not true; you know I kept myself just for you. You loved me. You told me so. The baby's yours, and you know it. All my free time I've spent with you, and I've never so much looked at another fella.' Her shawl fell onto her shoulders, and the rain and tears from her eyes mingled as she begged Joseph not to be so cruel.

'Me, love you, when I've a wife at home and a baby that is mine on the way. You fantasize, woman. Now let me be, and get home to your hovel.' Joseph prised her hand from its grasp on his cloak and started to walk away.

'I'll tell that wife of yours. I'll tell her everything: how you abused me, how this baby is yours and that

261

you are certainly no gentleman,' Betsy screamed in desperation above the rush of the storm waters.

'You'll tell her nothing, nor will you go anywhere near my home. Do you hear?' Joseph turned quickly on his heels and grabbed her throat. He breathed heavily as he held her tightly against him. 'You say a word, bitch, and it'll be the worse for you.'

'I don't need to say anything. All the mill knows I'm your fancy, and all of Langcliffe Lock cottages. You made sure of that, with all your comings and goings.' Betsy looked him straight in the eyes as she gasped for breath.

Joseph let go of her quickly, leaving her shaking on the wet slate path above the gushing millrace. Then, with a mighty strike, he brought down the silver head of his walking stick onto her skull, knocking her senseless and throwing her into the gushing waters of the race. He watched as the swirling waters dragged Betsy's body down, the current pulling and tugging her towards the sluice gate, where her body floated upwards, her dead eyes looking up at him, accusing him of her fate, with her haunting gaze. Quickly Joseph went to the crank handle driving the cogs that opened the sluice gate letting the excess water down into the flooded River Ribble. He swore as his walking stick slipped from his grasp, falling into the murky depths of the millpond as he quickly turned the crank handle to let Betsy's body wash down into the mighty roaring river. He watched as the body of his lover disappeared on the foaming waters, hopefully never to be seen again. Or at least not until the river reached the sea or until her body was unrecognizable, battered and broken by the power of the river forces. Quickly he wound the sluice gate closed, straining against the force of the water and swearing with panic at the thought that he might be found at the site of his crime.

Once the gate was closed he made his way to the mill, unlocking the great door with trembling hands and making his way in the quickening dusk to his office two storeys up. He dared not light the gas lamp in his office, for fear of somebody wondering who was at Ferndale at such an hour. Instead he sat shaking at his desk, taking a bottle of whisky from out of his bottom drawer and pouring an extra-large portion in the crystal hand-cut tumbler that he had bought before hard times hit the mill. He looked around him. This was his empire – his empire of nothing at the moment – and he'd just committed murder. He could be hanged at the gallows. The judges would show no mercy, especially if they were to start delving into the supposed death of his first wife. He gulped his drink back and went to the mill's safe. He turned the combination lock and lifted the mill workers' weekly wages out of it. It wasn't much to escape on, as he counted the few paltry pounds that his employees depended upon, but it was better than losing his life. To hell with it: a new life called. He'd made it on less in the past, and he'd build a new life again elsewhere.

Joseph looked around Ferndale for the last time and breathed a sigh of relief. What had started out so well had become a burden. Good riddance – he was glad to leave it all behind.

'Yates, Yates, did you hear my husband returning last night?' Charlotte questioned the butler as he experienced an exceptional bout of coughing in the middle of the hallway. Bert Bannister had just left her in a state of shock, after informing her that Joseph had not been at the mill that morning.

'No, ma'am, I never heard a thing. I'm sorry, ma'am, but if he'd wanted me I wouldn't have heard. I'm afraid this cold has left me a bit deaf.' Yates wiped his nose and watched as Charlotte looked at him, flustered.

'Some of the master's things have gone missing, namely his shaving equipment from our bedroom. And I've just looked into his bedroom and his shirts are missing from the wardrobe,' she said.

'Perhaps they are in the laundry, ma'am. Have you asked Mazy?' Yates felt fuzzy-headed with his cold and didn't know why his mistress was in such a way this morning.

'That's not all, Yates. Mr Dawson's not been at the mill this morning, and his favourite horse is not in the stable.' Charlotte was nearly in tears, remembering the mood he had been in the previous evening.

'Oh, ma'am, I'm sure there's an explanation. Perhaps he's gone to see the Jacksons on business in Long Preston and forgotten to tell you.' Yates came quickly to his senses and felt sorry for Charlotte, as she held back the tears in front of him. 'I'll get Lily to make you a cup of tea and I'll bring it to you in the morning room.'

'I don't want tea, I want to know where my husband is. He wouldn't take his shirts, just to go to Long Preston.' Charlotte sobbed and made her way into the morning room, sitting down at Joseph's desk. She ran her hand over the highly polished surface, expecting the top to be locked as usual. To her surprise, when she pulled at the lid, it opened, allowing her to look into the contents of the highly guarded desk. She gasped as it revealed its darkest secrets. Inside, the contents told her everything she feared: the mill was in bother; bank documents confirmed that Joseph had borrowed more than he could repay; and his debts were suffocating him. Charlotte sat with the latest letter in her hand, stating that if they didn't have at least some of their lending repaid, the bank would have no option but to foreclose on Joseph's debt and declare him bankrupt. Her hand shook as she read the stern, no-nonsense letter.

Yates came in with the tea tray. 'I'll ask Jethro to ride to Long Preston, if you want, ma'am, and check if he is at the Jacksons. The lad won't mind; it's a grand day for a ride out. You can never make sense of this weather. It was like the middle of winter yesterday and now look at it: as bonny a day as I've ever seen.' He placed the tea tray down in front of Charlotte, watching her shake as she reread the letter in her hand.

'There's no need, Yates, Mr Dawson won't be coming back, I know that now.' Charlotte breathed in deeply.

'Sorry, ma'am, I don't understand?' The butler looked puzzled.

'He's left, Yates. Leaving us all in a right state of affairs. It seems all was not as it seemed. You might as well know that Mr Dawson is in trouble with the bank.' Charlotte gazed out of the window and watched as the sun streamed in through it, highlighting the spot where a silver statue once stood on top of the desk.

'Ma'am, what are you going to do? You and the baby?'

'At this moment, Yates, I don't rightly know. However, perhaps now it is time for me to learn how the mill works and fight to keep it open. I owe it to all those who work there. I'm perhaps in a good enough position to be able to sort his mess out, if he has decided to leave.' Charlotte sighed. 'Yates, I'd appreciate it if you kept this quiet, just until I have confirmation that I can somehow cover my husband's debts.'

Charlotte was angry with herself for not realizing that she was being conned these past few months. All Joseph had told her about his wealth was lies, belittling her farm and savings. Thank God her solicitor had got the measure of him, holding back on revealing at her father's funeral her true wealth, to make Joseph think she wasn't worth much. Wesley Booth had been a very wealthy man and had monies wisely invested, which were now hers to do with as she pleased, unbeknown to the missing Joseph.

'Of course, ma'am. But, ma'am, you are a woman

with a baby on the way.' Yates looked at Charlotte as she stared at the letter in her hand.

'Aye, I'm a woman. But when threatened, we are at our strongest, especially when our offspring's going to suffer. I'm glad he's gone, Yates. He was no husband – you know it, and I know it. I hope I never hear of him again.' She spoke softly and looked at Yates in a fixed gaze as she thought of the future; a future without a husband and with a failing business. Could she face the world and do what she had spoken of so strongly? Only time would tell.

Jethro stopped the trap at the top of the bridge that spanned the River Ribble at the beginning of the town of Settle, on the way to a meeting with the bank. Charlotte and he watched as the local police carried a body out of the river. The crowds gathered around, as the body of the young woman was carried up onto the river bank in the blaze of the hot summer sun. There was a murmur throughout the locals as they realized that it was the body of missing mill worker Betsy Foster.

'Help me down, Jethro.' Charlotte asked for the footman's hand as she struggled to alight from the trap.

'Don't go there, ma'am, you don't want to see her – she looks in a right state.' He looked at his mistress.

'She worked at the mill, Jethro. The least I can do is tell them her full name and offer to pay for a decent burial.' Charlotte stood next to the trap and waited until the officers struggled up the banking with Betsy's body, now covered by blankets, the crowd parting as the body went past.

'Officers, is it true: is that Betsy Foster from Langcliffe Lock cottages, who worked for my husband at Ferndale?' Charlotte asked the officer taking up the rear, as the body passed her to be put on a waiting cart.

'Aye, that's right, Miss – drowned herself, we think. It looks like she'd got herself in the family way. A shame she never thought of her brother, as he's all alone in the world now.' The officer wiped his brow and walked on behind the corpse.

A man in the crowd spat loudly at Charlotte's feet and the women whispered around her, looking with both hatred and pity in their eyes.

'Why are they looking at me like that, Jethro? I'd nothing to do with her death.' Charlotte looked at the angry crowd.

'No, ma'am, but they have to blame someone and, as you say, she worked at the mill. She was one of Mr Dawson's favourites, ma'am, if I'm not speaking out of turn and saying too much.' Jethro blushed.

'What do you mean, Jethro? What are you trying to tell me?' Charlotte watched as the crowd moved on with the cart carrying the poor wretch's body.

'I'm not saying, ma'am, it isn't for me to say. But folk talk.' The footman held out his hand and helped Charlotte back up onto the trap.

Charlotte sat putting two and two together, and watched as people bowed their heads in respect and then shot dark glances back at her seated in her trap:

the wife from the big house, whose husband had had his way with one of his workers and got the poor lass in bother, giving Betsy no option but to take her own life by throwing herself into the raging river. What else, for the Lord's sake, had her husband been doing behind her back? Now she realized that it had not been just work that kept her from having Joseph lying in her bed. He'd been lying in the arms of poor Betsy. What a fool she'd been!

'Take me home, Jethro. I'll undertake my business in the morning. I'll not be welcome in Settle or Langcliffe today.' Charlotte bowed her head.

'Yes, ma'am. Sorry, ma'am, I didn't mean to speak out of turn.' Jethro flicked the reins, getting the horses to walk on.

'It's better I know, Jethro. Even at your young age, you seem to know more than me.' Charlotte mastered a smile.

'Me mam says I know too much, ma'am.' Jethro grinned.

'You can never know too much, Jethro, believe me. I am beginning to realize that quickly.' She sighed.

Back at Windfell, Charlotte lay on her bed and thought about Betsy's bedraggled body being pulled from the river. She tossed back and forth, trying to come to terms with the thought that the man she loved had been going with one of his lowly mill workers. Why? Had she not been good enough for him? Had she not been there when he needed her? A mill girl, of all people. Joseph had preached of his own high morals, but he was no more than a common guttersnipe. A common guttersnipe whose baby she was carrying.

The police inspector looked at the body of poor Betsy and shook his head, as he covered her battered body with a blanket in the cold of the mortuary's four walls.

'What a waste of a life – all for a bit of "how's your father".' Inspector Proctor shook his head. 'You say her brother's been taken in by the neighbours, Sergeant Capstick?'

'Yes, sir, up at Langcliffe Lock cottages.'

'And she worked at Ferndale. Is it right that the owner there had an eye for her, or is that just gossip?' Percy Proctor stood with his hands behind his back and thought for a minute, before uncovering Betsy's head for another look at her face. 'You know, I don't like the look of this bash on her head – it's not in keeping with the rest of the marks on her body.' He ran his hand over her skull and felt the indent where Joseph had struck her, before covering her face once more.

'Aye, that's right, sir. The locals are full of it seemingly, and he was never away from her cottage. Her brother's called Johnny, and he is with Gertie Potts now. She can verify anything that's being said about Joseph Dawson visiting. The lad and one of our officers found an accounting book in her bedroom; she'd listed in it every time he'd visited her and how much he'd given her. Let's say the lad won't want for nowt: she made more lying on her back than she would if she had worked every day of her life at the mill. Not speaking ill of the dead, sir.'

'I think we'd better make a call on Mr Dawson, see what he has to say for himself. These toffs – I can't stand them taking advantage of young lasses. He's a lot to answer for, if the gossip's right.' Inspector Proctor spat and lingered at the doorway, before turning round for a second. 'There's something wrong here, Sergeant. She wouldn't have left her brother alone. From what I've heard, she worshipped the ground he walked on.'

'That she did, sir; would do anything for him,' Sergeant Capstick confirmed.

'Then why throw yourself in the river, when she could have got rid of the baby at any old crone's house? There's always somebody that'll help a young lass dispose of a baby she doesn't want. Legal or not.' Inspector Proctor shook his head. 'I think we'll find out more at Ferndale.'

Inspector Proctor sat on the couch in the morning room of Windfell and looked around at the elegant furnishings of the manor. Ferndale Mill, which he had just visited, was a stark place compared to the luxury of the Dawsons' home. Riches made on the backs of the poor – he couldn't stand it.

'They said in the mill that they'd not seen Mr Dawson for two days now, not since the day of the storm. Is that right, Mrs Dawson? Do you know where he's gone, and is he responsible for emptying the mill's

271

safe?' The inspector waited, pencil ready and his notebook open.

'I'm sorry, Inspector, I had no idea. I've been such a fool!' Charlotte cried into her handkerchief. 'He said he was going to the Talbot Arms to meet Settle town council to discuss the ongoing crisis with the cotton supply, and he just never came back. It wasn't until the next morning that I realized some of his belongings were missing, along with his favourite horse. Then Bert Bannister came and told me yesterday morning that the safe had been emptied and the workers' wages taken. It could only have been Joseph. He was the only one who knew the combination.'

She sobbed. She'd never known such days. The whole bank had gone quiet when she had entered, to plead for understanding until her husband returned. The bank manager had given her seven days for Joseph to return and put his account in order, before fore-closing on the mill. This had left Charlotte in a state of panic, while watching eyes had pierced through her back, and ears had twitched to hear the business she was doing, and tongues wagged out of earshot.

'I'm sorry, ma'am, but I have to ask. Do you think your husband was having an affair with Betsy Foster?' Sometimes the inspector hated his job; it was obvious there were more people than just poor Johnny Foster left bereft in this affair. Charlotte Dawson and her unborn baby had been left high and dry, and the death of Betsy was beginning to look more suspicious by the minute.

'I believe he was, sir. He's never spoken of it, but I believe it is common knowledge among the servants and those employed at the mill. I knew nothing of it, until I saw poor Betsy being carried out of the river by your good sergeant here and his colleagues. Do you think she was carrying his child?' Charlotte held her breath as she watched Sergeant Capstick, who sat fidgeting in an armchair across from her.

'It's hard to say at this point, but it does look likely. I'm sorry, Mrs Dawson, you must be tired in your condition, and I'm upsetting you.' Percy Proctor had done a little research about Charlotte Dawson, the local lass made good, and hated the questions he was having to ask. 'Capstick and I will walk down to Langcliffe Locks and talk to the deceased's brother, see what he knows.' The inspector rose from his chair and urged Sergeant Capstick to join him.

'She's got a brother?' Charlotte asked.

'Aye, ma'am, the neighbour has taken him in, I believe. Betsy and Johnny have no parents, from what we can gather. She came from Skipton, after losing them both to cholera. What I can't understand is why she would leave her brother to fend for himself. It'll be the workhouse at Giggleswick for him, if nobody wants him.' Inspector Proctor took a final look around the stately room. 'Happen somebody will take pity on him – you can but hope. Thank you for your time, ma'am.'

'Thank you, Inspector. Please keep me informed, and if there is anything I can do for Betsy's brother, I will do it. After all, it sounds as if he is without any

273

family, thanks to my husband.' She stood up and caught her breath as the baby moved inside her.

'You take care of yourself first, ma'am. There's a word for your husband, but I'm too much of a gent to say it. I'll let you know of any developments.'

Charlotte stood at the same window that she had watched Joseph from and cried as the two policemen left the manor. Everything in her life was wrong: her husband had left her, the baby was nearly due, the mill was in the hands of an overseer, and the workers hated her. She had no idea how she was going to manage, but surely things could get no worse.

Percy Proctor stood in the kitchen of number two Langcliffe Lock cottages, making notes.

'He was never away, Officer. You don't have to look very far to find out who the father to the baby was. He paid her more to be his floozy than he did half his workers in the mill. Betsy changed from such a sweet lass to a hard-nosed cow. God have mercy on her soul and forgive me for saying that, but it's true.' Gertie Potts looked out into the garden, where she had sent Johnny to help her Stan weed the veg patch while she was interviewed by Inspector Proctor.

'And the lad, did he know? Where was he, when all these visits were going on?' The inspector watched the young lad helping the ageing mill worker in his garden, and thought how easy and at home they looked in one another's company.

'He knew nowt. He's virtually lived with us since all

this nonsense started; or Joseph Dawson visited when he was at school. Poor little bugger. The tears I've had on my shoulder this last day or two, he's broken-hearted.' Gertie breathed in deeply and sighed.

'Are you willing for him to stop with you a bit longer, or do you want me to make provision for him in the workhouse at Giggleswick?' Proctor looked out and watched as the two picked a lettuce for use in the kitchen, his mind going back to how he had helped his father garden, back when he was a lad.

'Aye, I couldn't do that to the lad – he loves my Bert. Neither of us are getting any younger, and he'll help us in our old age. We've no bairns of our own; we never seemed to be blessed with them.' Gertie stood behind the inspector and watched as the two planted new seeds in an already-raked patch of the garden, eventually to replace the cut lettuce.

'You'll happen be able to get some help with his keep from parish funds – he's a worthy case.' Inspector Proctor smiled at the old woman with a kind heart.

'We are not dependent on charity at this house. We'll bring him up like our own, and he'll not go hungry.' Gertie folded her arms, slightly offended at the suggestion that they might need an offering of charity.

The atmosphere was broken when an out-of-breath Sergeant Capstick came briskly in through the front door.

'Inspector, come quickly. There's something you need to see down by the millpond.' He caught his breath and then backtracked the way he had come, followed by the inspector.

'It's there – look! The water has gone down, with the warm weather and the mill using it. One of the mill workers noticed it on his way to work this morning and nearly pulled it out, and then he noticed the shawl caught in the sluice gate and recognized it as Betsy's. They thought it better not to pick it up, for want of being accused of anything that went on here.' Sergeant Capstick pointed down to the side of the millpond at the shadowy sight of Joseph's silver-topped cane, and then at the checked plaid of Betsy's shawl, caught in the sluice gates.

'Well, fish it out for me, man.' Proctor watched as his sergeant lay on his stomach with his sleeves rolled up, as he pulled the cane from the murky pond's depths. 'Now, this alters everything. This looks like a very well-to-do gentleman's cane. I'd say it probably belonged to Mr Dawson. If we put that with Betsy's shawl, it probably places them in the same place at the same time. What are the odds on this fancy silver handle matching the indent on Betsy's skull, Capstick? If I were a betting man, I'd say the odds were in my favour.' The inspector fingered the fine cane. This was now murder, not suicide, and he was going to get that posh bastard.

20

'Now, Miss Charlotte, how about you tell me why you are really here? You forget that I've known you since the day you were born, and I know this polite conversation and flirting around things is leading up to something more serious.' Lucy Cranston sat back in the Windsor chair in her small parlour and stirred her tea, waiting for Charlotte to tell her what was on her mind.

'Oh, Lucy, I just don't know where to start. My life's in turmoil. I wish I'd never set eyes on Joseph Dawson.' She broke down and, between sobs, told Lucy of the passing days and what had unfolded since Joseph's disappearance.

'Now, lass, don't take on so. I feel so bad, but I knew that bugger was a wrong 'un. Your father did too, towards the end of his life, but he said nowt. He just hoped he was wrong. Now, what are we to do? Between you and our Archie, there's been a lot of heartache, and

I don't know which way to turn.' Lucy puffed and then put her arm around the shaking Charlotte. 'Now give over, you'll only upset the baby with all this crying, and we've lost one. This one's got to sit tight until its time.'

Charlotte sighed and dried her eyes with her handkerchief. 'I just wondered, Lucy. Could you help by getting the bank off my back and lend me some of my father's money, to pay the workers this week? I wouldn't ask, but Joseph has left me penniless and I can't see all them workers out of work, for they depend on the mill.' She held her breath and watched as Lucy thought about it.

'Aye, Charlotte, it's a lot to ask. I was thinking of setting up Archie with his own farm. But I know your father would have left you the bulk of his money, if you hadn't have married that bloody man.' Lucy sighed and looked at the lass who was nearly begging her for support.

Charlotte dropped her head and whimpered, 'I'm sorry, I shouldn't have asked, but I'm desperate.'

'Well, as I said, it should rightfully have been yours. I'll give you half of what he left me. That should get you back in the good books of the bank and keep your workers fed. On the understanding, mind, that you pay me back when you can, and I expect a bit of interest.' Lucy sighed again; she could feel her heart fluttering, with the stress of losing her nest egg from under her bed. The nest egg that the bank had not wanted to give her in the first place, and now it was going back to them.

'Oh, Lucy, how can I ever thank you? You'll not be sorry, I promise you.' Charlotte sobbed and hugged the woman she loved.

'Aye, well, if things had been different, you could have been my daughter. And I loved your father, and it's what he would have wanted me to do. Brass doesn't mean a lot to me. It's nice, but I'd rather see you and that baby happy.'

'You'll not regret it, I promise.' Charlotte flopped in her chair and tried to control her sobs.

'Now give over, lass. That's your money worries sorted, but what about that man of yours? Where's he gone, the bastard?' Lucy watched as a cloud crossed Charlotte's face.

'I don't know, but I never want to see him again. I hope my baby never knows about its father. I'm ashamed. I've been conned into believing he was a good man.' Charlotte lifted her head and spoke the words that she'd been thinking ever since Joseph vanished.

Their conversation was halted by a knock at the door.

'My Lord, I don't have visitors for days, then everyone's knocking at my door.' Lucy rose from her chair and went to answer the fervent banging. She bustled back in, after answering the caller. 'Charlotte, come quickly – it's Arthur from Crummock. He recognized Jethro and the trap waiting outside. He thinks there's something wrong with the tenant at Crummock, and he wants someone to go there and see what's to do. He asked for Mr Dawson, not knowing your news.'

'I don't believe it! I've just solved one problem, then another raises its head.' Charlotte went to the door and Mrs Cranston stood behind her, as Arthur told her of his concerns.

'He's not answered the door for two days now and the window shutters are still closed. I've left the milk for the house on the back step for two days, but it's not been touched.' Arthur rubbed his head with his cap. 'Nothing would surprise me, though. I don't know who he is, but he's not a farmer, that is for sure. He's not lifted a hand since he was put in Crummock.' Arthur looked worried and pale.

'Don't worry, Arthur. I'll come back up to Crummock with you and Jethro and get to the bottom of Mr Wilson's disappearance. Perhaps he's ill?' Charlotte could tell that the farm lad was really concerned about the tenant, and this would give her a chance to meet him.

'Thank you, ma'am, I just didn't know what to do. I've been rushed off my feet ever since your poor father died. It's lambing time and I've had no help, and I need to get the meadows spread with muck. I can't do everything,' Arthur stressed, then went and mounted his horse.

'Aye, lass, you'd better go and see what's up. Call on your way back home, and I'll give you what you need to see you right. Sounds like another mess your man's left you.' Lucy hugged Charlotte as she lifted her skirts and climbed into her trap. What was she going to find at Crummock? God only knew!

All the doors at Crummock were locked and bolted and the window shutters of the kitchen were still closed, as Arthur had correctly informed Charlotte.

'Well, there's nothing else we can do but break in. Something is wrong. Either Mr Wilson is too ill to come to the door or he's left and not told anyone.' Charlotte stood looking in through the dining-room window and gasped quietly at the state of the room. 'He's certainly not looked after my old home, by the look of this room. Arthur, break the windowpane here, then put your hand in to lift the latch on this window. You should be able to climb in then.'

'Stand back, ma'am.' He picked up a stone from the garden wall and smashed the window, before putting his hand through to open the window and climb in. 'I'll go through the house and open the back door.' Arthur ran through the rooms and met Charlotte and Jethro at the back door, hesitating at what he found in the kitchen.

'I don't think you should go into the kitchen, ma'am. It's not a pleasant sight.' Arthur tried to stop Charlotte from entering the house.

'Nonsense, Arthur. I'll not be that upset that he's left the house in a state.' Charlotte pushed past him, angry that her old home was in such a mess.

'But, ma'am!'

It was too late.

Charlotte stopped in her tracks. Lying on the floor of the kitchen, in a pool of blood, lay the body of Roger Wilson. 'Is he dead?' she gasped.

Arthur opened the window shutters to bathe the body in daylight.

'I'd say well and truly dead.' Jethro bent over the body and pulled an empty port bottle from his hand. 'Looks like he drunk himself to oblivion, then fell and cracked his head.'

'That's all he ever did – drink. He had me running back and forth to The Gamecock like an idiot,' Arthur groaned.

'Well, you'll not be going there again. But, Arthur, can you go and get the doctor and explain the situation we are in here. We can't leave his body here for another minute.'

Charlotte looked at the corpse of Roger Wilson. She could tell he was one of Joseph's friends from Accrington; he was certainly no farmer, dressed like the dandy he was. Just how much more aggravation was her life going to have, before that scourge Joseph Dawson was caught and brought to trial for all his sins? No sooner had she solved one problem than another arose. What would happen now to her beloved Crummock?

Charlotte sat back and sighed. With the help of Lucy's money she'd finally cleared the backlog of outstanding bills, including the one from before Christmas when she had indulgently treated herself to the fur muff, gloves and hat. She sighed again. At least she was free of debt, and the bank knew that she would honour any commitments outstanding on Ferndale Mill. She could now hold her head up high, knowing that she owed nothing to no man. The death of Betsy Foster was another matter, however, for folk would never forget that. She leaned back and played with her pen. What was the way forward? She'd to keep the mill going – she couldn't live with herself if all those people were without wages and food on the table – but how?

Her thoughts returned to the day when Charles Walker had read her father's edited will to her and Joseph, and how touchy Joseph had been when Walker had mentioned new mill owner Lorenzo Christie knowing that the cotton industry was about to hit worrying times. Hmm . . . Perhaps she should make herself known to the hard-headed businessman; it couldn't hurt. She was a pregnant woman whose husband had just left her and a failing business – surely he'd show her some sympathy? Perhaps she could even play the sympathy card and see what Mr Christie thought of a woman running a cotton mill. Yes, that's what she would do. She'd make an appointment with Lorenzo Christie and see how the land lay.

Lorenzo sat back in his chair, looked at the bonny blonde woman in front of him, and puffed on his cigar.

'I thank you for giving me this time to talk to you. I realize you are extremely busy and that time is precious.' Charlotte looked across at the middle-aged dark-haired man, who seemed to be listening to her. 'I just wanted to introduce myself, as we are both in the same business and are only based a few miles from one another.'

'A woman in business – now that's a novelty. But then, from what I understand, you'd not much say in it.' Lorenzo flicked the ash from the end of his cigar and watched the colour rise in his visitor's face.

'No. As you say, Mr Christie, I don't have much choice. However, I do care about my husband's employees and I'm damned if I'm going to let them down.' She knew the gossip of her husband's deeds was spreading like a disease throughout the area and she wasn't about to be tarred with the same brush.

Lorenzo smiled. He liked a woman with fight and he could tell that, despite her condition, Mrs Dawson was a woman who could hold her own ground. 'Your husband cared a bit too much for a certain one of them, from what I hear. So much that his neck is in jeopardy, from what the gossips say.'

'I can't deny it. To be honest, Mr Christie, I hope he hangs. He's not done right by me, this baby I'm carrying or, indeed, anyone he's touched. I only wish my eyes had been opened to him before I married him, else I wouldn't be in this position.' Charlotte could feel her temper rising, but also that tears weren't far from falling.

'Aye and, like the fool I am, he bought and started a cotton mill at the worst possible time. Still, he had the foresight to see – as I had – the prospects of a good business, if we can ride out this upset in the Americas.

If you've enough brass, you'll make it and, like me, you'll keep the bellies of some of these locals fed. They had bleak enough times until we opened these mills. I remember walking around Langcliffe only a few months ago and the cobbles were green with grass growing amongst them, and the cottages empty. Now there's families in every one, and the cobbles are weeded, with bairns playing on them.'

'That is how I think, Mr Christie. I have more than a hundred and fifty souls working for me, and I can't let them down. My husband has done enough damage, and I don't want to see them thrown out of their homes, with no food on the table.' Charlotte looked down at her hands and fidgeted with her gloves.

'Have you enough raw cotton to keep your place going?' Lorenzo looked at the young woman, who had more spine and morals than her husband ever had.

'We have at the moment, but I don't know where to get ongoing quantities, to keep the mill running. Either I secure that or close down now, and my heart will not let me do that.' She let a tear roll down her cheek, hoping to tug on Lorenzo Christie's heart-strings.

'Well, happen you are best selling up. I'd offer to buy Ferndale from you, but it would only be at a low price. After all, a cotton mill without cotton is worth bugger-all. My lad Hector has just bought Bridge End at Settle, so I've enough outlay at the moment, especially in these troubled times.'

'I don't want to sell. I want to learn to run the mill. Bert Bannister is acting as manager at the moment, and

285

I'm to do the books. I'm good with figures – better than my husband was anyway.' Charlotte looked up at the smoke-shrouded businessman and decided to ask what she had come for. 'If you could give me some guidance on how to import raw cotton, and where to go in these troubled times, I'd be grateful. My solicitor, Charles Walker, talks highly of you and says that you are a very knowledgeable man.' She smiled and looked as the man leaned back and pondered on what she had asked.

'I tell you what, Mrs Dawson. If you can put some cash up front, Hector and I have a cargo of cotton hopefully outrunning the blockade on the Atlantic seaboard as we speak. Give me one-third of the cargo's price and one-third of it can be yours, on the understanding that if you can't make Ferndale profitable, I get first refusal.' Lorenzo stubbed out his cigar in the small brass ashtray on his leather-topped desk and waited.

'It's a deal, Mr Christie. I can't express how grateful I am for your offer. If we all pull together, we might just survive.' Charlotte rose from her chair and held her hand out to be shaken, smiling as Lorenzo was taken aback by a woman offering her hand over striking a deal. 'My father was a farmer, Mr Christie. He always shook hands on business, and he never backed down on his promises.'

'Tha's a different kettle of fish from your husband. I could never take to him. He was a flash devil – all talk, at the local business meetings.' Lorenzo shook her hand

and showed her to the door. 'You mind those steps, lady. You are carrying a precious load and you've had enough trauma in your life lately.' He watched as Charlotte carefully climbed down the stone steps from his office in High Mill to the warehouse floor below. He turned and went back into his office, with a satisfying feeling within him. Whatever happened, he was a winner: if she paid, it would help him with a full cargo of cotton that he hadn't really wanted; and if she didn't, he'd have first refusal on the mill. The cotton industry was his business, and hopefully he could ride out the impending storm from the Americas.

Charlotte looked at the angry crowd gathered in the mill yard and took courage as she stood on the loading-bay steps to talk to them.

'I know about the terrible thing that my husband is being accused of and, like you, I don't know if it's true or not. But I wasn't part of it, in any way. I'm as shocked and horrified as the rest of you.'

She stopped for a second and gulped for breath as someone shouted, 'Bastard!' at the top of his voice from within the crowd.

'However, you all need your wages and I, as well as you, need the mill to continue. From today I am putting Bert Bannister in charge, and I will be attending the mill every day to learn as much as I can and to run the finances. What I don't know, I promise you I will learn.'

'Tha's having a baby – what can you do? Tha's a

287

woman,' shouted the same man from the crowd, pointing out something that was obvious to everyone.

'I can run it better than my husband, and I will make sure you are all fed and paid, and your women not harassed. I've already joined forces with Lorenzo Christie, and we have paid for a new supply of cotton to get through the blockades that are currently in place. What I can't promise is to continue the daily supply of free bread. If I keep you all in work, I won't have time to help with that. But you'd be keeping your jobs. Now, are you working for me or not?'

She stood defiantly on the mill steps and listened to the surprised murmur that ran through the crowd. She'd bargained that the deal she had made with Lorenzo Christie at High Mill would win her workers back, even though it had depleted her funds badly, along with negotiating payments to the bank, to keep Ferndale in her ownership. She had hated going cap-in-hand to the clever old mill owner, who was known for his hard business head, but both of them were in the same boat and needed cotton at a reasonable price. So she had taken a chance on Christie, hoping that he'd take pity on a weak, feeble woman, and had made it sound as if she didn't know the first thing about finances. She knew he wanted to get his hands on Ferndale and could see the look in his eye as she told him of her plight, thinking that eventually the mill would fold and then he would be first in line with a low offer. *Wheels within wheels*, she thought, as she waited for an answer from her workers. She could play games as well as any man.

'Well, are you going to do a day's work or not? Or do I close the mill and evict all those in the cottages? Which helps no man or woman.' She looked around the murmuring crowd.

'Come on, you bloody lot. Things are different, now that bastard Dawson isn't in charge. No disrespect, ma'am.' Bannister doffed his cap at Charlotte. 'Mrs Dawson here wants you to work, and she'll be fair. She paid your wages out of her own pocket last week, if you did but know it, because he had pinched them. She's not like her bastard husband – she's a good woman.' Bert went to the warehouse doors and opened them. 'Not working doesn't bring Betsy back, it just gives you hungry bellies. And we all know what we are doing, so let's get on with it.'

Charlotte watched as, one by one, the workers turned to one another and then wandered through the mill doors, still discussing whether they were doing the right thing. She climbed down from the mill steps, her legs shaking like jelly. She was thankful that the situation hadn't turned nasty, which it could have done, in view of Betsy's death.

'Thank you, Bert, I couldn't have done that on my own.' Charlotte patted her new manager's hand and smiled.

'They are a good lot. They just need a bit of coaxing and a bit of stick. They are a little like sheep really.' Bert grinned, knowing that Charlotte could relate to farming analogies. 'Besides, it makes no difference to them who owns the mill; they just want their supper on the

289

table and a roof over their heads. They'll not forget about Betsy, though. Have the police found Mr Dawson yet? When they do, they'll hang him, you know.'

'No, I haven't heard anything. I think they are to visit the Talbot Arms for some reason; and Dora Dodgson, who used to be the housekeeper at Windfell. But they've not said anything to me. And then of course I had to tell the police about the death of Roger Wilson, although they don't think he has anything to do with Joseph's disappearance. He was seemingly hiding from the law in Accrington. It tells you everything about my husband's past life and his associates.' Charlotte sighed.

'You look tired. Go home – I'll look after this lot today. Come down tomorrow and we will go through everything together.' Bert turned and yelled at the carter for striking a horse that was playing up in its traces, stamping his authority on the situation straight away.

'Thank you, Bert, we'll do it together. This mill will make it through the next few months, of that I'm sure.' Charlotte smiled.

'Yes, it will indeed, ma'am, because we are going to show that bastard husband of yours. I never did like him.'

'No. It would seem that even my father had doubts about him towards the end of his life.'

'Aye, well, we are all wiser with hindsight. Go and get yourself home; we'll be fine here. There's folk down in Lancashire with no jobs. This lot are not daft. They know which side their bread's buttered. They'll not let you down, now you've shown them you are committed.' Bert turned to enter the mill.

'Thank you, Bert. I'm beholden to you.' She smiled.

'Just you look after that bairn – we'll need him or her to help run this place.' Bert grinned.

'I will. I'm going to have a lie-down as soon as I'm home.' Charlotte picked up her skirts and accepted Jethro's hand into the cart's front seat. 'Home, Jethro. My job is done here today.'

Percy Proctor talked to the landlord of the Talbot Arms over a gill of one of his finest ales and asked him when he had last seen Joseph Dawson.

'Nay, I've not seen him for a month or two, or even longer, now I think about it. It's like all them in business at the moment – they are keeping their heads low, while the ones that can't afford it turn to drink, 'cause there's nowt else for them to do. It makes no sense, but that's life for you.' The landlord hung up his clean tankards around the bar and then leaned over close to Percy and looked him in the eye, breath from his rotting teeth making Percy stand back from the offensive aroma.

'Did he kill that lass then? The posh bastard! I hope they hang him. Taking advantage of that poor lass. He always did think himself summat, with his posh bloody suits and his swaggering ways.' He leaned on the bar and waited for an answer.

'Looks that way. He seems to be our man, but that's

all I'm saying.' Percy swiftly drank the last few dregs of his gill and placed his bowler hat back on his head.

'It's always his sort. They make themselves out to be summat they aren't. The fellow that came from Accrington said Joseph Dawson was nowt, when he came asking for him way before Christmas. And by God he was right.'

'Which fella? Why didn't you mention this before?' Percy stopped in his tracks.

'A little fella. Came one afternoon and asked if Dawson drank here, and if I knew him. In his own words, he said, "Does that useless bag of shit, Joseph Dawson, drink here?" He threw me for a minute, and then I realized who he was talking about. It was the Lancie accent that made me think who he was after, for they both had the same twang.' The landlord leaned on his bar and waited for a response.

'And what happened after that?' Percy asked.

'I never saw him again. For all I know, he went back to Lancashire. I never thought about it again until now. And for the following day or two I was down at Lancaster, on business buying my ales, so I don't know if he came back in or not. What's that got to do with owt, anyway?'

'Probably nothing. But I'd like to know who he was, because he obviously wasn't a fan of Dawson's.' Percy put an extra sixpence on the bar. 'If you can think of anything, just let me know.'

'Aye, I will. Don't worry, sir, I'll tell you.' The landlord quickly slipped the sixpence in his trouser pocket as Percy made his way out of the Talbot's doorway.

'Psssh! Sir, sir, I can tell you summat.'

The spit lad from the Talbot Arms appeared from the cellar doorway, standing on the cobbled street shoeless and filthy, beckoning with his hands and obviously wanting to give the inspector some information.

'What, lad, what do you want to tell me?' Percy took him to one side of the busy street and looked at the thin waif. 'Tell me what you know and I'll give you thruppence.' He fumbled in his pocket and produced threepence, which he held in front of the lad's wide eyes.

'The posh fella from up at the mill had the other fella by the scruff of the neck. They were shouting and arguing, on the night they met up in the Talbot. The little fella threatened to tell everything about his wife, if he didn't give him some brass. I heard him whisper "thirty guineas", and then Mr Dawson told him to crawl back to Accrington and leave him alone. I think he called him Simmons or Simon, or something like that!' The spit boy concentrated on the threepence that still shone in front of him.

'Anything else, boy, think! Any more names?' Percy played with the coin, enticing more words from the youngster's mouth.

'Um, he said, "How's your sister?" and that he knew her to be with Mr Dawson.' The lad gazed at the coin. 'That's all I heard, and then the little man went.'

293

'Mmm. Well, that's good. I've got a name and a town. You were worth your thruppence, lad.' Percy ruffled the urchin's hair and thrust the coin in his hand. 'If you think of owt else, you let me know.'

'Yes, sir. I will, sir.' The lad grinned and then ran barefoot back into the inn.

Hmm . . . Accrington, Simmons and a sister. A few things to follow up, but he'd get the bastard yet.

21

'Oh, Lottie! I don't know who's the worse off. What a mess!' Archie sat in the parlour of Windfell and looked across at Charlotte, who was crying on the plush sofa across from him. 'I don't know what I can do for you.'

'You can't do anything. There's nothing anybody can do. Inspector Proctor is trying to track down Joseph now. He even came here yesterday to ask about Dora Dodgson, and what I knew about her. I don't know what she's got to do with all this. And Crummock is standing empty, with Arthur holding the fort, because until Joseph shows his face, there's nothing I can do with it. Anyway, enough of my worries. How is Daniel? Growing up quickly, I bet?' Charlotte sniffed and looked across at her best friend.

'He's driving Rosie's parents mad. They do love him, but it's such a small place that we live in and Rosie's father blames me for her death, which doesn't help. How are you feeling? You will take care, won't you?'

Archie put his teacup and saucer down and looked across at a worried Charlotte. He remembered the time when Rosie was heavily pregnant, just as Lottie was now, and the memories of that stricken day when he lost her flooded back to him.

'I'm fine. Not too long to go now. Dr Burrows says everything looks normal, and that he will be with me as soon as I need him, and I'm not to worry. It's just that all this with Joseph . . . I don't know if I can cope.' She looked across at Archie and started to sob again.

Archie jumped up from his seat and sat down next to her, placing his arm around her quivering body. 'Don't cry, Lottie. I know I'm not much good, but I'm here: you can count on me. I'll do whatever you want; you've always been there for me, through thick and thin. I've not got a penny to my name, but my heart's true.' Archie squeezed her tightly.

'Money's not everything. Look at us – both married, and our young with just one parent. Mine will never even see its father, unless Joseph returns like a bad penny, and he's hardly going to do that, with the hangman's noose waiting.' Charlotte sobbed and looked into Archie's eyes.

'Nay, he'll not land back. He's a bad man, Lottie, and you can do without him. The things I've heard about him would make your flesh crawl. Settle's full of gossip. I try not to listen, but you can't help it. I knew that you were married to a bastard, but there was nothing I could do. You were his, and Rosie was mine, and we'd both made our own decisions, no matter how wrong we both were.' He held Charlotte tight.

'Just what are the gossips saying? Is it so bad?' She wiped her eyes and looked at Archie.

'Aye, it is, lass. Nobody's saying a bad word about you, though. They know that you are from good stock and are trying your best to hold everything together. But if they could get hold of Joseph, that's a different matter. He'd be minus two of his assets, straight away. Archie looked at Charlotte's tear-stained face and watched her eyes brim with tears again, and decided not to say much more about local feeling towards her husband.

'I didn't know anything at all about the man I married – or should I say "the monster" I married. I'm just sorry, Archie, that I didn't realize how I felt about you, and Joseph turned my head with his flash ways.' Charlotte ran her hand down the ruff of Archie's shirt and felt a flutter in her heart as she looked into his blue eyes.

'Charlotte, don't. You are still married and I'm still missing Rosie – it isn't right. It's only three months since I buried her.' Archie had missed Charlotte's sweet kisses and winning smiles. He'd made a mistake in marrying Rosie, but he'd grown to love her, and now his heart was still tender from the loss of their baby.

'I'm sorry. I didn't mean to offend, and you are right.' Charlotte sat up straight. 'Of course you must go back to your home at Mewith and, once my baby is born, I'll be busy running the mill. The civil war in America can't go on forever. Besides, I've a delivery of

cotton due any day, which will get us through this year.
I can manage without a man in my life.' Charlotte felt
rejected by both Archie and Joseph, but wasn't going to
look vulnerable and lost; that had got her nowhere in
the past. 'I'm fine. Sorry, Archie. You are a true friend,
stopping me from making a fool of myself. I shouldn't
have put you in that position.'

'It was a nice position to be in, Charlotte, but too
early for both of us. Let us see what comes next, before jumping in with both feet.' He bent over and
kissed Charlotte on her brow, before rising and putting
his cap on. 'I'd better get back, before that lad of mine
has driven everyone mad. Besides, I need to tend to my
sheep before nightfall.'

'Thank you, Archie, thank you for being a good
friend.' Charlotte clung to his hand.

'I'm only a few miles away, don't you forget. And if
you need me, you send someone to get me.' He smiled
and let go of her hand before walking out of the parlour. Poor Charlotte. She was more alone than he would
ever be. He only hoped that her baby would arrive
safely.

Archie sat behind the drystone wall and looked down
upon the flock grazing contentedly in the pasture
below. The sun was slowly setting, but its warmth
could still be felt in the limestone rocks at his back, and
in the last lingering rays that warmed his face. He
breathed in and thought about Charlotte. She'd looked
unwell, and for once she had not been playing games

with him, like she had before she married. He couldn't help but think that life had dealt them both a hard hand, but at least he wouldn't be remembered for marrying a murderer. Poor Charlotte! He had thought she was going to kiss him, when she leaned over and fingered the ruff on his shirt, which would have been wrong for both of them.

'Aye up, lass.' Archie patted his sheepdog's head as she nudged his leg, impatiently wanting to move on to the next field and view the stock with her master. She panted with her mouth open in the heat, and stared faithfully into his eyes with a look of adoration for her young shepherd. 'I know, lass, you are wanting to be off. But bide with me a bit longer while I take in the day. You don't get many evenings like this.'

Archie looked around him: the cotton grass was in full bloom on the rough fell land and the white feathery heads flittered in the slight evening breeze. Above him skylarks sang and the smell of peat filled his nostrils.

'Aye, lass, I wish my Rosie was still with me. She'd know what to do for Lottie. She's in a bit of a mess. And I don't know what to do for her, except make the best of what I've got.' The dog nudged his leg again and barked sharply. 'Alright, alright, you win. Let's be away. I'll have to see that baby of mine before his bed anyway, but nowt beats a grand evening like this, with nobbut myself and thee for company.' Archie leaned on his crook and laughed as the dog barked and rushed back and forth around his legs. 'Alright, alright, I'm coming. I think I'm half-simple anyway, talking to a bloody dog. Folk have been locked up for less.'

He had a final look around him, across the wide valley and over the outstretched fields and fells towards the sea, which was just visible in the distance. No fancy manor or big house could outdo the vista at his feet. Lottie should have stayed at home and married him, and then everything would have been fine. 'I don't know, lass, do I want to get caught up with Lottie again?' He stomped his stick down into the sphagnum moss and looked down at his boots. 'We'll see, eh? Let's just take it steady.'

Charlotte lay in her bed and thought about Archie, her childhood sweetheart. She should have replied with her love for him, the morning of her grandfather's death, when Archie had declared his love for her. She wouldn't have had all this heartache and worry. She looked around her plush bedroom and rubbed her extended stomach. How she hated being pregnant, feeling huge and cumbersome. Thank heavens her time was nearly up, for she had so much to sort out and do. None of which anybody would take seriously, with a baby yet to be born. *Damn Joseph Dawson, let his soul burn in hell*, she thought, as she closed her eyes and tried to sleep.

22

'Push, Charlotte, we are nearly there.' Dr Burrows stood by the edge of the bed and watched as the off-spring of the most talked-about local murderer was born. Beside him was Mrs Briggs, a woman well known for her skill at bringing babies in the district safely into the world. She was issuing instructions to the straining woman.

'There now, just look what we've got. A finer baby girl I've yet to see.' Josephine Briggs quickly wrapped the squawking bundle in a blanket and placed her in Charlotte's arms, after Dr Burrows had supervised the cutting of the cord.

'There was no reason for me to be present at this birth. Mrs Briggs managed well, and I knew it was a perfect pregnancy. You have a beautiful baby girl, Charlotte. You must be proud of her.' Dr Burrows stood back and closed his bag, looking at mother and daughter over the edge of his spectacles.

Charlotte looked down on the dark-haired, red and wrinkly squirming baby who had come into her life that morning, after a night disturbed with birthing pains.

'I don't know. I'm so tired. Nobody told me how much it would hurt, and how long it would take.' Charlotte looked at Mrs Briggs, who held her hands out for the newborn.

'It took no time at all. Believe me, I've known some women go into labour for days, so you were lucky. Now give her to me and we'll give the lil' thing a quick wash, and then I'll see to you, once you've lost your afterbirth.' Mrs Briggs lifted the newborn from Charlotte and carefully unwrapped her, slowly lowering her into the basin of warm water on the marble washstand next to the bed. She carefully washed the birth membrane off the head of the baby, who smiled as she clenched her fingers and toes in reaction to the warm water.

'I'm going to leave now, Charlotte. Mrs Briggs will see to you, and it is no place for a man to be. Doctor or not, childbirth is a woman's job. You'll be fine. The baby looks healthy and you are healthy, so I can see no problems. But if there are, you know where I am.' Dr Burrows opened the bedroom door and looked back at the woman he'd known both as a girl and as a woman. 'Your father would be proud of his new granddaughter, you can be sure of that. Good day.' He smiled as he closed the door behind him, but in the back of his mind was the thought of Betsy Foster and the baby that never had the chance to live.

'Has she had the baby, Doctor? We thought we heard one crying.' Mrs Batty, Mazy, Lily and Yates looked rather sheepish in front of the doctor, waiting at the bottom of the stairs in anticipation of the announcement of a new presence in the manor.

'She has. You'll be glad to know that both mother and baby are doing well. And, as you've heard, the baby's got a good pair of lungs on her.' Dr Burrows smiled. 'Your mistress will need some hot water in her room, and I dare say a drink of tea would not go amiss.'

'I'll take it right away. I want to be the first to see this new soul. I wonder what she's going to be called?' Mrs Batty scurried off to the kitchen, followed quickly by Mazy and Lily, who were arguing between themselves over who would be first to see the new baby.

Yates remained silent as he walked with the doctor to the main entrance of the manor to open the door for him.

'You're still here then, Yates. Dawson didn't sack you for nearly killing his wife?' Dr Burrows took his top hat out of the butler's hands, as he picked it up from the hallway stand.

'I'd no hand in that night, Dr Burrows – it was his doing. He slapped her and then, near as damn it, threw her down the stairs. There was no loose stair rod when she climbed those stairs, and I was never asked to fix one. Betsy Foster might not have been the first person Joseph Dawson killed, if you had not been here so fast,

303

and if I hadn't seen what he did that night.' Yates looked at the doctor as he put on his hat and passed him his Gladstone bag from the hall floor.

'It's a bad do, is all this, Yates. I feel I'm partly to blame, because I thought it was none of my business when I saw the mark on Mrs Dawson's face, although I did make light of it to the dratted fellow. Perhaps I should mention it to the police – what do you think?' Dr Burrows looked at Yates, who hesitated as he opened the door for the doctor to leave.

'If you do, Dr Burrows, mention that there was more to his old housekeeper, Dora Dodgson, than meets the eye. He treated her different to the rest of us, and she was the one who made up the lie over the stair rod being loose. Aye, and she threatened me, if I said any different. Now why would an everyday housekeeper do something like that? She came with him from Accrington, did you know that? She knew his every move better than that good woman upstairs.' Yates opened up with everything that had been sitting heavily on his mind for the last few weeks. The truth was that it was a relief to do so.

'I will. I'll go and have a word with Inspector Proctor. That cad Dawson could do just the same thing to another woman. He needs to feel the noose around that neck of his, from what I've just heard.' Dr Burrows tipped his hat and turned for a second in the open doorway. 'And, Yates, please accept my apologies. I realize now that my words were hasty. The bounder had us all fooled.'

'Apologies accepted.' Yates smiled and closed the door behind him. Dora Dodgson – or, as she was now known, the newly-wed Mrs Bloomenber – was going to be receiving visitors, and not before time. She was a nasty, evil woman and he hoped a visit from the police would shake her up.

'Oh, ma'am, she's beautiful.' Lily, Mazy and Mrs Batty stood at the bottom of the bed and looked at the perfect picture of mother and baby, content and smiling.

'She is. Just look at her. Can you believe how small her fingers are? And look at her mop of hair, now that she has had her first bath.' Charlotte put her finger in the tiny outstretched hand and smiled as her baby grasped it firmly.

'What are you going to call her, ma'am? Have you thought of a name?' Lily stood closer and looked down at the round face of the newborn.

'I'm going to call her Isabelle, after my mother. I never knew my mother. She died when I was just a baby, but I know my father loved her dearly. There wasn't a day went by that he didn't mention her name. So I think it's fitting that I carry on her name in the family.'

'It is, ma'am. Isabelle will suit her perfectly.' Lily smiled.

'Isabelle Victoria, to be precise. I thought I'd call her after the Queen as well, because she's going to be queen of all she surveys when she grows up.' Charlotte smiled and then yawned. She was tired.

305

'Here, ma'am; give baby Isabelle here. I'll put her in her cot and you can have some sleep. You'll be no good to anyone if you don't get your rest.' Lily leaned over and gently picked up Isabelle. Mazy pulled back the covers of the cot and Isabelle was tucked up safe and sound at the side of her mother's bed.

'Thank you, everyone. I'm grateful for your support in these changing times.' Charlotte looked at her concerned servants.

'Yates says you've to take care of yourself as well,' Mrs Batty added.

'Tell him "Thank you".' Charlotte watched as her servants walked quietly out of her bedroom, then she slid under her bedclothes. She was on her own in the world. Even if Joseph did return, he'd be arrested for the death of Betsy. She lay on her side and looked at her new daughter, whispering quietly, 'I'm frightened, Isabelle Victoria. Can I raise you on my own? It was different for my father. He was a man and had the security of his farm and his own father. I've nobody, and I'm supposed to run a cotton mill that I only know the bare minimum about.' She sighed. She had a real responsibility now: a daughter who was totally dependent on her, and her alone. 'Please help me, Father,' she whispered under her breath. 'If you can hear me, give me some of your strength.' She turned over again in bed, hugging her pillow, and cried herself to sleep.

'The baby's the spit of her father. That black hair – you couldn't mistake that for anybody else but Joseph

Dawson's.' Mrs Batty was peeling the potatoes for supper.

'Aye, that one's his, just like poor Betsy Foster's was. He's a lot to answer for, has that one.' Lily sighed.

'And so will the so-called "Mrs Bloomenber" before too long. Dr Burrows is going to the police to tell them about the night Mr Dawson pushed Mrs Dawson down the stairs. I told the doctor that she covered things up for Dawson. No normal housekeeper would do that. Thick as thieves, those two were. The more I think about it, the more I think something weren't right there.' Yates sat back.

'Mrs bloody Bloomenber – Dora bloody Dodgson. Married to an old man of nearly seventy: now what can she be after? Not a bit of "how's your father", not at that age. Could it be his bank balance, I wonder?' said Mazy.

'Mazy Banks, will you wash your mouth out,' Mrs Batty scolded. 'But you are right, lass. Gold-digging bitch!'

'Now whose mouth wants washing out?' Yates grinned. 'What goes around, comes around. She'll get found out, whatever her game, you mark my words.'

A week went by in no time and Charlotte threw herself into motherhood, watching every move that baby Isabelle made. Every gurgle and cry made her love her daughter more, and even the night-feeds that she had been dreading weren't so bad. But in the back of her mind she knew that she was denying the obvious: that

307

her real place was at the helm of Ferndale Mill, even though it felt like a weight around her neck.

'What's up, ma'am? You look sad today, and baby Isabelle is such an angel, she hardly ever cries. Are you thinking about Mr Dawson? It's a pity he's never even seen the lil' lass.' Lily looked at her mistress. Her heart bled for her plight. Charlotte had always been so good to her, from the first day she'd set eyes on her.

'I doubt Mr Dawson will return. Let's face it, Lily, he was responsible for the death of Betsy, and he would be a fool to return to me and lose his own head. Besides, he never really loved me; he just used me. It was convenient for him to settle down with me, and then of course there was my father's money – or so he thought at the time. Looking back, he was after that, for sure.'

'You don't know that for certain. I'm sure he loved you in his own way.' Lily folded the nappies and placed them in the drawers next to the baby's cot.

'Loved me so much that he left me with his baby to raise, and his debts to pay. I do owe him something, though. I have the sweetest child anyone could wish for, and a grand house that I never in my wildest dreams thought I would own, now that I have managed to come to an agreement over Joseph's debts, with the help of Mrs Cranston. The one thing I could do without is Ferndale Mill, especially now that I have Isabelle. I don't want to leave her with some uncaring nanny, and that is what I'm going to have to do. And at this moment in time the mill isn't worth a penny. Nobody in their right mind wants a cotton mill in this economic climate, and while the Confederates and Unionists battle for power.'

'But, ma'am, the local people depend on you and that mill to keep themselves fed. Bert Bannister's a good man. He's well respected – he'll teach you all you need to know. The war over in America won't last forever, and then you'll have a thriving business in your hands. Something for baby Isabelle to inherit, when she's old enough.' Lily sat down next to her mistress, who was obviously suffering from baby-blues, along with her other worries.

'I don't want to leave my baby with someone I hardly know. That's the top and bottom of it, Lily. I owe her more than that.' Charlotte put her head in her hands and sighed.

'Then don't, ma'am! Why don't you promote Mazy to Nanny, instead of being a scullery maid. She's good with children; she's the oldest of five. What she doesn't know about babies, nobody does. And she's a local lass, so you know all about her. She's forever telling us what she's been up to, with her brothers and sisters. It would help them at home as well. There are seven of them, sleeping head to toe in a two-bedroomed house. Mazy would think she'd gone to heaven if you gave her her own room with baby Isabelle.' Lily couldn't believe she'd suggested that to her mistress. She'd always been proud that she was her mistress's earpiece, and now she was promoting Mazy as the answer to all Charlotte's worries. Mazy had a mouth on her like a sewer, but there was one thing she was good at, and that was looking after children, and everyone knew it.

'Mazy, little Mazy, who lights my fire in a morning and looks like she'd run a mile if I spoke out of turn to her? She's so timid.' Charlotte lifted her head up.

'You obviously don't know our Mazy, ma'am. Believe me, she says what she thinks. Her and Dora Dodgson hated one another. She'd have thrown a party, if she could have done, when Dora left. Come to think of it, we all would have done. No disrespect, ma'am. But, yes, Mazy is really good with children, and you will easily get a replacement scullery maid. Especially now Mr Dawson has left. You might have struggled beforehand, with his reputation—' Lily stopped herself from saying more.

'What do you mean, "with his reputation", Lily? Just say it. It makes no difference now. I can't be hurt any more than I already am. Send young Mazy up to see me, but don't say why. I just want to ask her a few questions. And, Lily, can you ask Mrs Batty for the menu for the week? Normality should be maintained, with or without my husband's presence. Could you also ask Jethro to take this note to Mewith and to wait for a reply from Mr Atkinson.' She passed a handwritten note to Lily, who curtsied as she left the room, making Charlotte smile. She was indeed the lady of the manor and should not forget it.

It was the writing of her note, announcing the birth of her child, that had darkened Charlotte's spirits. She had a beautiful baby, while Archie had neither wife nor newborn bairn. And there she was, having to leave her baby to be brought up by another woman, while she went about men's business. However, the mill could wait no longer. Bert Bannister knew about the functioning of the mill, but when it came to the accounts and the welfare of the staff, he knew nothing. She had to run the mill, or face more than a hundred locals losing their livelihoods; and she herself losing the mill to Lorenzo Christie, who she knew was just waiting for her to fail. She could never let that happen. She needed to prove a point. She could run the mill *and* keep her farm. And, by hook or by crook, she would do so, with or without a man by her side.

23

Inspector Proctor and Sergeant Capstick stood outside the padlocked mill gates of the Helene Mill, which had once been owned by the family of May Pilling, the first wife of Joseph Dawson. May's name was the only lead Charlotte had been able to give them, to her husband's past life. The four-storey-high, dark building lay silent, just like two-thirds of the other cotton mills in Accrington, throwing their starving workers onto the streets.

'Penny for an old woman, sir?' An old crone sat crouched next to the gates and shuffled in her rags, holding her hand out for any alms that might come her way.

'I'll give you a penny, if you can tell me about the mill owners and what became of them.' Percy went down on bended knee and looked at the old woman. He'd decided to come to Accrington after his conversation with the young lad at the Talbot Arms, but so far he'd found out nothing about Dawson.

'Do you mean the Pillings? They are long gone. Only poor May was left, and she married that bastard Joseph Dawson,' spat the old woman.

'Joseph Dawson?' Percy helped the old woman to her feet and questioned her more.

'I may be old and hungry, but I'll not forget his bloody name in a hurry. Right little bastard, he was, when he was growing up. Him and his sister terrified half of Accrington, and then poor May fell for his charms, and he took over this place until they moved.'

'Moved where? And are you sure his name was Dawson?' Percy squeezed the old woman's arm tightly, eager for more information.

'Get off me! It'll cost you more than a penny, if you are that desperate. What's the bastard done anyway? And aye, his name was Dawson all right; and his sister married Ted Dodgson, until he upped and left her. Ask anyone in Accrington. The bastard moved and took his sister with him to somewhere in Yorkshire, I think. God have mercy on their souls, wherever he's at.'

'This sounds like the man I'm after. We're not certain, but we believe he's killed one of his workers. We need to find him.' Percy tried to keep his voice calm.

'Killed someone! I bet it was a woman; he always had a nasty streak when it came to women. His mother was a prick-pincher, who stood on this very spot – the whore. He was brought up in the gutter, along with that thieving, lying sister of his. Everyone was thankful when he buggered off to Yorkshire, taking his sister

313

with him. Poor May, I don't know what became of her. He just used her to get his hands on her money, and to make money out of the poor buggers that worked at this place. He worked them until they dropped, and then sold the place to line his pocket. Now what's that worth to you? Hurry up, my belly is rumbling with anticipation.' The old woman looked up at the inspector with a keen eye.

'Is there anyone in Accrington you know who could be hiding him?' Percy rolled a coin between his fingers, the silver glinting in the sunlight. 'A friend or confidant?'

'For that threepence?' The old woman's eyes lit up.

'Aye, for that threepence. But make sure you tell me the truth, else it will be the worse for you!' He stood back and started to walk away.

'Go look for Arthur Simmons. He's a solicitor on Albert Street. He'll tell you all there is to know about Joseph Dawson. They were thick as thieves, until they fell out. He'll know all Dawson's old haunts and who would give him the time of day.' The old woman held her hand out and caught the coin as Percy flipped it up in the air to her. 'God bless you, sir, and I hope the lbastard hangs.'

'He will, if I catch him.' Percy and Sergeant Capstick walked quickly to interview the new lead, Arthur Simmons, in the knowledge that perhaps they had a double-murderer on their hands. What had happened to May Pilling? Was Dora Dodgson, the so-called 'housekeeper', really Joseph Dawson's sister? And where was the bastard?

Arthur Simmons sat behind his dingy desk, listening to the threats of being thrown into the cells overnight, as Inspector Proctor tried to draw out whatever information the solicitor knew about Joseph Dawson.

'I knew him. And aye, it was me the spit lad described to you. Dawson owed me some money, so I came up and frightened him. Told him I'd tell his pretty new wife about his old lifestyle. Plus I reckoned I knew what happened to his first wife.' Simmons leaned back in his chair, lifting his feet up onto the edge of the desk, and twiddled his thumbs while Sergeant Capstick took notes and Inspector Proctor leaned on the desk, looking at the piece of dirt he had quickly recognized Simmons to be. 'Has he killed that pretty wife of his? Is this what it's about? He never could keep his temper under control.'

'No, Mrs Dawson is well, but Mr Dawson is at the centre of our investigations. What do you mean by "I reckoned I knew what happened to his first wife"? Where is she, do you know?' Percy looked around the room and noticed the damp running down the dark walls. Even in the middle of summer the office looked dingy. God only knew what it looked like in the bleakness of a mill town's winter.

'No idea, Officer. One day she was here, and the next day gone. He could have thrown her in the cut, for all I know. He was that sort of fella – you didn't cross him. But he soon coughed up the money he owed me, when I mentioned May Pilling, and his sister Dora Dodgson. He wasn't going to be having his dirty washing waved in the faces of the good people of Settle. He had his new life to protect, with his bonny new wife, who was the talk of the county. Just because he'd moved to some backwater in Yorkshire, it didn't mean that I didn't keep my eye on him. I wanted my money back, and threats and violence are the only thing Joseph Dawson recognizes, believe me.'

'I could nick you, Simmons, for blackmailing Joseph Dawson.' Percy was beginning to realize just what a dark life the Dawsons had lived, and he didn't like it. Their lifestyle had started to come together in his mind, when the death of the rogue and thief Roger Wilson had been reported taking place at Crummock. No self-respecting businessman gave shelter to a common guttersnipe like Wilson.

'What for – for getting back the money Dawson owed me? That's not blackmail. It's his fault that he's got a past like hell behind him. I was only pointing out what could have happened. I walked away and came back to my offices to look after the poor, unfortunate people of Accrington.' Simmons grinned.

'Aye, the folk of Accrington are poor and unfortunate if they have to use you as their solicitor. Take care, sir, else you will one day be smiling from the wrong side of a cell's bars.' The inspector summoned Sergeant Capstick.

'Talk to his sister. She's the one you want, Inspector.

316

And let me earn my living here in peace. I washed my hands of the Dawsons the minute I got my money back off the lying bastard. If it's any consolation, I hope the lass that he married is safe and well, and I hope you find out what happened to May. She was a quiet, nervous woman, too well bred and flighty for the likes of him. She should never have met him. Their maid sensed something was wrong, but nobody listened and now she's moved away; gone where the work is, down south.' Simmons leaned back and watched as the two lawmen left his office. Well, that would be the last money he got out of Joseph Dawson. Dawson was a wanted man, and he couldn't afford to get his hands caught in such business. Because it would be dirty, no matter what Dawson had done. Of that Simmons was certain.

Percy Proctor walked up the pathway to Ingfield House. Up until a few months ago Dora Dodgson had been a humble housekeeper. He couldn't help but think she'd done well for herself, as he climbed the bleached white steps and stood to one side of the mock-Roman pillars to ring the bell-pull next to the green-painted door. He waited as he heard the patter of feet from behind the door, and doffed his hat as a maid answered the call.

'Good morning, what may I do for you, sir?' The pretty little maid curtsied and waited for a reply.

'Is Mrs Bloomenber at home, my dear? I need to speak to her.' Percy stepped close to the open doorway and tried to peer into the hallway.

'If you can give me your calling card, I will see if she is available to take visitors.' The maid reached for a silver tray, on which the visitor was expected to place a calling card.

'I don't need a calling card, my dear. She's no option but to see me, as I am the local constabulary. Now take me to her.' Percy wedged his foot in the doorway and pushed his way into the house.

'What's all the noise, Gladys? Who are you talking to?' Dora Bloomenber walked into the hallway and looked at the stranger there. 'Who are you? And have you no manners? Gladys, go and get my husband!' She stood back, affronted by the stranger standing in her hallway.

'But, ma'am, he's the police,' Gladys stuttered.

'Just bide your time, Gladys. I don't think Mr Bloomenber will be impressed, if he knows that a member of the West Yorkshire Constabulary is visiting his home. What do you think, Dora?' Percy stood his ground, watching the face of the woman, which looked as hard as nails.

'I'm sorry, Gladys, I'd forgotten this gentleman had said he was calling. It's a charity event you want us to sponsor. Is that right, Constable . . . ? I'm sorry, I've forgotten your name. Now, I must stop you from teasing my maid. Mr Bloomenber is all too happy to sponsor your event.'

'It's "Inspector" actually – Inspector Proctor. Now can we talk business somewhere private, perhaps?'

Percy watched as Dora dismissed her maid like a piece of dust from her highly polished shoes, telling her not to disturb them when an offer of morning tea was made. The woman could lie, there was no doubt of that. She'd have made an excellent card player, for there wasn't a sign of what was going on in that head of hers. Percy followed her across the hallway into the main living room. Ezera Bloomenber was obviously a man of great wealth and good taste, and had spent countless amounts of money on his comfortable home. The windows were draped in the finest material, and the walls were decorated with heavy coverings, while on top of the Adams fireplace a fine French timepiece kept the time with a steady tick.

'Nice home, Dora, you've done well for yourself.' Percy sat down on the couch and watched as the woman stood with her back to the fireplace.

'Stop the idle chatter. I know why you are here. It's about my brother, Joseph. I knew it would only be a matter of time before you put two and two together. I don't want my husband to know that I'm Joseph's sister. I'm trying to start a new life without him, and I don't want to lose all this. He won't look kindly on being married to the secret sister of a suspected mur-derer.' Dora folded her hands behind her back and stared at Percy.

'So, I take it he's not here then, and that you don't dispute that you are Joseph Dawson's sister?' He watched her as she put one hand on the mantelpiece and rubbed her brow.

319

'No, he's not here. And yes, we are brother and sister. We had a row before I left Windfell. I told Joseph I wanted a life of my own and was tired of living in his shadow. Besides, I'd met Ezera, and how could anyone turn this lifestyle down? There's a lot of difference between being housekeeper to the most dysfunctional household and being mistress of your own household. Joseph won't come here – he knows I've washed my hands of him.' Dora sat down next to Percy and watched him as he made notes.

'Did you know he was having an affair with Betsy Foster, when you worked at Windfell Manor?' He watched her closely.

'There was only that simpering wife of his who didn't know what he was up to. God knows why she stayed with him. He treated her like rubbish, poor cow, whilst he trailed in at all hours of the day and night and slept in a separate bedroom. It's our mother who is to blame. She treated him badly when he was young. He saw things no child should see and it's rubbed off on him. It warped him slightly; he doesn't respect women.' Dora twisted her handkerchief in her hands and looked at Percy.

'Mentioning wives, what became of May Pilling, Joseph's first wife?' Percy looked across at the surprisingly revealing woman.

'May, poor May, she didn't stand a chance. She was too vulnerable for a man like my brother not to exploit. Orphaned in the world, with all that money and property in her name: a prize plum ready for the picking, and pick her he did. She thought he was wonderful, but he soon wore her down, ground her to the floor and got her to transfer all her money and businesses to him, with the help of that weasel Simmons, his so-called solicitor. Then he played games with her, got her believing things weren't right – so bad that she thought she was going out of her head, poor cow.' Dora stopped for a second and composed herself, putting her hard face on again. She couldn't let anything slip.

'I appreciate you telling me all this. It is a help. I'm beginning to get the full story about Joseph Dawson.' Percy looked up. 'Why are you telling me this, though?'

'I don't want to lose all this. I've been at my brother's beck and call all my life, and I need some peace from him. Besides, it could have been me that he knocked on the head and threw in the mill race. There was many a time he gave me a good hiding. He had the brawn, but didn't have the brains. What do they say: "A fool and his money are soon parted"? Well, add charm and good looks, and you've got our Joseph, the idiot.' She sighed.

'I aim to track him down and bring him to justice, but at the moment he's disappeared. Nobody seems to have seen him since he walked out of Windfell on that stormy evening for a meeting in Settle. Is there anywhere you can think of that he would use as a bolthole? Anywhere he'd feel safe?' Percy waited.

'I'd say he'd try to contact his friend Richard Todd, on his plantation in Mississippi, but the plantation may well have been razed to the ground, with all the troubles in the Americas.'

'He'll not get a ship to take him anywhere near there, but he might make for the port of Liverpool. Surely he'll have contacts there?'

'My brother will only have contacts if he doesn't owe them money, and they are few and far apart. Most people gave up on him a long time ago. Folk only get taken for a ride once; they soon learn that his word is not his bond.' Dora sighed again.

'Well, it's somewhere I can send Sergeant Capstick to have a sniff around. But for now I think I'd better leave you, before that husband of yours comes in. As you say, he wouldn't take kindly to finding that Joseph is your kin. I'll keep you informed if we come across him – discreetly, that is.' Percy rose from his seat.

'Inspector Proctor, try Calderstone's down near Preston, for May. You'll hopefully find her there, but I warn you, you'll not get any sense from her.' Dora smiled. All she wanted was a respectable new life, and Joseph had always prevented that for her.

Percy walked to the hallway door and turned to be within earshot of the nosy maid. 'Thank you for your contribution to this most worthy cause. I'm sure the outcome will be satisfactory. Please pass on my best wishes to Mr Bloomenber.' He'd read Dora Dodgson incorrectly; she'd been used, just like every other woman Joseph Dawson had touched – used and abused, in more ways than he dared even think of.

Percy looked up at the huge clock tower in the centre of the forbidding red-bricked, three-storey institution.

The clock tower was there to instil order from chaos in the world of the mentally unstable and the dim-witted. The sound of its heavy ticking echoed around the asylum in which Dora had informed him May Dawson was a patient. A sense of fear filled him as he enquired at the desk if May was indeed an inmate of the notorious asylum. He felt uneasy as patients walked past him like spectres in the night, uncaring, unseeing and dressed in asylum uniform to mark their unfitness for the outside world.

'Yes, we have a May Dawson; she's been with us for nearly two years now. Her husband signed her in as being mentally unstable, with suicidal tendencies. She's one of the quieter ones, is May. Doesn't give us any problems. Not like Nora, who you can hear screaming now. I'm sure I'll end up in here myself, if she continues any longer.' The nurse on the desk sighed.

'May I see her? I just need to check that she is alright?' Percy looked around him, his senses on edge, with the smell of disinfectant and urine filling his nose.

'Yes, but you'll not get anything out of her. She just sits and holds the doll that she came in with. Even her husband couldn't part her from it. She's in her room on the third floor. We keep her there; it's less risk from some of the more unsavoury patients that we have here.' The nurse checked through her keys, then ushered Inspector Proctor up the steep stairs that led to a long landing with more than twenty single rooms, all with closed doors and peepholes through which to check on the occupants.

'This is May's room. Do you want me to open the door?' The nurse turned and looked at the inspector, who nodded his head.

She unlocked the door and let him step past her.

In the corner of the room sat a thin, grey-haired woman, rocking back and forth. She held a ragged, filthy hand-made doll, which had obviously been beautiful in its day.

'May, don't be frightened. I've just come to talk to you.' Percy knelt down and looked at the sad creature as she shuddered before him. Her hair was unbrushed and uncared for and the striped uniform of the asylum was stained. The eyes, which were the brightest cornflower-blue, looked at him with no feeling, her soul lost in agony. 'How long has she been like this?' Percy asked the nurse.

'Ever since her husband brought her in. He'd cared for her after her parents died, he told us. The poor man was a martyr. He told us he'd known that madness ran in the family and, even though he knew that, he had taken the chance and married her, because they had fallen madly in love. Unfortunately, as you can see, there is no preventing hereditary madness and that is why she's here. You are wasting your time, Inspector. She's not said a word in all the time she's been here.'

'Will you promise me something, Nurse? That as long as you work here, you'll make sure May is well looked after. She was once a lady of great beauty and wealth, until she was wronged by that so-called "husband", who used and abused her. He didn't love her, he loved her money, and I'm going to see him hang for what he's done to May and the other women he's used all his life.' Percy stood up and looked at the wretched creature that he was leaving behind. 'I'll get him, May – not just for you, but for Betsy Foster and Charlotte Booth, and even his sister, whose life he has made horrendous. May his soul rot in hell, because that's what he deserves.'

24

'Now, Mazy, Lily informs me that you are good with children. Is that right?' Charlotte sat in the parlour, with Mazy fidgeting nervously in front of her.

'I think I am, ma'am. My mother always trusts me with all my brothers and sisters, and there's enough of them.' Mazy looked at her mistress and didn't know quite what to say, for looking after children was second nature to her. Keep them fed, keep them clean and, most of all, keep a wary eye on them – that's what she'd always done.

'And babies, what about them? Have you patience enough to look after a baby?' Charlotte looked up and down at the slightly scruffy kitchen maid, visualizing her in a smarter outfit and with her hair tied back in a tight bun.

'Oh yes, ma'am, I love babies. My twin brothers are a dream. It's when the little buggers get cheeky enough to answer back that I lose a bit of interest.' She grinned.

'Well, Mazy, Lily thinks you'd be ideal for looking after baby Isabelle. However, there will be things for you to take into consideration. I would expect you to live in, like Lily and the rest of the staff do. And until Isabelle reaches an age when she knows her way around Windfell, I'd expect you to sleep in the adjoining room to the nursery, which is going to be made out of Mr Dawson's old room, now that he's gone. I'd expect you to be there for her twenty-four hours a day, and in return I'd pay you well for your services.'

'Me, ma'am, look after baby Isabelle? I'm only the scullery maid! But I could do it, I know I could, and me ma would be grateful to get rid of one of us. Our Lizzie is old enough to look after my lot. It'll do her bloomin' well good; she needs to grow up, she's nearly eleven.'

'Well, Mazy, how about we give it a go? We'll get you suitably attired tomorrow in Settle, and I'll ask Yates and Jethro to move the cot and Isabelle's things into Mr Dawson's old room and to dismantle his bed.' Charlotte looked at the amazement on Mazy's face, only for it to cloud over as fast as it had lit up.

'What if he bloody well comes back? I'll be in his bedroom, with baby Isabelle.' Mazy looked worried. 'Who's to know what he'd do to me, if he found me in there alone.'

'He'll not come back, Mazy. Mr Dawson is a wanted man – he'd lose his life if he returned.' Charlotte smiled at the straight-talking maid.

'And I'll get my own uniform and a room, and some more money?' Mazy smiled.

'Yes, you'll get all that. Should we say twenty-five pounds a year? That's not quite double what you are on now, and Sundays would be free to do as you like. You'll need to see your family, just as I will. But the job comes with a lot of responsibilities, Mazy. Isabelle is the most precious thing in my life, I can't emphasize that enough.'

'I'll look after her like one of my own, ma'am, don't you worry. She'll want for nothing, with me looking after her.' Mazy was over the moon.

'That's settled then. I'll give you a three-month trial, just in case it doesn't suit one or the other of us. And, Mazy, two things: try and stop swearing, for I don't want Isabelle growing up hearing such foul words; and secondly, let's get you in a bath before we go for those nanny's uniforms, eh?' Charlotte watched as Mazy's face went bright red.

'Yes, ma'am. Sorry, ma'am. My father says he's going to wash my mouth out with soap, and so does Mrs Batty. I'll get the tin bath out at home tonight and give myself a good scrub. I'll not let you down, ma'am, I promise. Baby Isabelle will be the best looked-after baby in Craven.' Mazy looked down at her feet.

'Very well. Go and tell downstairs the good news. And could you ask Mrs Batty to come up and see me? I need to put her mind at rest and tell her that I will find a replacement for your position.' Charlotte picked up the newspaper that she had discarded before she spoke to Mazy and glanced at the headlines: 'Confederates capture Fort Sunter from Union soldiers'. Would the cotton-driven civil war never end? Why was she fighting for a mill that was not worth fighting for? She sighed.

'Ma'am, I know somebody who would be perfect for the scullery-maid position. She used to work at Sidgwick's mill at Skipton, but they've laid a lot of people off. She's called Ruby Baxter and she lives back with her mother at Selside. They could do with the money, because her mother lost a hand when she caught it in the carding machine at Ferndale a few years ago.' Mazy hesitated.

'Was it when she worked for Mr Dawson?' Charlotte waited.

'No, it was the mill owner before him. There's always injuries in a mill, ma'am.' Mazy shrugged her shoulders.

'Not in mine – not if I can help it.' Charlotte uttered the words without thinking. Her mill, her headache; and hers to keep afloat through hard times. And by the looks of the headlines, harder ones still to come. Was she a fool, passing her baby over to a scullery maid to look after, while she ran a cotton mill? She was a farmer's daughter, not a mill owner. The only thing in her favour was her love of figures and a good way with people. Folk were the same, no matter what class; they just wanted to be treated right, no matter what their breeding. 'Tell this Ruby to come and see me and I'll see if she's suitable. If Ferndale took the bread off her table, then I should put it back on it, by employing the lass.'

'Yes, ma'am, I'll tell her. You'll not regret taking us

329

both on.' Mazy curtsied and then ran across the hall-way. Mistress Charlotte was a strong woman, now that her husband had left; she knew her mind and was kind. Just the opposite to the master they'd all hated.

'Mazy, for heaven's sake, calm down.' Mrs Batty sat down in her chair and watched the beaming girl dance around the kitchen.

'I'm Miss Isabelle's nanny. What do you think of that? I'm in charge of baby Isabelle, while the mistress goes to the mill each day. And I've my own room next to the new nursery, and tomorrow I'm going into Settle for a fitting for a uniform.' Mazy couldn't shut up.

'Well, ain't that just grand. And what am I supposed to do without a scullery maid? You just tell me that?' Mrs Batty crossed her arms and scowled at the excited lass in her kitchen.

'Don't worry, Mrs Batty, I told the mistress Ruby Baxter up at Stainforth would like to work here. I've to go and tell her to come and see the mistress. Anyway, she wants to see you too, to put your mind at rest. I've to tell you to go up and see her in the parlour.' Mazy flopped down in the opposite chair and grinned at the annoyed cook.

'For Lord's sake, Mazy, why didn't you tell me that first. Does my hair look alright?' Mrs Batty untied her apron and swept a stray grey hair behind her ear. 'And who's Ruby Baxter – do I know her family? And who are you to recommend who I have in my kitchen?' Mrs Batty raced to the bottom of the kitchen stairs.

'I'm the new nanny, That's bloody well who I am.' Mazy grinned.

'Soap and water, girl. Mind that mouth, else you'll soon be back downstairs, mark my words.' Mrs Batty grinned.

'Nah, I've got a good position now. I'm not daft. If the mistress can run a mill, then I can be nanny to that baby.' Mazy sat back in her chair.

'Aye, well, if you want my view, I think both of you will be up against it, but time will tell – we'll see. Now bide your tongue while I see the mistress, and put the kettle on the hob. You still work for me in the kitchen for now, and don't you forget it.'

Mazy watched Mrs Batty climb the stairs and waited till she heard the door at the top open into the hallway, before she stuck her tongue out and waggled it at the old cook, who always made sure Mazy kept her feet on the ground and was in her place. She'd show the old bat, of that she was sure.

'Well, Mazy, just look at you: don't you scrub up well.' Charlotte stood back and admired the pretty-looking nanny in her crisp, clean uniform as she smiled lovingly at baby Isabelle. 'And just look at Isabelle, she loves you already. Look at her smiling and blowing bubbles. I'm quite jealous of how fast she has taken to you.'

'I told you she was good with children, ma'am. I knew she'd be like a duck in water, given the right posi-tion.' Lily stood back and enjoyed the perfect picture of a respectable nanny with her ward, in the perfect nursery.

'I won't let you down, ma'am, don't you worry. Me and Isabelle are going to get on fine, she's such a good 'un. She's worth ten of my brothers.' Mazy looked down at a contented Isabelle and gurgled nonsensical baby-talk to the little one.

'You won't be saying that when she's screaming the house down for her two o'clock feed. And don't forget that she has to be kept in a routine – no deviating from it.' Charlotte wagged her finger and smiled at the besotted young nursemaid.

'I won't, ma'am, but I can't abide a baby crying. They only cry because something is wrong.' Mazy looked sheepishly at Charlotte.

'You'll only make a rod for your own back, if you forever nurse her. She is my precious darling, but I know a spoilt child can be an obnoxious, petty thing. Believe me, I went to school with plenty of them in Harrogate. Well, Mazy, that's you settled into your new post. And the nursery looks superb, now that everything is in place for you. I just had to buy the pram and rocking horse when I saw them in the toy shop in Settle. They make the nursery, and I'm sure Isabelle will love them when she's old enough.' Charlotte looked around her spotless nursery. 'Are you happy with your room, Mazy? I've tried to make it a home for you.' Every sign of her husband had been wiped from the adjoining bedroom. He no longer existed in her eyes. She could manage everything without him, and she secretly wished she would never hear of him again.

'It's perfect, ma'am, I don't want for anything.' Mazy smiled and then sniggered at the hypocrisy of Charlotte's words about not spoiling the child. She'd just bought the most expensive items in the toy shop, and the baby wasn't even walking.

'Right, Lily, let's go and see how Ruby is coping with her new life downstairs. I'm sure Mrs Batty will have her in hand.' Charlotte turned and gave another backward glance at the perfect nursery scene – one she thought she would never achieve.

'Ruby's just fine, ma'am, we are getting on famously. I've even realized that I know her uncle Bert at Lancaster. He used to be my next-door neighbour when I was married to the late Mr Batty, God rest his soul.' Mrs Batty was itching to get on with mixing her cake, before she could place it in the perfectly warmed oven. The kitchen was her domain, and the mistress's constant visits delayed her in her duties.

'Are you settling in, Ruby?' Charlotte looked at the mousy-haired young girl, who was washing the pans from luncheon in the shallow earthenware sink.

'Yes, ma'am. Thank you, ma'am.' Ruby curtsied and bobbed and then got on with her task in hand.

'See, you've much better manners than that Mazy upstairs.' Mrs Batty couldn't restrain herself any longer and started to fold the flour into her sandwich cake.

'Talking of manners, Mrs Batty, can I just dip my

finger into your cake mix? I loved doing that when I was a little girl, and Mrs Cranston always used to let me. I love the taste.' Charlotte took everyone aback by her request. Mrs Batty stopped in her tracks and offered her mistress the mixing bowl.

'Mmm. Lovely.' Charlotte ran her delicate finger around the inside of the bowl and licked it clean of the creamed eggy mixture. 'Sorry, I couldn't resist. It reminds me of home.'

Lily, Mrs Cranston and the newly employed Ruby looked at one another and then grinned. They'd all done that in their time; it was the best part of making a cake, and their mistress knew it. She was no snob, unlike her miserable rat of a husband.

'That's alright, ma'am, it's your cake to lick.' Mrs Batty grinned.

'I'll never be a lady, will I? Not with manners like that.' Charlotte looked at the innocent face of Ruby.

'You are every bit a lady, ma'am, and don't you change. You've a heart of gold and all of us know it.' Mrs Batty looked at the woman who had changed from a slip of a lass to someone with huge responsibilities. 'You can come and lick the cake bowl out any time you want. I'll tell you next time I'm making one.'

'Bless you, but no – that was just a quick indulgence. I should set a standard for Ruby, now, shouldn't I? No licking cake bowls out, do you hear, Ruby?' Charlotte looked stern.

'Yes, ma'am.' Ruby dutifully replied.

'That's that then. I'm going to walk down to the

mill now. I should be back for dinner, Mrs Batty. Six-thirty as usual?' Charlotte stood at the bottom of the stairs and looked around her happy, busy kitchen. Even though there was no master in the house, everyone was managing. The house was a better place without Joseph's presence. His moods had only brought the staff, and her, down.

'Yes, ma'am. Roast shoulder of lamb and new potatoes out of the garden, along with some mint sauce. Ruby picked the mint and chopped it so finely, before adding the vinegar and sugar, that I swear it was better made than my own.' Mrs Batty wiped her hands on her apron and reached for the cake tins that were waiting on the kitchen dresser.

'And a nice slice of cake, I hope, for dessert?' Charlotte grinned.

'Yes, ma'am. I think you've left enough for that.' Mrs Batty smiled.

'See you later then.' Charlotte lifted her skirts and climbed the stairs. If only the mill ran as smoothly as the house, she would be more than happy.

Charlotte walked slowly down the lane to the mill. Other women in her position would have been ordered to have bed rest after giving birth, but there she was, a month after having baby Isabelle, walking down the lane to talk to the manager of her mill. *Her* manager and *her* mill – the words still frightened her. She'd put nearly every pound of her father's hard-earned money, which Mrs Cranston had been kind enough to lend to her, into propping up the mill and paying off some of the mortgage on Windfell, the home that Joseph had spent so much of the bank's money on, trying to impress local folk. He should have realized that money did not make the man; it was actions that proved more, to the local folk. She didn't know what she'd seen in Joseph before, but life felt better now without him. Despite being left in debt, with a baby and no husband, she no longer had to walk on eggshells in her own home, and she knew her income exactly, and how much the mill was making.

The sun shone down, warming her skin and making her feel content. In the hay meadows lying on either side of the lane down to the mill, the farmers were turning the swathes of mown hay with their rakes. The sweet smell filled the air, reminding her of her old home at Crummock.

She'd not heard from Archie since she had sent him the letter informing him of Isabelle's birth. Perhaps he could not bear to see a newborn baby, after the loss of Rosie and his own baby. Added to that, he would be busy with his own haytime, eager to please his in-laws. She cast her mind back to her father and Crummock, and how he'd brought hired men to the farm to help with haytime, and with the clipping of the sheep in the warm summer months. He'd bedded them down in the loft above the cow biers and told her not to pester them, whilst he made sure they had everything they needed until the autumn weather came. For the few months they were with them, the men, who were invariably from Ireland, taught Charlotte new songs of an evening, and carved her tops and whips out of wasted pieces of wood.

It was with a heavy heart that she thought now of the once-loved farmhouse standing empty, for the sake of her foolish husband letting it to his criminal friend, and she only hoped that Arthur was managing to do as much as he could, until the present situation was resolved. She couldn't help but think that Isabelle was going to know nothing about a life of farming. She was going to be raised a lady, not a farmer's daughter. But would she be happy with all her finery?

Some tall swaying foxgloves flowering profusely in the hedge caught Charlotte's eye and she remembered how she used to put each individual flower on her fingers, making them look like gloves, just as their name suggested. That was until Mrs Cranston had chastised her for playing with them, saying they were poisonous and could stop her heart from beating. That had always made her cautious of the long, slim flower that grew in every hedgerow and in the long, curling fronds of musky bracken covering the fellsides. Her heart beat a little faster as the lane opened up to the cobbled yard of the mill and she walked up to the busy warehouse doors, where packed bales of cotton were being carted across to the main mill building.

The warehouse looked full as the workers hauled their loads, politely doffing their hats to the woman they now knew paid their wages.

'Ah, Mrs Dawson, I thought I saw you walking down

the lane from the office window. Come up to the office, and I'll ask one of the lasses to make us a cup of tea. We can at least offer you that.' Bert Bannister strode across the yard and smiled at his boss. 'We are busy, eh! It's good: we've plenty of cotton to last us a while, and the weaving shed next door is in full production. As long as we are careful, we should see into next spring, with what we've got.' He was eager to impress. 'The books are on the master's desk awaiting you, and once you've taken a look at those, I'll tell you where we stand in each department.'

Charlotte followed Bert up the steep stairs and walked into the office that overlooked the main spinning room. She stopped in the doorway and looked at the desk where her husband used to sit, king of his domain, cock of the midden; his lair, from which he preyed on poor Betsy and any other bright young thing that took his fancy.

'Thank you, Bert. I'll look at the books now. I take it these are the invoices and delivery notes from the last few weeks? They'll need entering, and then I'll balance them against any payments that have been made. Then I hope we will have enough left over to pay everybody for the next week or two.' Charlotte sat down in her high leather-backed chair and looked at her second-in-command.

'Aye, well, I'm not good with figures, but I know how this mill works and I know nearly everybody who works here, and you've a good lot, ma'am. They are all thankful that they've got jobs, they'll not let you down.' Bert rubbed his chin with his hands and looked at the woman in all her finery, who was going to run Ferndale.

'Well, I only hope I don't let you all down. This is new to me, but I'm going to run this mill like a well-run household, and then surely we won't go wrong. I'd like to walk around the mill every day that I am here, Bert, and for you to accompany me. I need to get to know everyone and exactly what they do in my mill. And when I do, I'll be satisfied. It's no good not knowing how your own mill functions.' She opened the sales ledger and then picked up the delivery note and invoice pile that had been left on her desk, awaiting her arrival.

'Yes, ma'am. I'll have to go and look at the carding room. As you can see, they were just unloading a new bale of cotton, and it's been full of rubbish lately. The pickers over there must have no pride in their work since this war, but still I'm not complaining; at least we have some cotton with this batch that you bought in.'

'Those pickers want to be free men, and not having to pick cotton just to survive, Bert. Can you blame them if they send us dirty cotton balls?' Charlotte looked up from her books.

'No, ma'am, can't say I'd want to be a slave and work for nowt.' The mistress was made from a different mould from her husband. Joseph Dawson would have played hell at the state of the cotton. 'I'll get away, if you don't mind.'

'Yes, you go, Bert. And as you offered, ask one of the lasses for a cup of tea; it would not go amiss.'

Charlotte put her head down and got on with the task in hand.

'Yes, ma'am, I'll ask one to be made for you straight away.'

She watched as Bert shouted instructions to one of the workers on the spinning machines. In another few months she would have the clout to do that, but today she would get the books in order. She would gain the knowledge to run this mill profitably and fairly, if it was the last thing she did. Life was going to be hard, corners were going to have to be cut and every penny watched, both at Ferndale and at Windfell, but she'd make it work.

'Oh, Mistress, just look at you. Come and sit down and put your feet up until dinner.' Lily plumped the cushion and watched as Charlotte slowly sat down on the sofa in the parlour.

'I'll be alright. I've just overdone it a little today. After all, it's my first day in Joseph's shoes, and I was catching up with the bookkeeping.' Charlotte yawned

'Pardon me for saying, ma'am, but do you not think you have taken on too much? I mean, you are only a woman.' The maid blushed.

'Only a woman, Lily! If we can bear children, we can do anything. Besides, look at the mess Mr Dawson left us in. I couldn't do any worse than him. How's my Isabelle? Has Mazy been good with her?' Charlotte had counted the minutes to getting back home and seeing her daughter.

'They've been fine, ma'am. Mazy took Isabelle a walk in her perambulator this afternoon. She had her bottle at the times you said, and now she's just been bathed and put in her cot. She's been so good, and Mazy's enjoyed every minute of it.'

'I should have done all that. But the mill will be her future, so I hope she will forgive me when she is old enough to understand the situation her father left me in.'

'Mentioning her father, ma'am, Inspector Proctor called while you were at Ferndale. He's left his calling card and will be coming back tomorrow afternoon, if it is convenient.' Lily looked at her exhausted mistress and felt a wave of sympathy for her.

'Oh, I could do without seeing him. I dread to think what he's going to tell me. I wonder if they have found that wastrel of a husband of mine?'

'He didn't say, ma'am, but Yates said he looked quite worried when you weren't available. I'm sure Yates would tell him to go away, if you are not up to seeing him,' Lily offered.

'No, let's see what the inspector has to say. Whatever it is, I should know. A good night's sleep and I'll be back to myself. Every day should get easier. It's just that I've so much to learn, and I feel all the workers at the mill are talking about me behind my back.'

'They probably are, ma'am. Only because they know you've saved them from the workhouse. Now, I'll tell Mrs Batty that you've returned, and ask Yates to lay the table.'

'I really should get changed for dinner, but I'm only on my own. Just this once I'll not bother, Lily.' She yawned again.

'No, don't you worry, ma'am. You are the mistress of your own house and what you say goes. There's no Dora Dodgson now.' Lily knew all too well that there was no love lost between the two women.

'Just don't remind me of that woman, Lily. She was a stickler. Thank God she left.' Charlotte closed her eyes.

'Yes, ma'am, she was indeed and, although I shouldn't say it, we were all thankful when she walked out on Mr Dawson,' whispered Lily.

'Perhaps they were too much alike, Lily. They were both unpredictable, let's face it.' Charlotte sighed, still keeping her eyes closed.

'Yes, ma'am. We are better off without the both of them, that we are.'

25

'Inspector Proctor, ma'am.' Yates showed Percy into the drawing room and announced his presence to Charlotte as she sat next to the window.

'Good afternoon, Inspector. I take it you have news of my husband, else you wouldn't be here?' Isabelle urged him to sit next to her. 'Would you like some tea?'

'Yes, ma'am, to both. Tea would be most welcome, and I do have some news regarding your husband, but unfortunately perhaps not what you want to hear.' Percy sat down next to the woman who was going to hear the shocking news that her husband had been not only a murderer, but a con-man and bigamist to boot.

'We'd better have that tea first then.' Charlotte rang the small bell next to her and Yates appeared like magic from the hallway. 'Tea for two, Yates, and a piece of the cake that Mrs Batty made yesterday. I fear I might need something to lift my spirits while Inspector Proctor gives me the latest information on my husband.'

'Yes, ma'am. Straight away, ma'am.' Yates looked at the inspector and knew things were grave.

'Now, Inspector, while Yates is out of earshot, tell me the worst. Is he dead? Have you found him? Or, even worse, is he still in the area?' Charlotte waited.

'None of those, I'm afraid. We haven't been able to track him down, but I do have reason to believe that he might have fled to Liverpool, seeking passage to America, of all places. I believe he has a friend there, a Mr Richard Todd in Mississippi. Have you heard of him?' Percy watched as Charlotte relaxed.

'Yes, Mr Todd is his contact at the Natchez Plantation, from which he used to buy cotton, but according to the newspaper reports, it may have been razed to the ground. There is fighting all around it – only a fool would attempt to go there. But tell me, how have you found out about him? He used to keep everything to himself.' She looked at the inspector, amazed at his knowledge of her husband.

The conversation stopped for a short while as Yates delicately placed a covered tea tray in front of them and waited for instructions, but when none were forthcoming he offered his services.

'Should I pour, ma'am?'

'No, thank you, Yates, I'll do it myself. Please thank Mrs Batty for her wonderful tea tray.' Charlotte smiled at the butler, who was itching to know the next chapter in the Dawson family scandal. She poured the tea and passed the delicate cup and saucer to Inspector Proctor, watching for Yates to disappear from view. 'Do help yourself to cake, Inspector, it is truly delicious.'

'Thank you, I don't mind if I do.' Percy took a mouthful and waited until he'd swallowed it, before telling her the facts that he had accumulated. 'I got the name from his sister.' He took another mouthful and watched Charlotte's face.

'His sister? Joseph didn't have a sister – he told me he was an only child. Was he lying yet again? Did he leave a sister back in Accrington?' Charlotte placed her cup and saucer back down on the tray and looked at the inspector, as crumbs fell from his mouth in a bid to eat his cake before the next round of talking.

'No, ma'am, she was a lot closer to home. I believe you know her as Dora Dodgson, your onetime housekeeper!'

Charlotte's face said it all. 'Dora Dodgson! I *knew* there was something about her. She knew everything about Joseph, more than I ever did. But he said she'd been with the family for years as a servant.' She gasped. 'Lily and I only commented yesterday how alike they were, but we never imagined they were brother and sister.'

'Well, she *had* been with the family for years – ever since she was born – and she *was* his servant in a way, because he used Dora just like he used everyone else. Until she met someone who could give her a decent life, and he hadn't bargained on that.' Percy sat back and waited, before he gave Charlotte the next shock.

'That would be Ezera Bloomenber, the poor man.

345

Does he know who he's married to?' Charlotte couldn't help but smile slightly. No wonder Joseph had been so upset the day Dora left.

'No, and I promised to keep the information about who she is a secret, because Dora gave me the information I needed, and there was no need to rattle her cage at this point. I might need to know more from her.' Percy watched and then decided to tell Charlotte the news he had been dreading. 'She did tell me that Joseph had got married to May Pilling while living in Accrington, as you informed me, when I asked you. However, the spit boy at the Talbot Arms had overheard a conversation between your husband and a Mr Simmons, a solicitor from Accrington, that got me looking into what exactly had become of his first wife.' Percy hesitated.

'She died, that's what Joseph told me. Don't say he killed her!' Charlotte held her breath.

'No, he didn't kill her physically, but mentally he did far worse. May Pilling is not dead, Mrs Dawson, she is locked in a room at Calderstone's asylum in Lancashire, incapable of even saying her name, let alone knowing anything about who she is. It's all his doing, from what I can understand, as a result of his desperation for power and money. You have had a very lucky escape from Joseph Dawson. Unlike May and Betsy Foster, you've got away with your life.' He waited as Charlotte took in the news.

'But he can't be still married – he married me. You must be wrong. That can't be his wife.' Charlotte didn't know what to say. What else was the man she had thought she loved going to do to her?

'There's no mistake, Mrs Dawson. Joseph Dawson is a bigamist. Your marriage to him was a sham. And as for poor May Pilling, she is never going to get her life back, locked in that asylum until she ends her natural days. The cad has a lot to answer for.'

'So my child does not have a legitimate father, and I'm not married in the eyes of the law. It couldn't get much worse. I don't know whether to cry or laugh. That poor woman locked away from the world, driven insane by that bastard. I don't know how I fell for his charms.' Charlotte sighed.

'It seems that he and his sister were brought up on the streets of Accrington. Their mother was a prostitute, and that's why he has no respect for women, or so Dora said. He's even treated her badly in the past. He's only got away with everything because of her cunning and his good looks and easy way with women. Apologies if I offend, Mrs Dawson.' Percy coughed slightly.

'I think you'll find that I'm still "Miss Booth", if what you say is true. However, I'd prefer it if we keep that to ourselves, for the sake of baby Isabelle. I know it is common in lower society that if a marriage doesn't work out, then you can go your own way and find another partner, but not in my circles. After all, Joseph would simply claim that his marriage to poor May was annulled, due to her madness. But technically my daughter is illegitimate. I only hope that she doesn't take after her father.'

'I don't think you need to fear that, for she will be brought up with love and care, from what I've seen – unlike Joseph. To reassure you that I'm still in pursuit of him, Sergeant Capstick is in Liverpool as we speak, trying to track the cad down. We will get him, of that I can assure you.'

'I hope he hangs. Not for me, but for Betsy and even more so for May Pilling; she must have been, and still is, in hell. I know what Joseph could do and how manipulative he was – and I'm a strong woman. To be quite honest, Inspector Proctor, it is a relief to know I'm not married to him, as I can restart my life. Especially now that I can own his house and mill; it's quite ironic really, when you think about it. And Crummock must be mine, so I can reclaim my family home. The relief of getting my life back quite undermines the wickedness that Joseph has dealt me.' She crossed her hands on her lap, looking out of the window and remembering the rainy night when Joseph walked out of her life forever.

'I thought you would take it a lot harder than that, Mrs Dawson, after all I've told you. It's everything a woman doesn't want to hear about her husband.' Percy rose from his seat.

'Nothing would surprise me about that man. To think that just over a year ago I was an innocent young lass. Now I am a shrewd, hard-headed woman with a business to run, and no time for fools, of which my husband is one. Do let me know if you find him, because I would like to visit him, once he's behind bars. Just to look at the dejected soul that he is, without a woman's skirts to hide behind.' Charlotte reached for the bell at her side and rang it. 'I'll ask Yates to see you out, Inspector.'

'I will indeed, ma'am, and thank you for your time. I'm sorry I've been the bearer of bad news.' Inspector Proctor lifted his bowler to his head and left her looking out of the window, as Yates escorted him to the door.

Charlotte watched him walking down the pathway, and then went up the stairs to the nursery.

'Miss Isabelle's asleep, ma'am. I've just put her down for her afternoon nap. She finished her bottle and is such a contented baby.' Mazy smiled at her ward. 'I'll leave you with her while I tidy my room.'

Charlotte didn't say anything to the attentive Mazy, but reached down and gently put her finger into Isabelle's limp pink hand. She looked the perfect baby: mop of dark hair, rosy cheeks and a rosebud mouth that was smiling slightly. 'I won't ever let anyone hurt you. You will be brought up the perfect lady, regardless of your father,' she whispered, as she tucked her baby's hands under the blankets. A tear fell down Charlotte's cheek. She would be there for Isabelle always, because there were only the two of them in the world, as far as she could see. She kissed her warm brow gently. 'Now, my darling, is the time to make something of our lives. I'm going to ensure we will be so wealthy and powerful that everyone will know our name, and will forget the

cad that was Joseph Dawson. It will be of no conse-
quence who your father is, and everyone will want to
marry you, I promise you that.'

26

Charles Walker leaned back in his chair and listened to what Charlotte had to say, each sentence astounding him more, as she told him of her situation. He had hated Joseph Dawson the moment he had set eyes on him, and now he knew his gut instincts had been right.

'Well, Charlotte, it seems quite clear to me: you are not legally married, so therefore Crummock is yours to do with as you wish. When it comes to Windfell and the mill, that's a little bit more complicated. However, with the help of Lucy Cranston, you have honoured Joseph's debts and are in a favourable position regarding ownership of both. Let's sort out Crummock first. I take it you want a tenant placing in it as soon as possible?' Charles smiled at the young woman, who had grown stronger with every blow that life had dealt her.

'I do indeed, and I can tell you just who I have in mind. I'm sure he will bite my hand off at the chance, or at least I hope so.' Charlotte had been waiting for this moment for so long. She had wanted Archie to farm Crummock ever since her father had died, and now his time had come. 'Archie Atkinson at Mewith. Joseph would not listen to my suggestion. If he had, everything would be running like clockwork up there. As it is, Arthur the farm boy is struggling to juggle everything and, after that guttersnipe Joseph placed in the house, it is in a right state – nothing that a bit of hard work wouldn't sort, mind you.' Charlotte leaned back, satisfied that at long last she was going to get her way.

'It was indeed a misfortunate episode, with the death of Mr Dawson's friend. "Birds of a feather" comes to mind. I must say I never did take to your husband. Now, would you like me to visit Mr Atkinson and draw up an agreement on your behalf? I think you've made a very wise choice; he's a good man and deserves bit of luck after the death of his wife.'

'Yes please, Mr Walker. The sooner my old home gets into safe hands, the better; and it's one less worry for me.' She rose and offered her hand to be shaken.

'Good luck, Charlotte, and keep strong. Things are bound to get better.' Charles shook her hand and showed her to the door. Charlotte Booth certainly knew her mind and had ten times more sense than her husband.

Charles knocked on the open door of the smallholding on the edge of Mewith Moor and smiled as a toddling Daniel gurgled and looked up at him, as he made good his escape into the farmyard. 'Is Mr Archie Atkinson available?' he asked as a red-faced, stressed-looking grandmother picked up the inquisitive toddler and placed him, complaining, under her arm.

'He's over there in the hay field. Who's asking?' Ruth Knowles looked suspiciously at the man in the suit asking for her son-in-law.

'I've come on behalf of Mrs Dawson with some news that I need to convey to him. I need an answer, so may I go and speak to him?' Charles looked at the young boy wriggling for freedom and thought how his life was just about to change.

'Aye, if you must. He's not done anything wrong with this Mrs Dawson?' Ruth looked worried.

'No, quite the contrary,' Charles replied and made his way to the young man scything the long grass meadow on the distant hillside. Every step he took brought Archie closer to a better life, with a farm of his own and better surroundings for his child.

Ruth Knowles watched as Archie leaned on his scythe, listening to what the man in the suit told him, and then she witnessed him throwing the scythe to the ground and shaking the visitor's hand fervently, before letting out a whoop of delight. 'Your father must have had some good news, little man. Mrs Dawson, it would seem, has made your father happy for the first time in ages in these long, dark days. Perhaps things are look-ing up for you and him.' Daniel looked innocently at his grandmother. 'Never forget your mother, little one, because she loved you more than life itself.'

*

'For heaven's sake, Lottie, I couldn't get here any earlier. Have you forgotten how busy the farm gets at this time of year? I had to take advantage of the good weather. It took me and Arthur the best part of a fortnight to mow and gather in the four hay meadows. We were both knackered.' Archie slung his cap down on the richly carpeted floor of the drawing room of Windfell Manor and looked at the most demanding woman he had ever known. After taking over Crummock a few weeks ago, her demands had never ceased.

'I'm sorry. I'd forgotten that my father always used to hire an Irishman at the fair in Settle. I can't believe you've managed all those meadows between you and Arthur.' She looked at the red-faced Archie. His skin shone from the sunburn he had endured while out in the fields. Another day or two and he would be bronzed, showing off his mop of bleached hair to best effect.

'I'm not your bloody father, and I got put into Crummock too late to do that. It's been me, Arthur and Mary. Yes, even Mary has raked and turned the hay for me so that it dried. Thank God Aunty Lucy moved back in with us; at least she's been keeping house and looking after Daniel, while bringing food out into the meadow for us all. It's been bloody hard work, but at least we have enough fodder for the stock to get us through the winter. That is, if you want me to stay there?' Archie flopped into the chair, not bothering that he was in one of the most stately homes in the district.

'Don't you swear about my father. I only said he would have done it that way. And of course I want you

354

to stay – even more so now that I'm on my own and have Isabelle to raise. How is Daniel? I'll ask Mazy to bring Isabelle down from the nursery and show you her in a moment.' Charlotte looked at the exhausted Archie and knew that Crummock was back in good hands.

'Daniel's fine, growing fast. Running rings around Aunty Lucy. I just feel so sad that he will never know or remember his mother. She was a fine woman.' Archie sighed and gazed down at his hands.

'I know. I wish I could have done more that day. Rosie was lovely – you were made for one another, un-like me and my husband. Well, I say "husband", but as you know he was never that.' Charlotte hesitated. 'You've kept it to yourself, haven't you? For the sake of Isabelle, I'm still "Mrs Dawson", to those who are not privy to my news,' she whispered.

'Aye, what a field day everybody would have, with that bit of gossip. Tha couldn't run the mill and hold your head up in polite society, if everybody found that out. What would your father have said? That puts him being a bit too friendly with my poor old aunt Lucy into the shade. And that bag of rubbish Joseph looked down his nose at both of them. The bloody hypocrite. Well-to-do gentleman, my arse!' Archie scoffed.

'Do you know who you sounded like then, Archie?' Charlotte grinned. 'My father – that was one of his favourite sayings, "my arse".' She giggled.

'Now then, Mrs Dawson, we'll have none of that vulgar talk. Remember your station in life.' Archie laughed and watched the first bit of colour in weeks return to Charlotte's cheeks. 'Let's see this baby then. If she's as bonny as her mother, she'll do.' He had never had time to see baby Isabelle before, and had been looking forward to seeing Charlotte's thriving baby.

'She's darker than me. She's got her father's black hair, but she's got my complexion.' Charlotte blushed as she rang the bell-pull at the side of the fireplace for Mazy to bring down baby Isabelle. It was good to hear kind words from a true friend.

Mazy entered the room and smiled at her mistress as she handed over her gurgling, contented ward. It was good to see the mistress smiling for once, she thought, as she left the threesome.

'Aye, Lottie, she's a bonny bit of a thing. Wouldn't your father have been proud? His first granddaughter. It makes no difference who her father is – she'll be a grand 'un. She'll bring you so much happiness in your life, just like my Daniel does. Once they get a bit bigger they can play together, just like we used to. Remember when we used to go tadpole-catching down at the Wash Dubbs and your father used to curse me, because you'd always fall in and get all your skirts and petticoats wet through?' Archie stroked Isabelle's cheek and then looked up at a contented Charlotte, hesitating for a moment as he remembered how much he had loved her. He wondered if he dared do the same again, before sitting back down in his chair.

'I remember. I also remember you getting me into

bother, scrumping apples down in Bernard Knowles's orchard in Feizor, when you left me halfway up the tree. My father was not impressed. No wonder he sent me off to school in Harrogate.' She smiled down at her daughter, wondering what sort of childhood Isabelle would have.

'I remember that. I could see your bloomers and everything. I was fascinated.' Archie laughed out loud.

'Archie Atkinson, you were no gentleman then and you certainly aren't one now.' Charlotte blushed even more deeply.

'I'm more of a gentleman than the one you married. But that doesn't take much doing, does it, Lottie? I'm really sorry you've got all these troubles. I'll try and make the running of Crummock no worry for you.'

'You are never any worry, Archie. I'm sorry I was so shallow with you when I was younger. My head was turned by things that I know now are not important.' She looked at her first love. She still felt something for the lad she had grown up with.

'Aye, but look where it's got you: mistress of the manor, mill owner and farm owner – you're a real woman of substance and power.'

'And I'd give it all away, apart from Isabelle here. I wish I was still stuck up that apple tree, with my bloomers showing and you laughing at me.' She wiped away a tear quickly.

'You can't turn back time, lass. It's time to look for- ward; things can't get much worse. We've a grand selection of lambs for sale this autumn – Arthur did you proud this spring, and we'll make some brass with them. You keep your head down and don't worry too much about this war over in the Americas. It'll all be over something and nowt in another week or two, and they'll all be fought out.' Archie knew nothing about world politics, but he knew it was causing hardship in the local cotton-mill villages and he needed to keep Charlotte positive.

'I don't think it will, Archie, but I've a good home and I've always got Crummock, even if I can't keep Ferndale going.'

'Aye, that's it, look on the bright side. Now I'll have to be going. I'm on my way to the Jacksons at Long Preston with my wool. I forgot to add that along with my hay-making, so you'll have your first bit of income from that at the end of the month.' He bent down and picked up his cap, hesitating at the doorway before leaving. 'You know where I am, lass, if you ever need me. Let me know if they find the bastard.'

Charlotte nodded. She couldn't reply. The words stuck in her throat as she gulped the tears back. She listened as Yates opened the door for Archie and then she let the tears out, once she knew no one could hear her sobs.

'He should have been your father, Isabelle. I'm sorry, I'm so very sorry.'

27

Sergeant Capstick was out of his depth in the busy port of Liverpool. He was used to the quiet backwaters of his home patch of Settle. He'd stood watching the world go by for the first day or two, amazed at the sights and sounds along Albert Dock and the quaysides of Liverpool.

He marvelled at the unloading of cargo, sugar, flour, wheat and molasses. Anything and everything was loaded and unloaded in the blink of an eye. The smell of the sea, mixed with spices and sweat, filled the air, and shouts and voices rang out around him. The rigging and sails filled the skyline of the busy docks, as the majestic sailing ships bobbed serenely in the quiet waters there. Not only were the cargo and ships fascinating to the eye, but there were people of all description, many of whom Sergeant Capstick had never seen the like in his life before. He had stared in disbelief at the first black man he had seen, not trusting his own eyes. How could a man's skin be that colour? He'd wanted to go and touch him, to see if he could rub the colour off, but at the same time he was frightened by the difference in the man's appearance. Children ran around his legs, and beggars and prostitutes gave him wide berth when they saw his uniform, while the wives and lovers of sailors waved their loved ones off as they went to sea.

How was he supposed to catch Joseph Dawson in this huge crowd of people? All he had was a rough sketch of the man and a description from Charlotte Dawson of what he looked like. It was obvious to the sergeant that it was going to be like looking for a needle in a haystack – any one of a hundred men could be Joseph Dawson, for so many met his description.

'Have you seen this man?' he asked a sailor as he swung his bag over his shoulder.

'Not seen anyone for six weeks, just come back from Jamaica. Why, what's he done?' the toothless tar asked as he offloaded his bag of belongings onto the dockside.

'Possibly murder,' said Sergeant Capstick, looking at the bronzed, wrinkled, wiry man, who was the only person who seemed to want to talk to him.

'He's either killed somebody or not. There's no "possibly" about it, if you bluebottles are looking for him. But no, can't say I know him. Have you got a fag?' The old man grinned.

'No, I don't.' Sergeant Capstick answered.

'Well, I don't ken him, so I'm on my way.'

Sergeant Capstick watched as the sailor picked his

bag up and made his way through the throng of crowds. Bugger it, he thought. I'm wasting my time here, I'm away home in the morning. If the bastard is here, he's welcome to the place. The green fields and fells of home were heaven, compared to the crowded streets and quaysides of Liverpool. This was no place for an ordinary Peeler.

Joseph Dawson sat back and finished his gill, before patting the backside of the saucy wench who had given him the eye as she cleared his plate away.

'Don't you touch what you can't afford!' The auburn-haired Scouser grinned at him.

'How do you know I can't afford you? I might be a wealthy man, for all you know.' Joseph grabbed her by the waist and pulled her onto his knee.

'Here, get your hands off! You're not wealthy, else you wouldn't be drinking in this one-hole place. Not unless you didn't want to be found, and someone was looking for you.' She made free from his arms, as Joseph was taken by surprise at her statement.

'What do you mean, somebody's looking for me? I'm just waiting for my ship to dock with a cargo of cotton.' Joseph said the first thing that came into his head and watched the girl as she stood, taking in his features.

'Well, that Peeler with the funny accent that's been sniffing around the docks this last day or two sure had a good likeness of you – wanted for murder, he said. Have you been a naughty boy? And if you are waiting for cotton, you'll have a bloody long wait. Don't you know there's a war on, across there in America?' The young woman sniggered as a look of panic crossed Joseph's face.

'It must be a lookalike. I'm a wealthy mill owner, not a murderer.' Joseph sat back and flashed his gold pocket watch to prove his wealth.

'The Peeler said that, and all. But that doesn't stop you from being a murderer. Looking for a ship to make good your escape, are you? Give us your pocket watch and I'll have a word with my brother – he's sailing out of port this evening.' The barmaid's eyes glinted at the fine watch in the hands of an obviously desperate man.

'Sailing where?'

'I don't know. He never says usually. He's been to America, or sometimes only to France; it depends what his cargo is. Where do you want to go? If I can arrange such a journey, of course.' She smiled.

'Tell him America, and the pocket watch is yours here and now. I'll pay him handsomely if he gives me safe passage.' Joseph waited as the young girl weighed up whether she could convince her brother to under- take such a journey.

'Meet him on Victoria Quay at nine tonight. I'll tell him you are coming, but show us your money first and give me your watch.'

The girl held her hand out. Joseph unhooked his pocket watch and quickly, without anyone noticing, passed it to her. As she hid the watch down between her breasts, he showed her the wodge of money he carried within his pocket.

'Nine o'clock tonight, look for the brig, the *Marie Rose*, and ask for Frank – he's the captain.'

Joseph watched as the barmaid smiled at her next customer and flirted with the sailors as they felt her breasts. He had to get out of Liverpool, for the Peelers were onto him. That meant they knew he had killed Betsy and he would surely hang, if caught. What was the loss of a watch, if it was a way of not losing your neck?

The moon was starting to rise over the rooftops of the red-bricked building of the docks as Joseph made his way down along the quayside. All his worldly goods were in his backpack, and a wodge of fifty pounds was in his inside pocket.

'Looking for tricks, darling?' A tight-laced prostitute made her way out of the shadows and stroked Joseph's face.

'Piss off! Go and find someone else to give the clap to.' He pushed her hand away from him and strode out down the quayside.

'Suit yourself. I know your sort – perhaps you fancy a young fag instead,' the prostitute shouted after him.

He was deaf to all insults shouted in his direction, his mind set on finding the *Marie Rose* and Frank, the captain. Then there she was, an older-looking vessel than he had expected, but still, what did it matter, if it was his way of escaping the gallows with no questions asked? Joseph walked down the gangplank and was about to yell into the cabin, when a hand grabbed him.

'Who are you?' The gruff, rough-looking sailor turned Joseph around quickly.

'I'm looking for Frank. His sister sent me; she said this ship's sailing tonight.'

'So you are the one our Mol's set me up with. Show us your cash, and then I'll show you your bunk.' The sailor lit a cigarette, by the light of which he watched Joseph reach for the money from his inside pocket.

'Eight pounds for a safe trip to America? No questions asked.' Joseph held his money out to the sailor and waited for a reply.

'Call it ten and you'll be out of here in the next hour. The brig's ready, the crew are just waiting for the tide to come in fully, and then we'll hoist sail and be on our way.' Without arguing, Joseph passed over the extra cash. The gold tooth that the sailor prided himself on shone in the moonlight as he smiled. 'That'll see you out of these waters and on your way. Here, I'll show you to your bunk. Mind your head, we only have cramped quarters.'

Frank led Joseph down into the bowels of the boat, into a small cabin with just a hammock swinging by hooks from the boat's skeleton, a chair and a roughly made desk.

'I know it's not much, but we aren't used to visitors. We are a trading ship – we haven't the space for niceties.' Frank sensed the look of horror on Joseph's face, as he lit an extra candle in a brass candlestick on the desk.

'It'll be fine, I'll get used to it.' Joseph sighed.

'Been to sea before, have you? Got good sea legs, I hope. You'll need them on this voyage.' Frank grinned.

'Never been to sea before, so we'll soon find out.' He sat down in the chair.

'Aye, we'll soon see. Right, I'm going up on deck to make ready the sails. It's best you stay here until we are out at sea. The less anybody sees of you, the better.' Frank turned and made his way through the darkness and back up onto the deck, where Joseph could hear him shouting at the rest of the crew. He listened as the ropes and rigging were hauled, in readiness for making sail.

He looked out of the small porthole into the darkness of the dock and felt the boat take the swell as it was unleashed from its moorings. He was leaving his worries behind him and starting a new life. Forget Windfell Manor, Charlotte and her baby, and his selfish sister Dora; he'd make a new name for himself in war-torn America, where nobody would ever find him. After making several attempts at climbing into the swinging hammock, he lay thinking of how to make his fortune, scheming and plotting his future until he felt his eyes drooping, in need of sleep. At last he could enjoy the first decent sleep he'd had since fleeing Langcliffe. He listened to the ship cutting its way out of the docks and into the open sea and closed his eyes.

*

The wind filled the sails and the sea lapped as the brig cut through waves, making its way out into the Irish Sea.

Joseph awoke, startled and in pain. 'Get off me, what are you doing?' He struggled as two burly sea dogs pinned him down, dragging him out of his hammock and holding his arms behind his back, as one punched him hard in the stomach, winding him and making him retch onto the sailor's foot. 'Do you know who I am, you bastards? I'll see you hang for this!' he gasped.

'I don't think you will, my friend. You are on the run, and nobody gives a damn about you.' Frank hit him hard and laughed as Joseph brushed his mouth and wiped away the remains of a broken tooth. 'I'm going to smash your bloody head in, you swanky bastard. So you'd better say your prayers now.'

Kicking and screaming, Joseph was hauled up onto the rough decking. His fingernails dug into the rough boards of the ship, in a vain attempt to save his life. Then, with ferocious cruelty, Frank stamped on his back, at the same time bringing down the full weight of a cudgel, battering again and again Joseph's dark-haired head and turning it into smashed blood and brains.

Two miles out into the Irish Sea, the crew of the *Marie Rose* quickly pilfered the battered and dead body of their not-so-wealthy passenger, before disposing of it over the edge of their brig.

'Nobody will miss him, lads. I know that look of desperation – he was running for his life. It's far better if we take care of his money and save him from a life of forever looking over his shoulder.' The captain shared the ill-gotten gains that had belonged to Joseph between his crew. 'God bless you, sir, and all who sail in you,' yelled Frank, as the body disappeared below the waves.

The crew roared with laughter and hid their stash about their bodies. In these hard times anyone could be a winner, especially as life was cheap. No one should be trusted, especially when a wad of cash had been waved under the nose of the most untrustworthy captain in the port of Liverpool.

'Right, lads, make sail for Dublin – or should I say America!'

28

Months had passed since Inspector Proctor's hunt for Joseph, and the storms of late autumn and winter of 1861 had set in. The rain had been persistent and had made the mood at Ferndale Mill heavy and oppressive. Christmas would soon be around the corner, and no soul – neither owner nor workers – had money to spare for frivolities.

'We aren't doing so badly, Bert. Other mills are being hit worse than us.' Charlotte looked up at the man who had helped her keep the mill afloat so far.

'Aye, at least we are holding our own.' Bert sat down.

'I've been talking to Lorenzo Christie. He's thinking of using something called "Surat cotton", which they grow in India apparently. Do you know anything about it, and would it be worth us looking at using it?' Charlotte leaned back into her office chair and watched Bert scratch his head.

'Aye, I know it, but you'll struggle using that on our machinery; it's better hand-woven. The fibres are short and break easily. Your young 'uns will be run off their feet mending breakages, and your weavers will not like it because the looms will have to be adjusted to a smaller throughput. It also likes the air humid, which is not what we exactly have here at the moment. This bloody rain, I'm sick of it. My missus is as well; the children are always around her feet, so I go back to her nagging tongue every night. As if I don't get enough earache here at the mill.'

'Perhaps we'll not go there then, Bert. I've told Mr Christie I'm willing to join forces with the other mill owners and run the blockade again, this coming spring. We should be alright until then. To think that when my husband took the mill on, he was full of hope and dreams, and now everything has turned to dust.' She sighed.

'Aye, well, if you don't mind me saying, ma'am, Mr Dawson was never a right good man for the job, more of a playboy than a worker. Full of bluff and puff. I never did like him.' Bert didn't hold back with his thoughts, making Charlotte like him even more. At least she knew where she stood with her second-in-command.

'What are you doing for Christmas, Bert? I know I've got baby Isabelle, but it'll be a year since I lost my father, and I don't feel like celebrating.'

'Nay, it'll be a quiet one for us too. No doubt the missus will ask some of our neighbours around. The

Spencers, at number five, lost their son last month when a runaway horse dragged him to his death, so it'll be a hard Christmas for them. Then we always have the missus's mother; she comes up from Settle and makes everyone's life hell by her constant moaning. I'll probably be glad to be back at work, the day after.'

'Make it the day after Boxing Day. I'm giving everybody both Christmas Day and Boxing Day off, with full pay, this year. I can barely afford it, but everybody has stood by me and I want to show my appreciation. Mr Dawson was a bit mean in the past, not giving everyone Boxing Day off. Besides, we aren't exactly run off our feet or overloaded with cotton at the moment.' She smiled as Bert's face brightened.

'Aye, ma'am, that'll lighten everybody's spirits. It's just what they need. God bless you, ma'am. When you first walked around the mill with me, that day when Mr Dawson was away, I thought then, aye; I even wished it was you who ran the mill. Now I know I was right to wish that – you'll get us through these dark days, I know you will.' Bert looked at the young woman with the weight of the world on her shoulders.

'I hope to, Bert. If I can get through this year, I can get through any year. Perhaps 1862 will be kinder to us.' Charlotte looked up suddenly as she heard somebody knocking on her office door.

'I'll get it, ma'am. You sit down.' Bert rose from his seat and opened the office door, revealing a bedraggled Inspector Proctor.

'Sorry to bother you, Mrs Dawson, but I've two

pieces of news I think you might want to hear.' The inspector took his rain cape from around his shoulders and shook it, before placing it in a heap on the office floor. He sat down in the chair that Bert had vacated.

'I'll leave you, ma'am. You know where I am, if you need me.' Bert quietly closed the door behind him and shook his head. The Peeler's face had bad news written all over it.

'What is it, Inspector? It must be urgent, if you have come out in weather like this.' Charlotte waited, silently praying that Joseph had not returned to the district.

'I'm sorry. I carry bad news, I'm afraid. May Pilling hanged herself in her room last week; she was found by one of her nurses.' Inspector Proctor looked at Charlotte and watched as she quickly brushed a solitary tear away.

'I'm sorry to hear that. Although I never knew her, I'm glad her soul may finally be at rest. My husband has a lot to answer for, Inspector, because he might as well have held a gun to her head and pulled the trigger, rather than put her through the mind-games that he obviously played with her. God rest her soul.' Charlotte blew her nose on her handkerchief and lifted her head up high. 'And the second piece of news? Have you found my husband – the one who has caused all this heartache?'

'We believe we have, ma'am.' Percy hesitated.

'Well, where is he? Locked up, I hope.' Charlotte waited.

'There's not much of him left to lock up, ma'am.

371

That's why I say I *think* we have found him, for the clothes that you described Mr Dawson leaving in and what was left of his hair make us believe it was him. The Lancashire Constabulary asked me over there, when a body was washed up on the beach near Southport. It matched your description of Mr Dawson and what he was wearing – it looks like he drowned himself.' Percy hesitated. 'It seems a long way to go to drown yourself, but I do believe it is him. Perhaps there was more to it than meets the eye. He was making his way to America, I assume. Knowing your husband, he was taking a way out. I am quite satisfied to say that your husband is dead. What's left of him in the morgue matches your description of him.'

Charlotte couldn't quite take it in. Joseph was dead, and she was free of him! She felt like celebrating the drowning of the man she had loved, just over a year ago. How her views, and her love, had changed in a matter of twelve months. The hurt and pain she had carried over recent months had made her feel hard towards the man she had once loved. However, she also felt a wave of grief wash over her, as her body started to shake and tears filled her eyes. It was over – Joseph was dead. No one would ever know of his past life, his dead wife and the fact that their marriage had been a sham. There was a closure to the hell she had endured, and perhaps a glimmer of hope for the future. She sobbed into her handkerchief and then composed herself, before pressing the embarrassed inspector's arm, holding it tight as if to squeeze the truth out of it.

'You are sure it's him – you are not mistaken?' Charlotte leaned forward and looked hard at Percy.

'As sure as we can be. I'm closing the case anyway, that's how confident I am that it is him.' He watched Charlotte, as she didn't quite know what to do with herself.

'Where is his body?' she asked.

'In the mortuary in Southport, awaiting my instructions.'

'Instructions? What do you mean?'

'Do you want to claim the body, or will he be staying there? If it's the latter, he'll be buried in a pauper's grave, unless you wish to pay for a grander affair.' Percy waited for an answer.

'Inspector, I hope he's burning in hell! A pauper's unmarked grave is just where he belongs.' She would never be able to forgive herself for wasting so much of her life on such a worthless man. She was not going to shed any more tears over someone who, she now knew, had never loved her.

'A wise decision, ma'am. It would only bring heartache to the young lad, Betsy's brother down at Langcliffe Locks, and upset your workers. I'll tell the mortuary to dispose of the body as soon as they can.' Percy looked around him. 'You look as if you were made for this office, ma'am, and there's a good atmosphere when you walk through the mill, if you don't mind me saying.'

'I'm learning fast. I just wish times were better. Joseph couldn't have walked out at a worse time. But

373

cometh the hour, cometh the woman.' Charlotte smiled and wiped away a lingering tear.

'You'll do it, Mrs Dawson. You are a determined soul, and you have your workers behind you.' Percy shook his cloak and wrapped it back around himself. 'I wish you a happy Christmas, if that doesn't sound uncaring, after just telling you of your husband's death.'

'Not at all. This time last year I would have been heartbroken. That was when I didn't know the real man I had married. Now I can go forward, forget the past, concentrate on my mill and farm, and just smother my Isabelle with love.' She opened the door for Percy.

'Good luck, and God be with you, Mrs Dawson.' He tipped his bowler and walked away from the woman who had been stronger in character than Joseph Dawson would ever be. Percy had listened to the local gossip: how the woman at the big house was working all the hours God gave; how she was making up – and more besides – for her bastard of a husband. The locals were behind her. After all, she was one of them: a farmer's lass who wanted to better herself. There was nowt wrong with that, he thought, as he walked out into the rain. He turned and looked at the tall, dark mill building, hearing the sound of the looms echoing around the valley. 'Good luck again, Mrs Dawson, because if anyone deserves it, you do,' he whispered, before turning his back on a closed crime scene.

Charlotte leaned back in her chair and wept openly. It was over; she could go forward with her life now, her own and Isabelle's.

Watching the inspector's departure, Bert knocked on the office door as soon as he saw that Charlotte was by herself, concerned by the sobs coming from within. Charlotte sobbed and shook as she informed Bert of her news. He'd been lurking outside the office as the inspector had told her his news, and had feared the worst when he'd heard Charlotte break down.

'It's over, Bert. They've found Joseph drowned, washed up on a beach in Southport. He's dead.' The words echoed around the office. 'He'll not be coming back, thank the Lord.'

'Thank the Lord indeed, ma'am. I don't think he'd have dared show his face in these parts. He'd have been lynched, for what he did to you and Betsy. Best end to him, ma'am. I hope he's stoking the fires of hell.' Bert looked at his boss, her face red and pained. 'Don't you shed another tear for that bastard. You can run this mill better than any fella, and everyone's behind you. It's time to go forward, ma'am.' He stood awkwardly in front of his employer.

'Thank you, Bert. And yes, you are right, it's time to look forward.' Charlotte sniffed and composed herself. 'If I can manage this year, I can manage anything.'

'Too true, ma'am, and don't you forget it.'

Charlotte looked at the note that bore Archie's sprawling handwriting upon it. It looked as if a wounded spider had limped across the page. Handwriting had never been his strongest point, she mused. She read the invitation again and smiled. She couldn't think of anything better than spending Christmas back at Crummock; it would be a welcome break for two days. She'd reply straight away.

Her mind wandered back in time to when Christmases at Crummock were filled with folk visiting, frivolity, food and laughter. Would those days ever return? Would she ever have Christmases like those, here at Windfell? She did love Windfell, but she still thought of Crummock as her true home. She quickly wrote her reply and sealed it lovingly, leaving it in the post box on the hallway table before climbing the stairs to her bed. Every day had been hard work lately and, as far as she could see, every day in the future was going to be hard work. Where had the carefree days of her youth gone? Thanks to Joseph Dawson, she'd grown up quickly, and she never wanted the same for her Isabelle.

'Goodnight, ma'am,' said Yates as she dragged her feet up the sweeping stairs.

'Goodnight, Yates. See you in the morning.' How she wished she could return to her old life, where she didn't have to stand on ceremony and she could disappear into her own little world without anyone judging her.

The mill's mighty water wheel ceased to turn and the tall chimney stopped its belching of steam as the looms and machines of Ferndale stopped for a two-day celebration for Christmas.

'God bless you, ma'am. Happy Christmas.' Charlotte watched as, one by one, her mill workers filed out of the mill gates, doffing their hats to her and then nearly running home as the sun began to set in the heavy grey sky of Christmas Eve.

'Merry Christmas, everyone.' Charlotte wrapped her shawl around her and shivered on the steps of the warehouse. Would she be saying those words at this time next year, or would the mill and the workers have disappeared into oblivion by then? She smiled quietly to herself. She'd come a long way in these last few months. Even Bert had said she was a quick learner, before adding sarcastically 'for a woman'. Good old Bert, she'd not have managed any of it without him. She watched as he locked the engine pump room and made safe the outbuildings, before nearly running over to her.

'All's made safe for the holiday, and we'll be up and running again as soon as Christmas is over, ma'am.' He blew on his ungloved hands and looked up at Charlotte. 'I'll be off now, if that's alright with you, ma'am. My old missus will be waiting.'

'Actually, Bert, I need to have words with you. Would you mind stepping inside the warehouse for a minute?' Charlotte's face was stern and she tried to hide a smirk as she saw Bert's disappointment when he realized he was not going to be able to make good his escape.

'But, ma'am . . .'

'Quiet! I need you to come in here.' Charlotte stepped into the warehouse and reached over to the hook where his Christmas treat hung. 'Happy Christmas, Bert. This should keep your family fed, and make your mother-in-law content.' She could barely lift the huge white goose that she had been hiding all day, as she lifted it from its hook and passed it to the dumb-struck overseer. 'It's a thank-you from me, for all your help. I'd not have managed without you.' She watched as the goose's bright-orange beak hung over Bert's shoulder, while he struggled to take his cap off in thanks.

'I don't know what to say, ma'am, but thank you. That puts our shoulder of mutton to shame. My old lass will be over the moon. You shouldn't have – you'll need your money,' he rambled on.

'Just go home, Bert, and enjoy your two days of peace because, believe me, I'll need you more than ever next year.' Charlotte smiled as she watched her loyal employee struggle to carry his prize home over the cobbles. He was good man. As he disappeared out of the yard, she locked the warehouse door and stood all alone in the yard, looking up and around at the huge buildings of Ferndale Mill. They stood silent against the background noise of the rushing River Ribble. God willing, the mill and her workers would still be going next Christmas. If not, well, there was always Crummock for her to escape to, if the going got too tough.

She walked steadily along the mill path, her mind now racing as she thought about getting baby Isabelle and herself ready for two days back at her beloved Crummock. Christmas with Mrs Cranston, Archie and Daniel was going to be a delight, but how she wished her father was still alive. How she missed his jovial spirit and his love. He'd rarely said that he loved her, but he never had any need to; she knew he had loved her, and she him.

Lost in her thoughts, she soon arrived back at Windfell to find her staff awaiting her return, as Lily, Mazy and Mrs Batty stood in the hallway wanting to wish her a happy Christmas before they returned to their families while the manor was empty. Yates had decided to remain at the manor, having nowhere else to go, but Mazy had insisted that he join her family for Christmas dinner, so even he had a home of his own that Christmas.

'Have a lovely Christmas, ma'am,' all three of her staff cheered as she entered the hallway.

Charlotte unwrapped her shawl and smiled at them all. 'Happy Christmas, everyone. Did Yates give you my presents? I'm sorry I'm a little later returning than planned. Thank you for waiting for me.' She looked at all the excited faces surrounding her.

'Yes, ma'am. Thank you very much, ma'am,' they all chorused.

'Well, go on then, get yourselves home. I know you can't wait. Mazy, before you go, is Isabelle changed, and have you prepared everything we will need for our days away up at Crummock?' Charlotte watched as the three women she had grown to respect scurried about the hall, trying to be polite, but wanting to get back to their own homes and families. Mazy hung back, knowing that her duty lay with baby Isabelle.

'Yes, ma'am. Her things are packed, and Mr Atkinson

is waiting for you in the drawing room. He insisted that he nursed her until you returned.' Mazy blushed.

'Thank you, Mazy. Have a good Christmas, and thank you for inviting Yates to your home at Christmas. I wouldn't have wanted him to be on his own in the manor then.'

'It's nothing, ma'am. My mother said another mouth to feed was no problem at Christmas, especially now I'm bringing good money home.' Mazy smiled and put her bonnet on hurriedly.

'Have a good Christmas. I'll enjoy every minute with Isabelle – it will be pure indulgence.' Charlotte watched as her nanny quickly made for the kitchen, before walking into the drawing room, where Archie sat burbling to Isabelle. She smiled as she remembered doubting Lily's recommendation of Mazy; she couldn't have wished for a better nanny.

'Ah, Lottie, Isabelle and I were just getting to know one another. I was telling her I'm her Uncle Archie. An Uncle Archie who brings her mother money, as we made a pretty penny with our lamb sales this year.' He balanced Isabelle in between his arm and lap and reached into his pocket for a handful of notes. 'Happy Christmas, Lottie. This will help you and your mill. I've included my rent for the coming year in that, as well.'

Charlotte looked at the bundle of notes that Archie handed her. 'You can't have made all this, surely – you've got it wrong?'

'Nay, I've just watched what we've spent and we had a good lambing, as I told you earlier on. Your

Uncle Archie's not that daft, is he now, Isabelle?' He tickled the contented baby under her chin and smiled down as she gurgled. 'But enough talk of brass, let's be away. Jethro's offered to take us up to Crummock in your carriage. I've tied my horse to it at the back and it will be getting bored. Yates has loaded everything you need, so all you've got to do is wish him a happy Christmas and we will be off.'

'But I've things to do. I can't just walk out of here.' Charlotte looked around her, still holding the money in her hand.

'You've nothing to do. Go and make safe that brass and let's be away. Aunt Lucy has a roast ham awaiting you, and I've been told not to dally.' Archie stood up and wrapped the shawl left by Mazy around Isabelle, then grinned at Charlotte. 'Come on, lass, get a move on; for once you are not in charge. It's only two days. The world's not going to end, without you giving orders. Come home and let us all look after you.' He walked to the doorway and waited as Charlotte locked her money in the desk in the morning room, then grabbed the bonnet that had been left in the hallway for her.

'Have a good Christmas, ma'am. Don't worry, I will look after the manor for you.' Yates appeared as if by magic out of the kitchen. 'You just enjoy the company you are with, and try and forget what a horrific year we have all had.'

'I will, Yates, and thank you for your support. I'd be lost without you.' Charlotte smiled as he held the door open for her.

'I'm sure you wouldn't, ma'am, but we would be lost without you. I look forward to your return.' Yates smiled, remembering the young woman he had first talked to, and how she was now a lady who was to be respected.

'I look forward to returning too, Yates, and I have a feeling that next year – no matter what is thrown at us – we will survive. Of that I'm sure.'

Assisted by Archie, she climbed into the carriage. Nursing Isabelle, she looked out of the window as the carriage made its way down the drive of Windfell.

Windfell, the manor she owned, along with Ferndale Mill. And now she was going home to Crummock, to spend Christmas with people she loved. The new year might bring fresh hardships and more worries, but she'd face them with new confidence and determination. Joseph Dawson had taught her a lot; if you treat people right, they'll be right with you. She smiled across at Archie as he patted her knee, seeing that she was near tears.

'Are you alright, Lottie?'

'I'm fine, Archie. I'm going home for Christmas, and I can't wait.'